PRAISE FOR *OUR POOL PARTY BUS FOREVER DAYS*

"The right to hit the road is our last unabridged freedom . . . to run from our failures, start over and fail bigger, faster, harder. Keaton's intro gives you fair warning that he looooooves him some car chases, and whether he's stalking stupid ducks or stupider cops or just prowling the irradiated wasteland of his own brain, every story is a white-line nightmare death-race, every hot-wired sentence supercharged with restless kinetic energy. *Our Pool Party Bus Forever Days* perfectly harnesses the rush of forever acceleration, the razor-sharp clarity of surreal details flying by, the fleeting promise of redemption (or just reinvention) in the vanishing point, the imminent peril of fatal impact the moment you stop to catch your breath . . . So don't."
—Cody Goodfellow, Wonderland Award-winning author of *All-Monster Action, Repo Shark*

"Like dropping acid and driving as fast as you can against one-way traffic with the windows down and Sinatra's "New York, New York" blasting at top volume, David James Keaton's *Our Pool Party Bus Forever Days* is strangely sophisticated, aggressively absurd, and so much fucking FUN. Buy it for the Greatest Introduction of All Time, stay for the weird, wild, winding trip down the darkly entertaining highways of a madman's mind."
—Jeremy Robert Johnson, Wonderland Award-winning author of author of *Skullcrack City, Entropy in Bloom*

PRAISE FOR DAVID JAMES KEATON

"The author's joy in his subject matter is obvious, often expressed with a sly wink and wicked smile. Decay, both existential and physical, has never looked so good."
—*Publishers Weekly* (Starred Review for *Stealing Propeller Hats from the Dead*)

"David James Keaton offers an insightful riff on trend horror and contemporary pop culture very much akin to that of an early-'90s Wes Craven." —*Fangoria Magazine*

"The universes David James Keaton creates have one foot in stark reality and the other in the oneiric realm of barroom stories and urban legends." —*Dead End Follies*

"David James Keaton is a writer to keep an eye on." —Frank Bill, author of *The Savage*

"David James Keaton's read his Beckett, sure. And he knows his Pynchon. But he also knows his Herschell Gordon Lewis, his Quentin Tarantino. Exquisite writing and fast-paced storytelling." —Stephen Graham Jones, author of *Mongrels*

"David James Keaton holds the lovechild of convention and expectations down to the hard, concrete floor, puts his hand over its mouth, and slits its throat."
—Michael Czyzniejewski, author of *Elephants in Our Bedroom*

"Keaton's stories are as sickly exuberant and gargantuan as gothic dirigibles, tall tales of teleportation into urban myth and mystery, post-truth, anti-reality, they break every rule of regular fiction and good taste." —Chuck Kinder, author of *The Honeymooners*

ALSO BY DAVID JAMES KEATON

NOVELS
The Last Projector
Pig Iron

SHORT STORY COLLECTIONS
Fish Bites Cop! Stories to Bash Authorities
Stealing Propeller Hats from the Dead

EDITOR
Dirty Boulevard: Crime Fiction Inspired by
the Songs of Lou Reed

CO-EDITOR
Hard Sentences: Crime Fiction Inspired by Alcatraz
Tales from the Crust: An Anthology of Pizza Horror

our pool party bus
forever days

road stories

david james keaton

Red Room Press

WWW.REDROOMPRESS.COM

First Red Room Press Trade Paperback Edition
October 2018

Our Pool Party Bus Forever Days copyright © 2018
by David James Keaton
All Rights Reserved.

This edition copyright © 2018
by Red Room Press
All Rights Reserved.

Cover artwork by Matt Revert & Tony McMillen
Fire Marshal Kill artwork by Tony McMillen

Red Room Press is an imprint of Comet Press

ISBN 13: 978-1-936964-08-6

Visit Red Room Press on the web at:
www.redroompress.com
facebook.com/redroompress
twitter.com/redroombooks

RED ROOM PRESS

WWW.REDROOMPRESS.COM

CREDITS

"First Story Ever" originally appeared in *Dogzplot,* 2011.

"The Ear Eater of Jasper County" was originally published as "The Best Chicken in Jasper County" in *States of Terror Vol. 3* (Ayahuasca Publishing, 2016).

"A Dull Boy" originally appeared in *Exigencies: A Neo-Noir Anthology* (Dark House Press, 2015).

"Ghost Pianos & Idle Hands" originally appeared in *PANK,* 2012.

"Egg Tooth" originally appeared in *Chicago Quarterly Review,* 2013.

"Movies for Milkweed" originally appeared in *Dark Highlands Anthology: Volume 1,* 2010.

"El Kabong" was originally published as "Lucha Horse" in *Wrestle Maniacs* (Honey Badger Press, 2017).

"Ha'penny Dreadfuller" originally appeared in *Burrow Press Review,* 2015.

"Dragon by the Dumpster" originally appeared in *Booked. The Anthology,* 2013.

"Wreckless Eyeballing" originally appeared in *It's a Weird Winter Wonderland* (Coffin Hop Press, 2017).

"Road Dirge" originally appeared in *Bluestem,* 2012.

"Up Down Up Right Down Left Up" originally appeared in *All Due Respect,* 2012.

"Spin the Throttle" originally appeared in *Tales from the Talking Board* (Word Horde, 2017).

"The Flowery" originally appeared in *Red Room Magazine* (Comet Press, 2017).

"Is That My Sandwich in There?" was originally published as "Yes, That's My Sandwich" in *Flywheel Magazine,* 2011.

"Forced Perspective" originally appeared in *Taut Lines: Extraordinary True Fishing Stories* (Constable & Robinson, 2016).

"Sharks with Thumbs" originally appeared in *Big Pulp,* 2009.

"Taco Hell" originally appeared in *Junk* (L.A.O.B., 2013).

"Double Piss Test" originally appeared in *Thunderdome,* 2012.

"A Gun Named Sioux" was originally published as "Smelt (or A Gun Named Sioux)" in *The Big Adios Western Digest,* 2014.

"Change Machine" originally appeared in *Floodwall,* 2012.

"Fasten Your Meat Belts" originally appeared in *Great Jones Street,* 2017.

"The Unforeseen Hazards of Hitchhiking" originally appeared in *Unloaded Volume 2* (Down & Out Books, 2017).

"Bad Reaction Shots" was originally published as "Reaction Shots" in *Burnt Bridge,* 2011.

"Rumble" was originally published as "Headless Hoggy Style" in *Hoods, Hot Rods & Hellcats* (Cathode Angel, 2014).

Dedicated to the lizard and the three big flips.

TABLE OF CONTENTS

INTRODUCTION: GASOLINE DREAMS

As I was poking around under the hood of this book and gathering up the stories and realizing that a theme had miraculously begun to emerge, I also understood that, at some point, a reader might find this supposed connection to the road a little . . . *abstract* in some tales. So I thought this introduction could serve as both a desperate rationalization and a bit of bonus material, or maybe just something like that first lap they take before a race where the cars do that little freaky waggle dance to heat up their tires and help them stick to the asphalt. Because even if a story doesn't have a literal car chase, or a figurative car chase, or sex with a tailpipe, maybe a "road story" can just be a state of mind? Or, to put it another way, what's the last thing that goes through your brain in a car crash? The fucking steering wheel! You see what I'm saying? I don't know what that means either.

So, I first got excited about car chases again, and by proxy stories about the road, when I saw Refn's wonderful throwback *Drive* and realized these sorts of movies were having a bit of a comeback. And they're still chugging along. This year, we'll actually have a road movie called *The Road Movie* to look forward to, which, near as I can tell, is some sorta hypnotic documentary made up entirely of crazy Russian dashboard cam footage that's being put out by the Beastie Boys' Oscilloscope Films, a company that's no stranger to the highway after distributing the mesmerizing, not-quite-post-apocalyptic (but those guys sure *wished* the world was ending) indie darling *Bellflower*. But have you seen *Drive*? I think it might actually be the adventures of a carjacking scorpion dressed as a man, but it reminded us again what was important in life. And as I said recently to a cab driver who wasn't really asking, it was a little bit of *Heat*, a lot of Hill's *The Driver*, a sprinkle of *Grand Theft Auto: Vice City*, dash of Tarantino's *Death Proof*, splash of Mann's *Thief*, smattering of *Vanishing Point*, as talky as the mute masterpiece *Two-Lane Blacktop*, and simmered in what sounds like the music from goddamn *Xanadu*, and, because it's the reason for the season, even a slice of Carpenter's *Halloween*-stalking action thrown in for kicks.

You *do* have to endure "The Frog and the Scorpion" fable for the millionth time, last heard in *The Crying Game,* and even *Skin Deep* fer chrissakes, but it's totally worth it because the scorpion in the movie (a childlike design embroidered on the back of the hero's satin jacket) should get a Best Supporting Actor nod for the emotion that creature brought to the silver screen. For example, after a particularly brutal elevator beating, I swear I saw that bug trying to catch its breath. Anyway, all this got me wondering where this movie might fall on a definitive, last-word inventory of car-chase flicks, and because I'll jump on any excuse to ponder this question forever, let's do it right now. I'm calling this list:

The Invention of the Wheel!

Mad Max told us the road was a "white-line nightmare," but it's more like a white-knuckle dream. Who was the first to do it? Invent the wheel, I mean. Someone, somewhere slid over their hood, dove into the driver's seat, then peeled out. Well, maybe not quite peeled out, since roads came later and the first chase probably involved horses instead of horsepower. Unless a horse can peel out on dust? Maybe on wet grass. The Duke Boys did it all the time, right? Anyhow. You know what happened right after that? Someone started chasing them! And this probably happened all over the world at the exact same time, just like those cave men who invented the wheels. Plural. See, it wasn't just one wheel, don't let 'em fool ya. They always talk about the invention of the *wheel,* singular, but it was definitely spontaneous wheels all over the damn place. And when four cave men in nearby caves rolled four wheels out into the sun at the same time, shit, they almost had a whole car. And then someone started chasing them! And then someone invented movies. And then came the lists. And the Lord did grin. It was just that simple. Trust me, I'm a scientist. Which brings us to . . .

The Best Car Chases of All Time. Or . . .
The Best Car Chases in Movies I Happen to Own

10.) *The Hidden*
The first chase in the movie, of course. The rest of the movie mostly feels like *Beastmaster*-era straight-to-cable stuff. See, aliens are among us. And we'd probably never realize it . . . until they start stealing high-end sports cars and rocking to bad heavy metal music while mowing down old people in wheelchairs. This is such a great opening to a movie (right up there with *The Last Boy Scout's* football game) that the audience is shocked into a satisfying kind of stupor thinking the movie will be better than it actually is. We

start off with some crazed-looking business man robbing a bank, motorvating down sidewalks in a black Ferrari, nodding along with the tunes and grinning all spooky while plowing through police road blocks. Stars *Twin Peaks'* Agent Cooper as the good alien, doing his spaced-out Agent Cooper thing two years earlier. The audience is as confused as the cops at first, and for a while you think you're strapping in for the greatest film of all time. And it isn't. But that's okay, because, for a second, you think it might be.

9.) *To Live and Die In L.A.*

The chase about halfway through. When the two "good" guys screw up their scam to steal drug money from one gang (actually undercover Feds) to buy counterfeit money from another gang, led by an utterly bonkers Willem Dafoe. Turns out the deal they were ambushing was staged by the FBI for a bust, so our heroes have to drive the wrong way through traffic to escape. Friedkin can do this sort of car chase in his sleep, but this one is something special. During the getaway, agents materialize around every corner (a decade before *The Matrix*), and it finally starts to dawn on our heroes that they fucked up pretty bad. At least it starts to dawn on *one* of them because the other guy, William Peterson from *Manhunter* (and, tragically, *CSI*, a show that will forever be remembered as confusing dumbass juries with a little bit of knowledge), flashes back to his recreational bungee jumping from the opening scene for some reason (the birth of extreme sports?), which, impossibly, helps him keep it together and follow the most important rule of the road, according to Tom Waits: "He don't lose his composure in a high speed chase." Of course he can't follow the second-most-important rule: "One-Way Traffic, yo."

8.) *Raiders of the Lost Ark*

No, I'm not calling it *Indiana Jones and the Whatever Whatever*. That re-naming was just more revisionist history from Lucas, but you almost forgive him and his buddy Spielberg when you see this scene. Good guy crawling all over that truck like a chimp, lots of goose-steppers slipping under the wheels, cheap shots and sucker punches from everyone. Maybe it's more like a fight scene than a chase scene, sure, but that truck is oh, so lovingly filmed and gives the sequence lots of momentum. And this chase is right after what is arguably one of the greatest fist fights of all time: Jones taking on a big, bald Nazi, then tag-teaming a propeller. Getting off track though. Gonna have to save the fist fight list for another time (where CGI and high-wire *Crouching Tiger, Floating Dragline* will be disqualified), and I will build another short-story collection around one to justify it.

7.) *The French Connection*

The only chase in the movie. Come on, you remember it. Where Gene Hackman steals a car to chase the bad guy riding the elevated train above him. And he seems to be killing or maiming several pedestrians during this pursuit. Hackman plays Popeye Doyle, the first of the Dirty Harry-type cops that bum-rushed the '70s, and he does a fantastic job gritting his teeth while he screams and honks that horn. And this horn is like its own character, too, as relentless and needy as the wailing baby in *Eraserhead*. Friedkin's sequence may be a little tame in this jaded age of videogamey pile-ups, but with today's movies you never get the pleasure of watching the cop shoot the bad guy in the back in frustration at the end of a chase. That's only on the 11 o'clock news.

6.) *Mad Max III: Beyond Thunderdome*

The last chase in the movie. The one where Max drives a train full of kids on a doomed, dead-end escape through the desert. More tricked-out dune-buggies ramming those metal wheels like moths to the flame. And maybe it was just the nostalgia of seeing desert + Max + wheels + Village People-lookin' bad guys and hoping that combination would still = magic. And maybe it doesn't quite pull it off. And maybe Max isn't all that "mad" in these movies anymore without the R rating (at least not as mad as a typical Mel Gibson phone call). And maybe the "last of the V-8s" is being pulled by horses (say it ain't so!), but this is George Miller and Mad friggin' Max we're talking about here, so it's guaranteed a spot on the list.

5 ½.) *Grand Theft Auto III*

This part of the list is like the half floor in *Being John Malkovich*, where *The Matrix Reloaded* chase would bump its head if it wasn't disqualified for turning into a videogame (and what's up with the CGI cars missing their mufflers when they flip over?). Equal parts satisfying and frustrating, kind of like the kinetic but artificial acrobatics in *Wanted*, which aped *The Matrix* fairly effectively. And I guess *John Wick* should go here in the half floor, too, even though, yes, Keanu Reeves was replaced with a more lethal avatar, his Mustang Mach 1, which they crunched in a tangible, off-the-hard drive, real-world fashion. Kind of like *Jack Reacher's* Chevelle bouncing around Pittsburg in a very appealing, sorta poor-man's San Francisco chase that was better than the whole movie. But then I thought about all this and decided I got waaaaaay off the reservation here, and that *Grand Theft Auto III,* an actual computer game, gets this half spot instead. Simply because in the game you can take your car chase into the park with a five-star wanted level and post up on this little island and shotgun cop cars and FBI SUVs out of the sky when the A.I. sends them flying off the bridge above you by mistake. It's a sweet glitch in the game that sends flaming cars screaming over your head while you just keep lighting them up over and over and over and over . . . Like an awestruck friend whispered when he saw this happen, "It's like the end of the world, dude." So it deserves the slot. Because *Matrix Reloaded* was just a videogame you couldn't play.

5.) *Bullitt*

You know what chase. Do I even have to say it? Mustang vs. Dodge Charger. Mustang wins. This chase has been overrated, then underrated, then overrated all over again. I put it at number five, like the porridge that's just wrong, because it effectively blurred the line between reality and fiction when Steve McQueen (like Burt Reynolds or Jackie Chan after him, really more a stuntman slumming as an actor) clicked on his seat beat and stabbed the gas, then continued to do all the driving and derring-do himself. It's not *really* a movie anymore after that, kind of like when McQueen slapped his wife/co-star in the face in *The Getaway*. It's really happening. And to Hell with *The Great Escape's* famous motorcycle jump (which he didn't even do). Peter Yates will always claim Steve's defining moment. Side note: all my life I thought this was a Dodge Challenger and not a Charger because I'm into roads, not cars, and I'm also an idiot, but I blame my confusion on years of hearing Super Soul in *Vanishing Point* announce, "Here comes the *challenger* . . ." which I didn't realize was also the name of a vehicle until decades later. I know. Shut up.

4.) *Mad Max II: The Road Warrior*

The last chase. Max trying to drive a decoy truck full of sand through about fifty screaming apocalyptic nutjobs (or "Smegma Crazies" if you dare to use subtitles) and their colorful array of custom, high-octane, teenage-wet-dream vehicular abominations. Bizarre muscle cars, spike-riddled dune buggies, harpoon-equipped El Caminos, and jet-powered forklifts all take their turn under Max's eighteen wheels. And watch close for what happens to The Humungous' two hostages when Max slams on the brakes. Oops. Sorry about the rescue, guys! The death of Max's own beloved ride ("Shoulda had a V-8!" my dad joked as he slapped his forehead while we all watched it five more times on his bootleg cable box) is even more tragic than when that tornado wiped out the *Little House on the Prairie* and Charles Ingalls lost his faith. But I have faith in George. To be honest, George Miller's dusty, hellish visions might be the most satisfying views of the future I've ever seen. And when I tell you that I want to collect gasoline from underneath car wrecks with my cracked Frisbee, trust me, I really do. Maybe someday we all will (checks gas prices, loads crossbow, adjusts football shoulder pads).

3.) The Driver

The big finale. Toothy goofy Camaro vs. cherry-red '74 Chevy C10 stepside pickup. Cat-and-mouse action in a warehouse with a very pleasing crunch when the mousetrap finally gets sprung. But what makes Hill's chase so satisfying is the buildup to it, the pre-game in the parking garage, when the bad guys make the mistake of having the hero test-drive a pumpkin orange Mercedes-Benz with them hunkered down in terror in the back seat. Ryan O'Neal's nameless "driver" bashes the stuffing out of their gleaming ride, scraping it against every sharp corner he can find. A beautiful, unnerving, weirdly punishing scene. Also watch for the end credits when the cop is left "holding the bag." Get it? I swear I'm not talking about testicles. Speaking of . . .

2 ½.) The Driver II (a.k.a. Drive)

Come on, it's pretty much the same damn movie, right down to someone at the end of the flick left holding their balls. But it's better, too. And the opening chase got my ladyfriend to turn to me and mutter, "You know, this is the first car chase I've ever cared about." I ended up marrying her! How did it do this, you ask? By doing the same things The Driver did. Cat-and-mouse moves (or cat-and-moose-and-squirrel moves really), slowing everything down, turning off the lights, then almost exclusively filming from behind the steering wheel. And the second chase in the movie ain't no slouch either. Looking a bit like the famous chase from The Seven-Ups, it was fast, hectic, with a brutal ending that shows a car simply stopped cold can be more effective than one that explodes.

2.) Mad Max

The first chase. Two ugly, piss-yellow, "bogan" wagons, a.k.a. police "interceptors," and a motorcycle driven by a guy named Goose (and anyone named Goose ain't gonna last long), all chasing someone calling himself "The Nightrider," who is never seen driving at night for some reason, and who gets oddly emotional during pursuits. A great chase and a real sense of danger for the stuntmen here. How many Aussie day-workers were "killed or injured during the making of this film?" Rumor has it they got paid in beer, too. George Miller starts his movie and his chases kind of lighthearted, then quickly escalates into some serious vehicular mayhem. A van, a camper, and a baby all wander onto "Anarchie" Road (hey, that's how they spelled it, not me) at the wrong time. And if you freeze-frame when The Nightrider is stomping the gas pedal, you'll see a tattoo on his toes! I'll let you discover what it says on your own. Also, here's another Easter Egg for ya; check behind the CD tray on your copy of Tool's *Undertow* and you'll see a cow licking its own ass. You're welcome! Seriously, what if this same picture is hiding under all of your CDs. Speaking of rimjobs . . .

1.) *Ronin*
The last chase in the movie. Rims flying everywhere. Mercedes vs. Audi, going Mach 12, lot's o' traffic, a real sense of danger for the characters, as well as the actors, pedestrians, and especially that dude on the bike that eats it. Too bad the movie kinda blows? Perfect chase though. Frankenheimer is inspired here by using no music at all for the first 2/3rds of this chase. Sure, maybe he should have stuck with no music the entire time, but still, this sequence is as close to perfection as a car chase in a movie (that I own) ever got. It'll have to do.

Runner-Ups (or is it Runners-Up? That never sounds right) . . .

11.) *Goldeneye*
Tank vs. Peugeot. Bit of a mismatch. Bond, driving the tank, accidentally destroys St. Petersburg as a result. But don't tell me those teeny tiny foreign cars sprinkled all over those streets weren't destined to be chewed under tank treads some day. I think they were trying to say something profound about the end of an era with all the Russian monuments and historic symbols being destroyed. And the message is clear: tanks fuck shit up.

12.) *Terminator II: Judgment Day*
Truck vs. Harley vs. mini-bike. I think the semi plowing through cars when the T-9000 first jumps on board is better than the famous chase through the reservoir, but still plenty of twisted metal for everyone, and the original *Terminator* chase isn't slacking either (*T3* might have made the list if it hadn't computer-faked its trucks). Hate the kid in this movie though, especially all his "catchphrases." Quit trying to make Tex-Mex teen slang happen, Mr. Cameron. Oh, yeah, the helicopter smashing into the S.W.A.T. van later is sweet, too. I remember people cheering in the theater when that happened, way back when. But they also cheered when I tripped on the way out.

13.) *The Blues Brothers*
It's just a comedy so it's easy to forget that John Landis' fever dream always seems to be on the brink of Carmageddon. Speaking of Biblical proportions, maybe *Death Proof* should be here instead, since this is where

the cars in *Bullitt* and *Vanishing Point* and *The Seven-Ups* ended up in the afterlife, or the ghost of every car a movie destroyed, doomed to chase each other's taillights and flip over and over forever.

13 ½.) *Highlander*

No one is really chasing anyone, so it doesn't really count (and I wanted to end the big list on a luckier number so saying 13 and a half makes even less sense). However, the bad guy jacking that car and playing chicken by plowing through pedestrians and oncoming traffic with a screaming passenger is just too much like *GTA: Vice City* to ignore. The bad guy is also singing like Tom Waits, which then morphs into Queen, and Queen wrote the song "I'm in Love with My Car," so there's some kind of synchronicity going on here that is bigger than all of us.

BONUS LISTS

The Best Anti-Chases!

3.) *Fargo*

Just when you think the big chase is about to start, the taillights flicker in the distance and one of the cars is upside-down in the snow. Tragic because two young lives, and, more importantly, a car chase, was cut short in its prime. Sniff. Only one of those things is *really* a tragedy though.

2.) *The Way of the Gun*

The chase right around the first third of the flick, when the two guys take turns sticking their feet out and walking their vehicles for some bizarre reason. Not sure if it works as a comprehensible scene, let alone a chase, and it probably only made sense on paper, but that car-walking deal has gotta be some kind of important milestone in chases.

1.) *Wages of Fear/Sorcerer*

Same movie done twice, more than 20 years apart. Both excellent. Trucks hauling old, soggy, nitroglycerine-sweating dynamite through the jungle at about 5 miles per hour. The building-the-trucks sequence in *Sorcerer* set to the sounds of Tangerine Dream makes me want to build a truck and die in it right now. The original film is a little Frenchified with scarves and striped shirts and time wasted on a romantic subplot, but both movies are twitchy masterpieces. And I'm convinced the remake ends up on the surface of the Moon somehow. Maybe I was hallucinating like Roy Scheider.

The Best Movies That Are Sort of One Big Chase but Don't Really Contain a Single Good Chase!

10.) *Mad Max: Fury Road*

Let me back up. It's not that it doesn't contain a single good chase. It's just that every inch of that movie is a chase and also perfect and I don't know how to deal with this. Okay, maybe the CGI lizard at the beginning wasn't perfect, but this movie, and 70-year-old George Miller, feel like they're somehow hovering above this list, spinning in a nuclear whirlwind. Because, at some point, if a movie is one big chase, the chase doesn't matter as much as the spectacle, right? Ripping ass down a road becomes as unremarkable as walking across the room, or even turning your head, because complete immersion has been achieved. Which is why this film will likely never be topped and should not be included here. Don't even look at it. It goes to eleven.

9.) *North by Northwest*

Arguably the first mindless action movie, as Hitchcock admitted the title meant nothing, the chase meant nothing, and nothing meant nothing. He just wanted to end a movie with a man hanging off Lincoln's nose at Mount Rushmore. You know what the movie was originally called? *The Man on Lincoln's Nose*. The prosecution rests. And no good chases to speak of here really. So why is it on this list you ask? Good question. Because Cary Grant does some excellent drunk driving in a jaw-droppingly irresponsible sequence. Today they'd call that shit "problematic."

8.) *Death Race 2000*

Some cool, goofy '80s Toledo Sports Arena Autorama-looking rides. But the creepiest thing might be the strange opening credits doodle. What the hell was that? Someone must have painted that on the side of a suspicious van at least once.

7.) *Baby Driver?*

Nope. This movie is completely disqualified for not having an actual baby drive a car. And for not using a Fisher Price baby dashboard. No excuse. So let's put *Speed* here instead. That was one big chase with no real "chase" chase. But how damn likable was Keanu Reeves in that movie? He's like our buddy!

6.) *The Hitcher*

Lots of cops get killed by C. Thomas Howell and the bad guy from *Blade*

Runner. Or is it the other way around? Or is the guy from *Blade Runner* just a figment of the kid's imagination and he's a one-man country-cop slaughterhouse? Is Eric Red pulling some sort of *Fight Club* thing here decades before *Fight Club?* Probably not, but I'm still hoping. "It's a drive-away," the whiny little punk keeps saying until he gets pennies on his eyelids. My favorite part is when the kid's covered in gas, and the match is falling, falling, and he can't catch his breath because of the fumes. You can still smell it.

5.) *Duel*

Cool, evil, very oily truck in this one. But it's a made-for-TV movie, so fuck it. Speaking of oil! I wanted to talk about *The Transporter* right here, too, but every time I try to watch a chase in those movies, I just rewind to the fist fight in the first one where Jason Statham is sliding around on bike pedals in a pool of 10W-30. It's so slippery it's like watching a fight give birth! To my penis.

4.) *The Getaway* (1972) & *The Getaway* (1993)

Both versions have great moments when the movie stops cold so the hero can shotgun the shit out of a cop car. So satisfying they had to do it again. And, of course, both movies stop cold so the leading men can pimp-smack their co-stars (wives in real life) across the face. What's up with that, guys? I think McQueen hits his wife twice! But Alec Baldwin gets smacked back by Basinger so the filmmakers can pretend it's all empowering to embattled wives slash crime molls or anyone else who's taken a wrong turn in a relationship and had hopes too high for a Peckinpah remake, so I'm leaning towards the original here? "Yeeesh" on those scenes either way. Hey! A little trivia you should already know: these were both written by Walter Hill, the man responsible for many an existential masterpiece, including number three on the big list up there, *The Driver*, and its illegitimate son, *Drive.*

3.) *Smokey and the Bandit*

You know, this movie holds up surprisingly well. Good wrecks and some great crunched metal, and Buford T. Justice's magically shrinking cop car is still quite funny to 10-year-old me. I'd even throw that chase from *Hooper* in this slot, too, since that's a videogame you can play if you still have your PS2 copy of *Stuntman.* But, yeah, these are all comedies and therefore make you long for the destruction that reached Old Testament proportions in *The Blues Brothers* if you're gonna be watching the funny pictures. Of course, if you *do* throw in *Smokey and the Bandit,* always be sure it's the old VHS version, not the retooled digital editions where Hal Needham added whimsical music to the surprisingly poignant final stretch. "We ain't gonna make it, son." Son? Yes, there's a 75% chance that Burt Reynolds is your father.

2.) *Vanishing Point*

How ridiculously symbolic is this? Dude takes "speed" then decides to drive from Denver to San Francisco in fifteen hours for no good reason. *Speed?* Get it? And he's helped by a psychic DJ named Super Soul. Could happen. And guess what? Another Dodge Challenger is involved. Remember it from *Bullitt*? Wait, no, that was a Charger? I still get confused. But the real problem here is the bastard keeps stopping and getting out of his car to flash back to his soft-lit, very soap-opera-looking life. Okay, there's a naked girl on a motorcycle rocking out to "Mississippi Queen," but if I wanted to see that, I wouldn't have watched a movie called *Vanishing Point*. Keep that channel tuned to highway oblivion, movie! Perfect ending though.

1.) *Two-Lane Blacktop*

I know this movie is about a race because that's what the nameless character said (damn, I sure love it when they go nameless). But, for some reason, I can't remember ever seeing this race occur. And I remember some mumbling about ripping out the heater in the heroes' car to make it faster, but I can't remember seeing that either. And I remember some tough talk from the rival driver, Warren Oates, every time James Taylor and Dennis Wilson stop for gas, but no one seems to be very passionate about any of this. But I do remember the cars. Bulky Chevy 150, the last thing you'd expect to be racing, and a GTO, driven by a guy the credits call "GTO" so we won't spend too much time thinking about it. You might remember him better as the guy that fell in love with the severed head of Alfredo Garica (Tarantino totally owes his sequence from *Sin City* to that movie, too). This is probably the slowest chase flick ever made. And, for some strange reason, against all of my instincts, one of my favorite movies.

Some Crazy Cars That Won My Heart!

1.) *The Car*

Big limousine-looking beastly thing with red-tinted windows. Driven by, uh, the Devil? Actually had a huge impact on me as a child. Because I thought we were rooting for The Car the whole time, until the end when the *Highlander*-looking tongue-wiggling explosion shows up and The Car loses. The equivalent of the Black Sox Scandal on my young mind. P.S. counting down like a bomb seemed dangerous all the sudden, so I'm counting up from here on out.

2.) *The Wraith*

Early Charlie Sheen classic (yes, that's a thing). Rips off *High Planes Drifter* so bad that some early reviews mocked it as *High Planes Dragster,* or *High Lanes Drifter.* Also features Audrey from *Twin Peaks* doing her Audrey thing two years early (between this and Agent Cooper in *The Hidden,* I think Lynch was watching a lot of shitty '80s movies). The plot goes like this; Charlie comes back to life as a combination space-alien slash Dodge Interceptor concept car. Jesus Chrysler, another friggin' Chrysler?! Well, at least it ain't another Challenger? Anyway, the car, er, half-car/half-Charlie hybrid, proceeds to hunt down and systematically murder the lamest gang since the home intruders in *Weird Science.* Features some very impressive fiery wrecks rolling down mountains. Too bad the car and Charlie look more like something out of *Tron.*

3.) *Christine*

Stephen King and John Carpenter rip off *The Car* but do enough cool stuff with the idea to be forgiven. The '58 Plymouth Fury pulsing and heaving and creaking to restore itself is practically orgasmic ("Show me . . ."). It's the best Cronenberg moment not in a Cronenberg movie. I'll bet he hit himself in the forehead and exclaimed, "I could have had a V-8!" Our house can't get enough of that joke. Hey, speaking of cargasms . . .

4.) *Crash*

Don't get this confused with the lame-ass Oscar-bait snoozefest of the same name. The cars in this movie kill, sure. But that is incidental. They're misunderstood. They really just want to fuck.

5.) *Freebie and the Bean*

Never mind, I thought this was the name of a porn. And, amazingly, *Dirty Mary Crazy Larry* isn't porn either? *Gone in 60 Seconds* (the original, not the crap remake) where the 40-minute chase wrecks 93 cars? Now that's porn.

6.) *Filthy Killer Trucks?*

Meat Loaf has a sweet Satanic semi in *Black Dog,* and this is Meat Loaf we're talking about, ambassador to the asphalt underworld and tour guide of dead-man's curves everywhere, and some of the trucks in this movie blowed up real good, but it all plays like a bargain-bin *Smokey and the Bandit,* right down to a blue Camaro running interference instead of a black Trans Am (even if it's funny to see Ned Ryerson as an ATF agent with one semester of psychology under his belt). Also, there was that sweet semi in *Maximum Overdrive,* with the grinning Green Goblin head on the grill (so my question is, why the hell did it keep killing with its ass end?), but, yeah, that filthy fucking milk truck from *Jeepers Creepers*, and the filthy semi in *Joy Ride*, those are my boys! Those trucks were kind of spiritual brothers, right? They both seemed to be the color of a grimy toilet you hope a bad guy's face gets slammed into. And, sure, both rip-off *Duel* and its patented filth wagon for the opening third of these movies. But both probably do it better. Too bad they start pulling over off the road and stepping out of their filthy trucks and running their mouths instead of their engines. Big mistake! However, this might be the best double feature since the crazy man-rabbit combo they served up with *Donnie Darko* and *Sexy Beast*.

7.) Bellflower

Motherfuckin' Mother Medusa! Staring into her headlights won't turn you to stone, but instead you'll turn to dangerous hobbies like shotgunning propane tanks, flamethrower construction, *Road Warrior* worship, and brain-damaged revenge fantasies.

8.) The Dead Pool

Teeny-tiny remote-control '63 Chevy Corvette vs. Dirty Harry's '98 Oldsmobile. Now that's a toy with personality. And one of those rare car-chase send-ups of the classic *Bullitt* chase that works both as satire and as a surprisingly effective pulse-pounder (almost had to put it in the Anti-Chase list). Seriously, just look at that little sucker catching air on those San Francisco hills! Also it's a fucking bomb, so Dirty Harry's unmarked Oldsmobile doesn't stay unmarked for long.

The Best Chase That Was Disqualified Because the Franchise Stole My Genius Idea (But Somehow Still Screwed It Up)

1.) The Fate of the Furious

For years I was telling anyone who would listen that the eighth *Fast and the Furious* movie should be called *F8*, and you'd pronounce it like, "Fate." No-brainer, right? Then have the poster's tagline say, "You Know Why *Fast 6* Was Afraid of *Fast 7*? Because *Fast 7* *ATE* 9!" Gold, I tell ya. But the official title, *"Fate of the Furious,"* makes even less sense than usual, even if they're still striving for that "smells 'gamey'" *Grand Theft Auto*-motive insanity. When they all parachuted out of that plane *in their cars* was a high-point though.

The Best Chase Where Corpses Are Treated With Little or No Respect!

1.) *Bad Boys II*

I used to call this a bad movie with good chases, but I've changed my mind on that lately. It's good chases with a bad movie! Wait, that's the same thing. But that chase with the embalmed bodies slapping around those hoods, or even the destruction of the shanty town? All minor masterpieces. I was tempted to add the dude from *Fame* getting windshield splooshed in *Robocop* to this slot, or the terrorist from *Die Hard* getting the "Welcome to the party, pal" safety-glass faceplant, but that's down the rabbit hole again. And even though *Die Hard 4: Die Hardier* had some of the best recent car action (smoking that helicopter at least), it was combined with some of the worst car CGI ever, so I came out disgruntled. There's just no getting around the fact that the best car chase in the *Die Hard* Trilogy is actually from Playstation's *Die Hard Trilogy* (what a twist!), and computer Sam Jackson clearly knew this when he shouted out during his voiceover work, "Slow down before we go back in time!"

The Best Chase Ruined by a Sound Effect

1.) *The Man with the Golden Gun*

As you already know, anyone who busts out a slide whistle at a party gets immediately waterboarded. It's almost as bad as someone playing acoustic guitar and gazing awkwardly into your eyes. Which is why when British stuntman Loren "Bumps" Willard (and either a mannequin or a corpse done up to look like a corpulent redneck) drove that AMC Hornet over a river to pull off a 270-degree barrel roll in one take (!) and in the process gave a hearty "fuck you" to a future full of CGI-addled action movies, people don't really talk about that scene in *The Man with the Golden Gun* as much as they should. Simply because there's a slide whistle in it. Rumor has it that Bumps was paid only £30,000 for nailing that stunt, which, coincidentally, is the price of 30,000 slide whistles. But the real cost will never be determined.

The Best Chase Where It Looked Like Someone Got Fucked Up for Real

1.) *The Seven-Ups*

For this movie, the stunt coordinator from *Bullitt* and *The French Connection* returned to drive the '73 Pontiac Grand Ville that goes up against Roy Scheider's Pontiac Ventura Custom Sprint, which was *probably* being driven by famous Hollywood stuntman Jerry Summers when it James Van Der Beaked into the back end of that semi and . . . oh my fucking God, look at Roy Scheider's face!

The Best "Chase" Where I Use Scare Quotes Around "Chase" Because Chases Get Sidelined When the Whole Thing Is Filmed Inside a Car

1.) *Locke*
Yes, I know there are no chases in this but I don't give a shit. This movie was amazing, and I learned so much about laying concrete that I could do that job *tomorrow.*

2.) *Wheelman*
I know I said earlier that I was frustrated whenever Barry Newman got out of the car in *Vanishing Point,* but this movie sort of proves, like the song says, sometimes you don't get what you want, you get what you need. But did we need Grillo to keep leaving his car like that when I was promised a car-bound movie? My real gripe with *Wheelman* in a nutshell is that, unlike *Locke,* this movie has all sorts of angles on the action going on around the vehicle (shots of the wheels, pursuers, top view, side view, etc.), which is intended to squeeze the most out of such a narrow focus, but, ironically, this makes the movie seem so much smaller, especially compared to static shots of Tom Hardy having intense conversations about pouring concrete, which (no joke) seemed epic and had me on the edge of my nuts. Maybe they should have had this guy alone the whole time, or mute, or only recording himself making enemies lists in between chases? Sort of like . . .

3.) *The Series of Embarrassing Videos . . .*
. . . that Dave made in high school where he drove around recording himself making enemies lists.

The Best Chase According to My Brother-In-Law

1.) So, my brother-in-law, for whatever reason, is a foolproof predictor of what films will be huge. For example, he was talking about sleeper hit *The Sixth Sense* before any critic caught wind. And his predictions are critic-proof, as well. Like when he was yammering about that horrible new *Ghost Rider* movie, specifically where Cage jumps a motorcycle over some helicopters or some nonsense, and we all scoffed at him. Then that movie went on to make almost 300 million dollars, with respectable reviewers still scratching their noggins. It's sort of an "everyman" gift he has (a sixth sense!) not burdened by taste or favorites or anything really, but he can pick the winners merely by buying a ticket. So when I was wrapping up this list, I decided to ask him what his favorite chase scene was, thinking there was no way I missed any. I was wrong, of course. He goes, "*The Fifth Element*, bro. With the flying taxis? That was the first three-dimensional chase without the stupid glasses." And holy shit, he was right again.

The Best Chases with Things That Don't Count!

10.) *No Clue What This Was*
Okay, I stumbled across this Hot Wheels slo-mo race video on You-Tube once, where it pit K.I.T.T. against Ecto-1 against *The A-Team's* "Free Candy" rape van and Doc Brown's DeLorean, and the *Scooby-Doo* Mystery Machine. The clip was this toy car chase with participants *almost* as tiny as the MINI Coopers in *The Italian Job(s)*. No clue what it was, but it still ended up replacing *The Italian Job* on these lists easily enough (maybe not the cliffhanger ending of the original though, where you know they used the grappling hook to grab that gold). So does TV qualify now all the sudden? No clue. So, basically, this spot is simply reserved for all those crazy clips you dig up in the dark recesses of the internet, snippets of Russian or Indian films where you never know what the hell is going on. Like that pile of Indian dudes in sunglasses with the skunk hair that turns into a massive, gun-spitting cobra or whatever? No clue what that was. We're just not ready for that. And you know what? Clicking through YouTube, I'm going to put the trailer for '80s classic *Short Time* here, too, because I just found it. Look at all those car crashes. Does this movie star *The Winnebago Man*? No clue!

9.) *The Long Riders*
Blatant *Wild Bunch* rip-off when the James Gang rides out of town after their botched robbery. Slo-mo bullet wounds and backward bullet noises are impressive as hell though, even if it is sloppy seconds (*Young Guns* stole this sequence, too, meaning Dirty Steve had dirty thirds). But, yeah, horses have horsepower, we established that earlier, but they're not technically cars because of all the defecating. That's science. But this *is* Walter Hill. And that scene is better than most movies. Especially this one.

8.) *Hard Rain*
The jet-ski chase through the flooded school. Who wouldn't want to do that? There's a kind of inspired madness to the scene, and any time you flood a house, strange things can and will happen. Just try it. *Deep Blue Sea* had

sharks slipping in and out of a flooded lab, opening doors, learning how to use ovens. Hell, I was waiting for a shark to get on a phone and try to sucker a pizza-delivery dude. And *Dagon* had people reverting back down the evolutionary ladder as soon as their living rooms overflowed. Also, on a side note, someone should make a movie called *Hard Black Rain* to cause even more confusion when I rent movies.

7.) *True Lies*

The horse chasing the motorcycle through the hotel. I know, stop with the stupid horses, but that was a weird chase, huh? But the best scene is really the two Harrier jets taking out the terrorists on that bridge. Pilot: "Will the nukes go off if we take out the bridge?" Schwarzenegger: "No." Then he turns and does this guilty shrug to Tom Arnold. That was funny stuff! The movie also scores points for featuring a loving kiss in front of a mushroom cloud, and, yes, we're sliding off the road again and I'm-a let you finish but didn't *Adaptation* get the last word on all this stuff with one line, "It's like a battle between motors and horses . . . like technology vs. horse."

6.) *Runaway Train*

Kurosawa wrote the script for this parable about a doomed train with escaped convicts heading for the big dead-end. So they're, like, really chasing *themselves?* Deep. Lots of satisfying arguments and twitchy eyelids (and Eddie "Mr. Blue" Bunker). And an oddly affecting fade-out ending and *Richard III* quote that wasn't "My kingdom for a horse!" for once. Thank Christ. What's next? A horse in the hospital?

5.) *Face-Off*

I'd kind of forgotten about the boat chase until my friend Jerry angrily described the climax of this movie as "the director jerking off onto my face." So any chase that gets that kind of reaction has to get a mention. I'd also like to throw *The Rock* in right about here because there might be a decent chase with the Hummer, but I couldn't tell with shaky cam strapped to that poltergeist. I did like how Cage and Travolta hovered in the air for about a year after the boats exploded. Points revoked for Cage's hilariously earnest titular line though: "I want to rip his face . . . [pause] . . . off." Ha ha shut the fuck up.

4.) *Black Rain*

That was a fulfilling little dirt-bike chase through that farmlands. Ends with a solid fist fight that shows how American right hands and cheap shots from a flabby, over-the-hill Michael Douglas can defeat that sneaky kung-fu any day! If there's anything more embarrassing than white people doing

Martian Arts it hasn't been invented yet.

3.) *The Abyss*

Decent little sub chase ending with Michael Biehn's wonderfully mustachioed bad guy getting smashed from the water pressure like an empty beer can. Question: How did they not predict a guy named "Coffey" was gonna get "the shakes"? Bonus points for Crazy Coffey elbowing that tape player into shards when the Linda Ronstadt song comes on in the middle of his chase. I'm right there with ya, buddy.

2.) *Ben-Hur*

Ever see that Roman transsexual porn called *Ben Her?* Speaking of jokes my former high-school classmates still post on Facebook in their 40's . . . not since high school boys cranked Queen's "We Will Rock You" before football games have straight males been so excited and confused at the same time. You've all seen this chariot race by now. But how about that rowing scene? That's technically a chase scene, too. At least I think they were being chased. But we weren't allowed to look since there aren't any windows in the bowels of a ship. I know I just said "bowels" but I'm not going to take the bait. Too many jokes . . . locking . . . up . . .

1.) *Darkman*

I got so excited that I forgot I was counting down again, but this movie has got to be the last word in superheroes hanging off helicopters, and when he's bouncing and running along the tops of all that traffic, it still makes me smile to this day. I did it again today. Smile, I mean.

So in summation, just remember that those crazy limeys in *An American Werewolf in London* said it best when they warned us to "stay off the moors and stick to the roads." I'm not sure what a "moor" is, but if it's anything like a "mook," definitely stay off them or you'll get your ass kicked like De Niro in *Mean Streets.* But I think we're done for now, even if this list changes again tomorrow, as it used to do almost hourly back when the first incarnation was parked in *Flywheel Magazine,* my now-defunct online rag chronicling my Toledo, Pittsburgh, and Louisville driving days, a project mostly dreamed up while pinballing around that rust belt and killing time in driver's seats, back seats, and trunks, surfing the same highways and backstreets where many of the stories in this collection were born. And even if we're all gathering more flies than wheels these days, luckily, it turns out tires really do screech on desert dust after all, and don't let anyone whose name isn't George Miller tell you any different.

FIRST STORY EVER

You were hysterical, so I jumped out and found it glowing red in the tail-lights, dead as hell, everything facing the wrong way. That's when you got out, too, and I thought our day would be ruined if you saw. We still had an hour before we were even close.

So I kicked the dog under the car. Then I ran to the ditch and acted like I watched it run away. I was like, "Damn, tough little bastard. Not even a limp."

You believed me, not knowing it was right by your feet. When you calmed down, we got back in, and I thought, "If I pull this off, I swear I'll tell the truth someday."

Right about then, the back tire rolled over its head.

If you knew, you gave no clue.

I was gonna write a story about it, get it off my chest, but it would be my first story ever, and you'd know something was up.

THE EAR EATER OF JASPER COUNTY

They joked about gas-station chicken for dinner again, until I explained I wasn't averse to eating birds from the same place you bought rubbers and motor oil. So when the Kum & Go sign boasted the "Best Fried Chicken in Nine Counties," I probably would have checked it out anyway. The fact that the light box also announced a "Big Foot Problem!" at the "Important Town Meeting 2night!" pretty much sealed the deal.

"Did you see that?" Mag asked.

"You know, sometimes it's tough to get motivated in the summer down here," Matt said. "Until you hear about a local town meeting regarding the . . . *Bigfoot Problem*. I know what we're doing tonight!"

"How do we know we haven't missed it?" she asked him.

"That's a very good question," I said, trying to side with Mag and score some points. Only I'd be dumb enough to pick up a hitchhiking couple and work on the girl. "How do we know what time the Bigfoot meeting is?"

"You know, I've *heard* about these meetings," Matt cautioned. "This could be going on from when it gets dark to when it gets light."

I must have looked skeptical.

"Well, if we're gonna do it, we gotta do it now," I said. "I don't want to crash through the door late to the Bigfoot Party and get shotgunned."

"Don't worry," Matt smiled. "I took a class on this in college. Cryptozoology 101. I learned a lot about Bigfeet, Littlefeets, all the feets."

"Let's do it. Leave Dave's cat in the car," Mag said.

"That's no cat," Matt reminded her.

"Shhh," I told them.

I opened the door, and the alarming jangle of the chimes signaled our arrival. Inside was like any other gas station slash convenience store, except for the conspicuous rows of heavily armed, camouflaged dudes taping up huge topographical maps and Polaroid pictures onto the foggy glass doors of the beer coolers. A dozen bloodshot eyeballs and cataracts rolled our way, beards working around chewing tobacco and toothpicks. They had a lot of rifles, which nervously switched shoulders as they looked us over.

"Hi, guys!" Matt said, cheerfully.

"I always wanted to go to a town meeting," Mag whispered. "It's got to be the closest you'll get to *Gilmore Girls*."

"Yeah, more like *Gary Gilmore's Girls*," I said, as we crept through the gauntlet, finding a spot near the snack cakes and overripe fruit baskets and trying to pretend we belonged there by putting on our best "Dealing with a Bigfoot problem" faces. Matt went off to get some peanuts.

"Just had a terrible thought."

"What's that?" Mag asked.

"What if it's a trap?" I asked.

"A Bigfoot trap! Even better! It would probably have huge shoes in it."

"No, like to sucker tourists."

"Like a bunch of Bigfoots are at the meeting undercover wearing trench coats?" Mag giggled. "Don't worry, tough guy. I'm a local. I'll protect ya."

"Bigfeets in the house!" Matt shouted as he came back, tearing into a bag of nuts with his teeth.

"Chill," Mag said, noticing side-eyes from more hunter-types still shoving their way through the doors, overworked chimes clanking their warning.

"Hey!" someone yelled, and in walked a goddamn Bigfoot, and even the chimes were suddenly spooked silent. He was a big, hairy dude in a black hunting vest. He stopped at the bubble-gum machine and palmed it like a basketball, pointing at us with the handle end of his axe.

"You," he said. He was all blacks and greens and dark eyes under a black leather baseball cap, and if anyone was actually a Bigfoot in disguise, it was this monster.

"Yeah. You. You drive a Volkswagen Rabbit, buddy?"

"Yes I do."

. . . because I just ate it, I thought, finishing his sentence in my head.

"You left your dog in the car. And that's animal cruelty. So I smashed your window to give it some air. You're welcome."

Then the axe man saw someone he knew by the microwave and trotted over for some monster high-fives. Two smaller hunters leaned on the bubblegum dome in his place, breath fogging the glass. These giants moved faster than I would have thought possible, down here on our end of the beanstalk. I tried to reassure myself with the knowledge that cops could pull the entire town's sweaty fingerprints from the bubblegum machine if we didn't survive this shit.

* * *

Even though my regular traveling companion was probably not a dog, or even a cat (and maybe something more like a rat) and even though he had a perfect name like "Zero" which would make you think he was tailor-made for low temperatures, I ran to my Rabbit and grabbed his cage so he wouldn't freeze. Glass crystals from the busted window dusted my driver's seat, and I brushed it all out onto the stones, tempted to drive off right then and there. The meeting hadn't started yet, and I'd only known Mag and Matt for only about 24 hours, and my car was already getting fucked up. But there was no way I was going to miss this meeting. Also, I figured if I hung around long enough, I'd get up the courage to confront the Axe Man about this smashed window bullshit. Even if he *was* strong enough to chop down trees with the wrong end of that thing.

This would impress Mag, a.k.a. "Magdalene," even if what she'd said at the state line was true about Matt having two penises.

No, that was definitely a joke. Had to be. Truth or Dare is always 50% bullshit, especially in a car.

*   *   *

When I got back inside, the Mississippi Militia were getting ready for something serious. They'd formed a half-circle, and on the imaginary stage inside this human amphitheater was a ruddy-faced, well-dressed man in crisp, un-tested hunting gear pointing up at the doors of the beer cooler, sometimes running his palms along the maps to help smooth them out. He looked even more out of place than us, and the group studied him skeptically as he snapped his fingers to get everyone's attention.

"Thank you, folks, for coming. My name is Henry Honeysuckle, founder of the B.F.G., Bigfoots and Phantasmagorics Gigantology . . ."

"'Phantasmagoric' doesn't start with an 'F'," someone near us corrected him, and I was impressed. Don't let the bumper stickers with the Union Jacks confused for Confederate flags fool ya.

". . . and this is our first time in Jasper County," he went on, undeterred. "We heard about your town meeting, and we were hoping you wouldn't mind if we shot some footage for our show, *MANSTERS: Half Man, Half Monster, All Terror.* Could I have a show of hands for anyone who has seen one, heard one, or found droppings of any, uh, Mansters?"

Mansters, I snickered to myself, as dozens of arms shot up, half of them holding high-powered rifles. Henry Honeysuckle took a pen from behind a purple, fleshy ear that looked more like a foot, and he tapped a map with it.

"Oh, no," Mag groaned. "This is one of those stupid reality shows."

"Great!" Henry grinned. "Now, speaking on behalf of the B.F.G., we have discovered through our research that many of these creatures have been sighted along the Mississippi River. So we have reason to believe that this river is being used as a 'highway' by the animals, a 'migration route' of North to South, 'depending' on the season, or their 'appetite' . . ."

His fingers were highlighted random words with air quotes as he traced a winding path on the map.

". . . so maybe you men can show me on here where the majority of your sightings have occurred."

A short man in camo from head to toe stepped up, snatched the pen from Honeysuckle's hand, and before I could make a joke about not being able to see the guy, and right about when Matt was puffing up and processing what Mag said about it being a reality show, Camo Man jacked Henry Honeysuckle right in the honey-sucker with a wild right hand, sending him headfirst through a spinner rack of beef jerky.

Holy hell.

Henry was still recovering, and the rack was still spinning, when Axe Man and his backwards axe stomped up next to Camo Man, held the axe handle under his chin like a microphone, and effectively took over the meeting. He cleared his throat for what seemed like ten minutes as his eyes scanned the crowd, and I stared at the blade of his axe balanced against his seven-point-buck belt buckle, wondering if he held phones upside down all his life, too, with no one daring to correct him. Then two men wearing a more reasonable amount of camouflage took Henry Honeysuckle by his arms, kicked the jerky rack out of their way, and dragged him out the door. A wormy little guy in glasses holding a GoPro that no one had noticed, presumably a member of the television crew, slunk out after him without a peep. Now that was real camouflage.

"I think someone misunderstood our ad in the paper," someone laughed, slapping the bubblegum machine like his favorite ass. Near the register was a bulletin board labeled "Wall of Fame," and pictures around its border showed hunters gathered around a human shape at their feet. Only they weren't in the woods, but photographed dead center in this very same candy aisle rainbow of colors.

"Are we gonna hash this out or what?" someone else wanted to know.

"Lock the door," Axe Man finally said, and I held my rat cage closer, trying to get smaller, wishing I could crawl inside with Zero, while Zero slept like it was his third Bigfoot meeting of the day.

"*Now* it's a reality show," Matt said, eyes wide and expectant.

"This is way better than I thought it was gonna be," Mag said, and the three of us backed up against a dessert cooler as far as we could. Still starving, I looked around us. Behind the glass and under my elbows was a row of evil-looking, blackberry snack-cake monstrosities and a handwritten sign that read, "Edgar Allan Pies." I swore I could feel their chilly, black hearts beating against my spine right as the real ruckus started.

*   *   *

It took us a minute to figure out what they were all arguing about, but eventually we realized these guys were real upset about something that, mercifully, wasn't us.

"It will not stand, boys!" Axe Man said, giving up the mic and letting his namesake bang on the tile floor. A smaller guy in fishing waders stepped up, holding a rawhide chew toy as a microphone, and I was reminded of the wrinkly seashell-looking "Fleshlight" they passed around in the porn parody *Lord of the Fries*.

"I got some more pictures to show y'all," MC Chew Toy said as he hitched the suspenders on his rubber pants, digging deep in a pocket.

"Robert Loon?" MC Chew Toy called out, head on a swivel. "Are you here tonight? Why don't you tell us what's going on in this one?"

His picture showed a huge, horned, six-limbed shape lying across a tree stump, hooves high in the air. It resembled a centaur, but with a sheep's body and the scaly torso of a man. One of the horns was cracked at the base, and half the face was blow away. A tiny hunter leaned on his rifle about ten feet behind the damned thing.

"I was driving down County Road 528144 after work," a voice came from the crowd. "When, all the sudden, something huge come up out of the thickets, and it covered both lanes in about three steps. Then it head-butted my car, sent it screeching into the ditch. I jumped out, and while it was gnawing my hood ornament like some Big League Chew, I pulled out my scattergun and blew its cursed head off."

"I've heard of this thing," Matt said to us. "They're talking about 'Randy the Ram Man of Chesapeake Bay!' But he lives on the East Coast. So what's he doing here . . . ?"

"Quite a story, Robert," the MC nodded. "Maybe you can tell us why you look to be sitting five clicks behind this critter when you had the picture taken?"

"Well, I . . ."

"We'll come back to that!" MC said, pulling another picture from his bottomless pocket. "How about Bobby Yupper? Where's The Yoop at tonight?"

"Right here, boss," said The Yoop, holding up a finger.

"Can you tell us what's happening in this shot?" MC asked, flipping a Polaroid back and forth like he was trying to coax out an image. When it stopped flapping in his hand, we squinted again and could barely discern another hazy behemoth, a low-backed, reptilian form with a man's fleshy arms, and something resembling a humanoid face. Again, a good deal of the visage had been removed with the indelicate assistance of a firearm.

"Fine," Yoop shrugged. "We were camping down by Arkabutla Lake, and suddenly we think we're in a hailstorm, until we start getting a whiff of it. Turned out something is throwing feces at our tent. Now this shit ain't normal size, so I come running out, and here's like this gator, but like a man-gator, rearing back and hissing, tryin' to get me. So I grab my peppergun and sent its face straight to hell."

"You sure did, Bobby!" someone agreed.

"Holy shit," Matt said, squeezing my tricep now. "You know what he bagged? That's the Mini-Minnehaha, the Microsaurus of McIntosh County! I wrote two papers on that thing. Got a C+."

"What the hell is a 'microsaurus,'" I asked him, pulling free.

"Most people took it for an alligator gar," Matt said, all authoritative. "In Georgia, there's been sightings of gars almost twenty feet in length, elongated necks, razor-sharp teeth, and long, prehensile tails . . . but this one is, like, half dude."

"Are you kids paying attention?" MC asked us, taking too many steps toward our spot near the dessert case for my comfort. I held up a hand and nodded.

"We're here to learn," Mag reminded us, and I made a motion like I was locking up my lip and throwing away the key.

"Good. Now, Bobby, how big would you say this creature was?"

"As you can see, about the size of a John Deere 8000. Same color, too."

"If this bugbear was the size of a John Deere, why is your boot in that picture there as large as a goddamn tractor tire?"

He held the picture high, and now we could see the hunter far back behind the creature, just like the guy in the first picture, but also with one leg absentmindedly extended to bring his shoe up near the monster's ruined face.

"I don't have an answer."

"Well, I do have an answer, Bobby. And I'll get to it in a minute . . ." He pulled out another picture. "How about Robbie Scruton? You here? Describe this scene, goddamn it."

This picture showed three men, arms crossed and proud, and a huge serpentine mass hanging from a construction crane in the foreground. The chimera seemed to be sporting what was left of a man's bloody face.

"Okay, I come around the corner of the garage, and this snake thing was bent down, choking and eating what had to be a dog."

"So it was bigger than a dog?"

"Oh, much bigger. Its tail was twice as thick as a Mastiff's ribcage."

"If this tail was bigger than a whole dog, then why is it draped across your feet and looking to me to be about as skinny as a garter snake?"

The crowd grew restless.

"What are you trying to say?" someone shouted as the agitation grew. Matt whispered something in my ear about that picture being the first definitive proof of "Volcano Vince," the half-man, half serpent formerly of Kansas City, Kansas, and partial to quarries, sinkholes, and blasted-out basements, but Mag shushed him with a hiss.

"Now, I know there's stiff competition this year for the trophy," MC said. *Trophy?*

"But an issue has been cropping up that we can't ignore any longer. Your feet have betrayed you, boys. Our judges have uncovered some serious chicanery."

A murmur swept through the group, and some men looked down at the floor, others cocked their weapons. I mapped the exits for the tenth time.

"That's right, men. We are dealing with the forced perspective."

The gas station exploded.

*   *   *

When the shouting died down a bit, and the dust from the ceiling tiles stopped raining from the bullet holes, we finally understood that this was not a *big* foot meeting after all, but a big *foot* meeting. Just like the sign advertised.

Voices were ramping back up, and I tried to pull Mag toward the door. She hissed again for me to be quiet, even though I'd said nothing.

"You keep hissing like that, you're gonna end up dead in a picture with a giant foot," I warned her.

"That is a serious accusation," a man shouted at MC as he worked the stock of his rifle with both hands, like the "snake bites" I routinely gave my steering wheel.

"You're right, Bob, it is," MC said, stepping forward.

I blinked as Matt left us and the relative safety of the dessert cooler and walked directly into the mob, palms open and up in the air.

"Excuse me," Matt said. "But what about those monsters?"

"What about those monsters?" Bob said.

"I mean, those are still a lot of impossible beasts you men have shot," Matt said. "You people have proven the existence of a half-dozen or more creatures that previously only existed in folklore."

"But these men cheated!" MC said, slapping Matt's cheek with a Polaroid depicting the murder of another fuzzy oddity.

"I understand that, but that's still a picture of a . . ."

"Doesn't matter," MC said with another slap.

"Your uncles are cool," I joked, leaning over to see if Mag was plotting our escape, and I was surprised to see her polish off a Yalobusha Milk Stout and crush the can in her small hand. I'd thought Mag was "shushing" me this whole time, but the sound had been the hiss of the beer tops she'd been popping. Around her feet, other half-crushed cans displayed long decals of animal scratches down their sides and all things "monster" related. I hoped ol' Mags wasn't mixing alcohol and power drinks. That stuff made people crazy. I watched her cracking knuckles instead of jokes now, ready to mix it up.

"What's your name, boy?" MC asked Matt, hand poised in mid-slap. Axe Man stood behind Matt, looking down, blinking slow.

"Uh . . . Bobert," Matt said, looking back at us, hand on his face and shrugging. "Gargantua slayer?"

"Why don't you have your friends come up here and join us. Show us what's in that cage of his."

Axe Man's cap angled toward me.

"You!" MC shouted, pointing at me and Mag, huddled on the floor. I slid Zero's cage behind me protectively.

"What did you bring in here?"

"I'm here for the trophy!" I announced, before I could think of anything better. But this gave the hunters pause, and Matt yanked the cage from my grip, holding Zero up high.

"Gentlemen," he said. "This here is Balabushka, the Russian Were-Beaver of the Bering Strait. It ran back and forth across that ancient bridge between Russia and Alaska, the very bridge that brought us all to this land."

"That shit doesn't connect," someone said.

Zero peered down from his cage, nervous tongue flicking.

"That's a goddamn possum," MC said.

"Were-Beaver, my ass," Axe Man agreed.

"Where beaver? There beaver!" someone else laughed.

"You want to hear my story or not?" I asked. "So, I was walking home from a party one night, and there was this thing running down the railroad tracks toward me, making train noises . . ."

"Bullshit!" one of them said. "That was a train."

". . . and it turned out to be a train. But when I got closer, I found this . . . thing, crouched overtop of another animal, eating its ears?"

I couldn't disguise the doubt in my voice, but at the word "ears," the men stopped and shared a worried glance. Then the far end of the mob parted to reveal a Hall of Fame poster board of photographs with the words "Pigzilla" and "Hogzilla" and "Big Fucking Swine!" scrawled above them. All of the pictures depicted barely-larger-than-normal wild boars in the foreground, with groups of hunters, arms crossed and defiant, way off in the background, but of course with their dumb legs thrust out in front of their bodies so that the corner of these pictures that supposedly proved the existence of school-bus-sized porkers inadvertently proved the existence of Peterbilt-sized work boots instead. But once I got past the trick photography, I noticed something else.

The ears were missing on all the monsters. It gave me an idea.

"You missing some ears around these part, men?"

"What do you know about ears?" Axe Man said, tipping up his leather cap.

"A lot," I said, waving Mag to head for the door, silently mouthing at her to start the car.

"You better start explaining yourself," MC said.

"I know where those ears went," I said, my fists and toes curling, realizing I was onto something.

"Where?"

"We took 'em."

Then I threw a punch that would have made a Bigfoot proud, if Bigfeets cared about that kind of thing. And there's no way to know for sure 'cause that shit don't exist.

* * *

We looked up the ear eater on Matt's phone later, and in the car we read all about the mysterious monster that had terrorized Jasper County, Mississippi, back in the summer of 1977. A series of livestock attacks that still haunted this town, maybe not as serious as forced-perspective photographs and the corruption of hunting competitions, and not nearly as conspicuous a monstrosity as the handful of other mythical beasts that seemed to still be plaguing residents, but at least a singular incident serious enough to have been immortalized on the internet, specifically the home page of Henry Honeysuckle's hit television show. It was a curiously outdated website, very '90s, all spinning pentagrams and spooky autoplay music, but it added to the overall effect.

The first reported encounter was by a man named Joseph Dickinson, who found one of his 50-pound hogs wandering around the pigpen one morning, seemingly healthy enough at first glance, but on closer inspection, missing both of its ears. No other extremity had been disturbed on the animal, and the hog was relatively unimpressed by its own mutilation, in spite of both ears having been completely severed with either knives, scissors, or teeth so sharp they'd sheared them off without so much as a whistle of fur or lacerations in the wounds. Mr. Dickinson corralled the rest of his livestock and made a more horrifying discovery; even more ears missing from each of his seven cattle, exactly one ear apiece.

The second report, and the first real sighting, came from a Robert Robertson, who owned a small farm about three miles down the road from Mr. Dickinson. He heard his pigs squealing the alarm and ran out to find a dark shape hunched over one of his animals, pinning it to the ground, both beasts writhing and thrashing up a storm of dust and blood. Mr. Robertson had the foresight to bring his biggest "fowling piece" up to the pens with him, freshly loaded with buckshot, and after discharging his weapon in the air, whatever had been molesting his swine's savory pink antennas thought better of it and took off in a tornado of screeches and dirt, taking the pig's left ear with it.

The third and final sighting was documented by Mr. Calvin Martin of Mary Martin's Dairy. He described finding one of his prized 300-pound sows missing its entire head. And when he came upon this gruesome sight, Mr. Martin maintained he witnessed a "largish" shape vault his chest-high perimeter fence and bolt off into the night. The morning revealed canine-like tracks, and when a constable's deputy shot a small, feral dog possibly hot on the trail of the creature, some townspeople hypothesized the attacks were the result of a pack of starving, wild mutts. But Mr. Martin swore to his grave that the creature in question was much larger than any mutt, larger than even a German Shepherd, which was the largest dog he knew of, and an animal he'd always adored in the World War II newsreels he collected. He swore it was able to "jump twice as high as anything on this Earth."

The head of Mr. Martin's 300-pound hog was never recovered, and local law-enforcement wondered whether the decapitation was the result of the mysterious creature growing bolder, or stronger. Or was it simply much harder to remove the ears from larger, prize-winning specimens?

All in all, the Ear Eater of Jasper County attacked nine different farms in the summer of 1977, and its whereabouts remained unknown.

Until tonight.

*   *   *

My punch was the stuff of legends!

When I was a little boy, I had some trouble making a believable fist whenever I tried to intimidate other kids, and sometimes my thumb stuck out like a hitchhiker, and my fingernails cut half-moons into my sweaty lifelines. But for once in my life, tonight my hand rolled up like my fingers never existed, turning my fist into something more like those round knobs of bone on the heads or tails of some of the cooler dinosaurs. You'd think a big beard like the one that adorned my target would have confused my fist where his jaw started and my punch began, but it was like my hand was working with sonar. I decided it was all the topographical maps I'd been in proximity to lately.

I caught him firmly in that circle of bone from the temple to the hinge, the ring that art teachers would typically start you with whenever you attempted to draw the perfect human face. But this face wasn't perfect for long, if it ever was, and my fist lost itself in his manicured beard, stretching the five o'clock stubble of the surrounding cheek like the distorted fabric of spacetime surrounding a black hole. I'm not a strong man, but my punch had a testosterone contact high or something on its side, and it launched MC Chew Toy a good ten feet in the air, his rawhide microphone failing to follow for long. His mouth motorboated so hard from the impact that it created a kind of impossible momentum, the wind from his lips surrounding him in a vacuum of velocity, like one of those comically-doomed, old-timey flying machines with some sort of mechanical hiccupping mechanism that no sane person would have bet on ever getting off the ground . . . but somehow ended up proudly airborne after all. His head took out the plastic arrow pointing to the ATM, then crashed through a closed-circuit camera, the umbilical of wires wrapping a noose around his neck. He came down camo-hat first into the impulse buys near the register, the bill of his cap snow-plowing through substandard *Duck Dynasty* and Union Jack lighters, 5-hour Energy Shots, now in healthy "green" flavor, and I swear he tried to catch one of those little bottles in his ruined mouth, maybe thinking it would re-activate him like Popeye's spinach. Then his shoulders wiped out the Duracell battery bin, and sent the "Under 18 No Tobacco" sign sailing up into the menthol cigarettes, until his limp Pete Rose slide finally stopped with his tongue unrolling like the red carpet at the Oscars to taste-test the pennies in the "Feed the Children" charity bucket.

No one believed I threw such a ridiculous, cinematic, positively *picturesque* punch, and later I wished a cop could have recorded it on his body camera for posterity. But at least I was there as a living witness, photographic evidence be damned. So I was as surprised as anyone when I blinked and MC Chew Toy and I were still nose-to-nose, and I realized without any proof that kind of punch just doesn't happen in real life.

And so it didn't, and he took my punch easy, then ducked the next, and had me around the neck like I was nothing, breathing Red Man up my nostrils like my sinuses were a chimney flue.

I looked for Mag but only saw Matt had been collared by the towering Axe Man himself, lifted off the ground as he windmilled and rattled off the names of every cryptid he could remember.

"Hey, man, you want monsters? I got monsters! You ever hear of the Spring Heel Jackalope? The Donkey Diva of East Texas? What about Bloody Mary? You guys must know about Bloody Mary! Heads up! Skunk Ape!"

Matt pointed to the fish-eye theft-deterrent mirror above them, and the

Axe Man caught his reflection, loosening his grip a bit, and Matt took a gasp, but I couldn't. MC Chew Toy had his arm around my throat, sinking it into my blood flow, and I thought I was going under.

Until I saw Mag in the anti-theft ball, coming down hard on the Axe Man's back. And even before she peeled off his leather baseball cap and sank her teeth into his ear, somehow I knew exactly what she was going to do.

*   *   *

At first, I didn't think she'd really do it. With all that talk about ears, I'd been targeting one of Axe Man's mud flaps in vain before she wrapped her beautiful mouth around the other one. And, yeah, it's actually *really* hard to rip off an ear with your hand.

But a mouth works just fine.

Well, hers did anyway. She bit and spit the first ear so fast he didn't seem to realize what had happened to him. But the second ear came off much harder, at least it came off much *longer*, pulling so much of his head and gristle off with it that I half expected his eyeball to be dangling from the lobe like an earring when it finally snapped loose.

Panicked, he made a grab for her, but she was up on the snack rack, the expensive snacks, the ones with all the nuts.

Not much bigger than a German Shepherd. And she could jump three times as high . . .

I watched her go head-to-head on these rubes, biting off ears like they were nothing. I got to my feet and found Zero's cage, cowering in the corner like a bunny, sometimes head up proud like a Jackalope. I saw Matt still on the ground.

Then I saw the axe, getting kicked around the brawl by some big-ass hiking boots, and I grabbed it, handle first, like you're supposed to.

There was a flash of light, and I thought it was a gunshot. Then another. And another. Camera flashes. I saw Axe Man standing up in shock, and Matt's phone an inch from his face, gripped tight in Matt's shaking hand.

The phone was displaying something strange, and Axe Man was gasping, hands over the new holes in his head. Other men stopped fighting and angled in, too, then looked away, visibly shaken.

"Is that what I think it is?" Axe Man asked, shouting because of his ear situation.

"It's the Loch Ness Monster!" someone shouted, and another camera flash went off.

"My God, there's two of them!"

It wasn't a forced-perspective shot, but it wasn't the Loch Ness Monster either. If I was a religious man, I would have prayed it was something less impressive like definitive proof of an extinct aquatic phenomenon on Matt's phone that made me drop my axe mid-swing, instead of what was really in that picture. But I'm not sure what I saw. Sure, it *could* have been the mythical double dick pic selfie, something I'd previously sworn impossible. Or maybe it was just Matt flashing a peace sign. Through his zipper. Either way, it worked.

Then someone blasted out the shoplifting mirror dome above us all, and it came straight down on the bubblegum machine, which detonated like a disco ball fucking a piñata.

"Take your Chupacabra, and get out of here," Axe Man said, and Mag hopped up off some squealing man's face, lobe stretching further than I thought possible. She let it snap back into his head, and we all glanced at my cage. I didn't know what Axe Man meant at first, then looked down at my own mystery animal, tiny hands on the bars of his prison. Poor unidentifiable Zero, whatever he was.

"It's just a cat, people!" I lied. "It's got some funky ears is all."

"I am not," Axe Man said, not hearing what I said, as he pulled out a camouflaged cellular and stabbed 911. He held the phone to his head right-side up, like a normal human being making a call, then screamed when it sunk into the hole.

*   *   *

We drove on, nursing our injuries and munching on some salty snacks. I still didn't know where they were going, but we'd crossed the Mississippi state line into that little Gulf nub of Alabama, so I could finally slow down on the gas. Mag was still hungry, winding down from mixing beer and Monster Energy. She found one pork rind at the bottom of the bag that was bigger than her hand. She gave it to me.

"Your trophy," she said.

Matt winced and gingerly tapped his swollen eyebrow in the mirror, then rose up off his passenger's seat. He brushed glass cubes and snow from under his jeans, then adjusted his crotch as I imagined something like the Rod of Asclepius going on in his blue jeans, and I forced myself to look away.

We drove on, and I thought of their Wall of Fame, imagining someone pinning a new Polaroid of her to their poster boards, or their coolers, or covering their maps or the holes where their ears used to be with her smile. Mouth streaked with gore, eyes blazing. I found her in the rearview mirror, and I made some wishes.

I wished for more monsters, and I wished I was in the picture with this one, because I knew that I'd be curled up in the background, trying to make her even bigger.

A DULL BOY

"All play and no work makes Jack a mere toy."
—Proverb

I'm telling a visibly bored class about immunostaining, the process for using colored dyes to gate out dead cells under a microscope and identify rare cellular populations, when the starstruck girl in the front row who had been giving me meaningful looks since day one, slowly and seductively blinks to reveal the words "Red" and "Rum" drawn on her eyelids.

* * *

My name is Danny Lloyd, and I'm a professor of biology at Elizabethtown Community College, although, when I lose my students' full attention, I've admittedly succumbed to the theatrics of chemistry demonstrations. When I was seven years old, I played the part of "Danny" in Kubrick's adaptation of Stephen King's *The Shining*. For months at a Colorado ski resort, I pretended to be a borderline psychotic but otherwise normal 5-year-old boy. The most distinguishing part of my performance, besides shivering and drooling like a rabid squirrel, was supplying the guttural voice of my index finger, Tony. This is the part of the film that is the most enduring, and that finger still follows me to work, decades later. For the record, I've never named any of my fingers. Not even whole hands, or fists, which seems to be in fashion here in the South, judging by some of the skirmishes in our hallways. When I began studying biology, I wasn't prepared for how self-conscious I'd feel whenever I'd use my finger to point out anything on the dry-erase board. To avoid any jokes, pretty early on in graduate school I stopped using that finger for essentially everything. And trying to indicate to someone to please, "Wait a minute" was always a mistake, even a noble "Watch out!" led to ridicule. And innocently scratching my ear was sometimes interpreted by King fans as Tony telling me a secret. Which was ridiculous because the finger thing wasn't even in the book, and real fans should know this.

I'd managed to lay low through my first several semesters at Elizabeth-town when my full-time teaching career began. Then, one day during the semester before all the rooms were finally outfitted with projectors, I made the mistake of writing something backwards on the overhead. A boy in the back had obviously heard from a friend of a friend of my short-lived movie career, and he shouted out in his best Tony growl:

"Redrum!"

I lost my temper that day, likely lost the respect of that class. But imagine how difficult it would be to kick someone out of the room without being able to point. However, there were plenty more classes to come, and hundreds more chances for that movie to disrupt my life even more.

*   *   *

It was about six years later, right after I received tenure, when technology introduced cell phone smuggling into classrooms. And with most instructors, me included, The Great Texting Cold War had finally begun. The policy on my syllabus was always, "Don't let me catch you texting. If I see this happening, you will lose all points for the day and could be asked to leave the classroom." I also explained that texting while driving was like having a 1.9 blood/alcohol level and illegal for this very reason. How could I have any confidence in their ability to follow my lectures if they were drunk? Someone grumbled something about Stephen King writing *Cujo* while drunk, and I moved on. But this one kid, Kevin, who sat in the back and should have been exhausted at the effort he put into entertaining everyone around him, was harder to catch than most. In fact, I lost a bit of ethos by demanding he stop playing with his phone, only to suffer the embarrassment of his slow, exaggerated removal of a phone that was buried deep in his book bag, which was actually a little plastic box of candy *shaped* like a phone. He claimed he'd been warming his hands between his legs, and that's why he looked so suspicious. Foolishly, I accused him of being covered in phones. And when he protested the unfairness of it all, I shrugged:

"The trust is gone, Kevin. I've busted you texting way too many times."

Hands were cold, my ass, I was thinking, *You want to talk about cold hands? Try eating ice cream for 47 takes while Kubrick makes the guy from* The Harlem Globetrotters *cartoon cry.*

*   *   *

"All work and no play makes Jack a dull boy."

The verse that everyone has recited at least a dozen times, those ten words that show up as jokes on most of my Teacher Evaluations, besides being that famous representation of writer's block in *The Shining*, was actually spoken in *The Bridge on the River Kwai, Buffy the Vampire Slayer,* an Alice in Chains song, *Twin Peaks, Melrose Place,* and it showed up on the chalkboard during an intro for *The Simpsons*, which means, of course, that it was in *Family Guy*, too. But it surprises some people to learn that this wasn't in King's original book either. Although he did jam it into *Pet Sematary*, I'm told.

Less frequently heard is a ten-word variation, the follow-up first recorded in 1825's *Harry and Lucy Concluded* by Maria Edgeworth, where she added, "All play and no work makes Jack a mere toy."

That's a line that could have really haunted someone later in life, so I guess I lucked out.

*   *   *

They hired me for that movie because of my name. The boy's name was Danny in the book, and they used my real name on the set, "Danny," so I wouldn't get confused.

So *I* wouldn't get confused? Maybe someone should have assured me it was only a movie and there would have been a lot less confusion.

"Jack" and I were the only ones that shared names with our characters. He must get confused easily, too, I figured. I had one up on him though, as there are two Dannys, two Jacks, *and* two Lloyds in that film. Therefore, my first and last name wraps around his Jack, mere toy or not, whether he had me on his lap or I was spilling Advocaat on his jacket.

Actually that was eggnog, and it was delicious.

I've read in interviews that I was supposedly told they were making a comedy, so I wouldn't be scared. Did they even wonder how my definition of comedy might be affected forever when I watched them filling an elevator with gallons of blood?

*   *   *

One time, I made the mistake of Googling my name and came across a blog post where a colleague at Elizabethtown wrote, "I ran into the kid from *The Shining* today at work. He had the same eyes. I knew him immediately. We're not supposed to talk about it, and it's driving me crazy."

I know there's little oversight in the Arts and Humanities, but I wonder if this instructor has considered how terrifying this might sound.

I understand that people want to talk about the movie all the time. And they never believe me, but I'd never even seen the entire thing until recently. I swear this is true. For my birthday, my sister was supposed to order me a copy of *Shine*, because the music instructor who shares our building's copy machine had been talking about the sudden burst of Rachmaninoff after that film's surprise Oscar wins. He said it was similar to the post-*Sideways* Pinot Noir upsurge (more like Merlot hatred), which was bad enough to endure. But my sister is a lot younger than I am, and she doesn't understand my lack of interest in the film, even if I wasn't starring in it. Actually, in her own way, she's the one who steered me towards my PhD, as she was the only one in the real world who insisted on calling me "Doc."

I guess I can understand her obsession, seeing my tricycle up on the little screen, then seeing it parked in our garage. Yes, it's a tricycle, not a "Big Wheel" like so many reviewers claim. That misidentification is why I no longer drive my Dodge 4x4. I thought it was a good choice for someone in Kentucky, but I switched to a Prius when my cousin laughed, "Look, Danny still likes Big Wheels!" Eagle-eyed viewers might notice that the path Jack takes us through the mountains, as well as the invisible maze I ride through the hotel, maps onto the hedge labyrinth exactly. Or at least it should.

The tricycle was a gift from Mr. Kubrick, and once it was handed down to my sister, it was easy to imagine her imagining herself peddling around those hallways, too. Anyhow, instead of *Shine*, she sent me *The Shining* and feigned ignorance (she made a similar joke when *Shining Through* came out, too), and I immediately printed out the proper return forms, repackaged it, and put it downstairs under our apartment's mailboxes to ship it back. But our vestibule doesn't lock, and someone stole the parcel. I know this because I placed it there at 9:00 p.m., walked down to C.C.'s on the corner for some ice cream, and when I returned at 9:25 p.m. it was gone. Maybe I shouldn't have autographed it. But infuriated, I sat in my living room and listened for any clues to the caper, immediately suspecting the kids who'd just moved in above me, and whose distracting bass-heavy sound system was usually all I could think about. So I listened for them to watch the movie, ignoring the much more likely scenario, that they'd sold it back to the Music & Movie Exchange for a quick five bucks of gas money. I sat on the couch all night, staring at the ceiling, careful my head was angled up and my eyes weren't rolling back in my head, never allowing myself that spaced-out look Kubrick had become famous for. I'd successfully avoided the film all my life, as I explained, but couldn't help catching sight once a year of my own five-year-old face drooling and contorted in seizures.

Eventually, I realized that I would have no idea if they were watching the movie or not. I only knew Jack's angry rant over the typewriter because I was on the set that day, pretending to nap on a nearby couch. And I only knew a spattering of my own lines. So I went down to the Music & Movie Exchange for my own copy. And I finally watched it.

It was a pretty good movie.

Jack went crazy kind of fast though. Every time a title card said "Monday," "Tuesday," "Wednesday," or "Two Months Later," I imagined it saying, "12:19," "12:25," "12:33," and "Five Minutes Later" instead. Can anyone switch gears that quickly from rational to homicidal? Kind of ridiculous.

* * *

Every year, our class takes a field trip to Kackleberry Farms to get some pumpkins for our hydrogen peroxide experiments, a variation on the classic Elephant's Toothpaste demo that you see in most grade schools. Hydrogen peroxide is mixed with liquid soap, then a catalyst like potassium iodide is added to make the hydrogen peroxide break down quickly. Then the foam puts on quite a show. Not enough foam to fill up an elevator, but it wakes them up for a day nonetheless, even keeps them from texting. More important, no one does a Tony imitation with their clamshell phone.

The formula, $2H2O2 \rightarrow 2H2O(l) + O2(g)$, is deceptively simple, considering how a bit of mad science actually opens their dead eyes for a week of lectures afterward. Something about that foam busting through the eyes and mouth of Halloween pumpkins makes my job fun all over again.

But this year the farm doesn't just have pumpkins.

They have a hedge maze, too.

* * *

Many times, people have congratulated me on my nine-year-old character's ingenuity, when we backtracked over our footprints in the snow to save Danny's life.

Now, I don't want to overanalyze the film. In fact, lately, there have been Post-it notes on my door with "Room 237!" scrawled on them, which steered me towards a recent documentary of the same name. I wasn't surprised by its popularity among my weakest students. From what I've seen, if it wouldn't be such a distraction to show it in class, I could have used it as a hilarious example of horrible inductive reasoning. It's bad enough they're using exclamation points on anything, since it's not only term papers that suffer from that sort of breathless punctuation. Each semester, I explain that students are allowed one exclamation point, whether it's in emails or more substantial assignments. I tell them not to waste it, in case they really need to scream about something important, like I do.

But now that I've finally viewed *The Shining*, I realize that it was never backtracking that saved me. If you look real close at what I was doing in the maze, if you squint right there in the bottom left corner of your screen, I was actually covering some of them up. I like this idea better.

* * *

Once, I had two sets of twins in my classroom. One set of twins was our turtles. I'd turned the corner at the Science Building one morning, and there in front of my huge off-road vehicle were two box turtles, side by side in the parking lot like they were going to live forever. I took them into our classroom, and with the students, we filled up the empty 20-gallon tank that had been gathering dust in the corner, and we gave our new turtles a home. I numbered their shells, "52" and "81" as part of an extra credit assignment. The numbers represented tellurium and thallium on the periodic table, two elements which produced a green flame when burned. Anyone who solved this riddle received fifty points, more than enough to cancel out a texting deficit. Despite the numbers, students would assign their own names, Kevin called them "Cuff" and "Link" every chance he got, and asked me how I could possibly tell them apart.

"Exactly," I'd say.

Someone drowned the turtles a month later, pinning them to the bottom of the tank with our textbooks. I upended the tank into the parking lot, not far from where I'd found them working their way through the cars for months, the creek they couldn't see mere feet from their heads at all times. I dream of their journey some nights. More often, I dream of the food in the freezer that Scatman Crothers showed Shelley Duvall and myself in the film. I would dream of sitting on a sack of coffee beans and eating peanut butter with my hands. Some days the dream comes back, only now I dream of hooking wires to the metal shelves and applying a series of electric shocks to rows of foods in that freezer, as well as thousands of shelves in hundreds of grocery stores. I would hit the switch and watch the sparks turn the labels first to numbers, then to white, then removing all identifiable features from every product.

My students joked that I'd numbered the turtles so I wouldn't get attached, as if I was going to experiment on them. As if they weren't the experiment from day one.

*   *   *

The other set of twins weren't twins exactly. Just two girls of the same height, color, and degree of disinterest. They fought the No Phone rule tooth and nail, maybe more like tooth and claw. They would see my own phone shining through my linen pants, and say sweetly, "Aren't you going to answer that?" They also worked for our campus newspaper, *The Street*, and one of them, possibly both of them, wrote about my brief acting career, violating the unwritten rule of avoiding the topic. The article said things like, "His only other film was an undistinguished role in *Will: The Autobiography of G. Gordon Liddy*, where he again played a boy named 'Danny.'" And, "Rumor has it that they told him he was in an adventure film, not a biography of the Watergate architect" and, my favorite, "Professor Lloyd wears checkered shirts every day, just like the carpet in the Overlook Hotel." I think the little shit was thinking of *Twin Peaks*.

Once the article hit, the jokes were more and more frequent. The "red" and "rum" on the eyelids of the twins mock me once a week now, and I understand that it's not due to my minor celebrity. Then there was the ridiculous unease when I used terms as innocuous as "Overview" on the top of my semester calendars, waiting for the snickers. Recently, there was one student who claimed he heard me say "gravy" instead of "grading," but I thought he said "Grady." As in Delbert Grady, the smooth-talking Iago of Kubrick's adaptation. I kicked him out, and later swore to my Division Chair that I'd caught him texting. I didn't feel bad about the misrepresentation. It probably saved his life.

I've been thinking about the pumpkin peroxide experiment more and more these days, even during the spring semester. It's fine to moonlight teaching chemistry when my degree is in biology, but I worry it's probably a little irresponsible to turn my classes into Pumpkin Carving 101 all year round, and Kackleberry Farms isn't open past November.

Still, I reserve the van for a brief field trip on Saturday.

I borrow the Science Department credit card from Connie, and I make sure that I fill the gas tank up near the school. I wave a couple of the texters up to my desk after class on Friday, and I ask each one if they want to earn some extra credit.

We'd need a lot more pumpkins if we were going to do the experiment every semester, so I figured they had to have some lying around the fields. Unless you gut them, vegetables don't rot very fast at all.

* * *

There's been talk of a new Stephen King book called *Doctor Sleep*, which is a sequel to *The Shining*, and this is another distraction that concerns me, especially after how the author flirted with putting multiple versions of himself into the *Dark Tower* series. And here we have a book that, at least in the minds of the masses, if not the author himself, is a sequel with not just the film adaptation in mind, but with his own miniseries, which he offered as a rebuttal to Kubrick's perceived failures. Combined with King's new fondness for meta-narratives, cracking open this novel feels like a game of Russian Roulette; another demonstration that sort of starts biological, but ultimately succumbs to the theatrics of chemistry.

* * *

Taking the kids to a hedge maze is probably a mistake.

Something about that environment opened the floodgates of conversations and questions that I'd managed to duck for thirty years. And something about getting lost in the maze together turned out to be the opposite of getting lost on the highway, something about being on foot, rather than on wheels. The maze made them oddly calm, and braver than ever, essentially the opposite of what I'd predicted using time-tested science and formulas.

My favorite line in the movie is when I say, "I don't want to talk about Tony." I had a good reason then, and I have a good reason now.

We enter the maze at around 2:00 p.m., but the days are short this time of year. The sun is going down, and there's a nervousness in their voices that they're trying to hide, or maybe it's my own. I explain that there has got to be a few pumpkins lying around in the maze where people have dropped them in exhaustion. And I tell them that I need the mallet to clear away the corn stalks without cutting them down. We're sneaking into a maze a little off-season, you see. No sense in drawing too much attention to our harvest.

The beauty of a croquet mallet is that anyone who saw the movie doesn't realize it's threatening. Only if you read the book. And it's hard enough to get these kids to read a textbook, let alone one for leisure, especially after its been at the bottom of a fish tank.

It's down to me and Kevin and the twins. Every year there are twins. I try to turn it into a lesson and keep them talking. I come up with a quiz, right off the cuff.

I ask things like, "What mineral boosts the immune system?" "What process is used to refine grains such as this corn?" "What are the dangers of going on a high-protein diet?" "Is it more dangerous than rampant cell-phone usage?" "What three vitamins are antioxidants? Are they oil or water-soluble? Are we oil or water-soluble?" I throw question after question at them as we back up and retrace our steps.

I carry many chemicals—ammonia, hydrogen peroxide, hydrochloric acid, all of which react better to blood than to pumpkins. I'll need all my chemicals if I'm going to put the mallet back on my wall for next semester.

They retrace their steps, but I cover up my own.

That night, the foam rolls out of their mouths like jack-o'-lanterns, which is much less alarming than their usual questions. But there are no screams. They'd wasted their exclamation points at the beginning of the semester, on the first research paper I'd assigned.

Like I said, I turn it into a lesson.

* * *

I used to read a lot of articles criticizing the casting, saying that I looked nothing like a young Jack Nicholson. Okay, maybe not when his face is at its most wicked, when we're in that yellow VW bug, navigating the maze of the mountains. But these comments always reminded me of my jealously regarding my younger brothers. The youngest was this lupine, grinning kid, looking and acting exactly like our father. I always felt like the mutant, the anomaly, as I was quiet, tight-lipped, white and smooth as a grub. Then one day, my dad showed me some grainy pictures of him hiding under the table at a wedding reception, and I saw that he started out in the same larvae stage, exactly like me. I was comforted for quite a while, then I was horrified, wondering how much scarier my brother was going to get. But the point is, what nobody understands, is that I was chosen for that movie for a reason. Because my father was the one who looked exactly like Jack. He was the one who named us all as easily as a boy can name his fingers. Not me.

I know all of these things are distractions, and I'm just as guilty as anyone. But I've figured out why my colleagues avoid the same topic that my students find so fascinating. There's an odd reluctance to congratulate you about anything you did as a child, as if my celebrated acting was accidental, simply because they lied about which genre I was pedaling through. But even back then, I always knew what I was doing.

GHOST PIANOS & IDLE HANDS

"Every day, it's a-getting closer, going faster than a roller coaster . . .
Every day, it's a-getting faster, everyone says go ahead and ask her."
—Buddy Holly— "Everyday"

A man, a woman, and her child, all walking too fast through a carnival. Jacki, a young Hispanic woman with that sweatshirt and black no-pants-pants thing going on, is dragging her toddler, Toni, by the arm. Jacki's boyfriend, Anthony, a red-faced, muscular punk, stomps along with a bundle of helium "Happy Birthday" balloons. He's the kind of asshole who wanted a boy so bad he named the girl after him anyway. They bounce lower and lower as they rebound through the crowd, the excitement hissing out of them every few feet or so. The balloons, too.

One particular balloon, just a crumpled bag of deflated silver scraping the gravel behind them, catches every sharp corner and ankle it can, as reluctant as a kid hanging onto a doorjamb.

Surrounded by bright colors, happy families and voices, this group stands out in their manic desperation to get on a ride, any ride.

Toni tugs, tugs, tugs on her mom when a shorter line of bodies suddenly catches her eye. She breaks free to run ahead, and Jacki watches her scamper up to the tail end of calmer family units waiting for some short kid with a stick and the audacity to check the height of others. Anthony takes advantage of the distraction to kick the rest of the sagging balloons away in disgust, and Jacki finally turns her full attention to him, eyes blazing in anger.

"What?"

"You know what."

The kid tries to measure Anthony to get a laugh from the crowd because Anthony is, of course, short as shit. But he knocks the stick out of the kid's hand and steps up to wait for a carny valet to bring around his car, arms crossed tight.

Ten minutes later, the three of them sit silent in a slow-moving Model-T, riding a rail around a track with no corner sharper than the curvature of the Earth. Toni hangs out the back window to stare at the other creeping cars, and Anthony sits brooding, his arms still locked and pale from loss of circulation. He watches the steering wheel turning on its own. He knew the ride with the shortest line was gonna be the worst.

"Bothers you not driving, doesn't it?" Jacki finally says without looking over.

No answer.

"Thought so," she sighs.

"What was *that* supposed to mean?"

Jacki thinks she hears the squeak of his brain working, then realizes it's just the steering wheel brushing his belly.

"This ride sucks!" Toni squawks. "Where's all the twists and turns?"

"It's not that kind of ride," her mother says.

"What was *that* supposed to mean?" Squeak.

"Where's the water?" Toni squeaks right back.

"It's not that kind of ride," Jacki repeats wearily, on autopilot, sort of like the car, more like those ghost pianos in the Westerns that play tired, tuneless carnival music.

"Does it go any faster?"

"Not that kinda ride."

"Oh, yeah?" Anthony says sarcastically. "Then what kind of ride was it?"

He's asking about something else, so Jacki answers like it's something else.

"A calmer, comforting, more realistic one."

"What are you talking about?" he suddenly wants to know.

"What are *you* talking about," she says without the question mark.

"Talking about this," Anthony hisses, suddenly headbutting the steering wheel. "Is *this* how it happened? Show me how it happened."

"Jesus Christ, calm down, asshole."

Jacki frowns and looks away out the window. She's had this conversation way too many times while driving and doesn't want to encourage him with too much attention. And the idea of this argument in a car that doesn't occupy his hands suddenly terrifies her.

But he says it again, and now she's feeling spiteful.

"Show me how it happened, Jacki."

"How what happened." Again, not really asking.

"You know what."

"Anthony, please, not now."

"Is that how it happened? Him behind the wheel? You on top? Just tell me. Is that how you two crashed that fucking car? Someone forgot to keep both hands on the wheel, didn't they? Then where the fuck were the hands?

That's why he ended up dead, swinging naked like a chimp from a fucking tree?" Pause. "You're lucky to be alive, huh?"

Jacki knows he's not talking about the crash. This is more like a threat. A lot more.

"Just shut up," she says, throwing a thumb back at Toni. "I'm not talking about this again. Not here. Not again. Not ever."

"Not ever, huh? You know," Anthony starts, eyes on the fake road, hands floating over the fake wheel out of habit. "If you two woulda been on this bullshit ride instead, that accident would never have happened. He'd still be alive, you two would still be fuckin', and I probably woulda never known shit. Would I?"

She says nothing, looking around to the families in the other cars. No one is smiling. And at least two couples have started arguing, too.

No wonder this line was so short, she thinks.

"That couldn't have been the first time. No fuckin' way, no fuckin' way. No. Fuckin'. Way," he goes on. "That's what it took, huh? Him to get fucking killed before I found out?"

"Is that why I have to hear about this shit every couple of months? Because you feel you were robbed of your chance to kick our ass?"

"I just want you to admit it."

"You don't want me to admit shit," Jacki turns full on him, furious. "You know how pathetic you sound? You're not angry because I cheated. You're angry because he's dead."

He considers this a second, eyes lingering on the line where her crotch was devouring her tights. Her clothes always seemed to get tighter when she was mad, even tighter when they were at an amusement park.

"Nah, I'm pretty happy he's dead actually."

"Anthony, you know what it is? You're just angry because you had to fake compassion by my hospital bed, right there in front of Mom and everyone. You don't think about how I was affected, or why any of it happened, or how someone actually *died* that day. And you don't care. You just feel like you were cheated out of a chance to hit somebody. Well, quit fucking whining about it and do something."

He considers this, hands greasing the fake steering wheel with a squeaky strangle.

"You can't stand the fact that what happened to him and what happened to me . . ." she pauses to make sure she gets the mouthful just right. ". . . was worse than what you think happened to you."

Proud of herself, she stops to watch his hands wring his sweat out of the plastic, laughing when he turns it hard left and the car doesn't do what he wants.

"Actually, you know what?" she says. "The more I think about you, the funnier you get."

"Where's the big twists!" Toni suddenly shouts from behind them. "I thought this was a ride!"

"It's not that kind of ride."

Jacki looks to the other rides on the horizon, wishes she would have picked any ride but this one. But it's been "Slim Pickens," ever since they walked in. And by that, she thought every one of these mutts manning controls reminded her of that hayseed asshole in *Blazing Saddles*.

She never feels she's in good hands at a fair so cheap and ugly.

Fair? Or was it an amusement park? she wonders. *Carnival? Anything but Theme Park, always hated that name.*

"So who was driving?" Anthony says, a bit quieter. "Just tell me that. Please. Then I'll drop it. Who was driving? You or him?"

"I don't want her to hear this, Anthony."

"Twists!" Toni stomps a foot.

"Not that kinda ride," she says. "This one's more like real life."

As if to prove this, Anthony actually reaches for a radio dial on the fake dashboard to drown out the child before he catches himself.

"Are you that fucking stupid?" Jacki laughs, then notices another couple's car off in the grass with their plastic hood up, the husband hunched over the space where the engine would be. He's looking all concerned, wife pouting.

"He was driving, wasn't he? So you fucked him while he was driving?" Anthony says, punching the speedometer sticker once, twice. The car shakes.

"Enough. Three years I've been listening to this. I'm not talking about it anymore."

"Three years and you've never given me any answers. I just want to know why you would even think about doing something like that, especially in a car."

Silence.

"Fucking *answer me!*"

Impossibly, oncoming traffic seems to be drifting into their lane, and the helpless drivers glance over at them nervously. The rest of the drivers are arguing now, a flurry of loose hands, profanity, and exasperation. One man leans out to eyeball Anthony. Forgetting it's a ride, Anthony reacts like he would on any road.

"What the fuck you lookin' at?"

The woman in that car reluctantly restrains her man.

"Keep driving asshole," Anthony mutters. Then, "Hey, did that motherfucker just cut me off?"

Anthony reaches for a rearview mirror to adjust to check the traffic behind him. He laughs when he sees there's no mirror, of course, but he's not very convincing.

Jacki tugs her leggings loose again and leans over.

"Are you losing your goddamn mind?"

"Could be."

He pulls hard on the fake steering wheel, and it turns out it isn't completely fake after all. The car bumps against the guide rail, and Toni giggles, finally excited.

"Do that again and we're getting out," Jacki warns him.

"No, do it again!" Toni squeals, clapping. He bumps the rail again.

"I'm pulling over so we can talk about this."

"You can't pull over, dumb ass," Jacki says "This isn't real. None of it."

Jacki slumps forward, her head in her hands in frustration. The sensation of a dashboard sinking into her chest is strange, but not unfamiliar. Not entirely unpleasant. She wishes it was dark enough to pull up her sweatshirt and feel the cold plastic on her skin again from the crash.

Staring at her, Anthony pulls on the wheel again and the car lurches harder against the rail, almost clearing it. Toni is actually clapping her feet now.

"You realize we aren't in a car, right?" she says softly. "You realize we're not pulling over on the side of the road to talk, right? You realize this is a fucking *ride*, right?"

Anthony ignores her and, with two more quick turns of the steering wheel, he finally jumps the rail. Other fake drivers stop punching their dashboards to voice their concern, and some kids even start crying as the renegade Model-T crushes its way through some ratty flower beds, cuts off the line of sputtering gridlock, and heads for the nearest fence. Jacki opens the door and jumps out, pulling her daughter with her.

"Where are you going?" Anthony pleads as they start running. "Please, just show me what you did. Show me on this ride and no one will get hurt, I promise. Show me. It's safer here. Think about it, this is the perfect place for it . . ."

Heads crane out of the other cars to watch Jacki with Toni in tow, and Anthony's car belches and bumps its way along the rope fence surrounding the track.

"Show me what you did!" he yells.

She says nothing, almost running now.

"Stop."

She still says nothing and gets ready to gather Toni up to run.

"How do I even know she's mine?"

Jacki is now holding her breath, the only way she can say less than nothing. Then she stops.

"Did you hear me?" he says, punching useless plastic over and over and over, fist running red.

"I heard you," she says. "Nobody's *yours*."

"I know what happened," he says. "So do you. You're not mine and neither is she. Tell me I'm wrong. You lied all these years."

"You're right. You know what? You're so good at predicting human nature, you should be named an honorary human being."

Anthony takes a moment to imagine himself at this ceremony and what that trophy would look like, then he jumps out of the fake car, too. He decides the "honorary human being" trophy would be waist-high and topped with a little gold man flexing a bicep.

Jacki and her daughter walk off the ride, out the entrance, brushing past a man who's trying to talk the slouching teenager with the measuring stick into letting him on the ride with his dog. The dog is almost tall enough.

That's when Anthony is in front of everyone at the gate, blocking the way out with a small revolver he's pulled from his skin-tight jeans like a magic trick. He doesn't have to look at the teenager for the barrel of his gun to find his forehead like a magnet.

The kid drops his stick. Then, suddenly unarmed and helpless, the kid decides to run. Anthony turns the barrel on Jacki. Toni bites her lip in excitement, and there is a rousing cheer from the back seats of the other Model-T's as the children mistake the action for part of the ride.

Theme park indeed, Jacki thinks.

"Get back in there. Move!" he tells her, obviously trying to sound like the movies. She wonders why he didn't just shout "movies!" instead.

But past the measuring sticks, real screams are starting. She looks up to see soap-white fists wrestling control from steering wheels and taking every car off the rails. Weapons are flashing everywhere now, snapping free of conceal-and-carry holsters or coming around from behind every back like that bouquet nobody wants. Pistols, rifles, even a buck knife, some jutting through the thin canvas roofs of the fake antique cars as work boots skid alongside in the dirt or sandals flip off and toes dig in like the fucking Flintstones. One vehicle gets stuck on the rope fence, fighting it like a bug strip until another car rear-ends it and flips it free and over.

What do they call this goddamn ride? Road Rage Rehearsals?

Jacki squeezes her face in her hands in disbelief as two men slide over the nearest hood, rabbit punching each other in the face until one of their boots hooks the grill and they wrench their sputtering vehicle completely sideways with them and disappear into a mushroom of dust.

Then it's just Anthony, his five-foot nothing blocking out the scene as he walks slowly up to Jacki, then behind her, pressing the gun to the small of her back, and she thinks about how the carnys should use metal detectors instead of rulers.

He pulls up Jacki's sweatshirt with the egg tooth on the barrel, and as the cold metal sinks into her skin, she inhales sharp and starts to walk.

A gun stashed in anybody else's shorts would have warmed up by now, she thinks.

Toni's eyes are positively glowing in excitement. Jacki's too.

"Do those come with the cars?" Toni whispers.

Her mother says nothing as they march forward. Back to the track.

"Mommy?" Toni sighs, tugging on the leg of her mother's tights and popping them out of the crack of her ass one last time. She's trying to make sense of everything she heard earlier from the back seat, some talk about her conception. "Was I born on these rides?"

"Maybe," Jacki says, still not afraid. She's never been afraid of anybody that short and wouldn't start today.

It's a hot afternoon, triple digits, and the cool kiss of the metal feels too good on her back.

The problem is the fake steering wheel, she realizes. *Ghost pianos and idle hands.*

Anthony pushes Jacki to move faster back to the ride. She drags her feet like that silver birthday balloon, and he's pulling her like she's pulling Toni when backfires from the tiny cars and their lawnmower engines start popping like bullets, but more like cheap fireworks. He says a line from a movie again, but he fucks it up.

"Show me on this ride or no one gets hurt."

RUBBING PETER
TO PAY PAUL

"To robbe Petyr & geve it Poule, it were non almesse but gret synne."
—*Jacob's Well: An English Treatise on the Cleansing of Man's Conscience*

"Clowns are not scary."

"No, they're scary, dude. I've been scared of clowns all my life, and . . ."

"What do you mean when you say 'clowns,' because these days assholes keep saying they're afraid of clowns, but they're always clowns that look like monsters. To this I say, 'No shit, you're afraid of an evil bozo beast with a shark mouth? Sounds like a real phobia, buddy.'"

"You don't understand, I'm talking about real clowns, a normal, everyday clown that . . ."

"What the fuck is a real *clown? Yes, you're right, clowns with six rows of teeth that kill people and creep around the woods are scary. I agree. You blew the lid off it. Nice work, man. Your unique fear makes you very special."*

"So scary, for real, dude. And it's totally a phobia."

"Hey, what's the name of that phobia where you can't stand to be around idiots who keep saying they're afraid of clowns?"

"I hate clowns."

"I hate people who say they hate clowns."

"Just keep rubbing the headstone, dummy . . ."

* * *

I never really hated clowns. They just confused me. I never understood how dozens of them could pile into that tiny VW Beetle, then drive off the stage. But then Paul explained there was a trap door in the floor, and they simply parked the car over top of it. He told me they weren't really climbing into anything, just climbing through it. So when the circus came back to town, I snuck under the tent one night and climbed onto that dark stage, and I jumped up and down, hopping two feet forward every time until I'd covered every inch of that sticky floor.

But it was solid.

When I told Paul this the next day, he said that was impossible. Then years later, he insisted I must have remembered it wrong. But I'm convinced it was the other way around.

* * *

"Do you think a grave rubbing is really worth anything?"

"Oh, definitely. I've seen people pay five-thousand bucks for a framed rubbing of James Dean's headstone."

"No shit? I tried to get a grave rubbing of Jimmy Dean's grave once myself. Felt kind of bad though, standing over that grave, wind in the beard, pondering existence and realizing it was really him down there, you know? I realized I'd never been over a tombstone I didn't deface."

"Grave rubbings aren't defacing anything."

"Okay, more like taking the face with me."

"But did you get it?"

"No, that's what I'm telling you. During my bungled attempts to transfer that legendary name onto my wrinkled sheets of parchment, I got red slashes all over the line between '1931' and '1955.'"

"Red slashes?"

"Yeah, at first I tried to rub with charcoal like you're supposed to, keep everything all neat and respectful, but it was raining so hard that it was washing all the rubs away, and I switched to crayons instead. And, man, I dare a grown man not to start giggling with crayons in his hands all serious, cemetery or not."

"Anybody buy it?"

"Hell, no. I did it in crayons, fer crissakes! Aren't you listening?"

"What did his grave look like?"

"Oh, you don't believe me? Well, I don't remember too much about it, except it was covered with pennies and half-buried in the mud, like it was sinking. Three years later, I made the five-hour drive back to Indiana to try some more rubbings, but it was raining again. Tried to sell them outside the Shell station on 51 anyway, but that particular get-rich-quick scheme ended up costing me about 90 bucks in gas alone, not including the goddamn Crayolas."

"Crazy talk."

"I'm telling you, I've seen someone sell one for five-thousand bucks."

"Impossible. Are you sure they weren't buying his skull?"

* * *

Even if you'll never convince me that clowns are scary, after actually being one for almost a decade, I can at least tell you with 100-percent certainty that they aren't funny. Though Fireball Paul would have probably said different.

I'd known Paul since we were kids, back when we went to all those sweet parties together, working so hard to keep everyone entertained. That was back when we were "circling airports," a phrase I'll explain later. I even shared a car with him, all the way back when Fireball Paul's name was still "Poindexter." Well, that was his last name anyway. His first name, like most first names around young males, meant nothing to us. And since his had too many syllables to boot, we just called him "Dexter" for about a day, then quickly switched that to "Pee" by the time the weekend rolled around, as in "The Princess and the Pee," a reference to the stain he'd left on our buddy Jay's mattress at a sleepover when we were grade school. This sleepover also went down in history as our very first official "Sweet Party," anointed by Paul himself. And both those names stuck to us like glue. Meaning, we just called him anything that started with a "P," and any time I attempted to plan something fun and it quickly turned to shit, it was known as a "Sweet Party." And they were typically my fault. So like if I said there was a gathering at so-and-so's house, and me and Paul got there and there were only about two people swaying back and forth in a driveway looking at their feet and no beer to be found . . . it was a "Sweet party, dude, thanks a lot." Or an "Ess Pee" for short.

Tired of ruining parties, we took the party mobile instead, putting our money together to buy a big boat of a car rusting on his uncle's lawn. It looked a lot like the big bastard in the *Evil Dead* movies, only bigger, and Paul's uncle had it first.

"Do you know how many people we could squeeze in there?" Paul whispered, eyes practically pinwheeling.

It was a '71 Oldsmobile Delta 88, about as confusing a name for a car you could get, compounded by the fact that Paul's uncle called it his Banana Mobile. But we christened it The Rhino Wagon instead, because of the broken horn of a hood ornament, and that first day we must have driven around at least 7 hours straight. Then even more the following weeks, like it was our job. In fact, we logged so many miles in that monster our hometown actually had to invent a law to stop us. The cops claimed there had always been this "cruising law" in our town, but we argued they simply couldn't stand to watch us drive around with nowhere to go. We said no law could justify their uncontrollable urge to pull us over and ask what the hell we thought we were doing. And the officer at the courthouse after our first run-in with the fuzz calmly explained this law was necessary because of the people who would drive up and down and around the runways at any airstrip, waiting for loved ones to finally land but not have to pay for parking. They said the official name for the infraction was "circling the airport," and whether we knew it or not, that's exactly what we were doing. But once we heard this, we decided to adopt this phrase to describe any endless teenage fornication where we struggled to get off, then we drove around for a day to celebrate our growing vocabulary. And this name stuck, too. Neither of us could sneak away with a girl without the other one interrupting with a rap on the Rhino Wagon's window with a shout of, "Quit circling the airport, asshole! That's a hundred-dollar fine plus court costs."

But we knew the cops didn't really give a shit about all our driving. They were just jealous of all the people we crammed in the back, or crammed in the front, or crammed in the trunk, sometimes even surfing on the hood. It seemed like hundreds of limbs on the best nights, and probably sounded like even more when we cranked our horrible power ballads and tried to sing along. Our car may have been rusty, but our speakers sure weren't.

We shared the Rhino Wagon for three years and thousands of miles, until the summer of the bubble in his brain changed everything.

*   *   *

"Don't dig. Rub."

"I'm tired of rubbing."

"Do it anyway."

"Why?"

"You know why. Hey, you know how much money we're gonna get? Rubbing the grave of Squeaky Pete?"

"You mean Fireball Paul."

"Whatever."

"Holy shit, look what I found."

"That's half a pinecone."

"Could be a skull. 'Yorick! I knew ye well!'"

"Why don't ya go get more charcoal from the car if you're going to fuck around."

"Did you know Yorick was a clown, too?"

"Nah, he was a jester."

"That's a clown, dumbass."

"So what."

"Did you know Hamlet was a slacker? They can tell by how old the skull of his jester was. No joke. Some scholar did the math. When the gravedigger holds up Yorick's skull and talks about him cracking jokes to make the baby Hamlet giggle, they just divided that birthday by the age Yorick died, multiplied by the Year of the Monkey or something, carry the two . . . and guess how old that makes him."

"How old?"

"*Thirty years old, dude! That's like 60 back then.*"

"*What's your point?*"

"*The point is, he still lived at home! It makes the play a whole different animal, man. Everybody always thinks Hamlet is this punk goth kid who's skulking around the castle, but he's a grown-ass man just fucking around, a midlife-crisis case, acting nuts to get out of doing any real work. Like I said, a slacker.*"

"*Sounds familiar.*"

*   *   *

The day of the bubble in his brain, Paul was at track practice, showing off, making people laugh. Later they told me no one knew it was a stroke, and figured he was just playing dead in the middle of the high-jump pit. He was laying there for at least an hour, and then his teammates thought he was pouting about not being able to clear nine feet, so they still didn't bother checking on him for half the day. When the coach came by to clean up and found him more unresponsive than usual, he finally called an ambulance. The paramedics cut him out of his track suit and took him away, leaving the whole gutted bundle of his uniform lying in the track's inside lane, complete with a new jagged slit winding a crooked path across the chest. This is where his girlfriend retrieved it that night, a seemingly innocent gesture that ended up causing quite a bit on controversy at our school later on.

See, before the stroke, Paul was dating this moody chick named Michelle, but we all called her "Nimbus." As in "Cumulonimbus." As in "Thunderheads." As in "the dark, depressing clouds you see right before it rains." This was because she moped around like she had a thunderstorm over her globe at all times. She wasn't even one of those all-black-wearing Hot Topic darklings you might expect something like this from either. She was small, blonde, partial to Easter-egg colored clothes, but she just seemed friggin' miserable. She drove me nuts, too, and I wasn't even dating her anymore. But Paul seemed to like her enough for both of us, and didn't seem to mind this perpetual frown painted across her face, at least for a while.

But right before his stroke, when we were driving around in the Rhino, he confided to me that he wanted to break up with her and was dreading having to actually do the deed. He told me that lately he'd been dreaming of dumping her almost once a day. And he may have pulled the trigger, if he hadn't bonked the high-jump bar at nine feet and ended up in the high jump pit with a partial loss of memory, muscular control, and the ability to speak.

When she came by my house to tell me about Paul having his stroke, I was standing in my garage and staring at her feet under the door slit and didn't answer her knocks. I'd heard the bad news already from my parents, and didn't want to have to react to it twice, certainly not to Nimbus. Instead, I waited until she drove away, and then I went through the workout routine with our dumbbells, a routine Paul and I had carefully designed to make us the most dangerous sophomores of all time. Or at least allowed us to systematically claim enough third-place finishes in the often-ignored hurdles, high jump, and pole vault to accumulate the points necessary to get our Varsity letter jackets two years earlier than the best bona fide athletes at our school. In other words, we totally *Moneyball*-ed that shit, and the vice-principal actually sighed in disgust when they called our names at the letterman ceremony. We just wanted the jackets. School spirit need not apply.

When I went to the hospital that night, I saw Nimbus weeping in the waiting room, then I sat down next to his bed and watched him roll his eyes trying to talk, until she ran in and pushed me aside to clutch his hand.

She said she'd never leave him, and that's when I realized how serious the situation actually was.

Right then, I decided it would be my mission to decipher whatever series of twitches, blinks, or grunts Paul managed to squeeze out in order to prove to Nimbus that he wanted to dump her ass. But it took weeks for him to identify common household objects on index cards for the therapists. I watched him move his thumb for "yes." Pinkie flick for "no," Barely perceptible nod for "No, that's not a hammer." I tried to explain to the nurse that maybe he couldn't identify her hammer because it was a shit drawing of a hammer and he was probably trying to say "mailbox," but they just kicked me out.

And during all this, I had to suffer through Nimbus and her baby talk, giving him crayons, feeding him Jell-O. It all made me furious, like she was doing it to me instead of him. Sulking near his right arm, I explained it was no easier to write with a crayon than it was to write with a pen. But over on his left arm, she proved me wrong by peeling a blue one and rubbing it over the bed sheet covering Paul's hand. But when the image slowly took shape under the blue streaks of her crayon, it revealed Paul's hand giving her the middle finger. I'd taught him that one.

She ran out crying, and in came the parents. Paul's parents, my parents, her parents, everyone's parents were looking at me like I was a villain. Except for Paul. He surprised everyone by reaching for my hand. That's all I needed. I swear, if angels existed, I would have heard them singing.

The next visit, I got there early, and they let me stay in the hospital room alone with him, so I asked the million-dollar question.

"Hey, do you want me to tell her to fuck off?"

By this time, he was saying a couple words and moving his left arm and left leg a bit. But for his answer, he just shook his hand "no" like it was on fire. I wasn't sure I translated this correctly, so I repeated myself.

"Just give me a sign, man. Anything."

He kept with the head shakes, so I said:

"Remember all those hours driving around with her, never able to pull the trigger? Now's your chance," I leaned in and whispered. "I will dump her for you, I swear."

His next response was a little more complicated because, unknown to the nurses and physical therapist, we'd already come up with a variety of complicated hand twitches for communication. Actual sign language was out of the question, of course, because that stuff was hard to learn, but I'd done some homework, grabbing some documentary on Marcel Marceau and watching him do his "Bip the Clown" bullshit, and the Ouija board I brought in was crucial, too, so when he wiggled his thumb up, down, up, right, down, left, up, I was surprised to translate . . .

"I said, 'no'."

Okay, there was a chance he was trying to say more than that, or something else entirely, like, "Why is there a scuba diver on that wall?" (which there wasn't), but this last "No" was all I needed. So I vowed to leave her alone, let her soak up the attention for his tragedy. I promised to stay out of it. And when we had more time alone days later, he twitched his thumb around the Ouija board to spell out something else:

"Sweet party, bro. This your idea?"

*　*　*

"*Did you hear about all the clowns jumping out of trees and trying to scare people?*"

"*Are they dressed as* clown *clowns or, you know, colorful monsters?*"

"*We've been through all this.*"

"*Apparently not.*"

"*It's the same thing.*"

"*God damn you.*"

"*Did you see that TV movie about that killer clown got remade? Now that's a scary-looking clown. But there was something about the original killer clown guy that's gonna be hard to top.*"

"*If you say they have some 'big shoes to fill' I might bury you here.*"

"*It's true though.*"

"*And for the record, no, it's* not *the same thing.*"

"*What's not the same thing?*"

"*Don't you understand? If they were real clowns hiding in everybody's trees, no one would give a shit.*"

"*What the fuck is a real clown?!*"

"Hey, was that thunder?"
"Yes, I think it's going to rain."
"Well, rub faster."
"Don't worry. One thing doesn't always follow the other."

* * *

Back at school, all that month, I started noticing Nimbus shuffling through the hallways, carrying what seemed to be a bundle of bloody rags wrapped around her schoolbooks. Behind her in the lunch line, I finally got a closer look and saw it was Paul's track suit, and she'd been cradling it all day. She'd carefully sewn it back together where the paramedics had cut it off his body, her bright red threads stitching up the ragged trail that had divided the front so everyone knew she'd repaired it. But these thick, crimson threads clashed with our blue-and-white school colors, and she'd sewed all these weird extra circles into the front, an unnecessary flourish that turned his track uniform into what could only be described as a costume, like something you'd find at the circus. I followed her to her lunch table, confident with every step I'd regret what I was about to do.

"Whatcha got there, Nimbus?"

"Don't call me that."

"What's this?"

"All four food groups."

"No, I mean right there. The pile of shit under your math book."

"A superhero uniform!" she said proudly. I was so annoyed I didn't even groan and said the word "groan" instead, and her friends started to chew on their lips, angrier by the second.

"But what's up with the stitches?"

"What are you talking about?"

"I'm talking about this clown suit . . ." I said, trying to grab it, and then her friends were around me, one of them hissing down my neck.

"What the hell is wrong with you?"

"What the hell is wrong with *her*?"

One of the girls shoved me, but I ignored her, not understanding why others weren't horrified by her conspicuous display. But every table within earshot was glaring at me in contempt , and I panicked. I grabbed a hand-ful of tater-tots from off their nearby trays, and I began to juggle. And the damndest thing happened. All the glares began to slide off their faces, frowns turning upside-down, as they say.

I was a natural.

"Did you ever notice it always rains when she walks by?" I said, and people were laughing. I should have stopped there.

"Oh, by the way, Paul was going to break up with her before this all happened!"

Then they were booing, and the tater-tots slipped through my fingers one by one, and the science teacher with the face like a tomato was leading me away by the arm. But not before I snatched the track suit right off her tray like a magic trick, all four food groups totally undisturbed.

I asked him sincerely, "Haven't you ever noticed a change in the weather when she's around?"

He just yanked harder. The science teacher always liked me, up until that day anyway. And you'd think a science teacher would have noticed an atmospheric phenomenon like that.

The next day, my locker was trashed. Graffiti calling me every name in the book. And when I say "in the book," I mean in my schoolbooks, too. Bunch of rotten fruit cups in my Varsity jacket pockets. Streaks of what I hoped were dried saliva on everything else. It was bad enough for the school to finally start assigning padlocks and combinations after that. So, kinda like the law against "Circling the Airport," that's another legacy we left behind, lockers finally getting locks. Metal detectors? That wasn't me.

I took Paul his track suit, after I may have tried it on, once or twice, and even though it was a struggle, he climbed out of his hospital bed to get in it. He'd lost so much weight he was swimming in it. But we were walking now, and together we danced down the hall best we could, and he made all the kids laugh. He was good at that.

* * *

"Did you hear about that gorilla they shot at the zoo?"

"Oh, yeah, everyone was talking about it."

"Lots of conversations lately about that gorilla. I heard they killed it to protect another dumb kid who wandered into the cage. Did you hear that? Well, luckily, I've solved this problem for everyone."

"How so?"

"Gorilla rodeo clowns, bro."

"Huh?"

"Think about it! If zookeepers want to screw around with dangerous, stressed-out animals in zoos, you just get ya some rodeo clowns."

"You might be making sense for once."

"Seriously, zoos are a real problem these days. Filthy, cruel to animals. Almost as frowned upon as the circus. So bring in the clowns, man. Part of your new job description as a zookeeper should include wearing goofy-ass clown outfits and running in there with a barrel and some fuckin' balloon animals at a moment's notice. This seems like a good compromise to me."

"I'm not gonna do that, but thanks."
"Just remember it was my idea."
"How much longer is this going to take?"
"Don't worry, this show's almost over."

*   *   *

After eight months of intense rehabilitation at a green, happy compound tucked away somewhere in the hills of Southern Michigan, Paul regained all his motor skills and memories, with the exception of his right arm. He was never again able to raise it higher than his shoulder, but I was surprised by his recovery and—as much as I hated to admit it—maybe a little disappointed because I'd spent so much time trying to enable him to communicate with just one hand, and just to me. His mouth was a little slacker than I remembered, too. And he seemed to spit a lot, like something in this throat didn't work quite as well anymore. Or maybe he just lost that part of the brain that reminded him to swallow. Or it could have been a new allergy? The doctor said that new allergies and aversions cropped up sometimes after strokes, so maybe he just got a little allergic to me, because whenever I asked him about his feelings for Michelle, I mean "Nimbus," back before the bubble in his brain, he'd just spit and change the subject.

They were together for another year, and I shouldn't minimize how effective she was in helping him recover. She brought in all these old 45's, and we listened to them through all his exercises. I'd hated her taste in music when we were all together, but now it didn't bother me so much. Anything that helped Paul, helped us all. Hey, that shit rhymes.

When they both started college in Cincinnati the following spring, I didn't see either of them that much anymore for quite a while. But, ironically, they broke up anyway, without needing my help after all, right about when his right arm started twitching again. And he came back home to us, wearing that track suit, and still swimming in it.

But the best thing that happened after that summer of the bubble in the brain was we didn't have to go into the Army anymore, even though he'd signed all the necessary paperwork weeks before he blew that fuse in the high jump pit, even though I'd called to meet with a recruiter myself, the day after he told me this. We had mixed feelings about not serving our country, but I reassured him that at least we broke up with Uncle Sam easier than we broke up with Nimbus.

"Dodged a bullet, you could say."

He laughed, but I never really talked to him about how I was still ducking the Army recruiter's phone calls ever since his stroke. No way I was gonna do it alone. That didn't make any sense to me. It was like that band we almost started back in the sixth grade, with all our joke songs like a poor-man's Weird Al. We quickly realized, even doing those parodies for our classmates, that a two-man band is about as welcome as a one-man band, which is as much of a pariah as the class clown. Meaning no one really wanted to hear those jokes. We just always thought they did.

The next summer, we joined the circus instead of the Army, and we were satisfied, because that shit was pretty much the same thing.

* * *

"For real, when are we gonna get to work?"

"Work? Hey, if I wanted to work, I wouldn't steal for a living!"

"If you wanted to go through life easy, you should have gotten a scholarship to Hamburger University."

"Don't you mean Clown College?"

"Same difference."

"How dark is it?"

"Dark enough to look at your face without screaming?"

"Any witnesses?"

"Nope, the place is ours."

"Good. Go ahead and put away the crayons. Grave rubbing is for pussies."

"Done."

"And get the shovels."

"Finally."

* * *

The circus drove us to drink, but Paul was better at this than me, just like most things, so when I say he was an alcoholic, I mean he was drinking straight-up poison like it was going out of style. Luckily, we were no longer concerned with style, or anything else respectable.

We were a couple of goddamn clowns, remember?

I was partial to ruining my life with beer, like a normal person, but Paul was drawn to the distinct plaid of that Luxco label, and the 190 Everclear grain alcohol wiggling its dick underneath that kilt. My only interaction with Everclear was that holy rite of passage—Purple Jesus: one bottle of Everclear and five packets of grape Kool-Aid. You bury it in an unused gas can for about three weeks, or however long the Bible said it took Jesus to rise again. Then you strain, serve, black out, and never, ever do that shit again.

Come to think of it, three weeks is about as long as I'm able keep Paul underground before someone's always kicking open his coffin, but I'll get to that in a minute. Sorry, if you thought we lived through this.

But as far as steady work, we did a lot of birthday parties, sure, usually for free, though Paul was fond of saying, "It may be charity, but it's also a great sin," whatever that meant. And we also did our share of "Sweet Parties," too, of course, but there was always a carnival somewhere in Ohio, and they always needed clowns.

We were real popular. Paul especially. People swore he could make balloon animals that no sane man would ever attempt. Complicated structures. The Golden Gate Bridge, but while it was under construction? Come on. The Empire State Building, but during the last reel of King Kong? An anatomically accurate balloon model of the circulatory system of the Great White Shark, which was very similar to a human being's circulatory system, except for six distinct differences, or two balloons . . .

Yeah, he didn't do any of those. I did. People are stupid. That's how I got my nickname, actually, but Paul didn't mess with balloon animals at all. Some other clowns frowned on this, but, hell, those assholes were always frowning anyway. Their faces were drawn that way. But Paul always said the bubble in his brain was his only balloon animal, and one was enough for him. He said he could still hear it sometimes, stretching through his oblongata, squeaking and swelling and curling its rubbery tail as it drove that highway of veins, dead-ending when it ran out of room in that clown car of his skull and then *POP!*

No, I was Squeaky Pete, so I stuck to the balloons, and Fireball Paul just stuck to his fireballs. Busting out his Everclear and his lighter, and blowing fireballs so big and bright that the drunks would swear the sun had come up early. And whenever he lit his right arm on fire by mistake, we never felt a thing.

And at first glance, we were pretty similar, too. More similar than we ever were in school. Rainbow wigs, red rubber noses, blue-and-white polka dot jumpsuits, with three big silver buttons right down the middle. No need for the greasepaint these days. Clown faces got easier every year. Bank robberies had even made the full-head rigs popular, where you just slipped the entire clown face over your own grin, nose horn, Ronald McDonald eyebrows, and all. There was a reason clowns opted for easy costumes. It was really Einstein's famous habit of having ten suits, ties, and slacks always ready to roll every morning. Or maybe it was the guy from *The Fly*. Either way, why waste brainpower you could be using on clown-related mugging, goofy knock-knock jokes, or intricate new balloon-animal concoctions?

But one suit was really all we needed. You know, a lot has been written about a clown's big nose, big hair, those big-ass shoes. But people forget about the three buttons. It was those three big buttons that made a clown suit distinctive, that made it recognizable from a distance, and it was Paul's buttons that made his suit even more distinctive than that. Normally, we'd just have pom-poms down the middle where the buttons would be. But Fireball Paul had been peeled open once before by those big paramedic shears, so the silver buttons on his suit were kind of his trademark, because they were actually 7-inch platinum records. No bullshit.

He thought it would be funny if they were clown songs, of course. One of them had to be Smokey Robinson's "Tears of a Clown," while the others were The Everly Brothers' "Cathy's Clown" and The Kinks' "Death of a Clown."

I always thought "Stuck in the Middle with You" would be funnier, but it wasn't my jumpsuit to adorn. I pretended I didn't remember Michelle playing all those songs in rehab.

How did he get real platinum phonographs, you ask? Well, snagging a vacuum-coated, metalized, platinum 45 rpm record wasn't that big a deal. You could buy them for about a hundred bucks on eBay, depending on the song. The plaque they usually got framed with were sometimes worth more money than the platter, depending on the artist, since they might be 24-karat gold instead. Plus they're rarely the song you think they are. They typically dip any ol' record in gold just to be more efficient in the trophy factories. In fact, rumor has it that when Billy Joel got mad at Christie Brinkley and smashed his framed gold record of "Uptown Girl," when they both calmed down, he put it on the record player to call a truce, but the song dipped in yellow turned out to be Randy Newman's "Short People" instead. And you know what happened to them.

The point is, there were a lot of clowns in the world wearing goofy costumes, but those big silver buttons on Paul's suit added a touch of distinction, as well as a bit of history, and, as impossible as it may sound, a touch of class. It kept us both in demand anyway, steady work long after a clown would normally be too old to half-ass a kid's birthday party.

Fireball Paul told his last stupid joke in the summer of '95, then died that same winter, a second bubble in his brain that popped and took the co-pilot of our clown car with it.

I thought about those bubbles in his brain a lot, even when I wasn't tying balloon knots, and decided that I was probably having them right along with him, only mine weren't fatal when they popped. But I was still changing every time.

And even though I gave Nimbus so much grief for dwelling on his stroke like she did, I carried around his jumpsuit, too, folded up in my trunk with all the respect and honor of an American flag. So it just seemed right to bury him in his uniform.

The rumors started soon after, and maybe I started them. Who can tell? But what if his platinum records were *really* platinum? I mean, with platinum going at about $1,500 an ounce, that meant almost 50 bucks a gram.

So 50 times 50 times 3. That's 7,500 bucks. Plus they said platinum was 11% denser than gold. So a record like that would weigh even more. Sure, I'm no mathematician, but I'm gonna go out on a limb and say that when we insisted on burying Fireball Paul in his suit, that clown might have been worth ten grand easy.

Unless it was just a rumor I'd started, of course. But true or not, we all still end up in a same place, am I right? Patrolling the final rest stop of our dead and speaking when they can no longer speak for themselves.

I know what you're thinking. If the songs really went platinum, and if these are really platinum records, then they wouldn't *be* platinum. I'm not even following what the fuck I'm saying anymore, but the question is . . . is it really worth the effort to find out? You know what I'm talking about.

Well, you'd be surprised. It turned out that quite a few people think it's worth a little effort, and worth a little digging. Unless you're not used to working for a living. But no one works harder than a clown.

*   *   *

"Did you know that typically when you're around the graves of famous people, there's a sign that warns of the penalties for defacing their tombstones."

"Fascinating."

"And because of this, every nearby headstone is covered in graffiti. As a kid, when the cops are trying to guilt you into not defiling graves anymore, you'll hear shit like, 'That was someone's brother, someone's son, someone's father, someone's grandfather . . .'"

"That's a good point."

"The problem with that argument is that the only thing you can be certain of is that it is someone's son. The other three are just guesses. And, honestly, who gives a fuck about someone else's son?"

"I sure don't."

"You should be ashamed of yourself."

"I am."

"Did you know that, besides Walmarts, the place most men masturbate is graveyards."

"No way."

"Yes. Way. It's because there are so many headstones at waist level. Way too easy to rub one out. And people will just think you're bowing your head to pay your respects."

"Do you think you'll enjoy hell?"

"Shut up. How much deeper do we have to go?"

"Until you hear his fucking nose honk."

"Wait, did you hear that?"

"Hear what?"
"Who's this guy in the trees . . . oh my God . . ."
"Dude, what the fuck is wrong with your face . . ."
POP! POP!

* * *

Looking at Fireball Paul's tombstone over the smoking barrels of my .45, I suddenly noticed the erratic scramble of insects along the edges, even though it was much too cold for them to be present. A swarm of black and blue flies have congregated around a tipped can of orange soda, occasionally dipping furry toes and noses in the sticky orange pool around the rim. I picked up the can and checked my reflection. What did they mean about my face? I guess it's like our mother always warned us.

Don't grimace too long or your mouth will stay that way.

Did they say they were grave robbers or grave rubbers? Doesn't matter. No one would miss either one.

I threw the can over my shoulder, and the flies stayed with me. I'm always amazed at what the cemetery crew doesn't clean up these days if they assume it's some sort of tribute. But what does a can of orange pop have to do with a dead clown? You could put an empty toilet-paper tube on a tombstone and forget the flowers and someone would still hesitate to throw it away. So it's good I'm out here to help out.

I jumped down into the pit of loose soil. The two grave robbers had gotten further than most, but it didn't matter. I'd dug up my better half so many times, I could do it in my sleep, and probably do. I liked their shovels though, and I kept the one with the price tag still on it. You get to appreciate a good shovel when you spend your weekends digging back up and digging back down.

When I hit Paul's casket, the lid was riding real high, like the top slice of a bulging club sandwich. Only this sandwich had arms and legs spilling out the sides instead of lettuce. And when I cleared enough dirt to swing the lid open, I saw the casket was way past capacity. But it's always been past capacity. With Paul down there on the bottom, buried under too many treasure-seekers to count. None of this mattered. They'd fit. They'd always fit, and I could do this forever.

Lightning flashed as I stuffed the two new bodies on top. I tossed their grave rubbings over their chests, and I let the rain fill the gape of their surprised mouths for a full minute before I swung the lid back over their mugs, then I started to shovel the dirt in again, racing the first splash of sunrise on the horizon. There were so many bodies, but it was getting easier to refill, so I wasn't worried. His grave would never really be full. I knew this because Paul had told me the secret of a clown car the first time I dug him up. He'd lied about that trap door in the stage, you see.

"You want to know how they really pile so many clowns into those tiny cars?" he whispered as I spun the silver record on his chest with my dirt-caked fingernail riding the groove, humming all the songs.

"The trick is that they pile on in, but it doesn't matter if they ever pile on out."

EGG TOOTH

No, I don't want to feed the goddamn ducks. Thanks, though.

Why would anyone not want to feed ducks in a park? Who would reject such a Normal Rockwell-esque moment of peace and introspection? Me, that's who. Too depressing, and I'll tell you why. I've had three ducks in my life. Five if you count the two ducks that Angie's dad shotgunned for us on Christmas Eve so he could dangle the damn things in our face first thing in the morning and be a tough guy. Thanks, New Dad! But as far as real live ducks, for some bizarre reason, my sister, my real dad, and myself all ended up with pet ducks instead of dogs running around our house.

It all started back in third grade when they brought a bunch of duck eggs into the classroom, and us kids forgot everything else we were supposed to be learning until they hatched. I'd picked an egg with a hole in it, initially because I thought it would never hatch and I'd get an automatic "A" out of sympathy. So when we were all told to carefully write our names on our eggs, I drew a sad monster face instead. But then when something started wiggling around inside that hole, I sorta started hoping it would hatch after all.

I began spending every second I could near the incubators, even recess, waiting to see what would pop out. I went from aloof to hopeful to scared as I started thinking the sad monster I scrawled on the shell might curse the egg to birth something deformed. Did all the kids get eggs? I think so. It seemed like there was one for every kid if they wanted one, and some didn't give a crap, of course, so the teacher even took at least five home for herself. She told us that if our parents said it was okay, we could keep the baby ducks when they hatched. Yeah, it was a different time back then. I don't think they still have the Elementary Duck Program, although they did do this with my sister, too, about ten years back. So maybe they still do. But I'll get to my sister's horror story in a second.

So, my broken egg hatched. And because I was leering over it when this happened, the poor little bastard imprinted on me immediately. The other kids weren't eclipsing their eggs quite as obsessively, or maybe their eggs just hatched when they were out on the swings, but I ended up the only instant father in the room. Problem was, after about a day of shivering and orienting itself with the world of a shoebox, this duck wouldn't stop screeching unless it could see me. If I went back to my desk, a steady, rising squawk would drown out the teacher. Miss Circle was her unlikely name, and that body was made of circles all right, high five! No, seriously, it might have been "Mr. Circle."

So, if I ran over to the box, the squeaking would quickly turn to these low, contented chirps and mutterings. Was it messed up somehow because of the hole in the egg? I don't think so. It looked like any old duck, I guess, after it dried out anyway. Boy or girl, I never solved that mystery, but it had these black circles around its eyes, so I called it "Masko." Circles everywhere. I lied to the other kids that I drew them on its face. And it had this weird tooth on the outside of its beak that gave me a scare at first, but they all had them. Miss Circle explained it was a temporary horn to help them crack the shell and get free of the egg, something Masko didn't need because of his hole.

This was the only thing we learned about ducks the whole year.

After all the ducks hatched, it started to get real noisy and stinky in the classroom, and Miss Circle had us all take them home. I'd never bothered to warn my parents, weeks earlier forging a permission slip like always. But after a raised eyebrow and a sigh in the car when he picked me up, my dad just shook his head and gave in. But the thing is, it's hard to take care of a friggin' duck, especially for a third grader. It's not like a dog, or even a cat. You can't really train a duck to do shit, *except* for shit, which it does about every seven seconds. And this little maniac followed me everywhere. Sliding and falling all over itself on hardwood floors, scrambling hopelessly at the side of the tub when I was in the shower until one time I finally plopped it in with me, so it could happily paddle around in the suds and fight the swirl of the drain. It even hopped in the toilet once, doing figure-eights and chirping away until my mom pretended to flush it to teach me a lesson. It worked. I never left the seat up again.

So Masko grew a bit bigger, eventually losing the egg tooth and starting to put on some weight, feathers turning from yellow to white. And that's right about when things turned bad.

You knew this story was too good to be true, right? Well, that's what I'm saying. Whose idea was it to give little kids goddamn birds? Fowl. Even the name sounds like bad news.

So I had no idea how to take care of it. When I let it outside, it ignored all the games a dog would play, so I guess I treated it a little more like a cat by default. But when water was around, it was more like a toy really. I'd be in the backyard, drawing treasure maps or whatever, and it would follow me awhile. Until it saw its first puddle. Holy balls, Masko loved puddles more than toilets. And this was about the time our neighborhood was flooding every year and had standing water in everyone's basements and around their foundations. So here's my duck frolicking in stagnant insect larvae and bacteria and who knows what else. But isn't that what they'd do in the wild, without third graders around? This is something I told myself as I watched it paddle around that black water. Now that I'm older, I realize a wild duck wouldn't be swimming near a house. A house is leaking all sorts of deadly stuff, which is exactly what was going on in the miniature swamp of oil-slicked rainbow water that the air-conditioning exhaust and gutters had created next door. Our neighbor's name was Bruce, or "The Big Indian," as my dad called him, and Masko loved Big Indian Swamp. So, yeah, of course the duck got sick.

Whatever ailment it picked up in that black water, it hit the legs first, and its pool-party days were over. I started noticing Masko couldn't follow me as fast anymore. Just got weaker and weaker, falling over, even on carpet where it got the best traction. We all thought it had a broken leg. But then the tail feathers stopped wagging, too. Something was shutting down the power from the bottom up. And after it stopped walking completely, it ended up back in that very first shoebox that I'd carried home. Now I had to haul that box all over, or else that steady, climbing squawk would drive everyone nuts, just like at the beginning of its life. So it was me and this box with my hand perpetually hanging in there to keep it muttering and clucking away, and that's the way we were for a couple weeks. Then it was lying on its side and couldn't flap its wings around anymore either. Just the neck and head moving. But it was still eating oatmeal and baby food, still seemed aware of everything, so I kept on feeding it until it was finally just a head, barely moving. Then it was dead. I'd tell you that this happened on my birthday if I didn't want to minimize the little fucker's struggle.

The next day, we buried him in the yard, and someone's cat dug him up about an hour later. That was fun. The duck's story was depressing enough without an epilogue where there's this tiny skeleton on our porch like something out of *Titus Andronicus* saying, "Remember me? Do not let your sorrow die. Read the instructions next time, asshole."

*   *   *

What about the other ducks in my life? Yeah, it gets better. About ten years later, my sister hit the third grade, and they were still handing out ducks like mad scientists, teachable moments for kids they thought might be too well-adjusted. Only this time, my sister doubled down with two eggs instead of one. Jesus Christ. Get comfortable for this part. I wasn't around for the hatching, obviously, so I wasn't as emotionally attached to these ducks, and there'd been no imprinting on me this time. Or so I thought.

She named them "Quack" and "Stupid," which just about covers every-thing you need to know about them. Simple creatures, maybe, but these boys could be endearing. Maybe because science had advanced enough for teachers to reveal their gender. The ducks gender, I mean. Mr. Circle was long gone.

And the ducks won over my dad, something that dozens of the cutest dogs, cats, and children could never do. Quack especially loved my dad and would nest on his feet whenever he stopped walking. But Stupid didn't seem to acknowledge his surroundings at all. Every minute was his first minute on Earth. They were funny in our above-ground pool though. And my dad really got into it, eventually building them their own pool out of some old tractor tires. And he built sort of a kennel, too, using all the construction supplies my grandpa stored on our property. My dad would go out every morning before work and hose down the tires and the doghouse, then he'd fill up their pool party with fresh water, and they'd sprint on in, gibbering away all happy as hell. Sometimes they'd hide until he put the hose away, thinking it was a snake, which was weird because they'd gone straight from my sister's classroom, to the car, then to our backyard, and I doubt there were any snakes during this journey. But once the hose was coiled up under the deck, they'd run out of their dog house, slipping and falling over each other in the excitement, then splash around in their truck-tire pool until the sun went down and my dad flipped over the wheel to drain it again. You know, people always act like it's so cute that ducks love water so much, but no one says that about fish. Like, "Oh, my fish are so adorable! They would just splash around in that puddle all day if you let them!"

They were ducks, and that's all they did. Every day splashing around. It's how they rolled.

Anyway, my sister moved out, and my dad inherited the two idiots, us-ing more lumber scraps to add onto their enclosure until this crazy duck hotel was as high as a man but twice as confusing. If you can picture this, it was like a double-decker dollhouse surrounded by a huge cage, sort of like the ones that separated dangerous inmates from each other in the prison exercise yard. And my dad started taking them to the vet, too, just like real animals, sitting in the waiting room with an upside-down duck hypnotized between his knees, since that was the only way they'd tolerate being held, the result of my sister cradling them like newborns all their lives. The vet told us this was also known as "holding them all wrong." My dad even started giving Quack some daily steroid injections, prescribed by one veterinarian who finally took the ducks and my dad's endless questions about their health seriously. I know what you're thinking, that maybe my dad was there when they hatched. That maybe my sister forgot her lunch money and he popped his head in the classroom and they imprinted on him or something. No, it wasn't like that. It was more like the ducks were there when my dad hatched.

With all this attention to their heath, these guys were getting real big, and turning white all over, outliving Masko by a long shot. And then the boys started laying eggs, too. Oops, so much for third-grade science. I panicked when I heard we had eggs, worrying we were heading for a swarm of ducks through the neighborhood. But the eggs couldn't be activated without any real males around, and my dad would just throw them out. If he didn't dispose of the eggs quickly enough, they'd sit on them until they turned rotten. And for awhile, our garbage cans were getting tipped over every night by animals in the neighborhood sniffing out those rotten eggs. It was happening so much, we thought we had a dog terrorizing our block. But eventually we found out that the ducks were actually tipping over the cans because they wanted their eggs back. They'd knock over a trashcan, root the eggs out of the bags with their beaks, then roll any unbroken ones across the grass with their faces, all the way back into their kennel. So my dad rigged a latch they couldn't nose open and started locking them into their kennel after dark. We even tried eating the eggs for awhile. Same as chicken eggs, better tasting really. Big, too, like Brontosaurus eggs (this was back when there were still Brontosauruses, and Pluto). But we stopped when some of the eggs gave me horrible diarrhea. That was my fault though. I must have left one incubating too long under their feathers before I grabbed it. So we gave up our giant pterodactyl omelets, and dad went back to throwing the eggs away. As soon as the ducks got out to roam in the morning while he was hosing everything down, they'd waddle over to the trash cans and start that shrill, climbing squawk we knew so well, and my dad had to start throwing the eggs over the back fence for a few days. But then they flattened themselves down and scurried under the fence into the noxious Big Indian Swamp to look for them. Eventually, my dad settled for herding the ducks over to the side of the shed so they could watch him whip the eggs against the wall one by one. This finally seemed to work.

A couple days later, even with them locked in every night and no more eggs in the trash, they somehow seemed to be knocking the trash cans over again. My dad started watching the cage with binoculars to see if they were standing on each other's head, maybe wearing a trench coat and sunglasses and picking the lock with their egg teeth. He never caught them in the act, but every morning, the cans would be tipped over.

This mystery was finally solved, or a new one was introduced, when one morning my dad found approximately half a bloody duck locked in the cage.

Something had eaten them. Both of them. Most of them. And the latch was still secure, a classic locked-room mystery. Eventually we put two and two together and realized whatever killed the ducks must have been the same whatever that was tipping over our garbage cans, and everybody felt even worse about blaming the deceased.

It was a dark couple days, and you could see by the way my dad was grinding his teeth that he was planning something. First, he lied to my sister about how they died. Having no time for a good alibi, he claimed they drank the black, poisoned yard water like mine did, then he quickly buried the evidence out by the fence. Then he dismantled the monstrous duck hotel with the reverence and ceremony of a decommissioned World War II battleship and burned everything but the tires.

He started sleeping on the deck with a rifle, talking about possible impossible cryptozoological culprits ("Do Bigfeets eat birds? Why not?") and waiting for the killer to show itself.

There was some collateral damage that week when my childhood friend Jesse, (after that day, shortened to "Jay" for the rest of his life), got the shock of his life, which probably shortened that, too. He was walking around our house one night to take a piss while dad was on monster duty, and Jesse had just started to unzip, heard that ominous click, and turned around to find himself staring down a rifle. My dad was sprawled out on our deck, flat on his stomach like one of those green plastic Army men. Clock radio, potato chips all around him, thumbing the metal tooth on the end of the barrel to keep his target sight clean. Jesse always had bad luck with my dad though, so don't feel too sorry for him. One time, Jesse made the mistake of driving by our house too slow to check out the scene after we got toilet-papered real bad by a rival school's football team, and my dad yanked open Jesse's door and dragged him out onto the road while the car was still rolling. He apologized, but Jesse had a slight lip twitch around my dad after that, always trying a little too hard to be funny when he talked to him.

"Hit the road, Jay," my dad said from the deck. No time for full names on monster duty, so it was officially "Jay" from then on.

Eventually a raccoon returned to the scene of its crime. Or maybe it was a badger. Either way, Dad got it. Well, sort of.

Remember the neighbor who had the drainage ditch with the *Toxic Avenger* water? Bruce, our big Indian? Well, Big Bruce always felt bad about that black-water incident, so when he heard about our latest duck casualties, he put out this big-ass raccoon trap next to his woodpile to catch the culprit. He was a hunter, always skinning something red and horrible in his backyard in full view of the neighborhood, but to us kids he was a nice guy who let us cut through his yard to get to the basketball court. And he'd actually cleaned out the stagnant air-conditioning swamp so any new ducks wouldn't be tempted to roll the dice. We never got the "Big Indian" thing though. He just looked like a regular blue-collar guy to all of us, except maybe for all the bloodstains on his grass. Or maybe because of them.

But one night, after my dad finally wasn't spending every waking minute scoping out the trash cans for clues, The Big Indian stopped by and said he'd caught the killer. We followed him next door, and there locked in the trap was this hissing, glowering raccoon only slightly smaller than a grizzly, and actually the spitting image of my dad with his newly cultivated black-and-gray, length-of-chin beard. The creature was easily big enough to lift up that huge cage like a blanket and crawl under. Big Bruce told my dad he didn't kill it because it was my dad's ducks, and he would let him do the honors. So my dad retrieved his rusty, never trusty .22 rifle, stood outside the cage, and stared at the raccoon for about five minutes.

Then he went home.

Later, he told me and my brother (but never my sister) that, "Bruce took care of it," whatever that meant. Then he said he was pretty sure it was a muskrat, and not a raccoon, which made for some terrifying moments where we wondered if it had actually been a cat. This species confusion would have helped explain his lack of vengeance or guilt about condemning the creature to Bruce's Death Row. His recent replacement in my life, my new, gun-toting Father-in-Law who thought of me not quite as the son he never had, but as a piss-poor replacement, never met an animal he couldn't kill with impunity.

But that's the last we heard of the dead duck killer, and we all figured it ended up in a Big Indian sandwich. So duck season in our household was over for good. And no one thought about them again until we heard Bruce killed himself out by that same woodpile about five years later. We were all off at college, but we got the story from my dad. Shotgun to the head. And when his sons came by to empty out his house, they told my dad that Bruce had been dealing with cancer, and they acted like their father's brutal suicide was the most normal thing in the world. Maybe that's why Bruce did it outside, so his grass would absorb the blood and hide the brains like it always did, and his sons would only be tasked with cleaning up material possessions.

One night some time after that, my dad confessed to me that he must have ridden the lawnmower past Bruce's headless body at least twice without knowing it was back there. Was he sorry he didn't see it? At the time we all thought he was. And I wished I could have asked him this question one more time before my dad died on the lawnmower the following year, which was better than dying in a car we decided. But sometimes I think his strange confession was just my dad-before-the-ducks talking, one last time.

MOVIES FOR MILKWEED

The third and final time I ruined a movie for someone was last year, at my old apartment. The parking lot in front of my place used to be sunk into the ground about five feet on all sides. It looked a bit like a huge community pool, maybe a bit more like the biggest cell in a TV dinner tray, the one that always held the meat. The inclines on the sides were gradual and only noticeable during the winter, when the tray filled with snow and slush and you needed a little extra gas to clear the entrance and hit the road.

New residents would spin their tires there for a couple days until they figured out the only way to start their day was to keep a routine, maintain that speed.

You'd think this obstacle would have made me late for work every day, and, yes, I had to dig myself out or give the car another running start to get up the hill every January. However, those inclines were the only reason I ever made it to work at all, because those slopes would encourage my legs to start running right before I reached my car, if only for about two or three steps at the most.

And I kept that momentum until the day she moved in.

*   *   *

In film class, we learned that the first movie ever made was really just a blurry, black-and-white series of images showing a horse running. It revealed for the first time that between gallops, every one of a horse's legs are off the ground at the same time. This is also true with humans, which the teacher proved in the *second* movie ever made, a man running. The third movie ever made, bizarrely enough, was some crazy short about electrocuting an elephant. It didn't mean much of anything to me. All the movies made after that involved car chases.

But according to those first two films, running is actually the act of throwing your body weight and catching it, if only for a second. Throwing and catching myself (something my brother could actually do with a football when, disgusted with my performance, he would try to play every position at once) was the one thing that gave me a sense of purpose or urgency in the morning. A jog of one, two, three steps tops, would wake me up enough to navigate the traffic and the red lights to get to work and behind that all-important cash register on time. I was actually running to my car to go to work without ever knowing it. I figured this out 28 jobs, 4 assumed names, and 13 different parking lots later, and I was never late for work again.

Until I moved here.

The day I bought that shovel was the worst. I was exactly nine minutes late.

At first, I blamed the landscapers and the smoothing out and slow death of that small hill near the TV tray, the one that had me flying to work like a racehorse and in the air for about zero point two seconds.

But it was mostly her. Once she moved in, she was always in front of me, just a couple steps ahead so that I couldn't pass. And she wasted even more time turning around and slowing down, as if I was trying to hide something or sneak up on her. I wanted to yell that she was making me late for work, that I needed to run for at least three steps to get up off the ground, that I needed that small hill for momentum.

But that would have taken way too long to explain.

That was the day I went to the hardware store with a nervousness I used to reserve for buying pornography.

*　*　*

Once upon a time, the theater in our town let the kids pay for their tickets in milkweed. The government was sponsoring a program to collect the fibers to make parachutes, and it was also a great recruiting tool for cannon fodder, similar to those captive-audience military commercials they'd been sneaking in after the candy-bar cartoon warned you to turn off your cell phone. Someone somewhere figured that any kid who collected plants to pay for a movie ticket would also be broke and hopeless enough to find the prospect of patrolling through hateful glares in a foreign land exciting. Sort of like the attention a 7-year-old boy gets when he takes his new toy and runs up and down the aisles making sputtering airplane noises during a Holocaust film. I can tell you this with certainty: someone will take that toy away.

But what better way than to let them start fulfilling this dream than by making parachutes? Hell, they'll probably claim that a few good-sized frogs could make ammunition. Or a cup of snails could be ground up into tank treads.

The movie theater actually handed out empty extra-large popcorn tubs to collect the milkweed, and you'd turn them in right where they normally tore a ticket, and they added it to a growing pile. I noticed the pyramid of empty popcorn tubs on the way in, but I just assumed it was some kind of popcorn-eating contest, or a creative display for a new botanical horror flick.

And when I laughed at some kid with his bucket of milkweed and cut in front of him in line, the kid went for my throat, face all red, fists balled up.

Later, I decided that the kid was so mad because, to him, the movie wasn't something you could watch again. It was a one-time event. The things happening on the screen were as fleeting as real life if some broke-ass kid could only see them once, and it would not happen again.

But even worse, he was angry because I was making him late.

* * *

Way later, after the parking lot was filled in and the girl was gone, a retired neighbor on the ground floor asked if I'd recently gotten a new job. She said I didn't seem as happy going to work as I used to. I tried to explain how I was still at the same job, that it was only the landscape that had changed. She just stared at me out her window, face framed between her lush hanging ferns, and silently sipped her coffee. I told her I could prove it, and the next morning dug through a pile of old photographs to find one that first girl had taken when she was watching me out the building's basement window, her tight, black curls cutting hieroglyphics through the fog of her breath on the glass.

The window was actually below ground level, peeking around one of those drainage boxes people sometimes fill with flowers, and if she was down there doing laundry, which was much too dangerous with all the exposed wiring.

But she liked to fling that window open near my feet and scare me when I got home from work. I fell for it every time. That final afternoon, she had decided to photograph my trek from the parking lot to the building, all the way up to the scare. The first picture in her series was supposed to show me getting out of my car, but the angle of the photo and the sunken parking lot revealed only my head floating in a sea of grass and asphalt. The girl was in the picture with me, but just like the first movie ever made, her legs didn't touch the ground.

* * *

Her photograph stayed on my refrigerator for an hour, surrounded by magnetic poetry I never used. Finally, I circled the girl's feet, put it in an envelope, and slid it under my neighbor's door. She never acknowledged the photograph, and she never greeted me with her morning coffee again. Her two ferns were even moved to her kitchen window around the corner of the building that faces the highway.

Maybe the reason that picture scared my neighbor wasn't the girl's feet not touching the ground. Maybe it was simply the same reason I jumped every time I used to look down and see my ex-girlfriend peeking out near my feet. There just aren't supposed to be heads down by the ground.

But they work just fine underneath it.

I still can't believe that she filled out my trail like that. It took years and about nine hundred pairs of shoes to wear it back down, but the morning after I buried her there, every blade of grass stood up straight and green, an effect I was unable to get from the milkweed seeds I dropped when no one is looking.

And there was still enough of an incline to get back my momentum. At least until the landscapers leveled it off. But like always, she stood back up, too, as straight as any goddamn flower.

The milkweed seeds worked , just not like the military advertised.

She moved back into the building the following Sunday. I knew it was her because she always carried the same number of boxes. And by Monday, she was slowing me down in the mornings.

I don't need to buy a new shovel every month, but I do.

EL KABONG

While I was still stumbling around trying to figure out why my pants suddenly didn't seem to have any leg holes, police officers were pounding on my door eager to tell me my wife was found dead in a guitar case. When I finally got dressed, I found them perched on my porch, rocking back and forth on their shoes, one big, one small, with a medium-sized buzzcut standing in the middle. The bookends were bright blue, wringing hats in their hands real noble, while the middle guy was the porridge that was just "white" apparently, wearing the sharp suit and a blood-red power tie which divided him neatly in half. He was clearly in charge, looking me up, down, up, right, down, left, up, head twitching like a thumb memorizing a videogame cheat code. Because of this grim trifecta of foreheads furrowed like fists and all the insufferably officious body language they were throwing at me, I knew they'd come to report something horrible. I knew this because, even though Angie hadn't been missing long enough for me to be prepared for the absolute worst, I'd actually watched a movie or two in my life. But in that moment, the worst was my certainty that these three cops were going to be comforted by their loved ones later on tonight about how hard their jobs were delivering tragic news.

I'd already imagined their dinner-table conversations, and I was convinced they got off on this stuff. I pictured them making sure their wives caught them staring pensively into the distance, a countdown to the sympathetic back rub or blowjob later, and, sure, I knew these guys were ready for my reaction, too. But only if it was a reasonable reaction.

I could feel the suspense coming off them like an audible hum. I also knew from watching a million true-crime shows that I, as the husband in the equation, was the prime suspect. The detective in the middle, with his bush-league semiotic strategies of interrogation, like a red power tie pointing at a belt buckle, for example, had it written all over his scowl, so our encounter was forever blighted by expectation.

But in spite of my confidence clocking all their motivations at 99% accuracy and my very real horror at the prospect of losing the love of my life, none of this mental chess stopped me from being the most suspicious spouse in the history of bad news delivered on doorsteps. I could feel misdirected rage boiling up and over and ricocheting in all the wrong directions before I could stop, even if I'd wanted to.

"Mr. James..." the small cop began. "We're sorry to inform you that..."

Somewhere in the thunder of blood rumbling in my ears, I heard the words "wife," "murdered," and "guitar" rolling off the hot breath of the dude, and I had questions. But I couldn't stop thinking how they were obviously relishing their roles as harbingers of doom. Who does this sort of work? And why did they need three of them to do it?

I was really stuck on all this.

Mainly because I knew they were watching me experience something I always found excruciating to witness in others, where a tragedy becomes an excuse to be a monster. And if it was two things all those crime shows had taught me, it was that monsters were typically ridiculous, and human beings didn't fit in guitar cases.

My first memory of this bad-reaction loophole goes back further, and involves much lower stakes. In high school when I delivered pizzas, a co-worker got the mirror knocked off her car by some bump-and-run, and she came running in yelling, "Call the cops!" But I hesitated, understandably wanting details, and she flipped, upending the perfectly symmetrical pizza I was crafting, screaming those words again, this time inches from my nose. I remember thinking, "No *way* you're this upset. You just wanted to trash my pizza 'cause we broke up." I understood the urge to launch a pre-cooked floppy disc across the room to see how they landed, but what I didn't understand then was, in a moment like that, you're hovering in a limbo of split-second understanding that you're going to take advantage of your new-found, tragedy-induced immunity in case it never happens again ... but you're also genuinely upset. So on my doorstep, I finally understood why she'd launched my first geometrically perfect pie into a ceiling fan, and I ground my teeth in a crimson haze of despair that was still coherent enough to hope these cops gave me any reason at all to flip my metaphorical pizza right the fuck out.

Later, I got more facts about the case, the horrible stuff, about how she likely survived in that guitar case for half a day, hogtied and folded up and running out of life while she listened to truck after truck piling the city's trash over her. But in that moment at the front door staring at this real-life representation of an Ascent of Man evolution poster, I just really wanted to lash out.

I scanned the big one, with his all-too-enthusiastic hat wringing, his lumpy blue shirt and matching tie, making it practically invisible and therefore powerless, and I imagined him using these encounters to explain away impotence, alcoholism, maybe missing his bully son's big moment of sanctioned assault in a hockey game.

"When did this happen?" I asked the big one, his mouth wriggling around so much it was practically eating itself. I squeezed my doorjamb and watched my own knuckles turn white, as he turned even whiter. I was extra strong in doorjambs, you see. Even though I hadn't gotten to the point where I could do 500 chin-ups on the bar I'd hung in our sagging bedroom-door frame, I was squeezing this wood so hard all three of them heard the cracking. But I wasn't sure this wasn't my knuckles.

"Well, sir, we don't know much," the detective in the middle answered, holding up a hand to keep Lumpy quiet. "But due to blood pooling on her right arm and leg, we believe, at this time, she was killed in another location, and, subsequently, brought to the garbage dump."

"No kidding," I said, not really asking, not really talking, just squeezing the door harder despite the forearm cramps. "So, you're saying she didn't live there? At the garbage dump, I mean. So you're saying you got cutting-edge forensics telling you her day didn't start on a mountain of beer cans and diapers and TV dinners? Thanks, Sherlock!"

"I'm sorry, sir, we're still trying to ascertain . . ."

"'Ascertain'? How about you stop bumbling over big words and just tell me what you know about my wife."

"We understand you're upset." The little one stepped forward, screwing his hat back on his pointed head to exert authority. "And you have our word, we will do everything in our power to . . ."

"Now, can you tell us . . ." Lumpy started to say over him, and at that I stepped onto the porch into their arena, eyeball to eyeball with the disheveled one, and, oh, he didn't like me in his bubble. But I figured I wouldn't get another chance like this to toss a perfect pizza into the fan blades, so I got even closer. Today was my diplomatic immunity, before my depression or their defensiveness took over. Like that moment you get pulled over for speeding, but your wife is going into labor, and they say, "Follow us!" and put on the sirens, and you all break the laws together, pizzas flying everywhere. All three of them were trapped with me in these bubbles of rising crust and huge, impervious, potentially nuclear explosions of ruby-red pizza goodness.

"Listen, please don't use the word 'power' when you stand there twisting the sweat out of your lid," I said up into his nose, considering a quick bite of the booze-busted blood vessels off the end of his beak. "You stand there fantasizing how you can tell this story over pork chops later, and I have to endure making you feeling okay about making me feel bad?"

The big one got a little fire back in his eyes, remembering I was just some citizen disrespecting him, and he was going for the mirror glasses so he could push back with his sovereignty, too. But a hand appeared on his shoulder, then his hand appeared on that guy's shoulder, then my own shoulder, then a couple more hands clapped over each other's chests, and miraculously this Twister party calmed everyone back down. We were all cupping hands and it was impossible to blow up now.

"Sir, we know how upsetting this must be . . ."

I tried out a small shove against the big guy's chest. He stumbled down a step, and the other two held up their hands.

"Whoa, whoa . . ."

Hands were back on everybody's shoulders but mine.

"Let's go, Joe," the small one said, pulling the big one away. I watched them get into their car, the detective looking like he still had a lot to say. So I pushed my luck and followed them to the cruiser, knocking on the window good and hard. I'd always wanted to do that, too. The detective stood with the door open, and the big cop, the driver, rolled down his window, holding his breath behind pursed lips.

That's when I saw their hands hadn't been clapping each other's chests and shoulders to restrain themselves, but instead they'd been covering up the electronic eyes of their body cameras in case one of them snapped.

A brave new world, I decided. *And a whole new kind of restraint.*

"Don't leave town, Mr. James," the detective said finally, climbed in. "Someone will be by to talk to you again."

I smiled. Even though I'd just found out my wife was dead, and even though I would begin the second half of my cursed life where things that made sense for half a minute when we were together wouldn't make sense anymore and happiness was only like that movie we saw once but couldn't remember the ending. I smiled because I could say something in that moment to make a cop feel foolish. And how often do you get the chance? This smile would cost me months of guilt and incrimination, and eventually something even worse, but I still believe it was worth it.

Then they were gone, and any dashboard cameras or body cameras or covert plastic eyeballs would miss my honest reaction, even if it was no different.

* * *

After the cops left, I may have stood there for an extra dozen deep breaths, even considered sticking around if I had any faith in the Louisville police department, or if I hadn't so effectively gotten the investigation off on the wrong foot by jamming mine in my mouth. I thought about my wife and our future baby curled up in a guitar case like grisly Russian nesting dolls, and I thought about how much she would have enjoyed that doorway exchange, considering her recent anti-authoritarian research for her dissertation , but mostly I stood there and thought about how we'd always joked about her height, about her being so short a hawk might swoop down to grab her on a jog. Which is kinda what happened after all. But she was no nesting doll. This didn't make any sense. A guitar case? Even Angie wasn't that small.

"Matryoshkas," she told me once. "That's what those dolls were called."

I'd mangled the word when we came across a pile of rusted playground hobby horses during our honeymoon trip to Corpus Christi, stacked up high under an overpass in order of decreasing size. She loved horses, even though she knew this was expected of females.

I thought about how impossibly small a guitar case was to comfortably house a human body, alive or dead, and remembered the time we'd watched guitar cases chase each other around a Louisville airport carousel after Texas as we waited for our lost luggage. We were getting frustrated by the passengers breathing down our necks and elbowing us in the ribs, all waiting for their lost bags, too. We got a good laugh when one little fiddle case got stuck on the conveyor belt and backed up the bags to upset everyone even more, until a guitar case slid down to knock it loose. I almost pulled the guitar out of it to pretend it was mine as an excuse to abandon our stuff and be done with the day. Until Angie asked me, "What if you have to prove you can play it?"

Eventually our heads were hanging low, and the sleepy tail-end of her wine buzz had quieted us both down to grumbling and teeth grinding. Then she pointed to a sign and laughed:

"Wouldn't it be more fun if this said 'Personal Baggage Claim' instead?"

It took me a second, but then I lost it, too, no matter how close to home that joke was. I said, "Oh, you mean you'd rather watch a turnstile full of exes, neglectful parents, missed birthdays, broken promises, minor scandals, Electra and Oedipal complexes, all rolling down the ramp?"

"Yes. That," she declared. "Then these people might hesitate to swarm this carousel so darn close!"

She always got away with stuff like that because of her height. And when she explained how "Matryoshka" didn't really mean "nesting doll" at all, that it was just a name for any little old Russian biddy, small but sturdy, I realized this was her in a nutshell. Curled up in a nutshell, I mean, feet pinned over her head forever.

But that day, strangers backed up from the turnstile when she shouted. She was small, but she had that kind of power.

*   *   *

Before I could come to my senses, I ran back inside and packed up all my stuff to leave town, jamming a couple head-to-toe changes of clothes into my suitcase with the ratty customs slips still attached, quickly realizing that a suitcase was almost too small to hold a textile facsimile of a human being, let alone the entire human, alive or otherwise.

And a guitar case was smaller than this? Insanity.

I also realized I'd lost my wallet somewhere in the chaos of the day, and for some reason, the loss of a valid I.D. helped to convince me in the moment that I was doing the right thing by getting the hell out of Dodge.

The streets of Kentucky were quiet, even with my windows down, and I drove holding my breath in my throat. I headed down Bardstown road, back to the alley near the Keep Louisville Weird shop with the cut-out circus-clown photo-op out front. This was the store where I used to make Angie laugh by putting on the same floppy horse's head, but never buying it. It was always her idea to do it, and I complained it would be terrible for a bank robbery because the animal's eyes never lined up with my own, and she'd say, "Ride your horse head for good, not evil."

I knew it was a borderline fetish for her though, because every Wednesday Angie and her girlfriends would head down to the Davis Arena for another Ohio Valley Wrestling moron-a-thon. The problem was Louisville's wrestling scene wasn't small enough for a bunch of PhD students to be there ironically, like Pittsburgh's ratty little Keystone State Wrestling Alliance had been, a weekend laugh where we'd hung out a couple times back in grad school just to watch assholes munch light bulbs and smack staples and thumbtacks into each other's heads, everything sinking into their skulls with the ease of December porch pumpkins. And Davis Arena wasn't big enough for the full-on kitsch factor either. Like Arena Football, and remember how embarrassing that shit was? It was kinda in the middle. The porridge that was just stupid?

Her girlfriends would tease her because she used to root for this big dude who was supposedly "half stallion." I hoped they meant his head. Seriously though, there really was this Mexican kid who called himself the "Lucha Horse." They bought her the T-shirt and everything. Maybe he was Mexican. No one would know with the mask, so it was a real mystery. Which meant, in the days of the internet, that nobody gave a shit enough to make anything up. At the time though, Angie had been practicing one of her Learn Spanish apps with me for so long that I did know his name in English translated as "Something Horse."

Goofy horse heads everywhere though! It was a big Derby town. It was also where I chatted up a clerk I called "'90s Ex-Girlfriend" because she had that reddish Kool-Aid colored hair so popular back then. I'd have that clerk repeat how much the horse head cost at least a dozen times because all I could ever think while looking at her was what I wanted to say to the real '90s ex-girlfriend who unceremoniously dumped me, like, "Sorry for all the free movies and orgasms!" This was also the joint where they had a terrifying life-size Walt Disney, who was sporting half a moustache and steadily disintegrating much faster than the real thing. They had some cool stuff, too, like a Spencer's Gifts from back before shopping malls morphed into boat shows, and Angie talked me into buying one of their ant farms, even after what horror befell my first ant farm back when I was a kid.

But I was circling their stomping grounds, and the musicians were gone. Calling them "musicians" was a stretch. In any warm state, they were a common infection, a topical rash. Where Angie had grown up in Minnesota, they called street musicians "buskers." This word made me homicidal the first time I heard it, and this was *before* I suspected one of murder.

Then I saw a conspicuously clean spot on the street where a guitar case used to be. A spot that at first glance resembled the curve of a woman's hips, and I remembered this particular guitar case on this particular corner because I was always amazed how little money the guy always made. I got out of the car and crouched down in the street to touch the edges of the sidewalk outline, still unable to comprehend how my wife could have fit inside. I glanced up at the Keep Louisville Weird store and wished I'd bought that horse head for Angie, and not just so I could be wearing it right now. It was supposed to be our final Kentucky Derby costume, "a jockey and her steed," she called it, and all she'd need was her '90s Fly Girl hat. But what turned out to be our final Derby had been a fiasco, so the idea was dropped.

Inside the store, I could see '90s Ex-Girlfriend rearranging the skintight hipster Mothman T-shirts for the window display, and I noticed she was about six months pregnant, but only three months from the Kool-Aid growing out of her hair. Then I heard the unmistakable sound of an instrument thrumming low inside its coffin as it bounced around off someone's scrawny knees, and I turned to see a musician slinking through the alley. He turned the corner, top hat all askew, carefully manicured orange beard and ragged accordion under one arm, metal triangle around his wrist, heavy instrument case of unknown origin clipping the brick road every third step. He saw me and set up shop, squeezing out a song in record time, tapping the triangle like Pavlov and bringing his fingers down on that tuneless monstrosity, and suddenly I was convinced he'd switched to the accordion because something had happened to his guitar.

I grabbed him around the collar and got right up in his coffee breath.

"Were you here this morning?"

He smiled and croaked a mournful note from the harmonic rig around his neck, it was almost enough for me to snap right there. Then I remembered the triangle.

The man has a triangle.

I buried my fist in his mouth, then kneed him in the gut, java breath covering us in a cloud. Then I put the toe of my boot through the teeth of the accordion's grill. Both of them made the same tortured squawk, and they both kept smiling. I'd never worn boots in my life until we moved down south, but after six months or so, Angie and I both ended up with a half dozen pairs each. Boots were required in Kentucky, even if it did mean you slipped all over the sidewalk when it was wet. But one benefit was made clear when I booted my first adversary with those sharp toes. That's when I was suddenly swarmed by a bevy of stinky street maestros avenging their friend, but I would have thought it was just one busker moving really, really fast all around me in a tornado of weed and onions if it wasn't for the colorful tinkling of holiday baubles in their beards. Trendy beard bling made for great targets, and my fists were finding them.

So much for never punching anyone in Kentucky . . .

But they seemed to be multiplying around me. A whole band now, including jug and spoon sections, and I beetled up on the street, realizing the alley would hide the brawl long enough for me to conceivably get hurt pretty severely by these dudes, though I was soaking up shots like they were barely there, their fists and hard-earned guitar-string calluses rebounding off my head like balloon animals. I wrote this off as adrenaline and their vegetarian diets, but I was still nervous enough to reach into my jacket for my secret weapon.

My hand went deep into my pocket, then *past* the pocket where the lining had torn, and my fingers found the extra pouch sewn into the back of the coat for hauling waterfowl. My duck coat was one of those big hunting jackets you'd find at Cabela's. Angie got it as a gift back when she still harbored dreams of me hunting with her dad and bonding someday. Her dad was one of those guys who practically lived at Cabela's and killed every animal that made the mistake of wandering onto his property, and he was always trying to goad me into going out and "getting us some ducks." But I'd had my fill of adventures with her dad ever since the first time I stayed at their cabin for Christmas and he went out for groceries and hit a deer with his car. He ran back inside asking someone for help, and Angie said, "Go with him. Bond!" So I dutifully rode back to the scene of his crime and tried to aim the headlights into the ditch as ordered, while he bumbled around with the .22 from his pile of pistols in the glove box. I heard a gunshot, then a "Damn!" then another shot and a panicked "Pop the trunk!"

Then he came back into the light dragging this gangly limp thing by the head, blood all over his chest. Her dad was a hairy man, and there were several times I'd seen him from a distance and thought, "Oh, man, now he's sleeveless?" but then he'd turn out to be shirtless instead. This night was no exception.

So I jumped out and ran behind the car and did what I was told, and there in the trunk was a coyote so frozen you could pick it up by the tail. He'd forgotten about the last thing he shot, or maybe hit with this car, and he was staring at it just as confused as I was. But I did take the expensive coat from Angie as a peace offering, pretending I might hit the woods with her dad one day after all. Because there was a silver lining to it all, literally. Hidden in the back of my jacket, for just the right opportunity.

The brass knuckles I'd bought for the best man at our wedding were illegal, but that's what I needed. I figured if you could commit a crime against humanity like playing an accordion in public, there was no reason they could outlaw such a beautiful natural extension of a man's hand. Originally, I'd gotten all my groomsmen the brass knuckles as a joke, but quickly realized there was a whole subculture of knuckles mania online, all custom made, all very serious. So once I secured some decent knuckles for my brother Lloyd, I couldn't just give everybody else the tin versions. So everybody got heavy-duty knuckles, forged from nautical brass and surrounded by warnings and disclaimers, and Lloyd's cost something like twice as much as the rest. Some of my groomsmen, the ones who'd driven to the wedding, they'd taken to displaying them on their coffee tables or man caves whenever I came to visit, which made it very easy to steal them all back, but I still hadn't got the knuckles back from my brother. He earned his though, being the first person I'd ever seen in a real fight. And on that day, he was smart enough to put in his plastic football mouthpiece before he ran into the mob, which was the next best thing to wearing a huge rubber horse's head in brawl.

But during the Apocalyptic Busker Beating, I grabbed my golden fist and worked on putting these musicians to sleep. Then I blew some blood out my nostril and moved on to the blackjack, from the *extra*-secret pocket. It might not have been as cinematic as a golden fist, but it sure as hell put people to sleep. A few cracks across the temple and half the musicians were on the ground in seconds, dreaming of album covers they'd never autograph, while the other half were running for their lives, long, thin beards trailing like silk scarves. It seemed like they were trying some made-for-TV moves on me during the battle, but maybe it was my imagination. Do buskers dig wrestling, too? They have that sort of earnest sincerity that they'd totally believe in it, I bet.

But there's one big clue wrestling is fake, only you'd have to be in a fight to realize it. When things end up on the ground in real life, they stay there forever.

I tried some moves myself just for kicks, things I remembered as a kid, or maybe from the half-ass talents of the Keystone Wrestling League. Cross chop, forehand chop, Mongolian chop. Wrestlers were always using a those open-fist chops instead of punches to minimize actual damage. But that shit changes real quick when you're chopping with a blackjack. In fact, if you handed every professional wrestler a blackjack instead of a feather boa, the sport would be more famous than *Rollerball,* or at least roller derby. Do they still have roller derby?

"Clotheslines," now *that* move was a great visual punch line on the television screen. Face down on the street though? With nowhere to fly, it breaks all the bones.

One move I did try to highlight was the Bronco Buster, since it seemed to fit the theme. It's where you ride a dude like a horse. Only I was the horse. What a twist. There was probably a Mule Kick in there, too, but that's as close as I came to a signature move. I guess a blackjack "Go to Sleep" move probably counts, too, but that move is universal, no matter the tool, and certainly not relegated to an arena.

It seems like a no-brainer, but the one thing I did not do was break a guitar over anyone's head.

Remember the ol' "El Kabong!" a shout made famous by the cartoon horse Quick Draw McGraw? More specifically his vigilante alter ego and his patented guitar smash over the bad guys' domes. I couldn't do it. It felt like way too much symmetry to risk it.

I crouched over Orange Accordion Man where he still laid and open-hand smacked him until he told me every corner where Louisville guitar players danced for their dinners. I wasn't even sure why I needed that info, because I'd come with the intention of accosting the first singer-songwriter I saw, but suddenly I had this fantasy about being a seedy, sweaty fuck of a private eye right out of the movies, bumbling my way around Kentucky, beating the treble clefs out of hippies and hipsters alike.

Afterwards, I went back to the guitar-shaped spot on the street. It was a huge mistake what I did next, but on the list of incriminating things I'd done since I'd received the news, it was barely in the top five.

I took out a piece of chalk and outlined the clean spot for real, like the crime scene it needed to be. I did it fast.

Quick Draw McGraw . . .

I outlined a guitar that wasn't there, then the shape of my wife within that outline to see if she'd fit.

I hoped this would help the police. Maybe one of the buskers was mad Angie didn't throw 'em a quarter, or maybe she threw the quarter too hard, or maybe our heated discussions outside Keep Louisville Weird about class theory and padlocks and doomed childhood ant farms drowned out all their terrible music.

Then I saw Orange Accordion Man wasn't getting right up, and the accordion wasn't smiling. So I ran across the street to the Smoothie King and asked for some ice, remembering how Angie did the same weeks earlier when she went jogging too far and almost stroked out, calling me from the shade of a trash can, scared her body had stopped sweating. That was the most terrified I'd ever been. Until this morning with the cops at my door.

I came back with the ice and poured some down the guy's shirt to see if he'd jump. Nothing. So I worked on the outline of the guitar some more, and Angie inside the guitar, then I laid down with them both and put my arm around her. I still wasn't entirely convinced my wife would fit inside. But it was close. Justice finally sorta served, I might have blacked out.

*   *   *

I came to my senses and rolled toward the prone tunesmith, his shirt wet from the melted ice, survival instincts beginning to kick in. I was no doctor, by any stretch of the definition, couldn't even claim the rhetoric-and-composition PhD loophole like my wife could, but my earlier ice-down-the-shirt diagnosis was good enough for me. I got out my throwback '90s clamshell phone and called the police, told them to check out some sidewalk art in the alley. Said it might help with their case, knowing full well it wouldn't. This, combined with skipping town before dusk on the same day I was informed of my new status as a widower, probably shot me right to the top of their list, of course. I imagined the head detective from my doorstep at that exact moment, taking my picture from the pile and pinning it to the tiptop of their pyramid of suspects, then taking a magic marker and drawing on a bridle. Seriously, I prayed it was my caller I.D. picture from Angie's phone, where I was wearing the leering rubber horse head from Keep Louisville Weird, because no way a picture like that ever gets demoted from the top spot, even if they ever catch the real killer.

Later I would read in the true-crime version of my story that the cops searched that alley real good, but instead of pondering my chalk outline, they found an innocent street musician in a coma, triangle somehow locked around his neck in a permanent chokehold, and an accordion that would need braces.

They also found the rubber horse head I was wearing throughout the assault, though I'd swear on a stack of telephone books I had no recollection of ever buying such a ridiculous thing, let alone putting it on when I stepped out of my car. But a splash-page sketch of my horse head askew on my shoulders, my golden fist clenched tight, my full uniform with my collar up high, would all be right there in the middle of that dog-eared paperback, where they always put eight pages of "shocking" photos. Then I'd vow to find a horse's head that would fit much better than that, one that wouldn't look quite so crazy.

HA'PENNY DREADFULLER

"In this town there lived a psycho by the name of Texas Red
Befriended by dead dogs, all were left for dead . . ."
—Arty Stealins— "Pig Iron"

Agua Fría, New Mexico, 9:09 a.m. Spring of 1878.

The coyote stopped at the edge of the well, a warning rumbling in her throat. On the way up the hill, her entire body telegraphed a change in the air. The smell of decay pulsed in her nostrils, and her tail was working overtime, whiplashing the flies from the furless patches of skin on her haunch. The signals ran from one end of her body to the other. Heat begat the scent, begat the flies, begat the tail. She was used to such stimuli and response hardwired into her frantic gait, even without the all-consuming hunger that clouded her mind.

At the rim of the stone circle, however, she found no evidence of water or the potentially nourishing rot her senses were screaming for. She leaned out to nose the rope creaking down in the darkness. The weight of a bucket hung suspended from it, now swaying over an empty hole, where it had previously bobbed and sloshed years before. Her snout nudged the rope to swinging, but the weight of the gold coins heaped inside slowed and stopped it pretty quick.

Before the well had dried up, when the bucket had still been half underwater, the waves of sunlight playing against these coins had kept most every horsefly at bay. Now the bucket hung limp and splintered, baking in the daylight and this new brick oven, and the gold coins had lost the dance of their former amplified reflection. The coyote didn't know a dance of light was an amazing natural deterrent to any insect. To her, everything was just a new source of agony.

And now, without the shine of the water, the flies could bite and sting her sores with impunity.

But she was ready to make the trade, winged torment for the promise of carrion. And although the coyote had no way of knowing this booty was the cause of today's misery, or at least these riches were no longer working with the shimmering well water to make her world more bearable, she had experienced a reprieve once before.

A week earlier, she'd swallowed a penny while lapping water from a teacup, one of fifty balanced along a rancher's fence posts. This rancher had left cups of water and copper along his border in order to keep his daughter from being troubled by flies at her upcoming nuptials. But the rancher had caught the coyote upending the cup, and had even taken a shot at her, despite his daughter's pleas to please, please leave her be, as the rancher's daughter had seen the low hang of the coyote's belly that concealed an imminent birth. This was a condition the rancher's daughter knew something about, also the reason her wedding was being held in a dusty backyard rather than a nearby church, or even the rancher's gun store, where his own brother had tied the knot two years before. But her wedding would never occur, not because of the swarms, but because the groom never showed. However, the rancher's daughter's belly wouldn't wait for another suitor.

The three of them would eventually gather the rest of the pennies in silence, the baby in her belly punching against the jostle of her sobs.

The pups inside the coyote kicked against dream space, as well, as their mother nosed the rope again, hoping for any last splash of moisture or mud to chew. But due to increasing desperation and the change in her center of gravity, she leaned too far over the edge of the well, and she tumbled on in.

The flies followed her down at their leisure.

Years later, the rancher would leave his dying crops behind and drag a cot into his bankrupt gun store, first uprooting his daughter and his strange grandson, then kicking them out of his life in disgrace. And this bucket of gold would go undiscovered for a decade, until drought turned every well in the state into a treasure hunt. The celebration of a local gang who would one day discover these riches would be muted due to drunkenness and dehydration, but the leader of the gang would be excited enough to lean over the rim when he caught a flash of gold on the bottom. Not realizing it was a copper Indian headdress circa 1893 rather than Lady Liberty's profile that shone in the rib cage of the coyote's ghostly outline, not far from the skulls of her litter, his greed would send him crashing to the bottom after it.

His gang would leave him down there for a long, long time, punishing him for grudges real and imagined, but mostly leaving him down there due to forgetfulness as they divided up the gold on booze and debts, fully expecting him to be dead when they returned, ready to pretend his death was a surprise.

But the leader of the gang had been underestimated since birth, weakness assigned by strangers due to pale skin prone to sunburn and blazing orange hair. He would survive his long nights in the well by counting the tiny skulls in the cradle of bones and sucking on that penny, fooling his body with the extra saliva that this created. He would survive months down there through pure force of will, amazed to find the well provided everything he needed. And every night would be a lesson in resentment, something he'd remember for the rest of the life. And although there were about a dozen other lessons he learned at the bottom of that well, like lessons in resilience, stubbornness, and determination, he would focus only on recitations that fortified him with hatred, the surprise secret of immortality, as he sucked on a penny and talked to his dogs.

DRAGON BY THE DUMPSTER

"Big gorilla at the L.A. Zoo snatched the glasses right off my face,
took the keys to my BMW, left me here to take his place."
—Warren Zevon— "Gorilla, You're a Desperado"

Besides when I blew my engine and had to walk to work every day down those railroad tracks with a shitty radio shaped like a hamburger for company, there was only one other time I was without a car. It was a strange summer, right after I'd been bounced out of school for vandalism, and I almost didn't get through it with my identity intact. Before I start this, I should mention that I changed the names of the vehicles in this story to protect their families. Less important, I also swapped the name Mike with Mark, I'm calling a bookstore a video store, and I'm not being honest about forgetting a girl's name. Worst of all, way later, I'll talk about a police sketch, and I'll lie about it looking like me. The rest of this shit is gospel.

So, first off, with all the cheap apartments I'd lived in, you'd think I'd have gotten used to a life of abrupt temperature changes with the water temperature by the time I hit college. You couldn't really blame anyone. It was kind of like the weather. You can't get too angry when the temperature drops outside, right? So, I was living in a tiny, converted-office building with this girl, unable to accurately forecast my next shower. The girl? I can't remember her name, but I almost remember her car. I remember both their colors though. One black, one white.

But next door was Crazy Mark, and I remember every inch of that motherfucker. Even though his real name was Mike Miller, I called him "Crazy Mark II" because I'd already known a Crazy Mark once in my life, and this was just easier. Besides, they're everywhere if you start looking.

But I'll talk about one Mark at a time. The first one, I'd managed to duck for about a decade. Then I ran into his car. Because it was my car. I'll explain.

It was sleeping in the exact same spot I saw it five years ago. A yellow dog curled up in the corner of the employee end of the parking lot at Ike's Truck

Stop off I-75, a garage-sized dive where Crazy Mark had been working his whole life. When I saw the car, my first instinct was to run over, low to the ground with a screwdriver in my teeth like I was in the trenches of World War II. As if they fought that war with screwdrivers. Careful not to wake it, I quickly removed the license plate from the Sundog, then replaced it with my own. It was scary but fun, and I figured he'd appreciate the joke. I felt like I was swapping collars on sleeping dinosaurs. See, I'd sold him this car the year before, and he'd never bothered to change the plate. And once my old plates were secured to my green Cavalry, I turned to stare at my old ride for a minute and thought, Crazy fuckin' Mark. What the hell happened to you?

I'd heard you were engaged to that girl we both dated (sometimes at the same time) and I also heard that you smacked her in the face when she broke up with you. I stepped closer and checked the rubber seal around the driver's-side window. It was still crusted with white, oil-based paint. I smiled, remembering the time when it was my turn to date that girl and I came out of the bookstore to find the words "Fuck You!" smeared angrily across the glass. I could never prove it was you, but I'm happy to see that you were never able to get all that paint off either.

I pulled my keychain from my pocket and found the extra key swinging right where I'd left it. The car opened without a protest, as if it was still mine. I felt bad for a second, like I should have hung onto this car after I paid it off, like I'd worked and earned the right to own this car only to decide in that exact instant I never wanted to see it again. How many times does that happen on a wedding night?

I climbed behind the wheel. I didn't even have time to look around before I knew that I do not like it back in this car at all. I felt like I was sitting in a cold puddle of something bad, and that something was slowly seeping through my jeans and crawling up the crack of my ass. It was almost as uncomfortable as the memory of that itchy hay ride in high school when another kid named Mark punched me in the face. Finally glancing around, I saw the most random, pointless collection of compact disc and cassettes cracked and scratched and littering the floor, and I needed out. Worst taste in music ever.

I decided this is what would have happened if I had stayed in this car, stayed in this town, stopped treating my music with respect and started smacking them around, too, just like he did to her.

How to Playfully Backhand a Friend

I thought about her often because I knew, and I'm sure she knew, she'd have been better off never crossing paths with either of us. The girl in question, we'll call her "Gee" in this story, as in the letter "G," because she had a license plate that me, Jerry, and Crazy Mark all got excited about, thinking it said GOD-LESS. With only a clever license plate, a pretty face, and a nice ass to go on (a "black girl's ass" according to Jerry), we thought this particular girl that stopped to rent movies every Thursday from the video store where we worked was the most utterly fascinating creature of all time. And even after a closer inspection revealed that her plate actually said GODD-ESS instead, we just chalked that up to her being ironic instead of just a shallow twit.

I dated her first. Then Crazy Mark about a year later. She didn't want anything to do with Jerry, and he's been in love with her ever since. But her and Mark didn't last too long, and when it was over, she stopped in the video store he'd long since quit (but I couldn't seem to break up with) and showed me some disturbing poetry she said Mark had been leaving in her bird bath when no one was home. I assured her that he was "harmless" and "a really bad poet" and then asked her who the fuck still has a bird bath? She muttered something about there being nothing harmless about bad poetry, using a Prince song as proof, and then she wandered out the "In" door, "In" door . . .

So I told Jerry all about this run-in, and that's when he decided it was a good time to tell *me* a story. Turned out Jerry was working at a restaurant near his new apartment in the city, a high-end spot named "Jerry's" which he claimed was completely coincidental, swearing to me up and down that he was not pretending it was actually his restaurant when he parked his car every morning. Yeah, right. Anyway, he said another guy in the kitchen, the head chef (this was Jerry's cooking phase, right before his park-ranger phase) was living with our girl, Gee, and guess what his boss had been up to? Jerry explained it all with at least three sound effects:

"He's fucking at least three chicks on a regular basis. Bam! He comes back from the parking lot on his 15-minute break and brags about it, shaking my hands all proud, sometimes shaking my head, then wiping who-knows-what sticky shit all over my shoulders. Slorp! Sure, he might be lying. But he's elbow-deep in something out there. His face comes back grinning like a glazed doughnut and his fingers look like he just waxed a car. Once he playfully backhanded me in the face. Splotch! It was like that time the giraffe woke me up with its tongue when we passed out in the zoo."

"*You* passed out in the zoo," I reminded him. "And how do you 'playfully' backhand someone?"

"That's what I'm saying, dude!"

So I filed this information away, along with Jerry telling me about Head

Chef trying to sell him a bunch of guns (!) because it turned out, he was also this survival nut, and me and Jerry were on the cusp of his phase, too (right before his military phase), which that lasted one whole trip to a shooting range where we got kicked the fuck out for pulling quick-draw contests with the targets inches from our faces while a cop was adjusting his laser site two targets down.

So, rewind the videotape, and I've started seeing Gee regularly at the video store for the first time in a couple years. Her plate never said GOD-LESS no matter how hard I prayed, but now, after I watched her put her movies in the return slot and try not to make any noise doing it, I started liking her all over again. I think it was just from thinking about all the conversations and drama going on around her that she was unaware of, maybe my knowledge of her Head Chef's secret recipes, or maybe just the way she was being wronged, I don't know. But I wanted her just like the old days, so I decided to strike up conversations every chance I got. It was fun for a couple of weeks, even though she had no mysterious poetry bombs to report.

Then one night it was all awkward, and she told me that she'd seen me "driving behind her the other day." What? Then she nervously asked if I knew anyone else that lived on her street because she thought she saw my car there, too. I immediately understood that this was Crazy Mark driving the car I'd sold to him, the car I'd owned when me and Gee (and Jerry) were hanging out together. I tried to explain all this to her, but she seemed unconvinced. Then, the next time she came in, she admitted that, yes, Mark had been around recently. He'd walked straight into her house a couple weeks ago, and Head Chef had to "gently" restrain him until the cops showed up.

"No shit?" I asked her if she saw my car, then said, "Remember how I told you I sold him my car?" Then I asked, quite sincerely, if she thought Mark was mistreating it. She blinked, frowned, sighed and left, clearly tired as fuck of us crazy bastards. And right then, I made a decision that I knew I'd probably be punished for some day. But it hasn't happened yet! We'll see if he reads this.

So I called up Crazy Mark with this bad idea in my head. First, I got the scoop on that incident. Of course, his version of events was radically different than hers. He claimed that he'd only stopped by as an afterthought to give her another small, 42-page poem about Sir Gaiwan and the Green Knight, and that Head Chef attacked him for no reason, holding him on the ground at gunpoint with a knee on his throat. No "gently" anywhere to be found in his version. Then Mark went on to say that when the cops showed up, that gun had mysteriously vanished, and that he was going to be charged with trespassing, assault, and attempted kidnapping. If he could just "prove there was a gun involved," he was sure he could get all those charges thrown out. I said, "Holy shit, dude, Jerry works with this asshole, and he's trying to sell him guns all the time." I actually heard Mark's brain shifting gears on the other end of the phone with a dull metal clank. So I threw a little more sugar into his gas tank and go . . .

"Hey, did you know that this cocksucker is fucking around on her, too? Nails everything in town on his smoke breaks? Pow. Laughs about it to everyone in the kitchen where he works. Someone should do something. None of my business though. Anyway, how about those Red Wings . . ."

Crazy Mark cleared his throat and calmly said, "No, I didn't know that," then got off the phone.

So I went on with my life for a while, and everyone sort of disappeared. Then I'd heard Gee was single again, that she'd caught the Head Chef cheating. So I called Jerry to get the scoop.

First thing he asked me was, "Where you been?"

I said, "Nowhere. Where *you* been?"

He said, "Court."

Then he told me that he kinda lost his mind after I told him about the Head Chef cheating on Gee. After that, compounded with the trespassing, assault, and attempted kidnapping charges (most of them dismissed, however, when Jerry was called in to testify about the guns), Mark decided to get some righteous revenge. Just like I knew he would, fucking poet that he was.

Apparently, he popped out of the bushes and bashed the Head Chef within an inch of his life with a convenient block of nearby firewood. Then he might have bashed him that extra inch.

Mark had gone over there with the intent of breaking his arms so that he was unable to "make a proper omelet ever again" (Jerry's words) and sent him crawling down the street screaming he was being mugged. Some "strange" that the Head Chef had been banging came running out of a parked car all blustering, and Mark started working his way up his shoulders towards the Head itself with that hefty piece of wood. Then he found it. The commotion woke up Gee, who finally caught him red-handed. And red-headed. Red fucking everything.

Covered in blood and spouting sonnets, Crazy Mark was arrested running down the street naked, and Gee came around asking questions. I acted all shocked, and even though I finally seemed to convince her that it wasn't me following her around in the Sundog, I know all that time that she thought it *was* me made a lasting impression that the truth could never erase. It's like starting off a conversation with bad news, an insult, or a horrible lie and then quickly adding, "just kidding." Sure, you might get the laugh, but that split-second that they thought you were serious stays with them forever, even if they never recognize why their feelings for you have changed just that teeeeeny tiny bit.

My fingers are about an inch apart.

Turn off the Water!

Anyway, things were normal for awhile, and then suddenly I was kicked out of school. I also didn't have a car again, and those are the worst times for me.

When I moved in next door to this nut we called Crazy Mark "Too," I was shacked up with the girl whose name I can't remember, and I'd recently been fired from some bush-league carpet cleaning business/chop-shop garage and couldn't afford to get my car fixed anytime soon. And without a job or transportation, me and the apartment with bad weather in the pipes began to merge into one. I didn't do anything for weeks at a time, barely grunting hello and goodbye to the girl I was sharing those days with. All I could tell you about her now is she was taller than me, had dark hair, fucked up my VHS copy of *Highlander*, and she didn't really have any favorite things of her own. Movies, music, nothing.

So, I was in the shower one morning and could hear my neighbor through our ridiculously thin walls fumbling around in his tub, chasing the soap or a toy boat or a girl scout or something. Then he bellowed so loud I thought he was standing there under the spray with me.

"Turn off the water!"

I must have been in shock because I did exactly what I was told before I could stop myself. Then I toweled off and spent the rest of the day with my ear to the wall, listening for any more instructions. I didn't tell my roommate, but confused her when I got up early the next morning to see her off. Suddenly, I had a mission. I waited until I heard my neighbor's shower running and quickly turned on my own hot water. Right on cue:

"Turn off the water!"

I turned it off. Then turned it on again.

"Turn off the water!"

Turned it on . . .

"Turn off . . ."

. . . then off again real quick.

". . . the water!"

Sometimes I experimented with different ratios of hot and cold and different levels of pressure. It didn't matter. It all made him furious. I smiled and listened while this monster crashed and banged his way through the most frustrating thunderstorm of his life, then went on with my day of doing nothing. The next morning I was up before the crack of noon. "Have a good day at work, hon!" Smooch. Ran right to the bathroom.

"Turn off the water!" and so on.

I was having fun with this new routine until I noticed something that was happening on my girlfriend's way out the door. Whenever she would leave, I would hear the neighbor stumble across his apartment, open his door, then quickly close it again. When she got home, I asked her if someone was walking out with her every morning, maybe leaving for work when she did? She sighed and looked down at the ground.

"Well, I didn't want to get you all upset, but the neighbor peeks his head out and watches me walk down the hall."

I dropped whatever I was holding. It was probably a remote, but I wish it had been a drink for dramatic effect. Or maybe a basketball so I could keep dropping it over and over.

"Are you fucking kidding me?! Wait, what does he look like?"

I was protective of her, but understandably curious about this voice I'd been tormenting.

"I don't know. I just saw this big mop of curly hair, then he was gone."

"No shit. No. Shit." I pondered the new info.

The next morning. "Good day, baby." Big smooch. Then I was peeking out the door watching her walk down the hall, ass shaking like she was all business, headed out to bring home the bacon to her deadbeat boyfriend. And after she was about halfway to the stairs, I heard bumbling footsteps and saw that mop of curls framing the back of some large man's blunt profile, peering out to watch her along with me. I shouted:

"Hey!"

Both of them turned around, but his door slammed before I could see his eyes. I smiled and yelled to her surprised face.

"Hey, baby, could you grab some more Lava soap on the way home?"

That night, we shared theories about him and wondered how he could afford to stay home all day without a job or school. We got so excited that we were a happy couple for about 48 hours before I started sulking again about my employment situation and ruined both our moods. And the next morning in the shower, the booming voice confused me with a question instead:

"Why aren't you in class?!"

I yelled back through the wall:

"Fuck do you care?!" Then, "If I was in class, who would turn off the water!"

He was stumped. I heard him mumbling to himself and stomping around, and eventually I pounded on the wall to stop his tantrum.

I eagerly told my girlfriend all about it when she got home. And we were up all night with brand-new theories, so late, in fact, that she had no time to take a shower before work the next day. Her sudden change of schedule right after mine must have thrown my neighbor way off because his head was nowhere to be seen when I watched her walk down the hall. However, I did notice an envelope peeking out from under his door. My curiosity overwhelmed me, and shirtless and shoeless, I tip-toed down to peek at it. It wasn't sealed, and inside was a note from his caseworker (wait, his what?) saying that she'd be around next week to make sure he "got his groceries okay." I guessed the caseworker was a "she" by the optimistic handwriting. The letterhead on top read "Maumee Mental Health Board." And this is where I discovered his name, "Mike M. Miller," but it was way too late for that shit. He was Crazy Mark II, damn it. Better than Crazy Mark Also.

But some other things start making sense, too. Like the envelopes under half the doors, like no one else ever leaving for work in the morning, like the fact that most people down this length of hall left their doors open all day, visible on their beds, arms crossed behind their heads like they were in a dorm or, more likely, lockdown.

"How many fuckin' mental patients are in this joint?" I asked Jerry. I'd started going to his house every day instead of a job, carrying a giant hockey bag of blue jeans and boots and playing hours of *Battletoads* and *Blades of Steel,* sometimes watching him die on *Mega Man,* which was way too hard for me, too. I was over there every day like clockwork. Almost started wearing a tie.

But I didn't tell my girlfriend what I'd found since I didn't want to scare her with all those alarming "M's" in the same letter and, even more important, I didn't want her to insist that we move.

So, I'm in the shower again, and now we were having almost entire conversations through the wall, not knowing quite where he stopped and I started.

"Turn off the water!"

"It *is* off!"

"Why aren't you in class?!"

"I *am* in class!"

"Why aren't you at work?!"

"*This* is where I work."

"Leave me alone!"

"You started it."

"Turn off the water!"

"Turn off the weather!"

That night, the landlord called. Before he could speak, I was all over him.

"What's going on with you housing mental patients here? Do you get a discount? You realize that crazy fucker stares at my girlfriend every day, right? How would you like me to bring him over to live in your goddamn garage instead?"

The landlord waited for me to finish, then explained that he'd been receiving complaints about me, not Mr. Miller. "Mr. M. M. M. Miller," I corrected him like a crazy person, but no amount of explaining could convince him that I wasn't the one yelling about water, weather, and class schedules every morning because I kinda was.

"In fact," he told me, "Your neighbors have started a petition to get you evicted."

At 3:05 p.m. the next day, Crazy Mark: The Sequel actually stepped out of the apartment for the first time. I hoped he was trying his luck at "getting those groceries okay," and jumped up on red alert.

I'd never seen him out in the wild, so I was dressed and running out my door right behind him. I almost wore a suit I was so goddamn excited. But it was an unremarkable trip, and for some reason his appearance was even harder to remember in the sunlight. Except for the curly rat's nest of hair, I wouldn't be able to pick him out of a crowd of babbling mental patients, even if they were all in the shower.

But things got real interesting at the end of our walk.

When we turned the corner around our apartment building, he yelped in fear, dumped half his food, and bolted up the stairs. Half hour later, his caseworker stopped by, and I listened with a glass to the wall. Her voice was so smooth and soothing, I wanted her to work on me next. Told you it was a "she."

"Shhh. There is no dragon, Mike."

"There's a dragon by the dumpster. I saw it."

His voice was high and girlish when he talked to her, not the guttural trumpeting I got through my shower wall every day. He always sounded small on the phone, too, which made him more terrifying.

"There's nothing out there, remember?"

"There's a dragon there right now, I swear!"

What the hell is he talking about? I needed to know.

I went back out to take a look, and next to the dumpster was a rolled-up mattress wrapped in black garbage bags and rope. Nearby was a pile of moldy pickles and the shattered remains of a jar. *Must be the dragon,* I decided. *Was this waterhead trying to feed it?* Once I looked around, it was clear it wasn't the first time he'd dumped his groceries. He'd been scared so many times there were enough meats and vegetables laying there to make a week's worth of tacos.

That night, I told my girl about all of this, and she finally started getting scared. For all the wrong reasons.

"You followed him?" She was actually shaking.

"Yeah."

"Why?"

"I was looking for a job."

That wasn't really a lie, if you think about it.

The next day, my neighbor went to get more groceries to feed his monster, so I followed him again. When we got to the dumpster, I couldn't help it. I screamed:

"Look out, Mark! Mattress dragons!"

He dumped his milk and orange juice and pickles again and ran up the steps to his room, slipping to his knees twice on the way, screeching over his shoulder in his little voice this time:

"My name's not Mark!"

Crazy fucker, I thought. *How does he even know what his name is?*

The day after that, I followed him again. My landlord would have said we were in love. He didn't get groceries anymore though. The caseworker would leave a bag in front of his door, either sick of the argument or finally acknowledging the very real dangers of dragons by dumpsters. No, these walks were different, all straight lines, purposeful, like he was working up his courage. But mostly we just walked around the block three or four times. He never noticed me following him either, and maybe any former classmates that recognized me and said "hello" never seemed to see him either. I followed him for weeks.

The last day I saw him, we didn't walk toward the center of town. Instead, we wove our way around miles of residential houses, sometimes taking shortcuts through backyards and bushes. His apartment door stood open all night. Then a padlock appeared on his lock in the morning.

That afternoon, my girlfriend showed me the newspaper and announced she was moving out. There was a sketch on the front page, and she was convinced it was me. The fucker looked like me, no denying that, especially with all my broken noses. And under the drawing was an article about a man peeping in windows all around campus. Oh, yeah, it also talked about how he might be responsible for a couple rapes. And maybe a missing girl or two.

I swore to her that I was only following our neighbor, and okay maybe they did see us in their yards, but only remembered me instead. Or some combination of me or him. "Maybe this is why the sketch resembled me so closely?" I pleaded. "It's both of us!"

She wasn't buy anything I was selling.

Years later, I moved into an efficiency apartment by myself and, maybe because of my mental patient neighbor's constant pep talks and reassurance, I set about finishing that last class I'd dropped. It was an art class, The Female Body 101, and the teacher kept trying in vain to convince me to start my sketches with the line down a woman's back, even if she was facing forward.

I, however, always started at the eyes, and so my proportions suffered, my creatures ending up confused, sad mutations that could have grown up near reactors or power lines. Like a child's drawing of a five-pointed star when they're afraid to cross over their own lines with that single unbroken trail, all five points of the face hung and curled like limp swastikas.

I would have been a terrible sketch artist.

I ended up passing the class and graduating, barely, and during this time, I noticed a classmate opening and closing the trunk of his car every day, caught in some helpless, hopeless, obsessive compulsive loop. I started to imitate him, parking right next to him whenever I could and slamming my trunk, too, hoping he'd notice and resist doing it so much. Instead, the other classmates started looking at me more and more suspiciously, until the teacher cautiously approached one night to finally ask what I was doing. Halfway through my description of him, she stopped me and said, "Who are you talking about?"

I was never able to sell her any of it either.

Cars with Thumbs

I've always been annoyed by people who exaggerate the importance of their mailbox by saying with a sniffle, "It's a federal offense!" whenever you vandalized one. So you can imagine how surprised I was at the guilt I felt for ripping the mailboxes for my apartment building off the wall.

I was going down to get the check they sent me for groceries, reaching inside and fully expecting a mousetrap. Instead, I found a check for 50 cents. Seriously. 50 cents. Someone from the post office actually took the time to write out a check for "50 cents and 0/100ths" and mailed it off with a 40-cent "America: Love it or Leave it!" stamp in the corner. I flashed back to all that arguing with the postal clerk when their machine stole my money, and I wished I'd squeezed his neck a little harder.

Instead, I embraced the entire bank of mailboxes like I was hugging the biggest grandma ever (the one on my dad's side of the family), and I wrestled the entire thing off the wall. It came down easily, leaving behind six baseball-sized holes in the plaster from the bolts.

And there was another letter back there behind my box, pinned up high where I couldn't see it. No return address, but I knew who it was from. It was about my old car, of course, and I was disappointed the letter wasn't *from* my old car.

I read it anyway. It was old, and the envelope had gotten wet, so there was no telling when she'd sent it. But in the world of the letter, Mark is still stalking her, still driving my old car. And she "just doesn't know who it is anymore." In the world of the letter, she explains that the only thing she's sure of is it's my car. And it will have been so long since I've seen him, that I'll wonder how much he looks like me these days, wonder how much he looked like me back then, if he hugs the steering wheel too close, as tight as a mailbox or his last girlfriend. In the world of the letter, she's threatening me with a restraining order if I don't quit cruising her job, her school, her bird bath. She says she's really getting scared. She says she sees my car everywhere, and she says I'll have to pay for what my tires did to her yard.

If I had time, if I wasn't moving so soon, I'd explain to her, to clear this all up, that she doesn't need to talk to me, or Mark, but obviously to the car in question. Hell, a car doesn't even need a thumb to make a phone call anymore. Most already have phones in them. Or worse.

I could call either of those guys, maybe shame them into not following her anymore, but I don't. I deserve this letter. And I always have. Here's why. Wait, I already told you about that.

WRECKLESS EYEBALLING

Our mother was the one who ruined Christmas for everybody. Here in the hometown we never left, she came up with this idea of dialing license numbers so you could talk to any car on the highway. Here's how it worked: As long as you could see the plate, you could punch in the combination of letters or numbers on your phone and be instantly connected to another driver. It was more like calling the car than the driver, which made you more likely to do it. It also seemed like a match made in heaven, as most phone numbers and most plates both had seven characters. Our mother got the idea from the orientation video they showed her at her new job for the Kentucky License Bureau—a quick history of license plates and how, before there were so many cars on the road, the identification tag was just a short series of letters, almost always a word that could be easily remembered.

She worked there at least 48 hours, the longest she'd ever remained employed, and, coincidentally, the average amount of time between gun-related road-rage encounters in the United States.

"License plates are just like the first phone numbers!" our mother announced to that VCR/TV combo in the License Bureau break room, as the light bulb began flashing over her head. She tried to get through her next two days of training, but she found this impossible when her brain was storming with new ideas. She was obsessed with the new phones, small and thin as Communion wafers now. She remembered when the wafers were as thick as Christmas cookies, but everyone told her this was a false memory from growing up broke and small.

Most cars were given names, she realized, phones too, like pets or wives. Our mother decided this was probably why those older vehicles in movies were in such pristine condition, since you were more likely to take care of a machine with a name instead of a number. If it had a name, you might even be inclined to give a neighbor's car an affectionate pat on the hood on the way by, maybe tell them damn kids to stop throwing their football over it, maybe even stop to wipe off a patch of bird shit with your own hand. Seemed reasonable. But we didn't have the heart to tell her the only reason cars were so shiny in the movies was because those were toys lining streets no bigger than a sandbox. They were merely playthings, as new as the ones piled up under the Christmas tree. And one day, every car ended up rusted out, in garages or abandoned car washes, no matter what name you gave it. But toys looked big from the right angle, just like the trees, just like the Priest who laid that delicious Frisbee on her tongue, and our mother never understood a forced perspective. Only her own.

She told us that once she stole a whole bag of Communion wafers, and when she got busted, she piled them on a plate on Christmas Eve, next to a tall glass of milk, spilling over the brim. It was all gone in the morning, she said, which didn't help her confusion. That's right around when she started trying to call Santa on the telephone, accusing whoever answered of vast conspiracy. And that was on a huge, rotary phone, too, and awkard technology that meant commitment.

But despite our bizarre urge to spin such a complicated lie as Santa Claus during our children's formative years, our mother made connections other people didn't. And she was convinced her new idea would catch on fast, just like that nutty text messaging all us kids were doing these days, and several cellular companies agreed with her. Even NORAD had already developed a Santa Sleigh Tracker, which, embarrassingly enough, had already been mistaken for a Russian first-strike at least twice by our President.

Similar to texting, her concept turned out to be the absolute worst of all worlds, not only causing a driver's terrible instincts to quickly surface, but giving a convenient voice to the worst urges, as well. People discovered the only reason highways weren't piled even higher with more gun-toting, trigger-twitching, road-rage wreckage was because that anger for every perceived insult—cutting people off, driving too slow, driving too fast, just driving too *wrong*, etc.—was usually quenched harmlessly with a rehearsed glare or obscene gesture from the relative safety of your own rolling cell. Sure, the gestures increased exponentially depending on one driver's percep- tion of weakness, "babies on board," or new car smells still perceptible on the highway from three car lengths away (the exact distance recommended to avoid tailgating), but—excepting the off chance that two deaf people would have a clash on the turnpike and start throwing page after page of hand signs and shadow animals out their windows—drivers normally had no real voice for their frustrations, except for a fast "Fuck you" followed by the only logical response, "Fuck you, too!".

Message sent. Message received.

Dialing the license plate in front of you and instantly getting a car on the phone changed everything. They never should have debuted it during the holidays, when traffic and people were at rock-bottom.

* * *

Our mother's brainchild went nationwide on Christmas Eve 2018, and within 24 hours, bodies filled the gutters.

Okay, maybe not quite nationwide. Still, a nightmarishly ambitious tech-*bro*—inspired by "Hubris," the hugely popular app that accidently turned the average Joe into a taxi driver/rapist—jumped on board to help connect every stranger on the road in the state. She always resented joining forces with this guy, but considered him a necessary evil. They had big plans, treating our small town like a canary in a coalmine. More like a canary someone forgot on the hood of their car, come to think of it. She felt like it was taking back the road, opening lines of communication, a good-hearted disarmament pact. Or something. Because while, on the surface it seemed like the highways were a playground for us boys, women dominated every road. This wasn't wishful thinking or a political statement, our mother explained. This was simple statistics. Hard numbers. Hidden Figures. It was just hard to see them because, even with their driver's seats up straight as an arrow, they laid low. "But this will change," she told us.

She didn't make a whole lot of money at this venture, but it was enough to divorce my dad, and certainly enough cash to ignore the collateral damage. We thought she'd be sensitive to actually causing road-rage incidents, especially after her injury.

The rest of the population didn't have her special sort of tunnel vision, her *drive*. So, after lots of hand-wringing and bullet-riddled pile-ups in the drainage ditches, after all the fist fights through the flowers and cat tails along the sides of the roads, the blood-n-oil Jackson Pollocks across the yellow lines, and the strips of chrome decorating every gas-reeking bush along the highway, a new law was passed fast. It said you couldn't talk on your phone anymore while driving, and call another car? That would be insane.

It was quickly passed in other States, too, under the reasonable assumption that phones had always been a dangerous distraction, like listening to headphones, doing crossword puzzles, thumb wrestling, you name it. But few people knew the real reason for the law, fewer than the fools who still believed Santa Claus could navigate that level of holiday traffic.

It was all because of our mother.

All because a phone was more like a weapon than a tool during that one terrible winter in our hometown.

Even now, if a cop sees you answer your phone too fast around here, or even standing next to a parked vehicle while flipping open your cell fast as Captain Kirk, you might find yourself in a quick-draw situation with a state trooper before you know it. Or, if you bring that phone up to your head a little too quickly, you could be tackled to thwart a suicide attempt. But who are we kidding? Those motherfuckers will probably shoot you anyways and write it up as "Seasonal Defective Disorder."

To this day, people on the street are pushing for more restrictions to curb road rage. There's talk of the law against tinted windows being repealed, massive subwoofer installations rewarded, and people are encouraged to have as many suction-cup teddy bears clinging to their back windshields as possible, in order to distract drivers from locking eyes at dangerous speeds, maybe to encourage fuzzier, happier thoughts on the roads. We even heard rumors of them bringing back that show *Pimp My Ride*, and a documentary on prostitution was shown at our last town hall meeting, where college students—half-jokingly at best—suggested we adopt the hustler's blanket policy of "no reckless eyeballing" for their stable, sometimes referred to as their "Elves on the Shelves," women who had to learn quickly the golden rule about keeping their gaze focused solely on the curb.

While we learned a lot that day during the Q&A, like how a citizen's arrest might never be quite as serious as young women being put under "pimp arrest," both punishments turned out to be surprisingly similar when pranksters listed them side-by-side next to those double doors of our courthouse, right under the Ten Commandments:

"Look down at your feet, your hands, or the road at all times. And do not make eye contact with the mark unless there is a car coming toward you. Do not make eye contact with a pimp, under any circumstances."

Our mother bragged that she had precisely the same rules stamped on a business card, long before local governments adopted them, and we decided to believe her. Rules to live by, we agreed.

They still call the DMV the "DMZ" around here, and in driver's ed. class, you now hear recent statistics suggesting you're just as likely to have your eyes enucleated by the car keys clenched in someone's fist during a road-rage experience as you are to be struck by lightning. Something that happens constantly when you're in a car. Only we cannot feel this. One of the benefits of being electrically grounded by rubber tires—which, it turns out—was almost as important to our successful upbringing as being grounded by our mother. But the silver lining they don't mention when you receive your license is that a human eye hanging from its optic nerve (as long as it retains some of the ciliary muscle around the cornea, of course) makes a handy and expressive souvenir for your vehicle. It can hang from your key chain at least as long as your car alarm fob. Maybe not as personalized as those tiny state license plates you can pick up in gas stations—the ones they never seem to have with *your* first name (and our mother knows this because she looked through every damn one of them)—but some religions maintain that memories are stored in the iris, rather than the brain, so, even better. Of course, some believe that a Christmas cookie is a fucking corpse, so who are we to play favorites. Believe in what you want.

As horrific as this kind of injury seems, in our town it brought us all closer together. This sort of injury was somehow best. You aim better with one eye.

They say the human head can send signals to the body for up to five minutes after it's detached. But it turned out an eyeball can report back to your brain for years. Getting one plucked out during an assault is the ultimate handshake. More than a handshake, actually. More of a hazy impression lingering in your good eye of someone else's life. Or at least their car's. For anyone carrying those key chains, this is a sort of a deterrent. Like the fake testicles the female squid flash so the males leave them the fuck alone. Like those eyes on the backs of caterpillars that trick birds into thinking they're snakes. Like the reindeer's nose that glows as red as a taillight if a bumper punches the little bastard just right. Too hard and the noses blink out forever. Too soft and it doesn't learn anything.

Our mother recently tried to pitch her original idea to another phone company, in the next state over this time, where they shoot holes in streetlights just to make them change. And even though the glut of vanity plates across the country might pose a problem, she was pretty sure they were gonna go for it, despite the fact that it might be doomed by complication one day, without enough numbers to play with. Communication was traditionally revered, she admitted, but calling the wrong number could be fatal for both drivers, no matter how much road was between them.

She couldn't, in good conscious, play matchmaker to humanity forever.

But she'd continue to sell her key chains. They were great stocking stuffers, she would explain, and they'd always made her enough money to get by, certainly more money than the jewelry she used to create, and there was always plenty to harvest on the sides of the roads during the holidays when everyone was looking at everyone all wrong, especially when she saw herself reflected in their anger, or reflected in the change in their pockets. Selling them was always going to be a little trickier than plucking them in the wild though, not just because Christmas was forever fucked after what she'd done, but she swore people trusted her more than most, let her get close.

We certainly did, and not just because of her eye patch. And she'd remind us that when you see the lights on the horizon, those aren't motorcycles coming down the road. It's just every car in the world with one eye out, a small price to pay to forever aim for the future. And we believed her. Believed in her, you could say.

BODY CAM CROSSES

All my life, I've been convinced that describing a dream to someone is the most torturous experience for all involved. I also think this applies to describing a fight. So I'm going to just give you the greatest hits, so to speak. And I'll probably leave out the dream sequence. But if someone explodes into insects mid-punch and then someone has sex with a motorcycle, or it sounds more like a movie than real life, feel free to ignore everything that preceded it. Luckily though, it all started off predictably enough. Or at least more linear anyway. And a dead-end still has the comfort of being a straight line.

I rolled into town right before the sun came up, stuck in some construction and trying to get past an old pickup truck rattling like an empty train. For miles, I'd been swerving to avoid blown-out chunks of tire, thinking, damn, that's more exploded tread than you'd normally see, right? But as I got closer to this pickup, before the eyes in its rearview mirror saw my car swerving back here trying to peek past them, I watched some guy in the bed first toss out a beer can, quickly followed by strip after strip of that jagged black mystery rubber. He stopped when we got bunched up real close by a gaggle of orange barrels, and we just sat there a minute. The guy bouncing in the bed was what we used to call in the Midwest a "stunted man," one of those smallish, white-trash dudes who never grew much bigger than a teenager, even at 50 years old, wirey with the muscles they built from fast-talking and bullshitting all their lives, creases around their mouths from sucking off authority figures, arms streaked with shitty tattoos, beards struggling to grow along their jaw lines, forever riding bikes or truck beds. He crouched with his back to the cab, glaring at me as he re-lit a cigarette, and it really felt like I'd busted these guys doing something they shouldn't.

Then we started moving again, and I hoped we'd find a red light soon so I could pass the pickup, but now maybe lean out to ask the hard questions. I had a lot of questions. I mean, what if those tire strips I'd been seeing all my driving life weren't from 18-wheeler blowouts? But now that I thought about it while I limped along at 5 miles an hour, I couldn't remember seeing a truck tire actually *pop*. Not ever. It was the opposite of the road skunks you always smelled but never saw. But then again, I saw dead dogs on the highway all the time, and I never noticed any of those critters actually getting smoked either. Maybe stunted men dumped all the dead dogs in the world, too? "There were worse jobs," they'd shrug. "Hey, you like this tattoo? It's a bald eagle hatching the White House like a turd."

Eventually, we did slow down enough to stretch my head out the window, but I'd already overthought everything so much that my questions probably made little sense, at least judging by the lack of response.

"Hey, man, you throwing dead dogs out on the roads, too?" I asked him. "Or you just collect all the skunks?"

He just bounced his cigarette butt off my hood with a splash of sparks, and I brought my head back inside. A road sign screamed, "Chilo! Stay for our Yurts!"

What the fuck?

Another fifty orange barrels, and time got even slower, down to about two miles an hour tops. I mistook the red glow of emergency lights on the horizon for the sunrise, another disappointment.

Once we were up on the accident, I realized by the lack of urgency that it was a bad one. That might seem like a contradiction, but first-responders only moved this slow when someone was dead. So I got out to stretch my legs, and the guy in the back of the pickup immediately got into the cab with his buddy, either to get away from me or to get another butt. So I walked up to see how close I could get to the crash, try to give myself something unhealthy to think about.

And it was a death all right. That's the only time they leave you laying in the road like that, put to bed forever on the yellow lines with a dozen people trying not to stare. At least they're usually nice enough to tuck you in with those heavy blankets.

She wasn't tucked in very well though, because I could see it was a girl in an orange jumpsuit sprawled out on the asphalt. Judging by the comet streaks of gore leading up to her tennis shoes, she'd been run over by something, ground down, not just clipped. The fleece blanket was still mostly folded, and only draped across her diagonal, haphazard like she'd been in a beauty pageant, or just lost one. I saw there was no crash at all, at least no heavy metal besides emergency vehicles. I glanced around for more info, saw tire tracks but no tread, and a big black garbage bag on the edge of the ditch. Then more black bags up and down the horizon. I'd been driving past these garbage bags for miles. Like the black-rubber tire chunks, those black bags were something I'd filtered out, I guessed, like haphazard crap was just the natural fauna of American highways.

In fact, you could line the roads in this country with all sorts of horrible, even Sleeping Beauties like this one, and it wouldn't seem out of place, if anybody saw anything at all. Something about the sides of the roads was fair game for refuse and ruin, and the Fifth Circle of Hell could break loose and dance for hours in those ditches before anyone even turned their heads. Well, more like the Seventh Circle of Hell, the one with the poets who get turned to trees and pissed on by dogs.

That's probably why I'd obsessed over those rubber strips all my life. Because they were in the middle of the road. Drive long enough and someone gets understandably protective of their lane. But *along* the road? You could have as much black rubber and dead dogs and wailing poets as you could pile up and torch and nobody would notice until the fire showed up in their rearview.

I looked back behind my VW Rabbit to see if any cars were starting to stack up in the bottleneck. It was too late or too early for traffic yet though, so I crept up closer to the body. I could see the girl more clearly now, the long, blonde hair flared out over the road like she was on her back in a swimming pool and had just kicked away from the side and would never sink. So I stopped right there, not wanting to see more than that. Then I saw a cop notice me for the first time and start that purposeful asshole march straight towards me. I leaned against a mile marker and tried to look like I belonged with the rest of the litter.

"What do you think you're doing there?" the cop asked, barely containing his anger at a civilian showing interest in a crime.

"Legs cramped up. Had to stand up a second."

He just stared, mirrored glasses mercifully up on his head, making him blink and maybe throw him off his game.

"No, I mean what the hell do you think you're doing *there*?" He reached past me and slapped the "mile marker" with the heel of his hand, and I saw it wasn't a mile marker at all. It was one of those roadside crosses, a monument to mark the spot where a loved one died. To be fair, the arm of the cross was loose and swinging, or I might have noticed it quicker, but I probably should have realized mile markers didn't have teddy bears duct-taped to the bottom. Now I could see the name.

"Christy Briggs?" I read to the cop. "Check it out, 'Christy.' What are the chances of that?"

"What do you mean?" the cop asked, and he put his hand over his heart. I thought he was covering his badge, getting ready to do something terrible and anonymous, but his number was still clearly visible. Number Five. Was the town so small they only had a single-digit force?

"You know like, 'Key-rice-tee'?" I went on. "Christy on the cross? Get it? Never mind."

"Get back in your car. And shitcan the attitude."

I smiled. He had no way to know this, but I loved it when people used the word "shitcan" as a verb. I still held out hope I'd see one on the side of the road one day.

"Was she picking up trash?" I asked, not walking. "Community service or whatever?"

"What's it to you, boy?" the cop grunted, almost up my nose after that.

"The orange jumpsuit? Trash bags? Someone hit her?"

"Go. Right now."

"Thanks for your help, Number Five!" I said, backing up. "Since you got it under control, why don't you scrape her the hell off the road and I'll be on my way. Or you guys wanna stand around another six years."

His nostrils told me to switch gears.

"Sorry, sorry, sorry," I said, putting a hand up, smiling. "I thought I knew her, so I walked over. Got my heart beating is all."

"Really? Who did you think she was?" He sounded interested, like if he'd been a movie cop, he'd have flipped over a fresh page in a tiny notebook. I hadn't had to think on my feet for about three states, so I said the first name that came to mind.

"Well, I thought it was Christy."

"Wait here," he said, marching back into the mob.

I looked up and down the highway for escape routes, saw the stunted men in the pickup shaking their heads. But the cop was back too fast, this time with a man in a suit and all sorts of tiny notebooks. He also had two wallets in his hand, one of them purple plastic, one black leather and sagging with importance.

"Heard you knew the deceased," the detective asked, clapping shut the badge, sounding both impatient and interested at the same time. A miracle of science, this guy.

"Who? Her? I was joking . . ."

He flipped the purple wallet out so I could see the license.

"Christy Briggs," it read. Just like the cross.

"Whoa, wait a second. The girl on the highway, she has the same name as . . .?"

Right as I pointed to the cross, another guy in a suit kicked the base to work it up out of the ground. Once loose, he folded up the wood, then punted the teddy bear into the weeds. It flew like it was made to be punted, and I imagined how satisfying it would be to kick a can down the road.

"There are approximately one hundred 'Briggses' in this town," the detective said. "That part was just a coincidence."

"But that's a hell of a coincidence."

"Already said that. Did you know the deceased? Do you have some kind of I.D.?"

"Funny story, I lost my license back in Kentucky. Not *lost it* lost it, but you know, *lost it*. I'm in the system though, just check my plates."

"Yeah, we're doing all that."

The cop and the detective stared at me like they were waiting for me to solve it all, so I started off with one of those "listens" law enforcement loved. I felt myself shrinking with every word.

"Listen, I was only reading the name off the cross, man. I didn't realize that was actually her name. But isn't that the freaky thing here? Seriously, man. Not that I'm able to read, but the fact that you have a memorial set up before the person was even killed?"

"Don't get carried away, sir. She was picking up garbage, yes. And maybe she lingered near this cross because she shared the name. But I need to know how you knew her."

"Jesus Christ, I didn't." I spit towards the crater in the stones where the cross had been.

"Show some respect," the cop yelled. "Crosses are everywhere."

I could feel myself treading water in that dangerous limbo where authority figures didn't want to you to say another word, even to answer their questions. But after another few minutes, they'd loaded up the body, and the first cop cleared me.

"Get the hell out of here," Johnny Five, the silver-eyed supercop said, and I was back in my bunny and creeping through construction before I caught a boot. But he was right. They *were* everywhere. Maybe it was the Red Car Syndrome again, but I saw miles of those crosses after that. Usually first names, but lots of full names, too. Vaguely ethnic. Mostly men, the white stunted kind, as well as, you know, the Presidents:

"Stack Washington," "Terry Lee Lewis," "Bonita Jefferson," "Dino Goodfellow," which still seemed like a fake name, "Kenny Thompson," "Sean" going left to right and "Leonard" going up and down, like two first names nailed together, like maybe a road crew busted two crosses and mixed and matched during reassembly, "My Beloved Joey," a mile later, "Our Beloved Billy . . ."

Have there always been this many? Seemed like hundreds.

And between every teddy bear crucifixion, black bags for miles.

*   *   *

Construction hung me up so long I got hungry. And between all those cock-eyed crosses and invisible martyrs, I found a bar with a picture of a real-live chicken, and it gave me high-hopes for food, or at least the safety of a bar full of cowards. But as I stepped out, I saw a grown-ass man revving his motorcycle. Or making engine noises with his mouth, which was even scarier.. On the wall was a sign that read, "We Welcome Soldiers and our Boys in Blue!" and I thought, "Wow, way to take a stand on the riff-raff."

I went in anyway, remembering something a terrible teacher told me once. She said, "If you spend a day in a town, you can write a book about it. Spend a week and you can write a letter. Spend a year and you can't write jack. Unless Jack's in prison."

Inside, the dripping bag of fried chicken came way too quick, and I considered making exactly this complaint because of how funny that stuff would sound out loud. Also any chicken that" came that quick" was tough and stringy, like trying to eat an old man, and it gave me plenty to concentrate on. I was on my fifth finger when I saw who was having lunch with me. Holy hell, Johnny Five, sans sunglasses but still in uniform. I dragged my stool and my octogenarian remains next to him.

"Hi!"

Johnny Five turned, eyes locked like they were pinned open with toothpicks. Up close, I saw for the first time he wasn't just wearing a shiny badge and a lot of black and blue.

He was wearing a camera on his shirt.

I'd heard about that, something about a test run of camera cops in New Orleans.

"Are you recording?" I pointed a bone at the tiny black eye on his pocket.

I swear it blinked, and he spun his stool and took a long swig of his beer. I don't know why, but I'd expected him to talk a little more human, with me catching him out in the wild and all? Impossibly, he sounded even more alien.

"When an individual or party is responsible for willful deception directed towards a second individual or party, the former is culpable," he said. "When such deception is repeated subsequently, the latter is no longer excused of liability."

"What?" I laughed, chicken hanging from my teeth. His delivery was stiff enough on the road, but here in the bar he was absolutely mushfaking. In prison lingo, a "mushfaker" cobbled together contraband out of any material available. But in schools around "discourse types," it just meant "faking it," like lawyer-speak you'd hear from cops in court, chronic D students all, as they floundered to describe simple scenarios on the witness stand and tied their tongue into knots.

Mercifully, he translated.

"Fool me once, shame on me. Fool me twice . . ."

"Oh, gotcha," I said to make it stop. I looked back down at the camera eye on his shirt. It had to be the camera that caused this. When I first heard about cameras on police uniforms in The Big Easy, I thought it would be a good idea to stop back-of-the-cruiser beatings. But now I was starting to think it was the worst thing to happen to these fools since Tasers, and I was suddenly convinced everything he was saying was really about the camera. But the bartender brought him another Coors and I noticed there were enough empties that I started believing we could be buddies, or at least work this case together.

"So, what was going on today on the side of the road?"

He cleared his throat and got comfortable. I closed my eyes, suddenly sure that, despite the beers, a straight answer would never come easy. I was right.

"One time on the beat, an account was related by another officer in which a parcel of methamphetamine crystals was placed on the roof of an automobile during a suspect interaction. The alleged criminal, a real Adam Henry, forthwith headed E.B. from the scene, while the parcel remained on the exterior of his vehicle, inadvertently distributing said crystals across a three-mile expanse. In a subsequent unrelated incident, five individuals accused and convicted of minor misdemeanor offenses were rendering service to their community in recompense for their crimes by collecting garbage from said highway, when . . ."

This was worse than a backseat beating. The bartender asked if I needed anything, and I pleaded.

"A shotgun?"

"Like I said earlier," Johnny Five went on. "When an individual or party is responsible for willful deception . . ."

"Oh, man. Shut the fuck up!"

"Excuse me?" He covered the camera's eye like it was underage.

"It's just . . . come on! There's gotta be easier ways to say things, dude."

"I've told you everything," he said, hand still over his tiny, black heart. "Do you understand?"

"Understand what? That a bag of crystal was left on the hood of somebody's car? And that five people pick up just the right amount of petty crimes to receive a community service sentence and clean up the highway? Wait . . ."

A light flashed on the trivia machine and over my head.

". . . so they pick up rocks and shitcans or whatever, and they stick the bags on the side of the road to get collected later, right? 'Cause the guy picking up those bags is in on it, too, am I right? Am I close? See that though? There's an easier way to say stuff. Why do you have to overcomplicate it?"

Johnny Five, more machine than man, actually smiled. A couple beers after that and Johnny stopped talking for a stretch, so I started listening in to whatever the hell barflies near the trivia machine were yammering about.

". . . so if someone tells you they're getting their uterus removed, never ask if you can have it."

"Ain't that the truth!"

"Uh . . ."

And a couple beers after that, I was wiping the cop's half-empty Coors off the edge of the bar and standing up to kick the can into the wall with a satisfying explosion of suds. He'd actually stood up before me, but I still had the advantage. See, cops probably fight real hard with a camera attached to them, but the camera also makes them fight fair. Big mistake.

* * *

I promised earlier that I would never think of punishing someone with a detailed description of a dream sequence or a fist fight. Well, I've since learned you don't dream when you're knocked unconscious, so that won't be a problem. And as far as the fight, here's a highlight reel instead . . .

He protected the camera on his shirt like it was an extra testicle. I learned early in the fight that a punch to this new plastic heart would make him deflate to lessen the blow on his space-age technology. After I realized this, I wanted more cameras in the fight immediately. I wished there would have been five or six good angles to document the world's first battle with the future of law enforcement.

I actually waited for him to drain about eight beer cans before I took my first swing because I am a cheap, sucker-punching motherfucker. But attacking a police officer after drinking with him all morning was a new one to me, and I couldn't wait to tell people about it. This was plenty of incentive.

I'm not sure if cops work out like they used to, but they must brush their teeth, because I left about a half pound of knuckle bacon on those rock-hard incisors of his, and that beautiful white smile was unsullied when it was over.

I'm about 6 foot, 200 pounds, pretty unremarkable before this new generation started shrinking and stunted men became the norm. And Johnny was relatively average-sized, even with his technology and extra testicles. But here's the thing, alcohol doesn't really affect me. And I can take a punch, especially if I think there's a camera nearby. Well, alcohol probably does affect me quite a bit, but I can't tell. I realize I've just described every alcoholic's impression of their own illness.

At one point, I tried to fishhook the cop and cut a thumbnail across his cheek, considering brawls in monster movies, how Godzilla vs. Ghidorah the Three-Headed Motherfucker was the best by far. Because, if you think about it, that was a dinosaur against a dragon. Which makes it like Evolution versus Creationism? And that was important. And I told the cop *all* this shit while I started choking him.

I looked up and the bartender seemed genuinely excited, and I fantasized

I was doing the town a favor by kicking a cop's ass. You know, community service.

Oh, yeah, toward the end, it ended up on the ground like all fights that aren't in rubber suits or CGI or burned onto celluloid. I was hugging his waist and trying to pick him up like an idiot, while he sent a special delivery of elbows to the back of my head, and I saw that his gun was out of his holster. Later, I found out he'd given it to the bartender about three beers earlier, just like outta some Western. I found this out at exactly the moment when the bartender tapped the butt of the revolver against my head to turn out the lights.

*   *   *

As I started coming back, I could hear the cop and the bartender talking about crosses and the garbage bags and orange jump suits, and I tried to keep my eyes closed to catch as much as I could.

"Right next to a highway cross and teddy bear," Johnny Five told him, talking normal all the sudden. "We thought we had them dead to rights, but all we found in the bag was papers. Custodial trash from the local schools..."

Clues! I thought. I wished I had a tiny notebook to write everything down.

"... one time, they cut up a man and left him along the road in fifteen plastic bags..."

Then someone had scruffed my collar like a kitten and I was outside in a heap. I sat up and blinked until I could see my rabbit, waiting patiently to get the hell outta Deadwood and try another town.

As I fumbled with my car keys, I looked down at my knuckles and saw that, despite the pain, there was no blood at all. My hands were soaked, but clear, like I was bleeding water. For some reason, this didn't surprise me, like if I ever had my chest X-rayed I'd see my backbone was missing completely. Then I noticed something in my other hand and was a little happier. I sorta remembered grabbing for that camera on the cop's shirt during the brawl, but I'd come up with something else entirely. A souvenir, proof I went on the ride anyway.

I walked past the police cruiser and noticed the dash cam. I hoped his sergeant watched all the videos and they got his ass fired. What's another word for fired? Shitcanned? No, don't even say it. But if that didn't get him in trouble, maybe there'd at least be some hard questions when they realized his badge was missing.

*   *   *

The rabbit's engine was knocking, so I stopped to get some oil, and a couple other things. I considered flashing my new badge to try for a *Thin*

Blue Line discount. But I forgot about Johnny Five's badge for a second when I discovered that not only do they sell plastic and wooden highway memorial crosses in department stores, complete with a squirt of glue and some plastic flowers or something snuggly, they were in the goddamn automotive section.

Of course they were.

Even though some came with stickers to create your own recently deceased loved one, they had a variety of ready-made names already stamped on those crosses, too. Like those novelty license plates you could get in the souvenir shop at the amusement park. They served the same purpose really, proof you went on a ride.

* * *

I was within sight of the city limits when I saw there was another accident. Another orange jump suit smeared on the road, a guy this time. And I didn't have to get out of my car to guess that his name would match the memorial cross not more than ten feet from his fractured skull.

I'm not saying my detective work was gold, but I was onto something, I'm telling you. But I never got to verify this because Johnny Five showed up.

When he stepped out, I saw the sunglasses covered his black eye, but my black eyes were frying like eggs in the sunlight, so balance had resumed. But I was too excited about solving stuff, so I didn't even give him a chance to tell me to move on before I was already telling him how I'd cracked the case. Don't you see? The pickup truck. The garbage bags. The rubber on the road. The crosses . . .

"And remember the bag of meth on the roof of the car you were talking about?"

"Yes," he answered.

"Well, what if you misheard that story. What if they were saying . . . 'math.'"

"What? 'Mash?'"

"No, no, no. It wasn't a bag of 'meth.' It was a bag of 'math.'"

"What are you talking about? What are 'math crystals?'"

"No, math questions. And answers. See, in the bar you guys said it was custodial trash from school. What if it was SAT's, the ACT's, whatever, and what you need to test out of the developmental math courses was in those bags?" I was losing him, so I patted my badge. I cracked the case, damn it.

"Think about it. Two grand a class? You save yourself a ton of money. That's worth the cover-up, right? That's worth more than a bag of drugs, right?"

He put his hand over his heart, either unaware of the torn piece of shirt on his other pocket where the badge had been, or not caring at all.

"Are you talking to me or the camera?" he asked.

"Huh?"

"There's nothing to solve here, asshole. Do us a favor. Try the next town."

"You kicking me out?" I asked, as sincere as I was able, which was about 25% less sincere than normal, well-adjusted people.

"You kicked yourself out."

"There were tire tracks but no tread. The construction slowed down the stunted men, see, and they had no time to drop some off, so why don't—"

"Listen. Stop helping us."

I got back in my car.

When my wife was in school, she used to talk about something called the Dunning-Kruger Effect. I only had to hear her bring it up a dozen or so times until I realized she was talking about me. It meant that, if you're incompetent at anything you are passionate about, you can't know you're incompetent. The skills you need to produce a right answer are exactly the skills you need to recognize what a right answer is. I was pretty sure she'd take all that back if she saw me cracking all these cases.

I knew now that driving too long made crosses, and crosses beget more crosses, and eventually everybody kicked the can, so I stopped after I crossed the state line. Then I backed the rabbit up a bit, just like a guy who gets bounced from a bar but keeps tapping his foot barely inside the doorway to be a prick. I popped my trunk and dug around my pile of empty 5W-30s to get my shiny, new crucifix, price tag still attached where a big nail would be pounded through the teddy bear's feet. I planted it as deep as I could in the stones, propping the dead-eyed toy up against the base. I'd almost bought one with my name on it because who could resist that shit? I pinned the cop's badge to the bear's ear instead. Looking at the memorial, I thought it probably read like a threat, but it was more like regret really. Engine no longer knocking, I got back in my car to see how fast my rabbit could run with its black blood pumping freely again. For miles, I chewed my lizard tongue and never thought about my cross stabbed deep down there in that ditch, or my badge, or pesos over eyeballs, or any currency at all, because chances were slim that anyone but me would ever bother using them again.

ROAD DIRGE

All night you're typing captions for television shows, sometimes well into the morning.

The captions look a lot like this actually. The rule is one thought and one line at a time.

You get on the road late and stop to eat at one of those UFO-looking food stations. There's a row of five fast-food counters with no dividers behind the beams that separate them.

When the employees move around, it's like the movies when the camera follows people through the walls. The kids should at least switch hats and put on fake beards when they do this.

You browse the glowing burgers over your head, and total up as many cheap items as you can, like it's some kind of contest, and you think how the invention of dollar menus was some serious, next-level Don Draper-type shit.

Back on the road, you pay the turnpike guy and want to ask him what someone does if they don't have money at the booth. But you forget to do this and vow to find the answer on the way back to Pittsburgh. You've always wondered about that.

Back in college when you used to take road trips to Cleveland, there was a rest stop that had a fence behind it where you could creep out with your car, take a dirt road up through some farmer's field, and then you wouldn't have to stop at the last tollbooth to exit. Except it was on the wrong side, sending you the opposite way you'd intended.

It got to where you wouldn't even factor in that five bucks toll coming back. You'd count on that fence never being locked, driving back to Toledo with a quarter to your name, and back then it never once crossed your mind you might have to stop at that tollbooth without any money.

You were going to call your dad to say when you'd be there, but your cell phone died for the fifth time. Pulling into his house at 5:45 a.m., the road out front that seemed so huge when you were growing up looks as small as a sidewalk now. You're about three hours later than he thought you'd be.

You consider sneaking in with the claw end of a hammer, like you used to in high school when you were late coming home, but that garage door has been fixed for years. In fact, everything's different. No stones in the driveway, and three security lights pop on like you're scaling a fence at Alcatraz. You ring the bell expecting him to be annoyed, but he opens up in a dazed stupor and goes back to bed.

You stand in a kitchen that looks totally different and drink some water. You see they've got a fish tank now. You sit in front of it and watch the tiny snails slide around the glass. You're not tired, but you have to try to sleep because the funeral's in like three hours. Heading to your old bedroom, you seem to be making slightly less noise than a man wearing a suit of armor. There's no carpet anymore. Just wood everywhere, and every movement is as loud as a factory floor.

You lie down on a bed that's way too small and smack the pillow over your face when you realize you forgot your headphones. You can't sleep without music. You're thinking about sleeping in the car and listening to the radio, but it's getting light outside and it's too hot. And the noise you would make trying to get out of the house would be deafening. You discover that the 1940s-looking radio in this spare bedroom is not just for show. It actually has a CD player in it. You stick in a calming Neil Diamond mix, thinking about what songs would be played at his funeral, and you decide "Hell, Yeah" would be the best choice. You're finally just starting to fall asleep when . . .

. . . suddenly it's time to go. Your dad's in the doorway. You let him say your name one more time than he needs to. You're totally swimming in nostalgia thinking about him trying in vain to wake you up so you won't miss the bus. You see your stepmom in the hall and ask her where the toothpaste is. She's too shocked to see you, but still explains that "It's in the shower!" like that's completely normal and looks at you a bit longer. Then she adds ominously, "That's so you can go ahead and spit as much as you want."

You try to brush your teeth in the shower, but toothpaste foam running down your groin seems potentially dangerous, so you creep out and brush your teeth in their new perfectly polished sink. When you spit, you find that you can do it completely silent, and you feel like you're getting away with murder. You wonder when you'll get to use this newly-discovered skill again.

You sit over by the fish tank and wait for them both to finish getting ready for the funeral. You tell your stepmom that you like all her cool little snails. You start to tell her how snails can no longer form hard enough shells because of the acid in the oceans from all the factories, and how that could screw up a food chain involving more than half of the creatures in the sea. But she just starts freaking out that there are snails in there.

She calls your dad over to ask how the snails got in the tank. You all debate it awhile as he tries to tie your necktie like you're a little kid. You decide the snails rode on one of the plants. You tell them that they just eat algae and won't be a problem. You have no idea if that's true, and you imagine their fish tank six months later in the middle of the night boiling over with snails. There's a huge brass snail sculpture the size of a bowling bowl on the floor in the same room as the fish tank, and you point and say, "Hey! It looks like you love snails!" Your stepmom just stares.

On the way to the funeral, you don't even have time to think about your uncle dying because it turns out the funeral home is only two blocks from your dad's house. You're completely unprepared to get out of the car so soon. You had at least three songs you wanted to listen to before this happened. Inside, you have about five mini-reunions in various doorways with the relatives that actually remember you. Half ask if you've become a football fan since you moved to Pittsburgh. You just sum it up with, "If you lived there, you'd be sick of that bullshit in zero point two seconds."

You compare back surgeries and jammed fingers and other injuries with your Uncle Bob. You're thinking you're winning until he busts out, "The other day, they went through my leg with a wire to burn off a piece of my heart." You admit defeat. You sit with your dad and wait for your brother and sister. Your whole family's late, everywhere you go, and you know he'll be as late as you'd hoped to be. You're hoping he's late enough that you can move and sit with him in the back row out of sight.

You feel small around your dad's seven surviving brothers and your fifty or so cousins. You were so small growing up and they seemed huge, always telling epic fight stories and towering over backyard grills. You were always so scrawny. You remember your cousin Mike telling you about beating up someone, and during the story you looked down at your fist, and it looked like a girl's fist to you. Then you looked at Mike's fist, and it was so hairy you thought you'd just had a Sasquatch sighting. Your first, but not your last. You don't see Mike anywhere at the funeral.

Then you do. You've got about 3 feet and 50 pounds on him now. You wonder if he still thinks of you as that skinny little kid frying ants with a magnifying glass, or worse, playing Vietnam Bug Hockey while everyone else threw around the football. When you threw the football it always went sideways. But you have hair on your knuckles now. Between the top two knuckles, too, which you've heard only happens in 7% of the population. Since a funeral is a good time for a confession, you'll also say that you have two stray hairs near the hole you piss out of and a couple even more bizarre places. You fully expect a hair to be growing out of an eyeball within a year.

You go to look at pictures of your uncle that are lined up all around the casket. Now you feel sad like you're supposed to. Drunk or sober, your uncles were always good to you. You remember one of them throwing another one into a lit grill in your backyard. They stopped fighting to send all you kids around front. Near the coffin, there's a big board with old snapshots glued all over it. There's a picture of your Uncle Ron , shirtless, next to a boat with a beer in his hand and a cigarette hanging out of his mouth. He looks like Steve McQueen. You realize that you're standing right next to his dead body. Yep, there he is.

Your brother finally shows up, and you go talk to him. He's so late he doesn't have anywhere to sit. You want to joke, "You'd be late to your own funeral!" but you don't. You go back and sit with your dad and stepmom and watch them unfold some more chairs for more stragglers. Then you see a bunch of relatives trying to figure out who the hell you are. But you know them all. Your grandma comes in with your two aunts and your cousin. Your cousin has the same ring-of-fire tattoo on his arm that your brother has. Him and your brother were similar in a lot of ways, lots of sports and friends. You have no trophies or tattoos. Your grandma is 99, and her body doesn't work anymore, but her brain is perfectly fine. You love talking to her, and you want to go talk to her, but you hate to see her with her head bent down like that and crying. Everyone says that no one should outlive their children but your grandma might outlive everyone.

Your grandma had this nasty little Yorkie named "Mitsy" that lived to be 23 years old. Just died last year. You're not exaggerating, you explain to someone. What's the math on that? Something like 400 in dog years? This dog was blind and mean as can be, too. It wouldn't let anyone near your grandma. It would just sit under her chair in that smoky kitchen and growl. It must have set some kind of record hanging on past five generations of dogs, but it still couldn't outlive your grandma. This is what you're thinking about when they roll your grandma up to the coffin and stop. Your alpha aunt starts looking around the room and shouting orders. She locks eyes with you and says, "Dude! Come here!" You know it sounds weird that she's calling you "Dude," as if she's a surfer, but that's just your name on your dad's side of the family. Your aunts rename all the boys, but all the girls are called "Sissy." You're told that you are all now going to lift your grandma's wheelchair so that she can see your uncle and kiss him goodbye. "Holy shit," you're thinking. Your cousin grabs one side, you grab another, your aunt's got a wheel, Uncle Chuck's got a wheel, and up you go. She's much lighter that you thought.

A hundred relatives are looking at you wide-eyed now, and you feel big, like you were chosen over all these bigger cousins. You have fantasies of defending your grandma from some rival funeral next door that wants to take all your folding chairs. Then the coffin starts wobbling alarmingly on its stand. You're leaning the wheelchair over too far, and you have to keep one arm on the coffin to keep it steady. "This is going to be a disaster," you're thinking. But there's nothing else you'd rather be doing. Your grandma wants to see your uncle's face, and God damn it, you're going to make that happen. Everyone's straining and the coffin's shaking, and the wheelchair's creaking, and you've got her in there close, but you hear grandma keep saying. "I can't see him." No matter how hard you strain, the angle just isn't working, and her face won't line up with his. The coffin slides away from you all as you lean into it. "This thing's gonna crash," you think. You look at your uncle. Yep, there he is.

You're getting ready to suggest that you pick up his hand or something for grandma to touch instead when suddenly she says, "Okay, put me down." You guess you're done. Did she kiss him like she wanted? You must have missed it, you decide, too busy keeping the coffin steady. You turn to your cousin and say, "I can't believe that worked." He smiles and shakes his head. He still lives near everybody. He's seen it all. You sit back down, sweat on the end of your nose, and the preacher is up there pretending like he knew your uncle, but he's not doing a very good job. Later you find out the motherfucker was a half-hour late and only looked at the some biographical information your aunt handed to him for about 30 seconds before he started talking.

When you were all little, whenever there was a tornado warning, you and all your cousins would end up at your Uncle Ron's house because he was the only one with a basement. The adults would play cards while the kids watched the windows, scared shitless. But it was still kind of fun, and the memory is powerful as hell. You wish that you were around everyone enough so that you could be able to go up there and remind them about the tornado warnings, but you moved away and find it hard to say much around them these days. You head to the grave site. Your sister wants to ride with you. You're the only one parked facing the wrong way, so you have to back out and turn around to get in the procession. Your sister is trying to figure out a way to keep the magnetic flag they stick to the car. You saw her covet that flag as soon as the guy smacked it on the roof. You look up at the magnetic sign and are reminded of the three pizza delivery jobs you used to have.

On the way to the grave, you pass a field of migrant workers who are all leaning on their shovels with their hats off while you drive by. You're so impressed by this show of respect from strangers that you momentarily have faith in the human race again. You tell your sister to take a picture of those workers, but she's slow on the draw and only gets a blurry picture right as her battery dies. You go over to your dad sitting on his car. He's upset, and he talks about how his uncle used to give him and all his younger brothers whatever money he had in his pocket so he could go get candy and pop and other stuff. He tells you how his uncle would throw him his keys and let him use his car, even though his uncle needed it for work. When your dad asked him about it later, he said he did this because your dad was "a good kid." You're trying to imagine a man who always thought of your dad as a kid.

Your dad's upset, and that's tough to see. And your sister's crying because she can't stand to see your dad like this. Dad tells another story about how they had a bench-clearing brawl at a baseball game and how your Uncle Ron had someone by the neck up against the backstop and was punching him in the face. Your dad says his brother was the strongest person he knew. He says, in awe, "That kid that he was punching and holding with one arm? His feet weren't even touching the ground." You all laugh at that, and your dad's not so upset anymore. You walk past another uncle and find out that he recently had a grandson named after him. You wonder whether this was because he wanted a son but had three daughters instead. And you wonder how the daughters feel about this. Your brother has two daughters, and, the most recent, a son that looks and acts just like him. You see that more and more, where the youngest child is always a boy. Like they said, "Finally."

Back at your dad's house, everyone tries to watch a movie, but you fall asleep. When you wake up, your dad says your sister walked down to your grandma's and that you're supposed to meet her there. You change clothes and head over. You see from the cars in the yard that there are a couple uncles and cousins there, too. You walk in and sit down on the floor of the kitchen next to the fridge like you're five years old again. You can't begin to explain how comfortable it is to sit there on the floor for the first time in decades. You sat there for approximately the first third of your life. Your grandma falls asleep in her chair, and as soon as everyone sees this, they immediately start talking about how grandma told them that she couldn't see her son in the coffin until he turned his head to look at her. They say that grandma said that she felt so much better once Uncle Ron turned his head so that she could see him, and that's why she stopped crying and told everyone to put her down. You don't believe in anything remotely supernatural, but you find yourself trying to remember which way his head was turned when you were wrestling with the wheelchair and steadying the coffin. Your cousin says, "That cemetery's gonna be full of us one day." You tell him that you were thinking the exact same thing, but you can't stop thinking about the wife of your other Uncle Larry who was divorced, but still had a tombstone in the family plot. You wonder how weird she feels, both seeing a tombstone while she's still alive, and seeing it next to her ex-husband's name, who she grew to hate. Then someone makes a comment about the "Mexicans in the field staring at the cars all weird," and thankfully someone defends them and explains they were just paying their respects. "Oh," the other cousin says, still doubtful.

Back at your dad's house late, you and your sister get a little punchy and proceed to eat every goddamn thing in the kitchen. Cereal, old pizza, some cheese popper things in a carry-out box, some spare ribs, strawberries, some nasty-ass cookies with walnuts in them. It's a leftover feast of Biblical proportions. Your dad comes out to tell you to keep it down. Your sister talks about that magnetic funeral flag she wanted, and you tell her that you tried to keep one of those flags when your aunt died years ago. But when you were on the way to her grave site, you realized you were almost out of gas and had to sneak out of the line of cars when they turned so that you could go to the gas station. Then, when you went to meet up with everyone after they left the cemetery, you saw you still had that flag and didn't want anyone to see it and realize you didn't go to the grave site. So you stopped your car, pulled it off the roof, and stuck it down out of sight on the side of a small metal bridge. You try to remember where that bridge is so she can go back and get it.

Back in the old bedroom again, you try to stretch out on the bed but knock over something again. You go to get it and knock over something else. It's like trying to curl up in the middle of a fucking domino tournament, you decide, like you're simply not meant to sleep in that room anymore. You turn on the light and look around. It's so small, and, impossibly, at one time both you and your brother were living in there together? Unbelievable. You decide to go see your grandpa on your mom's side of the family, your real mom, because he stays up late like you. Looks a lot like you, too, everyone says. Once there, he lets you in, smiling, and you ask him where all grandma's frogs are now that she's gone. Your grandpa takes you to the garden and insists that you take this giant blue concrete frog and find it a home. You put it in the trunk. Then he shows you this peanut he's glued to a small piece of wood with a small splash of red paint on the end of it that looks like blood. "Guess what this is!" he asks, smiling bigger. You give up. He declares proudly, "It's an assaulted peanut!" and gives it to you to keep the 100-pound frog company. Back inside, you put batteries in grandpa's TV remote to turn on the closed-captions and show him what you're doing for work these days. He tells you that the cable guy took the batteries out so that he wouldn't get his remotes confused. You suddenly feel the urge to call the cable guy and explain that your grandpa isn't one of those stupid customers that need their shit disabled like that, and that if he disrespects him again in that way, you'll kill him. Then you find a documentary on the Wildlife Channel and yell, "See that! I typed those words!" He seems disinterested, but has you leave the captions on anyway. Well, not always on, he decides, just when he hits the mute button. Then he takes the batteries out again. You tell him how your captioning always seems to have an extra word hanging down into the next line of text. Sometimes two words. Sometimes three. You tell him that, at work, you dream of your captions starting small, one line like they're supposed to, then slowly covering the screen from top to bottom, filling the space under the glass with a pile of words fighting each other for room to be seen. Then you leave and drive around for an hour looking at people's houses that you used to know. You think about work tomorrow, how you've been typing things before they happen lately. It's getting real late, and you're not sure whether to stay another night or head back. You feel satisfied that you've fulfilled your obligations for the funeral. You weren't sure you were going to try. Then you turn the car too sharply, and the 600-pound concrete frog in the trunk rolls over. It scares the shit out of you, and for a second you think you have a flat tire. Then you see a turnpike sign, and you decide to head back to Pittsburgh right then. Four more hours and you'll be home. You call your sister and tell her that grandpa gave you an "assaulted peanut." She's very disappointed and tells you, sighing, "No fair, all I got was a 'quarter pounder' and a 'cartridge in a pear tree.'" But you know she's happy you showed up. You drive on, trying to picture that last thing your grandpa made, and you decide it must be a bullet stuck in some fruit or something.

As you drive, you pass the long stretch of spinning windmills near Chicago. And in the light of the sunrise, you can just barely make out the hundreds of dead birds littering the ground beneath them like apples under a tree. You remember something a trucker told you once, how their forearms twitch and spasm on their days off, how invisible wide-right turns invade their sleep. Through the windshield you marvel at the landscape. Padlocks and elbow tattoos and cameras and road crosses and prisons are everywhere these days. You want to gather all you are able.

You consider a road trip to Lovelock, Mississippi, the largest river in the United States. According to your new girlfriend's father, this means it contains "the universe." You're not sure what he meant, or why he's so big on rivers, but you're sure you're going to like him. You need new influences in your life to replace the old ones, and you remember loving fishing as a child.

Hours later, you stop at the last turnpike booth and remember to ask the guy what happens if you don't have enough money for the toll. He looks surprised, laughs and says, "You fill out a form and pay it later. It just happened, actually."

UP DOWN UP RIGHT DOWN LEFT UP

"Ironically, in my solitude, I had created something that could only be used in concert with another human being."
—Kurt Vonnegut— *Mother Night*

Diamond Mining

The headlights behind me continue to mirror everything I do. Every swerve, sway, weave, drift, and jerk. On the last hill, I put my car in neutral and let it drift backwards a quarter mile but they never got any closer.

I reach up and flick the rearview with a finger, expecting the headlights to disappear. But they keep pace a steady half mile back. I jam the brakes with both heels, step onto the road, and look back down the moonlit vanishing point. The headlights have stopped, too. Too far back to see anything but those unblinking white eyes, I can't tell if the driver has stepped out on the road with me. I walk to the front of my car and slowly cross in front of my own highbeams.

In the distance, the headlights finally wink at me, one at a time.

* * *

Back in the car, Jay's calling again.

"What up."

"What up."

"Jay, what's the most chrome you've ever seen on a car?"

"The whole thing."

"Seriously?"

"Yeah. Guy I knew. He started with the rims, moved to the bumpers, the hood scoop, then his hair, then the whole fucking car. When he hit the road, no one could see him. He crashed immediately."

"I doubt it would be completely invisible. I'm thinking it would be like a mirror, everyone would see their reflections."

"I was joking."

"Oh."

Right before I left Toledo the first time, Jay met this girl we (I) called "Tea" because she had this gigantic pyramid of tea tins filled with weed, various drug paraphernalia, and grayish hard candy that had long since lost its rainbow colors. She was what kids these days call a "fake-ass hippie." More bandannas than '80s gang movies, tie-dyed crap everywhere, style-over-movement gear, you know the type. But besides all that, I never really liked her to begin with. For me, it was something about the way she transformed herself into what Jay seemed to want, even though the smart, sharp-dressed pictures all around her (soon to be "their") apartment told another story. And she also started blaming me for every irresponsible thing Jay ever did, even though, ironically, every girl I've known has blamed Jay for every stupid thing I've ever done. The truth lies somewhere in the middle. Just like her actual personality, probably. Jay's tendency to date this fake counter-culture type was as confusing to him as it was to me. But she must have seen a police lineup of his former girlfriends to start her campaign. And I probably could stomach some of this if her insatiable quest for a wedding ring from my boy wasn't so goddamn transparent.

I studied her hands when I first met her, just like she studied mine. And I could tell her third finger was desperate for a diamond ring just by the way it twitched and pointed at him every time a smile cracked his orange beard in her direction. The rest of her fingers were covered in silver and stone, hip, non-precious stones, of course. But not that one. That finger was thinner than the rest, atrophied, impatiently waiting with a white band between those gnarly knuckles. I could tell it carried more than its share of engagement rings through the years, and it wouldn't stop fucking twitching until it got another one to weigh it back into submission. I remember sitting at their house one time, playing that videogame where the little man with the light on his helmet has to navigate collapsing tunnels and gather as many jewels as he can. I called Tea into the room and told her to watch the screen. Then my thumb tapped the direction arrows on the controller rapid-fire with a carefully rehearsed "up, left, down, right, up, down, up" and the television screen was suddenly filled with hundreds of glittering digital diamonds for my little dude to gather at his leisure. "Which one do you want?" I asked her, grinning through my bubble gum. Jay didn't get the joke, but I know she did.

"Hey, Jay, can you call me back later?"

"Yeah, man, got a story for you. Don't want to waste this alone time . . ."

He's gone, and I check my speedometer. Jay's phone calls seem to ratchet up my driving to dangerous levels. I look up to the mirror, and behind me I see the headlights taking each turn as expert and reckless as I do. I also see the heartbeat in my neck throbbing alarmingly, pushing blood, paranoia, and bad thoughts into my head. I remember the first time I heard a teacher talk about that artery, how I thought she was calling it "corroded" and how that name made perfect sense.

I turn on the radio, fan, and windshield wipers, a combination of buttons, joysticks and switches that I know will momentarily overwhelm the car's electrical system and draw off the battery, making all my lights dim.

The headlights behind me pulse in the rearview mirror just like my dashboard.

Autoinfanticide

A horse pulling an Amish carriage clomps next to me, and I'm grateful they don't have headlights or I'd prove them right about us asshole "English."

See, the thing about jerking off is, if you wait long enough to do it, you don't have to fantasize about anything.

You don't need the face or body of an ex-girlfriend in your brain or what you always did together or even the image of someone else doing the same thing on the page or a videotape. Wait long enough and you won't need anything at all. It'll be like blowing your nose, more like a sneeze actually, and with approximately the same level of collateral damage to the environment. And the thing about jerking off in a car, however, is that no matter what you do, you seem to let pressure off the gas pedal and slow to about five miles per hour without even realizing it. I swear I didn't see that bandanna when I closed my eyes. You couldn't prove it anyway.

When I flick a ticking pendulum of semen off the rearview mirror and stop fantasizing about grandfather clocks winding down, I see the eyes idling and waiting patiently for me to finish. We both ease carefully back onto the highway and start driving again.

Then I turn off the fan, windshield wipers, and radio in a different order this time to see what happens. I'm convinced that by doing this, I've somehow just made this car faster, as least for the moment. I remember the chase scenes and cheat codes from my favorite videogames, glance up at the eyes behind me, and feel the blood returning to my brain and feet until I can finally bury the gas pedal.

Crayon Rubbings

Doing research for a paper around my ninth year of undergrad at the

University of Toledo, I saw a framed charcoal grave rubbing of horror writer H.P Lovecraft lording over a selection of his books in our town's library. The price tag on it was eighty bucks. Dollar signs in my eyes, cash register noises in my ears, I immediately checked online and saw that grave rubbings of celebrities of James Dean's stature were going for fifty to a hundred bucks on eBay. See, me and Jay had gone there once before just for the hell of it, and I asked him if he still had the map. He sure did. Road trip! We'd actually driven to Shipshewana first to try and find a Amish barn-building in progress, maybe lend a hand. Like we were the first clowns ever to see the movie *Witness*.

No luck. So we went for the grave and took a couple Polaroids.

I quickly tried to gather as many people as possible to spread the misery in case shit went wrong, but Jay and Rachel were the only ones up for it, "Ray" being the essential member of the crew as she was always all "organ-i-zized" (her word) and, as I anticipated, already had a bag of paper and supplies happily swinging at her knees when I picked her up.

On this particular day, Jay had plans with Tea for later that night, who he'd just met, and you could see from his furrowed, newborn, fist-like face that he needed shit to go smooth so that he could get back in time or else he was going to pull the pin on a grenade. Anticipating Jay's need for distractions, I brought along my former favorite handheld videogame, the short-lived Atari Lynx, just to keep his hands busy. I would have brought him one of those fake preschool dashboards so he could honk the horn and pretend to drive, if I could have found mine in time, but a tiny hockey game kept his thumbs busy just fine.

Five hours later, I still couldn't find the graveyard. I swear you could light a city with the electricity coming off the back of Jay's head when he realized I'd been circling the same block.

We were going by the old snapshot I had taken and hoping the flat skyline in the background of the photo would be enough of a landmark to go by. But suddenly there were *two* graveyards in Shipshewana, Indiana, maybe more. The Amish apparently had the lifespan of mayflies. Out of the car, me and Ray were running giddy figure-eights in and out of gravestones as Jay watched the sun sink and started to lose his mind. We started weaving slower on purpose and peeking out from behind granite obelisks, trying to eavesdrop on the conversation Jay was having with himself, which was more of a debate really, each mutter punctuated with a savage rocket of saliva between his own feet. And when we finally found James Dean's grave, it started raining real hard. Jay didn't even bother to look at it. He was clearly nearing a breaking point. I could tell by the way the rain turned to steam before it even hit his head. Ray was frantic, too. If the grave got soaked, the entire trip would be a bust. I didn't care though, and I figured Ray would get over it. But for Jay, wasting this much time was incomprehensible.

Turned out the grave was covered with so much bullshit that it actually helped our cause; big plastic flowers and glossy pictures of Jimmy Dean in gunfights poses and at least fifty bucks worth of pennies. I tried wiping it off with the towel I'd kept in my trunk for exactly this kind of emergency, and now Jay was stomping around the cemetery, smacking himself in the head. Then he started running around the graves, calling everyone names, screaming at the sky as we gave chase. The only thing that calmed him down was his discovery of a giant, refrigerator-sized tombstone, too big for a grave rubbing, marked with the hilarious name, "Wigger." Ray started taking pictures while me and Jay struck white-boy gangster poses in front of it, of course, and eventually we all succumbed to playing the inevitable "let's find our own names!" game.

No luck.

Jay probably would have been okay and resigned to the fact that he would never get back to Toledo anytime before midnight, but I decided to wind him up again. Ignoring the expression on his face that was saying "*this* close to attacking you, dude," I walked over to my car, stopped, looked around in horror, and pretended I'd locked my keys inside. He was in slow-motion going for my throat when I ducked for cover and held up my keychain crucifix-style to ward him off. He spit again and closed his eyes to make me go away. At some point, I saw him playing with one of her bandannas, tying it to a tree. I would have fucked with him for this if he wasn't on such a hair trigger.

Anyway, the grave was way too wet for charcoal, so we tried to do it with crayons instead. Our soggy wrinkly rubbings looked more like psych-ward art therapy than anything framable, but I carefully rolled up rubbing after rubbing until we represented each color in the crayon box. Even the white one. I figured it was worth a try, in case the invisible letters showed up after they dried.

Postscript to the trip. The soggy grave rubbings eventually got posted on an online auction, but, unfortunately, I included a picture next to the description. A couple weeks later, I got a dollar thirty taken from my checking account for eBay fees, which put my account under zero because I routinely took my accounts right down to the fucking nub (still do). So I got a fifty dollar insufficient-funds fee. I tried explaining the situation to my "personal banker," but despite that title, she wasn't all that interested in the details of my life. I still have a stack of sad, wrinkled grave rubbings stashed somewhere in a poster tube waiting for a good home, just like the mangiest cats at the shelter. I've tried to give them away now and again at various sweet parties, but people always seem to forget to pick them back up on their way out the door. That's okay though. It wasn't the last scheme to crash and burn. But it's for the best. The only thing I might handle worse than disappointment is success. And the only thing I handle worse than that is everything else.

Hockey Strikes

Jay almost got away from her at least twice. He actually dumped her so many times that it got to be a running joke, even with her. One time, I stopped by to finish our real-time six-month videogame hockey tournament. Reports in the real world were saying the Red Wings had just lost the Cup to the Penguins, and even though we ended up living in Pittsburgh, we could give a fuck about those idiots. We considered videogames much more important.

Right before I got there, unknown to me, Jay had gone out the back door down to the dumpster. Tea buzzed me up, thinking I was him coming back from taking out the trash.

I walked in saying "Where's Jay?" a split second before I noticed the boxes everywhere. She looked at me all serious and goes, "He left me again. Thanks for asking, asshole." And I didn't know what to say and just started mumbling, "Uhhh, really sorry to hear that. I didn't mean to . . . uh . . ." as I backed out the door.

She got so close she was almost on my toes, and she said, "Have you ever thought about us?"

And right before I said something I would have regretted forever, Jay kicked the back of my knee behind me as he came back in and goes, "What up, fool?" She laughed and said, "Got ya!" and poked me in the chest and then went on with whatever she was packing, more than likely more evidence she needed to destroy to complete another personality change. I had to give her a little credit for the joke and thinking on her feet like that, and I think it illustrates our little not-so-friendly competition for our boy.

But I'd really love for her to know as much about him as I do. About how he values his relationship with certain videogames so much that he would never ever *ever* consider cheating. This really isn't the case with her.

The rules for playing our beloved hockey tournaments were complicated. In spite of them involving a decade-old, out-of-date system and a very unsuccessful and inaccurate depiction of the sport, for nostalgia's sake it was our favorite, and we took playing it very seriously. Way past its six-month expiration date. However, my own relationship with that game wasn't too serious for me to try cheating every chance I got. Not Jay. The closest he'd come to cheating was denying that I would score, regardless of what the game was telling him. Bastard would yank on his controller cord and say, "Look, it wasn't even plugged in! It's cool. We'll just adjust the score in our heads. Okay, that says 5 to 19. So it's actually tied up 3 to 3. Let's go . . ."

His fear of the popular myth that one limb grows stronger with the loss of its equal prevented him from playing the game, as I requested, with one thumb tied behind his back. But I do know he used a cheat code at least once. Problem was, I could never prove it because I wasn't sure what the code actually did. At first, I thought it was for invincibility. But that made no sense and could never really be tested because there were no weapons or fatalities on that virtual ice, and, of course, most hockey games aren't played to the death. Then I thought it was for infinite lives. Again, no way to test that. Finally, I was convinced it was for slow motion, and that it only affected my skaters, and that it was a change almost indistinguishable by the human eye. The cheat code could have slowed me down just enough to miss intercepting that pass, just enough for him to get the jump on a computerized goalie that had memorized his every tactic, just enough for me to miss snagging an elusive loose puck in a corner that was rendered on the screen only slightly smaller than a garbage can and with the same level of maneuverability. This sneaky slow-motion cheat code would be undetectable if I didn't check the game clock on the screen with the one on my wrist. Games that should have been over by midnight would creep over into daylight, and I could never figure out why. Just like a three-hour drive that, for some reason, seems to last three days instead.

The only cheat I've ever seen successfully applied to that particular game was one of those joke codes that the programmers slipped in to entertain themselves while clacking away on potato-chip covered keyboards in their cubicles. It was referred to as the "Lamaze Cheat" and if you tapped the right sequence of buttons, the tournament slots would fill up with games already played and jump straight to the final face-off. If you were playing "real-time" as me and Jay did, this would eliminate a six-month season, or, in the event of the hockey strikes that were a running gag in the League in meatspace, a nine-month season. You'd think this inside joke would be enough for it to earn its nickname. Not quite. You see, besides jumping ahead nine-months to game seven of the finals, this code would also afflict every member of both teams with large, bulbous stomachs that hindered game play so severely that it was never worth bothering to cheat at all. The huge, pregnant bellies on the digital men was funny enough, but soon we understood that either these little players couldn't take a hard check to the midsection as successfully as before or, at least, our subconscious was making us flinch every time it happened so that all momentum of the match was lost. This was more than enough to psychologically fuck up our thumbs and make the game unplayable.

Jay claimed he knew a code that gave you a gun, but he said it was a secret.

Cheat Code Ethics

I'm unsuccessfully trying to trick the mirror car into taking on-ramps with tiny squirts of turn signals and random swerves when the phone starts bouncing impatiently on my seat again. I answer it and hope the shadow in the car behind me has to deal with the same phone call.

"Duuuuuude, got some strange!"

"From a stranger, I take it."

"Stranger and stranger! Where you at?"

"Outside of Pittsburgh."

"Holy fuck you drive slow. So, get this, I'm at work . . ."

"Since when?"

"That hotel bar. I told you about that."

"You got a job in the last three hours since I left and had some kind of adventure, huh?"

"No, man. This happened a couple days ago. Anyway, there's this girl there for a convention, so I chattered her up a little bit at the bar while she waited for her team or whatever, and she's telling me she's there for a seminar on environmental stress as a PR person for this mining company. And I start telling her all about hiking and being 'at one with nature,' too, you know? And I ask her about what she thinks about mining diamonds. And get this! She tells me that she thinks it's ridiculous 'cause they can be man-made without seriously damaging the eco-structure, but no one ever bothers to do it that way. So, dude, I'm all excited because, *dude,* she works for a mining company and she agrees with me about the evils of mining diamonds? What are the chances?!"

"Can I call you back? I have a situation with this rearview mirror that . . ."

". . . so I buy her drinks for a couple hours, and I start to realize that she ain't leaving! Seminar's way over, and she actually ends up staying until I get off work. And we grab a table while they're vacuuming and talk more about how our personalities and philosophies and respect for all living creatures is similar and how, at our respective jobs, we're basically doing the same thing to . . ."

"What? How are you in any way 'doing the same thing?'"

". . . and pretty soon we're back up in her hotel room where I start fucking the shit out of this silly bitch. She tells me that she hasn't been fucked like that in a long time even though she has a serious boyfriend at home in

Canada that she's been with for years. And she's fucking *hot*."

"What exactly does she look like? You?"

"Dude, she's hot. Kinda big, but cute. It's not as important as what I'm about to tell you. So, while she's working on me, dude . . ."

He pauses a moment, thinking he's adding some suspense.

"Dude. Dude. Dude. I decide to stick a finger up her ass. You know, for kicks?"

At this moment I glance up and see a sign, of course, telling us both that we're going the "Wrong Way."

"I'm, like, laughing and I tell her, 'Invader, sector nine!' and make this cute little alarm noise at the top of my lungs. And she starts going, 'Oh, my god, what are you doing?' And I'm cramming my finger up there like I'm scratching a stack of lottery tickets and holding up the line at the gas station. And now she's like, 'Oh, shit. That's not bad. I'm embarrassed because no one's ever done that.' So I say to her, 'Well, if you think that feels good, you're going to *love* this.' And I flip her over on her back and *doink!* jam my shit up her ass. She's all squirming around at first, but then gets into it, saying the same nonsense, 'I can't believe I actually like this,' and 'I don't know why I never thought of this before,' and 'Is this a good idea medically?' and yap, yap, yap . . ."

At this point I think I hear a voice in the background and ask him where Tea's at, worried that he's going to get busted.

"I don't know. No, that's not her. She's out of town, looking for another house. Did I tell you she's knocked up? Maybe both of them. I'm gonna be a dad. Hold on . . ."

That's not how babies work.

I hear a long string of keypad tones as he pushes buttons on his phone.

"Who are you calling, man, I'm still . . ."

"Shhh!"

He pushes about nine more buttons then sighs in my ear.

"Was that supposed to be a song?"

"No, dude. You don't remember? That was the code for invincibility from *Carjacker*, the greatest game of all time."

"Really."

"No, I don't remember. Maybe it's the code that gives you another car just like the one you're driving. Anyway! Where was I?"

"You had fingers working her ass like a grave rubbing."

"So I'm hooking my thumb in her mouth and I'm cracking this ass for hours, dude! It's in-fucking-credible. But when I leave, I sneak out thinking I can't have her looking me up or I'll get caught. So I don't leave a name or nothin'. And on the way home, I stop at a gas station to wash my face since it looks like a week-old glazed donut so I can risk creeping back in the house. But dude, dude . . ."

Now he's finally whispering.

". . . dude, she's *cool.* You know why? Think about it. She's a PR person for a mining company and she totally agrees with me about the environmental distress caused by diamond mining and the rape of the environment and the impact of our . . ."

"What would your girlfriend think if she knew all this? Or how about the guy who sent his princess off to her seminar with a tender kiss at the airport, and she comes home fucking reamed and acting different somehow that he just can't put his finger on?"

Jay starts laughing and describing tiresome reunion scenarios.

"Put his finger on! No shit! Yeah, like, what's up with the weird way she's started bringing him his beer . . . in her ass! And how lately he keeps losing the remote control . . . in her ass! Poor Canadian bastard, but he really should have been taking care of business instead of just watching all that hockey. Hold on, man . . ."

He starts pretending we were talking hockey as he's setting the phone down.

". . . so, if Detroit loads that team like Colorado did back in '99, hell, like we did with the '98 version of the same season, they wouldn't need to stack so many defensemen up against . . ."

The end of his phone thuds again, and I hear his voice fade off around a corner. Then, I hear the distinct sound of someone breathing who's trying not to breathe. I stop making airplane noises with my lips and yell out:

"Hey! Finish the story about fucking that chick in the ass!"

A girl's voice. Slow and sinister. And a question with no question mark:

"What did you just say."

"Wrong number."

I hang up. Oops. The phone starts hopping in my hand. I hit the button but luckily don't get it up to my ear quick enough.

"What the fuck?!"

"Sorry, Jay. Thought we got unplugged. You'll make a great dad, motherfucker."

I hang up again. And again. And again.

Strange, Stranger, Strangest

When I hit Fairmount, Indiana, I think that it makes sense that I'm back at this grave one more time. So many people fuck around with it, I'm surprised nobody's tried digging anything up. Or digging anything down.

Up down up right down left up . . .

I always regretted not taking a handful of pennies off that headstone to cover some of the expenses of those road trips. I don't make that mistake again. Even if it just pays for a couple feet of gasoline, it's worth it just for how wrong it feels to steal them.

I glance up to my rearview mirror, and the sight of the headlights makes me hit the brakes with both feet. My car pitches sideways and almost into a ditch. Looking back, the eyes are gone. I can't believe it. I count to a hundred and look back again. Still gone. I step out onto the road. My first footsteps in another state. I start walking back down the punctuation matrix of dots and dashes on the blacktop and stop when I hear the rumble of the car. It's sideways, too. That's why I couldn't see its eyes. And there's the shadow of someone on the road, exactly halfway to me. I wave. It waves. I hold up my other hand. It does, too. We're not close enough to make out any details like sex, race, or number of fingers. I put my bad hand down. It follows. Then I put my hand up. I get an idea.

Up, down, left, right, down, left, up. Now there's four headlights behind the shadow. I do it again. Now there's six lights. One more time. Up, down, left, right, down, left, up. Now there's eight. I think I hear a laugh, and then we're both running back to our cars.

Inside, I delete Jay's number from my phone.

A mile later, I follow those same directions, of course substituting "down" with "neutral" and rolling backwards at a couple red lights until the cars behind me honk in fear and anger. After I complete all those turns, I look to the clock on the stereo to see if it's slowed down. It's blinking zeros, as if the girl who I stole it from it never bothered to set it, so I can't tell. It could be the battery finally giving out. I hope that I didn't accidentally speed everything up with the wrong code. I promised myself I'd only drive for three hours, not three days. So I type the last code into my phone and stop my car.

On the road, I walk around my car to see if anything in the distance winks, and near the graveyard, I notice a pink-and-purple bandanna tied to the lowest limb of a dying tree near the ditch.

The bandanna is at face level. Closer until it's at eye level. Bend my knees until it's nose level. The sweet rain and sweat and the idea of breathing in the scent of my first local redlines my senses so fast that I have to put a hand on the trunk to stable myself. The tree rocks under my weight. Leaning forward, I see a ring that the salt of her perspiration has burned deep into the bark. I bury my face and smell deeper. Deeper until I sneeze.

The distant headlights flicker to get my attention, and I'm halfway to the other car before I notice a gun has appeared in my hand from nowhere. And I'm halfway home before I stop seeing the disbelief in her eyes, her naked hand up in horror like a child who thinks if she can't see you, you can't see her. And I'm halfway to the state line before I stop thinking about the bullet and that bandanna detonating behind her windshield like a burrito in the microwave. I'm halfway to Hell when I realize I'll never stop this car again.

SPIN THE THROTTLE

To play their games, they used the first bottle of whiskey they'd all drained together, back when the fire truck first rolled out. They'd passed it around their circle and then tossed it into a corner of the pool, forgotten. But now this empty bottle of Jim Beam Devil's Cut bourbon refused to cease spinning, and though no one was into the party games as much anymore, the clear violation of the laws of physics got to Beth, who couldn't bear the scrutiny if it stopped to point at her. So she seized it from the waves, and then screwed some sort of tiny message into its neck and tossed it out into the night. Reeves made a half-hearted slap to intercept it, but he was way too far gone by now. They all heard the bottle shatter on the road, message lost.

Their party had been going for at least seven hours, though it was hard to be certain. A dozen of them were crammed and shivering in a hot tub in the back of a 1955 American LaFrance Series 700 pumper that had been haphazardly Dr. Moreau'd into a garish party wagon, one of those ancient fire trucks with a pug nose for a cab and more than a passing resemblance to the hippy buses popularized in the psychedelic '60s, but now decked out with speakers, Christmas lights, and American flags. They'd started out in good spirits, but sometime around the third hour and the driver's refusal to pull over, they seriously began to worry the party would never end. Though some of them had become more mentally and physiologically accustomed to their situation.

"What did that say?" Jill asked Beth.

"It was a map."

"To what?"

"Treasure!"

"Oh my god," Angie said. "We need you acting crazy like we need a hole in our head."

"We need a hole in this boat!" someone shouted, half underwater, probably Reeves, by far the drunkest of them all.

Jill shook her head and rubbed Angie's shoulders, trying to keep her spirits up after the loss of Amy, who had panicked and jumped off into the dark about fifty miles earlier. And, hey, it was *still* her birthday, Jill tried to remind them all, and she wanted people to make the most of it. Hell, parties were supposed to be dangerous. Away from the others, Jill gently assured Angie that people would know they were missing soon enough.

Reeves surged up between them right then, and maybe it was because they'd been driving in the dark for so long and all their pupils were so dilated, but Angie could have sworn his eyes rolled over black when he smiled and slid backwards under the water again to swim.

*   *   *

Their circle constricted for a bit, increasing the heat, but Angie shivered when someone spun another bottle. Every time one of the dudes tried to get a game of Spin the Bottle going, the driver seemed to sense it and whipped the red, air-horned beast back to full throttle. So their resulting panic meant any game quickly degenerated into Truth or Dare instead, which was sort of a mob-mentality comfort food, and a welcome distraction. But every time one of the females tried to keep that game going, they just ended up trading injury stories all over again.

This time it was Holly, Gaddy, and Sherry trading scars, and, listening to them, Angie realized why fairy tales always started with the same word.

"Once, I sprained both wrists and ruptured a disc in my back by moving boxes of books at work," Holly said. "Ended up having surgery on my spine and spent months of rehab in a pool with weights around my ankles. The retired Olympic psycho in charge of my rehabilitation seemed to develop a crush on me, and I started getting worried that she didn't want to see me get better and kept trying to injure me again. Seriously, who puts weights on someone's legs in a pool? How dangerous is that? That's like putting a goddamn pool on a fire truck!"

The group snickered at that.

"Once, I fell about a hundred feet out of this tree at our family's first house," Gaddy said. "It was this huge weeping willow with a broken branch at the top that laid flat across two splits in the trunk. After a week of intense debate, we named it 'The Bridge,' and we would climb up there and stand and look out at everyone's rooftops. And, of course, it finally collapsed when I was on it, dropping me down through about a hundred limbs like someone had just hit the multi-ball reward on a pinball machine. I ended up tangled and hanging upside down over a thick bottom branch, slowly rocking back and forth, trying to cry with the wind knocked out of me. Then I untangled, dropped to the grass, and saw a layer of skin sheered off my left forearm, wrist, and fingertips. I couldn't touch anything for weeks, it stung so bad. See that right above the elbow? Where I'm the wrong color?"

"Racist!" someone laughed.

"Speaking of pinball machines!" Sherry said, going for the one-up. "Our dad actually got us a pinball machine for Christmas once. It was a weird one, though. You know how pinball machines usually have themes, like movies or musicians? Well, this one's theme seemed to be 'pinball,' as it had pictures of '70s-looking guys playing pinball on it! Therefore, I can only assume that the machines *they* were playing also had little dudes playing pinball on them. Turtles all the way down. But me and my brother loved it, and we must have played with it for a whole six to nine minutes. Once, we tried to take it apart. I was reaching up inside to try to get the metal balls out—I had to, had to get them out—and my brother hit the buttons, and something inside blinked, squawked, gave me 500 points, and quickly sliced the top off one of my knuckles. I still have this white line across the bone to this day . . ."

"I wanna go home," Beth cried behind them, fingers in her ears. It wasn't just the chatter. The party music the driver had started their trip with was blasting was even louder now. They instinctually circled the wagons again, around another Devil's Cut empty nodding in the water. Jill used the opportunity to spin it once, twice, three times, until it finally slowed to point somewhere near her, and they all got the idea at the same time.

"So, do you wanna play or what?" she asked them, already knowing the answer.

"I think everybody's already kissed everybody," Reeves said, half under water where he lived now.

"Let's do a Ouija board," Angie said, and those who knew her well groaned. She was always keen on this idea, had been all her life really. Besides the fact that Ouija-ing it up was her preferred party game (because it didn't pair everyone off like Spin the Bottle), she also had the sort of love for the game that automatically came from parents throwing the boards in the trash as fast as she could buy them.

Before her mother regretted finally giving in to buy her an "official" one, Angie had played her own version of the "game" with a variety of other objects, some even alive. Like the time she gently laid her fingers on the back of the turtle she'd found on the Morse code of their street, letting it guide them both to the safety of the gutter, asking the question in her head:

"If he steps on that cigarette, I'll die before I'm 20. If he steps on that candy wrapper, I'll live forever . . ."

But her favorite early incarnation was modifying a 1975 Milton Bradley board game called The Bermuda Triangle, which handily supplied its own version of a planchette, a blue, amoeba-like cloud with a magnet hidden on the bottom. And when you spun the wrong numbers (or the right numbers depending on your recklessness) this dark cloud slid over your tiny, metal-capped ships and plucked them from the game board unseen under your hands, vanishing from their shipping fleets forever. Angie lost the spinner eventually, and she and her friends resorted to a more cooperative form of game play, all of them with their tiny fingertips just brushing the edges of the thundercloud as it swept the entire game triangle free of ships. Because of this modification, most of their games lasted one round, or approximately fifteen minutes. So, except for the delicious sense of doom, sort of the opposite of their predicament, at least when it came to duration.

"How the hell would we play that game, stuck in the back of a hot tub, lost on the back roads of Kentucky?" Lund scoffed, always a problem.

"I don't think the driver's lost," Beth hissed.

"What part is the 'Ouija' though?" Jill asked. She seemed game, as usual. "The thing or the board?"

"I think it's the board?" someone muttered.

"Yeah, all the letters," someone agreed.

"So even if you could play it without the thing," Jill said. "You can't play without the board."

"Planchette!" someone shouted, probably Lund.

"Sounds like lunch," Jill laughed.

"It's shaped like a heart."

"With a few more splinters."

"We don't need a board. The board is the water. And the thing . . ."

"Planchette!"

". . . can be a bottle."

They remained skeptical.

"No, no, this can work," Angie said, desperate now. "We can designate one person 'yes' and one person 'no,' but, wait, what do we do about the letters?"

"Easy, there's, what, nine of us left?" Lund said. "That's three letters each, like how you had to text before smart phones! So 'one' is 'A-B-C' . . ."

"'Two' would be 'A-B-C,' bro," Reeves spit from a wave as the fire truck took another unlit turn. "'One' didn't have any letters on it. I know my phone is old as fuck."

"And four letters were on number 'seven.'"

"Fine! Forget it. We'll just do 'yes' or 'no.'"

"You can't play Ouija boards without the board," someone muttered again, but it was too dark to know who, and they did it anyway.

*   *   *

Trapped in the tub, they drank, then drank some more. Then they drank like their lives depended on it. When the alcohol was mostly gone, they found themselves drinking whatever had filled the bottles and cans that bobbed past their faces. When they studied their hands, they found that all their soaking had shriveled their fingertips to tire treads, which gripped the slippery bottles wonderfully now, and, in turn, made their bodies even more conducive to systematic inebriation, even if someone of it was imaginary.

They tried using the Devil's Cut as their planchette, and realized it was surprisingly effective. There was less resistance in the water than on a table surrounded by skeptics, and their hands moved it easily three times as fast. In no time they were deciphering messages.

"There Is No Fire," was the first one they translated, which was a head-scratcher. Angie guessed it had something to do with alerting people to a fire truck that refused to stop. But it would have made more sense if the sirens were flashing, or if the message was delivered to anyone except some drunken hostages.

"Most people think Ouija boards are a modern-day lie detector," Beth said. "Though you can beat both of them the exact same way."

"Oh no," Holly laughed. "Watch her butt for bubbles!" and Beth slugged her in the arm.

"Wait, huh?" Dan was baffled and angry. He was a bit of a bully, like a B-side Reeves.

"She's serious," Gaddy said. "Like, say, if you answer the question, 'Have you been to the Moon,' you just answer, 'Yes,' but then finish in your head with 'Moon Township, Pennsylvania' . . ."

"Where the heck is that?" Lund asked.

"Have we already started?" Dan asked.

"I think she already lost," Reeves said, blowing bubbles like a baby.

"Have you ever been to Mars?" Lund asked.

"Mars, Pennsylvania, yes," she smiled.

"What the heck is going on in Pennsylvania?" Lund laughed.

They all studied his face a moment, then threw up their hands and burst out laughing.

"Whoops, there's another loophole," Angie said. "Be an idiot!"

"All right, since we clearly have all night to burn, did we do this yet?" Jill asked. "I'd like to propose a toast. To myself and another successful journey around the sun!"

"Someone already said that," Lund mumbled, not confident enough to say it was him.

"That is some deep shit," Dan said.

"Huh?"

"I said, that is some deep shit!" Dan yelled.

"Yes, we are in some deep shit!" Lund yelled back.

"I can't take much more of this fucking music!" Reeves said, punching the side of the truck hard enough that they felt it in the water around them.

They went back to their games.

At some point, the bottle spelled out "Yield." Or maybe it was "Wield." But there was enough of a debate for the bullies to start rummaging the back of the truck for weapons again.

*   *   *

Messages in bottles and "yes" and "no" questions became the thing for a little while after that argument, which Angie considered a waste of time as Reeves just asked everyone if they wanted to die, then struggled to point the bottle at himself, who had been designated the "Yes" as long as he wasn't trying to swim and bump into everyone's legs. Angie wished they'd hoisted Reeves up on some shoulders to play "Chicken," like they had when the night started. Then someone could flush him over the side instead, to get sucked under those awful wheels in turn, just like Amy, slurped up like a gnat vacuumed in your yawn.

But Reeves just kept getting pats on the back for his jokes, and his vigorous laps, until she saw Jill recoil at something she felt between his shoulder blades.

"What the hell is that!" Jill said, looking at her hand like she'd been bit.

"I don't know. A scab or something. I musta got cut . . ."

"Do you see that on his back?" Jill said, almost falling over to move away from him. "What's growing on his back?"

Angie was convinced it was a fin, but he'd vanished under the waves again. People started talking about their drinks being spiked and all measure of hallucinations, and Angie was colder than she'd ever been in her life.

"I think we've been poisoned," Beth said. "If not by the beers, then by this gross water."

Jill snorted at this, and Angie looked her over, noticing her carefully cultivated "Hitchcock" look tonight, the "suicide blonde," head down and eyes perpetually narrowed, like she was always gazing over an invisible newspaper.

"Maybe we're on a prison bus right now, headed for jail for our crimes," Angie said. "And we're not in a pool at all. This is just a bus filled with urine and sweat, and we're all handcuffed to each other and pissing all over the floor . . ."

"Stop!" Beth said, fingers in her ears again.

"Are our crimes really so bad?" Jill asked them all.

The bottle floated towards where Reeves was kicking in the corner, and Jill, Beth, and Angie recoiled from it as if burned.

Finally they were out of all alcohol for good, no bottles or beer cans to warm their bellies or their brains, and Angie closed her eyes with both hands on the rail, feeling the rumble of the road, understanding that she now knew these invisible wheels even more intimately than her own body.

* * *

They wouldn't have known it, but it was an uncharacteristically hot night, for that time of year anyway. But certainly not too hot for Kentucky, and once they left Bardstown Road, and once she counted the shadows of nineteen overpasses without ever turning, Angie knew the party had to be heading for somewhere even colder for their final destination. True Hell on Earth. Indiana.

Few people remembered that the final circle in Dante's *Inferno* was actually ice, but she did. And Indiana was Hell all right. Or worse, maybe they were headed for the Tenth Circle, that redneck baby-talk-y hybrid of a name, the DMZ where the worst people she'd ever known lived and breathed (but rarely worked), a limbo they referred to as "Kentuckiana," where she'd been drunkenly assaulted by authority figures at least twice while passing through.

There would be no help there, she decided, and she vowed to end the journey, by any means necessary, before she crossed that line. But she was too tired to plot, and Angie was well on her way to the sweet comfort of hypothermic sleep when she saw Lund using a broken bottle to cut a stretch of fire hose. They'd long since stopped playing their game by then, as too many planchettes floated and clinked in their midst, seemingly desperate for more terrifying questions, but the acceleration of the truck when they played also was a strong deterrent.

Angie watched Lund labor another moment, confused. They'd recently abandoned climbing off as a viable option, as a driver barreling along at breakneck speed was suicide. Then she finally understood what he was doing.

He wanted to drain the pool.

As she watched, Lund sucked on one end of the hose, and successfully siphoned the green soup from the pool around them to splash out onto the street, but people weren't feeling the plan like he'd hoped. And once the pool water was down to their ankles and their bodies were even more at the mercy of a wind that whisked the moisture from their swim suits and damp underwear, no one was looking at Lund like a hero. And just that quickly, his party was over.

Chubby Spencer S. Lundergaard, the only reveler wearing glasses, sometimes referred to as *Lord of the Fries* while growing up, became the party's next distraction. And he wasn't even targeted by the regular assailants, Reeves and Dan, but by everyone else instead. It was Beth who punched him in the mouth first, with a fist full of bottle. It shattered and his eye rode the shards over the rail, a comet trail of optic nerve and white lidless surprise. Beth stepped back in surprise, hands out in surrender.

More joined the fight, but so far away from civilization, and so far into the depressing blackened, blasted-out strip-mall void that was Kentuckiana, Angie couldn't really see who was who anymore. But she heard three or four wet bodies tackle Lund and drag him toward the taillights over his protests.

She tried to cover her eyes with her hand before the ritual was illuminated in red, but she couldn't help but peek through her wrinkled fingers before it was over, and she saw Lund's glasses divided as neatly as his head as he was hurled off the truck and headfirst, but with one headlight out, straight into a "Yield" sign. And, agreeable to the end, this was exactly what his skull did to comply under its yellow metal blade.

*   *   *

It didn't seem possible, but the driver sped up even more, and Angie felt her ears pop from a change in air pressure. Angie could sometimes make out the black of Reeves' eyes and the whites of Jill's teeth, and she guessed she was smiling at the very real possibility of time travel on her unique leap-day birthday, probably the most memorable birthday party of all time. For the rest of them, though, panic was in full swing, which was its own sort of party.

And in the dark, after battling the rumbles of the road for so long, they'd somehow developed a new form of communication, one that lacked language but was no less clear to them all. At first, she'd assumed there were too many bottles for their game, but now she realized they were all still playing. Hugging their own chests, corralling floating cans and bottles between their legs, periodically holding their breath to stop their chattering teeth, and long, slow blinks, occasionally flicking a bottle and mouthing the letters as it pointed at them all in turn, speaking to them more clearly than anyone could have predicted.

Angie read their bodies, all of them roughly translated as, "We're in this together," or maybe "We're fucked," which meant the same thing really.

After a silence that felt like five years and five hundred more miles, Jill whispered that she missed her cat, wondering who would feed him.

"A cat's future is even more limited than our own," Jill went on. "You know why? Because of one simple fact. If you hold them like toddlers with their feet barely touching the ground, a cat can only walk backwards. Did you know that the only instance of this affliction recorded in human beings is in a swimming pool?"

This all sounded reasonable, and even like something Lund would have said, but he was long gone. Angie tried to get a head count, and she thought about how there were more women than men left in the end. She attributed this to the hidden exercises they could always do under the waves, to tread water forever, those muscles they develop in secret when they were cutting zen gardens into their palms with their own fingernails under the covers while their fathers over-explain things, all the while smiling, smiling, smiling through their eyeteeth.

Jill grabbed Angie's face, and she tried real hard to keep listening, but she was captivated by a sleek, slack-jawed visage, somewhat resembling Dan's grinning, catatonic face, sinking beneath the suds, dragged down to be consumed by an unseen force, never to resurface.

"You see, in a pool it's almost impossible to walk forward when your body divides the surface of the water between the tips of your toes and your nostrils," Jill explained like this was the answer to everything. "You have no choice but to never go forward. You will back up forever."

Angie believed her, ever before her embrace, even before their kiss, and together they discovered the last two warm places in the world.

* * *

They flew past something huge, some sort of gargantuan illumination on the horizon. And it was moving. Then they saw the rectangle flickering like a massive television through the trees, and they understood it was the drive-in movie again, and they could just make out the end credits scrolling up the screen.

Some of them stopped shivering in the wind, focusing through their shock and haze, and some finally realized that only an hour and a half could have passed if the movie was just ending, a maximum of three hours if it was a typical double-feature, the requisite running time of a motion picture and exactly the amount of time they had paid the driver for.

Then they forgot all this math just as quickly, as if their thoughts drained out their ears and onto the asphalt as freely as the last of their fetid pool water.

Someone sprang up like a porpoise, saluted anyone who remained, and then someone jumped off into the night. It was so dark, and it happened so fast, there was no time for her to ascertain the identity, even illuminated by the occasional lightning flash that she swore originated eleven hundred miles away in Bermuda. But if Angie had to hazard a guess, she would have said it was Reeves. Even after all the death at his hands, she was sorry to see him go. The pool would miss his body heat and manic exercises dearly.

At some point, Beth cracked and never came back, screaming until she was hoarse. And when she hit top volume and some of the bottles shattered in the puddles at their feet, they were suddenly driving past a real-live school bus full of kids' butts and faces on their way home from some other game, a pink-and-yellow flash of skin heading in the opposite direction, like a snapshot from the yearbook of their former lives, and those kids just screamed back at Beth, thinking it was a party, which it was, of course.

It was the last party, where every party in the world had the potential to end up if it tried hard enough.

* * *

They all held hands in the glow of the taillights, a red haze that signaled death for most of the ride, but now marked a doorway to possible escape. Their eyes watered, but their blinking was stolid.

They all jumped together.

And they landed not on the road, but on the grass, intact, alive.

The truck had stopped.

For how long, no one knew, with their bodies so numb from the wind and the drink and the time that had long ago been rendered meaningless.

They were deep in the woods, but still in someone's yard.

At a party.

Colorful streamers and balloons were tangled in the trees, huge "Happy Birthdays!" scrawled in childlike letters and glimmering in the flickering light of a tall bonfire, and the remaining partiers silently circled it to get warm. Or maybe they were circling Jill. Angie couldn't be sure. Further off on the horizon were some power lines, and a bundle of transformers, possibly a tall fence surrounded by barbed wire. It was tough to see in the dark and her bloodshot eyes had yet to adjust to a world not made of taillights.

The cab door opened, and the driver stepped out. He was a huge man, wearing headphones, unplugged and dangling, and a black eyepatch hovered indecisive between his eyebrows. The bundle of dollars they'd paid him at the beginning of the night fluttered from the chest pocket of his overalls, ends flapping in the wind like a rattlesnake. Then the money flew free from his pocket, one dollar after the other, leaving a wake of cash behind him, and he made no attempt to retrieve it. On the dashboard, a crackling TV monitor was visible, with the now-empty party pool flickering on the screen.

The driver frowned and looked over the group, mouth working as he scanned their bodies, naked and streaked with blood, piss, and beer. Sexless and indistinguishable.

"Goddamn, you kids sure know how to celebrate," the driver said, sliding the eyepatch over his left eye, then his right. He laughed. "Though some people would argue a surprise party is a form of aggression."

Though no one could see it happen, they all imperceptibly turned to each other, fingertips gently caressing the rough, heart-shaped edges of their worst ideas, and though no one could hear it, a message was both sent, and received.

And everyone who was left fell upon the driver, ripping and piercing, sometimes with broken bottle shards for teeth, tearing him down to the ground, down to their level of understanding to render him recognizable as the perfect asset for any party:

Ribbons.

Once transformed into warm pile of red, streaming party favors, they placed his body on top of the long metal coffin behind the cab, and one of them came from the bonfire with a flaming branch, green end popping and cracking as it blackened.

The fire truck burned like it was born to. But there were other trucks at the party, too. New trucks with gleaming chrome and no rust, not burdened by the embarrassment of a conversion to a bullshit party pool or undergrad dance wagon, and well-muscled men sat in the trailers, coils of hose between their legs, drinking beer and eating popcorn, but making no effort to stop the blaze. Eventually, more vehicles arrived, and faceless men in jumpsuits and fogged-up visors began to douse the flames, the torrents from their hoses filling their pool back up to the brim. Naked and against all instincts, Angie ran through the roar and glare of the sirens to climb aboard the nearest fire truck she could find. And on this truck, black now instead of red, she sat in a seat facing the wrong way, next to more astronauts and anonymous shades, and she squeezed her hands locked behind her back, smoothing valleys back in her fingerprints, dreaming of rolling through bright-lit streets and crowds very soon, speaking silently with those fingers, her breath and the tip of her nose drawing hearts on her window, dreaming of more celebrations, in places teeming with secret highway rites, the wind blowing the blood from her dirty-blonde hair before it could dry as she breathed in a world she was no longer convinced existed.

Behind her, within the black husk of the smoldering party bus, she saw Reeves reemerge from the trees, slick and gray, striding through the billows of smoke and the bonfire now turned wildfire, to climb back onto their engine. Indifferent to the pyre, he stepped up the chrome stairs, back up into the boiling cauldron, now overflowing with water and flame. She watched the fin on his back and his perfect body cut through the waves like he was claiming the deep end of any pool, and Angie leaned out into the wind as far as she could without falling, still able to sense him through the growing distance and fading distortion and shimmer of heat. She could still feel his cold skin pressed against her own, warming her, then cooling them both, then perfectly acclimating to the world until they were invisible.

THE FLOWERY

"Wear your heart on your skin in this life,
I'm the man can give you a deal."
—Sylvia Plath— "The Fifteen-Dollar Eagle"

I was so rattled from getting my ass kicked in Ohio that I drove through at least three states before I looked up at any signs. Okay I do remember "Nashville," and thinking I could search for clues there, but then I realized every corner of that town would be adorned with some earnest asshole and his guitar case. And I didn't need any more red herrings in my life. Shit, I'd bet real money that there was a band in Nashville right now called The Red Herrings, and they'd be playing their asses off, hungry. Making eye contact.

When I did look up, a sign said, "Welcome to Florida!" which I was pretty sure was in the wrong direction from where I was supposed to be going, but then I remembered that, because I didn't have any idea what I should be doing, let alone where I should be going, I could do my investigating in any order really. So I might as well check out what that last cryptic note in my wife's address book meant before she vanished. I thought about Florida a bit, Florida as a concept, as I slowed down and fumbled with my road map, looking out at some dead grass and what I swear was some kind of mosquito tornado, and I remembered my dad explaining to me one time how Juan Ponce de León's christening of the state translated into Spanish, how sweet and innocent it sounded in another language, and how that shit didn't fit at all with the buggy wasteland out my windshield.

I folded the map back up, content that I was just clipping the top corner of Florida, right where it touched that little tumor protruding from the ass of Alabama, the "panhandle," they called it, which I'm pretty sure was what Alex called an erection in *A Clockwork Orange*. But I really could have sworn I was in Mississippi when I'd stopped paying attention, you know, all overalls and Huck Finn 'n' shit? But, no, this was definitely Florida because there were at least three mosquito tornados outside my window now. And this being Florida, and me having spent way too much time online, I did know some hard stats about the place: I knew this state had 56 state prisons, and seven creepy-ass private prisons, housing something like 150,000 offenders.

So I decided to do an experiment to take my mind off the mosquitoes, and I tried counting in my head before I saw my first official Florida prison, to see how far I would get.

I only got to one-thousand-and-one before I saw a "Don't Give Rides To Hitchhikers" sign. I knew those signs usually meant "prison," but when I hit one-thousand-and-two I got bored with the game, so I stopped to get my cat-thing, Zero, some food. Instead, I found myself milling around a Native American gift shop for way too long. And that's when I saw something weird on a T-shirt they were selling, and after a quick talk with a clerk, and the last surprise translation of the day, I was running back for my car so fast that I almost knocked over a fat kid on crutches. I fell instead, and he never slowed down.

*   *   *

I don't think I can overstate how excited I was to decipher my first legitimate clue. Follow me here for a second. You remember that my wife had "Clearwater" written on her address book before she took off, and I assumed that must mean "Florida," right? I never told you that? Well, it was Florida, yes, but not "Clearwater," Florida. See, she also had that little Indian drawing next to the big clue. And "Clearwater" in Creek Indian apparently means "Shambia." And "Shambia," that turns into "Escambia." And that was the name of the county I was in at that precise moment.

I won't bother detailing the half day I wasted when I thought it was the code written on the front of ambulances. That's "Ecnalubma," in case you're wondering.

I'm not sure how long I drove around, but at some point I found myself staring at the gates to my first Florida jail.

I mean, there it was, a jail popped up right in front of my face as soon as I wished for one, just a couple miles from where they sold cheapjack dreamcatchers and "rattlesnake egg" rubber-band gags. I wondered why they didn't sell jailhouse souvenirs, too. But I was about to find out.

The sign read, in reasonably large letters, "Escambia County Corrections." But above that, for the dumbasses I guess, in letters twice as big, screamed, "JAIL." I thought about driving up a little closer, but not having any idea what to say to whoever might ask me questions, I parked right next to the heavily fortified fence and idled there awhile.

That's when the red pickup truck zipped up next to my car, and a huge guy in overalls and no shirt (of course) opened up my passenger door and plopped down in the seat next to me before I could even react. Zero was confused, too, and bumped my feet as he zipped under the seats to the front of the car.

"Hi," this guy said, leaning forward and squeezing the top of the passenger's seat. I'm guessing he did this so I could gasp at the size of the motherfucker's hand, a pink mitt that compressed the headrest like an office stress toy.

"How ya doing. Uh, can I help you with something?"

"Why you hanging around outside the gate, sir?"

"Why not."

"You here to pick somebody up?" the man smiled, lots of teeth on this guy, and goddamn if he didn't seem friendly though, besides the fact that he'd invaded my car and was working my headrest like a toothpaste tube. I could feel Zero circling my feet in alarm.

"No, I am not. Do you work for the Department of Corrections, uh, I mean, *jail?*"

"Kinda." Impossibly, even more teeth now.

"Are you waiting to pick anybody up?" I asked him, unable to not smile back.

"Nope. I mean, I hope not!" he said, meaning me, I think. His smile reached the maximum capacity before someone would have to start laughing. But he never did.

"Tell me sir," he went on. "You aren't mad about nothin', are ya?"

"Mad?" I wished he'd clarify which definition he was referring to, so I just went with the denial, almost but not quite laughing, too. "No, I'm not mad. I mean, I don't think so. But I don't know why you jumped in my car, and, to be honest I'm just waiting to see how this shit pans out."

"Okay, here's the deal, the name's Cort. And I'm the, uh, V.P. of this particular prison. Off the books, I keep a lookout for people looking to bushwhack new releases."

He tapped an angry red brand scarring his fuzzy pink shoulder that indeed read, "V.P."

"Do you mean V.I.P.?"

"Naw, man, 'Vengeance Patrol'! You like it? I made that up."

"I see. Yeah, that's a good name. And you do what again, Cort?"

"Well, when people camp outside these gates, maybe waiting for someone to get released, someone who did something wrong to them or a loved one, that's when I gently get them to move on. Ask them real nice to, say, get their revenge somewhere else, know what I mean?"

"Why don't they just move the fence back to the street? Then put up a 'No Parking' sign?"

"What is this? Russia! No, no, we let you park here. We just make you move as soon as you do."

"Even if I'm not here for revenge?"

"Vengeance," he said.

"'Revengeance!'" I laughed, and he nodded.

"There ain't no such word, sir."

"See that?" I said. "You *are* in the Department of Corrections!"

His smile slipped a little.

"So, why don't you move along then, buddy."

"But I told you, I'm not waiting to jump anybody."

"Doesn't matter. We have a protocol."

"Protocol means you have an official procedure, like a list of steps. You're just saying, 'Move!' That could easily be taken care of with that 'No Parking' sign I was talking about."

"I am much more effective than a sign." Big, big smile now.

"Okay, so you want me to move then. You got it. Or what if I just plant my feet here and don't do anything wrong?"

"How do you know that's what 'protocol' means?" he asked, still squeezing my headrest like it owed him money, but he seemed genuinely interested in my answer.

"Huh? I don't know. I looked it up?"

"Not on the internet, I hope. Internet don't do shit."

"No, it was probably a real, live dictionary. But what do you have against the internet? It hasn't wronged me yet."

"Well, it's wronged me on occasion," Cort said, letting the air and shape back into the headrest and abruptly stepping out of my car. He headed back to his truck and popped open a tool box in the bed. I got out to follow, and listened with mounting concern as he clanked around with something unseen.

"The internet has wronged you?" I repeated, confused by the turn in the conversation and his scrounging in the back of his truck.

"It has," he said, head still buried in the tool box. "For example, the internet might be able to define a word here or there, but it certainly can't tell you what, unequivocally, a jackhammer would do to a person's foot. Because looking at all that information on the internet, and reading about details such as how they aren't really 'hammering' anything, well, the real life repercussions might just be different than what we'd expect."

"What are we talking about again?"

"Jackhammers."

"How about you ask a jackhammerist?"

"Right now?"

"Yeah, call 'em up!" I shrugged, still not sure where this was going.

"Well, a jackhammerist may have difficulty both hearing the phone and feeling it vibrate," he said, peeking up to lock eyes. Cort the V.P. had one of those meaty heads, "big Irish face" syndrome, but with a bit of Cuban stirred in. I walked a little closer, not quite getting the angle to see what he was wrestling with.

"One day someone will make a phone app of a jackhammer that vibrates when you get a call," I told him. "Maybe it'll be me. Instant millionaire!"

"Excellent," he laughed. "I love it." He leaned into the shade of his truck bed tool box and banged around some more. His voice called out, "Here's the thing, since they're designed to break up pavement and concrete, I suspect a jackhammer'd reduce a foot to a bloody sack of sinew and shattered bone."

"Now I'm thinking about that visual, so thanks for that, buddy!" I laughed.

"But would it really do that?" he wondered, head back up. "What if it just makes your feet stronger? I think I need some volunteers."

"I've looked up a lot of stuff lately, online and in books," I told him, feeling like sharing but keeping my eye on my escape route back to my driver's seat. "In fact, you might say I'm a born-again scholar when it comes to research. And the only injury reports I've stumbled across on my web surfing regarding jackhammers is when some construction guy in our town dropped one on his toe. But the tool itself is heavy of course, so it crushes the foot anyway. So I'm not really talking about a sustained 'jackhammering' of one spot on the body, with just the vibration of the tool but no hard rock to vibrate apart." The tool box lid slammed shut, so I talked a little faster.

"However! I'm no expert," I said. "And I think your description is probably really, really close to accurate. I've never actually seen a jack hammer taken to a foot. So . . . I might be surprised."

He came around from the back of his truck and held up his monster hands to reveal nothing at all, and he laughed even harder. I tried laughing back.

"If this were a movie, the camera would pan down your body and reveal . . . *pow!* Two wooden legs."

"I don't understand," he said. "But I like your moxie, kid."

"I totally thought you were going to jackhammer my ass."

"I don't need to do anything like that to send you on your way. Describing things is sometimes enough."

"You might be right. I've never seen a man hanging a foot in the air by a meat hook in his ass, but I bet it hurts."

"Well, I have seen that . . ."

Of course you have, I thought.

". . . and let me tell you one more thing. If you decide you really want to plant your feet here outside this gate? Those feet will 'vibrate apart' just as easily as any rock, if not more so."

I had no idea why, but I felt like arguing a little more about jackhammer injuries. I can't explain it.

"You never know!" I said. "What if it just harmlessly transformed a foot into two perfect feet?"

"Good point," he said. "Probably depends on the bit. Carbide-tipped, diamond point, clay, hand chisels, rock hammers, finishing hammers, wedges and shims. They're all gonna do different damage . . ."

"Cort, are you trying to sell me a jackhammer?!" I tried to smile as big as him, but he just kept talking.

". . . but the feet will all end up looking the same when I'm done."

"Transformed into tiny rocks!"

The smile was finally gone.

"Get the fuck out of here."

"You got it."

*   *   *

I left the prison gates, but I couldn't *leave* leave. I didn't want to get hypothetically jackhammered by Cort the V.P. though, so I drove around in circles. Eventually, I came back, creeping my Rabbit back up to the fence. Well, sorta. I idled back on the road, keeping the gate within sight. Cort's pickup was visible around a storage shed, but he was nowhere to be seen. I didn't want to get on his bad side, but I kind of wanted him to deal out some vengeance on somebody. I figured this must be one of those days when people were getting out of jail. And I was just getting ready to admit I was wrong and drive off when a buzzer sounded and Zero, my cat-thing, zipped under the seats, and the gates creaked open.

And out walked a grown man in a cape, and I knew I'd made the right decision.

Okay, it wasn't really a cape. It was his winter clothes thrown over his back, the clothes he must have been arrested in, likely in some colder part of the country. He'd tied a heavy yellow sweater over his shoulders, which looked to all the world like a big ol' cape. And with that spring in his step, it wouldn't have surprised me if he flew off into the bright blue sky. I couldn't see his face, but his eyes were buried in the shade provided by a Cro-Magnon, "early man" kinda forehead, so I just assumed he did something terrible to someone (sorry, I mean, "wronged someone"), and I suddenly felt like a failure for not being there to get revenge on some prisoner who did one of my loved ones wrong. So I thought he might do for practice.

I decided to follow him. See, I grew up in the '80s, before the internet, when you had to follow people around for awhile if you wanted to peek into their private lives. You couldn't just click a few keys to creep on a potential girlfriend. You had to physically follow them from place to place, go through their lockers, garbage cans. Yes, we stalked people in the snow, both ways, and we liked it! What I'm saying is this wasn't the first time I pressured myself into stalking somebody, and technology be damned, it probably wouldn't be my last.

I wasn't dumb enough to pull up to the prison gate again, so I backed off about a hundred yards to see who came to pick him up. Imagine my surprise when Cort screeched up, then screeched back out onto the highway, his passenger's yellow cape trailing out the pickup's window.

I followed them. How could I not follow them? All sorts of thoughts going through my head. Was Crazy Cort waiting for him the whole time? Was all that verbal intimidation just for my benefit but essentially a bullshit story? I had to know, so I followed them a long time, about sixty miles along the Conecuh River until we ended up in some town without a sign, behind a bar with a row of Harleys and a smashed-up barber pole wearily spinning out front, all surrounded by about ten kilowatts of blinking red Christmas lights. A sign along the building read, "The Bowery." There was something like an airplane hanger out back, past what looked like an overgrown vegetable garden, and that's where I saw Cort had parked his truck.

I rolled up my windows to keep Zero safe, then went inside. I probably would have stood out more if I hadn't lost my previous bar fight and gained these scabs and bruises. I was suddenly thankful that cops and bartenders had done a little damage on my travels already so that these bikers would possibly do a little less. It felt like progress.

At a long metal bar, also covered in winking Christmas decorations, I jawed with some bearded older dudes about the area. At first, the conversations were mostly about an oil pipeline, where they'd all worked, and their dads worked, and their dads' dads. Something about another pipeline coming through Florida to take it over, something about jobs being lost, then something about hiring all the cons and ex-cons for cheap, farmed out by the glut of private prisons in the state. I tried to keep them talking about that, but then one of them was explaining to me that the name "Clearwater" was "pretty ironic," considering a flood of sewage that had engulfed the county jail, a disaster which resulted in a fire in the prison laundry room which blew the facility sky-high, killing two inmates and injuring over a hundred more. I slid up next to them to hear everything I could about that action-packed story.

"No, that didn't happen," a second old biker leaned in to correct the first one.

"Fuck it didn't," the first one said, slamming his beer.

"No, that was Santa Rosa County Jail, nowhere near here. 600 inmates were missing for a day and a night."

"How the fuck do you know that?" the second biker demanded.

"Because they only rounded up 599," the first biker said, smiling.

I smiled, too, not because of the tall tales of escape and intrigue, but because I was remembering how full of shit conspicuous tough guys always were, and it was reminding me of my reason for coming in there in the first place.

"Hey, men," I said, cheerful. "Do you know who drives that gray pickup out there?"

Their faces dropped.

"Why."

It was one of those "whys" without the question mark again.

"I was supposed to meet him here."

"Uh huh."

One of them clapped me on the back, but kept his hand on my jean jacket collar afterwards, and the other one pulled out my stool, forcing me to stand up. I finished my beer and tried to shrug off the hand, but it stayed put and the bikers suddenly seemed to be multiplying. Somehow, I was now dead center in a circle of ten or more Santas gone to seed, white beards working around their mouths all excitable. I tried negotiation.

"So all your families worked on the pipeline, huh? Sounds like hard work. Honest work."

A few of them squinted, but we still weren't moving.

"You know," I went on. "If working on a pipeline didn't sound so noble, people might be more aware of how bad they're being exploited. Like imagine someone saying, 'Man, our family has been sucking horses' cocks for years! My dad, and his dad, and his dad's dad, shit, all practically *born* sucking off horses. It's in our blood!"

I caught a furry fist in the back of the skull, and the Christmas lights went out.

*　*　*

When I woke up, I marveled at how I was getting used to having my ass kicked in bars, places I'd never frequented in the first thirty years of my life. I looked up and saw written on the curved metal wall in blinking red light bulbs, "Disgraceland." Then I looked around and realized I was in the hanger behind The Bowery. It didn't take me long to pick Cort out of the shuffling crowd, as he stood a good foot taller than his gang. He was still in his overalls, but now he had a leather vest over his bare shoulders. There were a lot of patches on this vest, including one that read, "V.P.," and revelations started to dawn on me.

"So . . . where's your President?" I asked him, grimacing and rubbing the back of my head.

Cort stepped forward and offered me a giant hand. When I took it, he helped me get my legs out in front of my body, but shoved me back down on my ass. Then he gave me a finger to sit still, tapping his lips to signal that I shut up. I assessed my situation. Cort was the V.P. alright, Vice President of a motorcycle gang by the looks of it, a gang that was named, from the looks of the jackets, the "Jobshitters."

No, wait, another jacket said, "Mobshitters." No, hold on, the patches surrounding me had a ton of names. The Beelzebugs, The Christ Munchers, even one that read, "Heaven's Devils," which, being not quite the Hell's Angels, seemed like a baffling choice for a real gang, like starting out in movies and calling yourself "Donny Jepp."

Then I saw "Bowery Boys" on someone's back, and I started thinking melodramatic *Gangs of New York* thoughts instead of campy *The Warriors* thoughts, and I worried this wasn't some kind of summit meeting after all. I sat up a little straighter.

"That's right," Cort said. "You're hanging with the Bowery Boys, real-life descendents of the original Six Points Crew."

"Don't you mean Five Points," I said.

"Who told you that?" he smiled. "Thought I told you not to trust that internet."

"But I can read a New York map . . ." I tried.

"The Bowery Boys, represent!" Cort bellowed, arms out wide.

"More like the Flowery Boys," someone muttered, but it was impossible to tell who'd said it in the hurricane of facial hair. A dangerous electric hum danced around the crowd for a second, then dissipated, as Cort pulled another Mobshitter close to him and gave him a hug around the neck.

"Liam here, he's one of our Australian brothers, ain't that right, Liam?"

"Good-o," Liam said, giving me the thick accent I'd hoped for. "Australia is a lot like your Florida, to tell the truth, a state of mind more than the weather, you dig? But, like, if Florida was an entire continent."

They stared at me awhile, and it like it was my turn to say something.

"You got a lot going on here," I said.

"Sure do." More time ticked by.

"Welp, sorry to disturb ya, everybody!" I said, starting to get up. Liam and Cort quickly put hands on my shoulders and sat me back down.

"Just hang on there a second, boy. Why did you follow us?"

"Well, I just followed you."

"Why?"

" I can't explain it."

"That's okay, how about I just explain something to you instead. See, you've stumbled into something here, and we were thinking about killing your ass, but I think we can salvage this situation." He snapped his fingers. "Jason! Come up here. I think you've already met Jason . . ."

The inmate I'd watched stride out of the jail with the yellow sweater over his shoulders pushed through the crowd. They all pulled back to make a circle around the three of us. Jason had lost the cape and was wearing the sweater like a normal person now, tied around his waist. That was when I noticed the cracks in the floor at our feet, and the strange Rorschach test of split concrete spreading out all around us.

"Jason here, was a member of The Lose Lose, a motorcycle club out of Tulsa."

"Let me guess," I said, emboldened by his talk of "salvage" and "not killing my ass." "They're the mortal enemies of The Win Wins?"

"Yes." Cort said, deadly serious. "Exactly, right. And we've brought him here to deal with his patch."

Cort spun Jason around to reveal an intricate tattoo that depicted a red, plump, very butt-like apple, vigorously fucking the incisors of a grinning skull with its hearty rump. I had to nod, as this was probably the most succinct illustration of a win/win scenario that I'd ever seen.

"You already heard about the flood from our sergeant-at-arms back there at the bar. What people don't know is that a lotta guys escaped under cover of that disaster. Jason here, he got out during the flood, too, along with 500 or so gang members—accounts vary—who had their personal information erased when the computers sparked out underwater. We all got caught pretty quick after that, so don't let the movies fool you when they act like water is the best way to lose a dog's scent! But Jason, he was re-incarcerated under the wrong name. Like a lot of guys. See, in their rush to wrangle us back up and cover their asses, hundreds of affiliates were incorrectly logged back into the system, names changed, numbers changed, and no amount of protests could straighten this out, not with the crushing bureaucracy of the prison system. Especially here in Florida where, as you probably heard, there are more prisons than post offices. You ever seen the movie *Brazil*? No? No, it has nothing to do with this story, I'm just curious, my copy got ruined in the flood, and I don't know how it ended. Anyhow! After a couple months of beatings and trying to convince guards that identities had been swapped, those 500 guys went back to biding their time, adopting their new roles, temporarily. This meeting here is where we decided that they'd only turned their backs on the brothers due to impossible circumstances. And we're here to clean up the mess. Get everybody sorted back out."

"I don't get it."

"Listen, in prison, if you adopted another name, that means you adopted another patch, and that means we got hundreds of motherfuckers with the wrong tattoos! We've all gathered here to set things right."

"So this is like a tattoo removal thing you're doing?"

"Sorta."

"So, that talk of a Vengeance Patrol was bullshit."

"Sorta."

"And what does this have to do with me again?"

"Sorta. Wait, what? Shut the fuck up."

I noticed one of the men in the circle passing around earmuffs. Cort, clearly more V.I.P. than V.P., got his earmuffs before anybody else, big ones, fuzzy and pink, and he snapped them over his ears like a king.

I was gearing up to endure the rough road of listening to him explaining ever-increasingly complicated reasons for all this insanity, but this time a whole lot louder because of the giant earmuffs, when all the sudden the crowd parted and out came the jackhammer for real this time.

* * *

Of course he's the one doing the hammering, I thought. *It wasn't like he didn't try to warn me.*

There were only enough earmuffs for about ten guys in the crowd, so I guessed they were the ten most important guys. I wasn't sure what to do with this information, but filed it away in case it became important during a quick getaway, along with the detail that only one guy was wearing a surgical mask, and that was Cort, too. It had a big lop-sided grin drawn on it in lipstick.

One of his Mobshitters, shirtless and sweaty, with a tattoo of either Florida or a fucked-up pistol on his back, passed him the huge industrial tool, a yellow and black beast with purple stains halfway up the bit, "Bosch Brute" in white Impact font on the side, a name I assumed was a preview of the squishy sounds it was about to make when it started dancing. Cort spun the power cord out and away from his body with the panache of a lead-singer working a microphone stand, and then started squeezing and twisting the two handgrips. I fully expected him to straddle his legs around the machine's torso and drive away into the night, or at least make some motorcycle noises with his mouth. Then the jackhammer was making the motorcycle noises for all of them, and I wondered why all biker gangs didn't ride these things when they were out of the saddle. Maybe they did.

A Jobshitter slid an open can of black latex paint in front of Cort, and he dipped the tip, shooting black flecks onto everyone, including myself. I spit some paint off my lip as Jason of The Win Wins, formally of the Lose Lose, laid himself out willingly on the floor in the middle of the goons, arms and legs splayed like a martyr ready to be drawn and quartered. I didn't understand his lack of resistance. I started to think they really believed you could walk away from a jackhammering, despite the internet warnings, and I held my breath along with Jason as his chest rose to present his ribs and his jailhouse tattoo to the machine. Cort mounted him wide, revved the engine, and brought the tool down.

In spite of the conversation we'd had earlier outside the prison gates, a jackhammer's effects on a human body were not that surprising. It did exactly what I thought it would, deep in my heart of hearts. Speaking of, holy shit, you should see what's inside a heart. But you probably don't want to. Wait, there's still some confusion? That's understandable, I guess, but, come on, you don't really need a play-by-play, do you? Great, let's move on. Just kidding, here you go:

I'm no doctor, but the best way I can describe it was like the root beer I dumped on the subwoofers I installed in my trunk once, and how I stood there watching the soda hop and bubble around the bass of whatever shitty Kottonmouth Kings song was playing and how, even though I knew it would ruin my speakers, I felt compelled to pour the rest of the root beer right into that fluttering ring to see what else might happen. It only ended up ruining the speakers, of course, but while the dance of root beer lasted, I thought of the valve on my own heart, and that congenital heart defect that always caused me to get a little dizzy and the beats to skip, something my wife always joked meant my heart was shrinking away to nothing. And I thought of all this again, right up until the biker's heart of hearts was revealed in all its squirming glory. His heart was bigger than I thought, certainly bigger than mine, and no doubt a lot tougher, because the jackhammer had a hell of a time pinning it down. The tip kept slipping to the sides of the organ, over and over, due to density, or all that hemorrhaging, but it looked like the sucker was protecting itself with invisible stiff-arms, imperceptible defensive movements. Like there was this force field around the heart for something just like this, possibly the unlikeliest of all situations. Either way, it was a good thirty seconds before the point penetrated and reduced his pump to a whiplashing water balloon. And that gave me plenty of time to find the right words, because I realized it was tougher than I ever thought to describe such a horrendous image. And, since I already said I was no doctor, later in life I finally had to ask a real, live doctor friend of mine what he thought might happen if, say, you tried to jackhammer a human body. I presented the question like I was really curious, like the internet was broken and I couldn't look it up, not like I needed to describe it if I ever told this story. And he told me something like this:

If you pressed this tool on the abdomen, starting centrally, say in the periumbilical region, which is exactly what happened, those 1,500 thrusts per minute essentially macerate the shit out of the soft tissues. For my doctor friend, it was a question of how quickly the muscular abdominal wall would perforate, and he really gave this the most thought. He decided that if the jackhammer had a tip like a screwdriver, tapered, which was exactly what this jackhammer was sporting, combined with the weight of that particular model, it basically would just go right through the body without looking back, that tapered tip rushing headlong in its quest for a hard surface underneath something as insignificant as a human body. And once it was through, it would tear the floor up just as vigorously, if not as colorfully. And while it was dancing on a concrete floor like the one I was watching from, it would be a veritable shower of liquids, really nasty fireworks, too, given that, according to my doctor friend, this would mostly be small intestine getting skewered, centrally, along with the colon, peripherally. Then it would hit that subwoofer I was talking about, I mean, the branching aorta being cradled by the L4-5 disc.

He said death would probably come pretty quick once the jackhammer got to the chest, and I hoped he was right. He said that a person could remain conscious for maybe a minute while the jackhammer pulled a Sherman's March to the Sea through the abdomen, but once it crunched through those ribs like old toast, there would be fountains big as the Bellagio as that heart pumped off into nobody. My doctor friend said there may even be a sucking sound as the pleural cavity opened up with a *swoosh!* and the lungs popped, but who would hear that shit with a jackhammer running? Especially a top-of-the-line jackhammer like a Bosch Brute. But go big or go home, right . . .

Go big or go home! He wasn't kidding. But, yeah, he said there would be blood. He said there would be bone. He said there would be stool. He said there would be a slurry of fecal matter and pre-stool and blood and bone chips, and it would be like a stinky 4th of July. And he said there wouldn't be any conceivable way, even dipped in ink, that it could stain anything resembling an intact human body with anything resembling what we considered a tattoo. But he did concede that all of these fluids would possibly stamp a stain into whatever concrete floor wasn't reduced to rubble.

"You really want to know if someone could use a jackhammer for tattoos?" my doctor friend asked.

"More like tattoo removal," I said.

"More like life removal!" he laughed.

Wiping some bile from my eyes and spitting some blood from my mouth, I tried again to stand.

"I'm having a hard time following exactly what you're doing here . . ."

I said to the Mobshitters dancing around the middle of this anatomical massacre, but a shot in the teeth shut me back up. Then I was mesmerized because Jason had been cut clean in two by the tool, and the vibrations seemed to be moving those two halves out of the way of the endless hammering. I could see Cort working those fluids into the floor after all, very much like the world's biggest, ugliest tattoo. It looked like he was trying to trace the state of Kentucky, but it came out more like Hawaii. When he pulled back and wiped the strip of intestine from his grin, I saw that he had been attempting to draw the entire United States on that floor. Or maybe it was a dinosaur. Or maybe it was a United States made up entirely of Floridas or dinosaurs, kind of what you'd expect from a horde of dudes with only a passing knowledge of their home state. Rest of the map be damned! I decided that with enough tattoo removals like this one, their map would probably resemble an elephant-shitting contest more than anything. Or, you know, Florida.

Since no one could hear it, I started singing a variation of the '60s *Spider-Man* cartoon theme song to hang onto sanity.

"Florida man . . . does everything a Florida can . . ."

Then Cort switched off the jackhammer, and the rumbling revved back on down to a clock-like tick. He kicked a bit of Jason to the side and shrugged.

"The funniest thing about all this is 'Lose Lose' here should never have left that jail. He was ready to be released tomorrow!"

A man with either a tattoo of Florida or a flaccid penis across his shoulder blades laughed so hard that he doubled over and puked right into the middle of Cort's handiwork, not really affecting it in the least. I'd made it up to one knee and was thinking about bolting for the door first chance I got, but a Jobshitter with an Australian accent and either a tattoo of Florida or a broken boomerang over his trapezius shoved me back down.

"Sit still," he reminded me as Cort walked up, pink earmuffs around his neck like a fuzzy ascot.

"What'd you think?" he asked me, eyes gleaming. He dropped the jackhammer to the floor with a crash and held out a hand. Someone slapped his palm with a shotgun, and he cocked it and brought it up, not quite on me but the meaning was clear.

"You know," I said, figuring this was it. "There is a tendency for people to overdramatize their final moments before death. I wish they would understand it's virtually impossible to understate the importance of last words. I'm not going to remember what you said. You aren't going anywhere. And you couldn't take anything with you if you were."

"Well said," Cort laughed, clapping his giant hands, and I decided that must have saved me. "That would be a sneaky way to get in some powerful last words, I must admit. If I was gonna kill ya."

* * *

His arm around my neck, Cort walked me outside. He got right in my face, breathing up my nose what must have been the remnants of a squirrel-shit sandwich as he told me all his ideas. He seemed happiest when I agreed that a jackhammer should be able to make a decent tattoo, or remove one, with enough practice. He told me that a tattoo needle under a microscope looks just like a baby jackhammer and that was science, goddammit. He told me about flowers you could only grow in the Sunshine State. He told me his master plans.

"We're going to use you, I think, for a probationary period," he told me. "Gonna turn that frown upside down!"

Then he showed me his garden. I tried and failed not to look.

* * *

When he brought me back into the hanger, he said they could use all the help they could get, "straightening out the rosters." He said this was a win/win situation for everybody.

I cocked a thumb at the huge stain on the floor and said if that was a "win win," I'd hate to see a "lose lose."

Cort sighed, and I looked around for any sign of "Jason," and all I saw was his yellow sweater knotted up into a ball in the corner, the cape he'd worn over his shoulders as he walked out of jail. I realized a man with the cape didn't have any superpowers after all, or if he did, they were skills that did not include invincibility, or foresight, because he was everywhere now, as far as the eye could see, split wide open from this throat to his groin, exploded like a Thanksgiving turkey on Black Friday. Someone dragged his top half past us, and I saw there was another tattoo on his back, amateurish but huge, but comparably professional to the haphazard gutting of Cort's paint-soaked jackhammer that I'd just witnessed. It was still hard to make out through all the busted capillaries, but the artwork seemed to depict something long, sagging, surrounded by roses.

"What is that? Is that another state?"

"It's a state of mind."

I snickered.

"Don't make me plant you," Cort said, with a bit of regret in his voice. "And I do mean 'plant.'" He cocked the shotgun I hadn't forgotten. "These shells here are loaded with seeds instead of buckshot."

"You'll be pushing up daisies fer real!" someone in some gang with a stupid name shouted from his fuzzy, toothless maw.

"That was funny the first six times you said it, Snoopy," Cort yelled back. Then, to me, knocking the shotgun against his own temple, "No, not daisies. Orange blossoms, of course, our state tree. Sounds nice, I know, but it does plenty of damage just the same. At one time, we thought it might mean we didn't have to bury someone afterwards, like they'd just be some cool landscaping . . ."

Someone snickered.

"Zip it," Cort said, then back at me again. "It doesn't work as well on people. We aren't soil, as much as we try. These seeds are probably a bad idea, definitely a mistake for someone, that's for sure. But our garden's getting better. Anyhow! Why don't you get going. And remember what we talked about."

On my way out, I walked past his garden again, trying not to notice the orange flowers lining the side of the hanger, obviously daisies and not orange trees, crown-rot afflicted Gerberas, suffering from being planted too deep, but still sprouting strong from leather jackets and motorcycle helmets and twitching with the morning rain, almost perceptively straining for some elusive sunshine. I couldn't look at them for long without getting dizzy.

A shotgun blast snapped me out of it.

*   *   *

Cort and his gang sent me on to another jail, as promised, to sit outside the gate and wait for the next guy to come out, the next sorry son of a bitch to be flying the wrong colors after the flood. My job was to bring them to the abattoir behind The Bowery, an airplane hanger where there weren't any airplanes and Christmas never ended and the craziest motorcycle gangs in the land dreamed of baby jackhammers and green thumbs and sending a bouquet with a shotgun. Where the state flower was blood oranges.

IS THAT MY SANDWICH IN THERE?

The first time I ruined a movie for someone it was one of those real heavy, holiday-season, Oscar-bait crime dramas up on the screen, and the theater was packed. We wouldn't even have gone to see it, but we'd missed a plane coming back from a friend's wedding in Louisiana (the summer when there were way too many weddings) and we had four hours to kill. We walked into a cinema next door to the airport, a great money-making location that took advantage of weary layovers, and asked for two tickets to the longest piece of shit they had. Jesse tried to duck me by hiding in the bar, but I drug him reluctantly away from the local news, which turned out to be better than the movie actually. Louisiana news was crazy. They had gator alerts at the top of the hour instead of weather reports.

I barely remember the flick we watched since we only saw a third of it before the outburst, but I do know it was a murder mystery.

It happened during this scene where a frantic father is trying to break through a protective line of police to see if his daughter is the dead body inside some monkey house or reptile pit in a zoo or something. The hard-ass dad is fighting with these cops and screaming over and over, "Is that my daughter in there? Is that my daughter in there?!" And there's this pileup of about 625 uniformed cops restraining him as he screams in anguish at the sky, then the camera soars above the scene and the music swells and then . . .

Then Jesse leans over to me, almost upending my Dr. Pepper, and whispers, serious as hell:

"You know what would make that scene very different emotionally? What if instead the dad was screaming, 'Is that my sandwich in there?'"

I stared at him a minute and tried to stifle a laugh and blew snot out my nose. His comment didn't make much sense, and probably wasn't that funny, but both of us started sniggering uncontrollably, and we could actually feel the anger of the crowd rising around us like a tsunami.

If you've ever thought of a perfectly hilarious comment while watching a movie in a theater and couldn't help but share it with an auditorium full of strangers, you would have quickly realized that no one wants to hear it. No one. No matter how clever you know you were. There are few venues in the world where an outburst is less welcome. Think of it as church with arm rests, whistling through Twizzlers instead of faking the words to hymns.

But after some hateful glares and a "Shhh!" or two, we got it under control. And we were doing fine until the movie came to the scene where the father has to identify his daughter's body in the morgue. They pull back the sheet, and her face is twisted forever in a grimace of pain, and the father mutters:

"Yes, that's my daughter."

And right then, me and Jesse look at each other, both knowing we're, of course, thinking the exact same thing. Instead we had heard the manly, distraught father say, clear as day and solemn as a sermon:

"Yes, that's my sandwich."

We both lost it, barking loud laughter that made my stomach ache as if I'd dry heaved all night or did a thousand sit-ups. Angry moviegoers muttered and *tisked* and stomped out the door to demand our ejection, and we were still convulsing even as flashlight-wielding security manhandled us through the exit stage left of the screen. The sunlight that blasted onto the furious faces in those seats made everything worth it.

I still think they got lucky. Who knows what would have happened if we'd made it to the second act, to the inevitable autopsy scene where the medical examiner would start cutting a perfect diagonal line through the center of that sandwich, something any coroner or restaurant owner will tell you maximizes the exposure of the contents. If we'd made it that far into the movie, I might have shit myself holding in the giggles.

Outside we heard our plane was delayed, so we tried to eat up more of the clock by heading back to the beach. We decided it would be fun to shake sand out of our asses when the TSA put us in the airport microwaves and grabbed our balls. We never saw the kid follow us out.

*   *   *

Back on the street with the Louisiana anvil of sunshine on our shoulders, right when we could smell the Gulf of Mexico but still couldn't see it, we came across a crowd around an alligator that had wandered down the road and into a supermarket parking lot. I saw an old biddy, way too old to be wearing cowboy boots and a mini-skirt, and I asked her what was up.

"I don't know," the Biddy said. "It must have walked a mile inland. Maybe it smelled the deli counter."

"Does this happen a lot?" I asked.

"About twice a day," the Biddy shrugged, twenty bracelets crashing down to her elbows.

Me and Jesse looked at each other in shock, and she laughed.

"Just kidding, suckers! Stick around though. They'll be by to shoot it any second."

"Wait, what? They're gonna kill it?!" Jesse was horrified.

"Of course. How do you think they make boots!" she said, punctuating her point by tapping her heel on the asphalt. I chewed on my bottom lip and checked my watch. Jesse looked up and down the street, then stared at me with his hands on his hips.

Five minutes later, Jesse's in the middle of the road trying to drag an angry gator by the tail, the toothy top half of the beastie whiplashing around his feet, and I'm screaming for a cab. The cab was for me, not for Jesse and the gator. I was gonna leave both of them. I knew we were in over our heads. We'd only made it a block past the supermarket and could just barely hear the beach, but I knew we'd gone too far.

That's when the knuckles found my jaw, and I was suddenly looking straight up in the air, wondering what happened. When my vision cleared, I saw the kid. A wiry little bastard, cherry-red fists as balled up as his forehead. He grabbed my neck and I truly thought he was going to climb up my shirt and hit me again. Beak to beak, breathing in my face, I smelled it and figured it out.

Popcorn.

He'd come from the movie. The little fucker had actually followed us halfway to Last Island, angry that we'd disrupted his flick, just to punch one of us in the grill. And now he was standing on his tip-toes promising even more. He was little, and he was skinny, but his veins were out, and he clearly had a righteous cause. Sort of like Jesse. I didn't want any part of it. I turned to my friend fighting with his dinosaur.

"Trade ya?"

Jesse looked down at the hissing, snapping gator between his legs, then back at the kid.

"No way," Jesse said, and he started trying to drag it again, sweat pouring off his nose in an unbroken stream. That's when the creature locked onto his ankle, and Jesse screamed. He sat down hard, trying to kick himself loose as blood seeped through the stripes in his tube sock. I would have laughed if I didn't have my hands full.

I tried to grab the kid and calm him down, but he'd lost his shirt at some point and was about as slippery as a bar of soap. And he was punching me at will. And this kid bit, too. I watched him catch a mouthful of my tricep and thought: *He's gonna brand me for the rest of my life. I'm gonna have to tell everyone at every party all about how a kid weighing a buck 'o two kicked my ass.*

So I grabbed his face like a bowling ball, thumb in for the fish hook, middle finger in a nostril, and I flipped him onto his back. Someone in the crowd grunted their approval.

At some point, I caught a glimpse of the old biddy sitting on a speed bump with her cowboy boots off, painting her toenails, every so often glancing up and cheering for someone. I pouted as I worried it wasn't for me, and I tried harder.

But both me and Jesse were losing interest fast. It reminded me of this fight Jesse got in at graduation. How it started in the living room, went through a cheap table, down the hall, knocking over some framed Springsteen albums on the wall, then ended up in the bathroom, where Jesse's head cracked open the PVC trap under the sink. He needed six stitches, but his mom found her engagement ring. We measured the fight later. It lasted thirty feet.

This fight lasted a thousand and one.

* * *

Things we learned on vacation. Don't tug on Superman's wheelchair. Don't spit into the wind. Don't try to drag an alligator by the tail. And don't fuck with someone's movie.

No bullshit, we all made it to the beach. Miles down the road with the sun going down, and I could barely see through the sweat and the blood, but we got lucky when we all hit the sand and I caught the kid's head on one of those dog-shit stations and had the upper hand for the split second I needed. I used my weight to steamroll him while I tried to sit on his chicken arms.

"What the hell, kid?" I had time to ask.

"That was my sister in there," he said.

I still don't know what he meant. In the movie? Was that a true story? No way. I had another theory. I'd heard about violence in theaters before, and when families are broke, I truly believe that they'll attack you, even shoot your ass, for interrupting.

I've been in fights over way less than that.

Jesse's alligator had calmed down, went into some sort of reptilian shutdown. And Jesse was actually petting it with its head still locked on his ankle.

"Surf and turf!" someone was shouting nonsensically. And that's about the time we were flooded with blue uniforms. I gave some trouble to a chubby cop in a crew cut. The kid tangled up the rest of them, all the while screaming at the sky. And at some point, a zookeeper took a shot. In the papers, they swore they were aiming for the gator, but the kid took the dart square in his back, right next to my handprint.

I'm pretty sure there was a cheer from the crowd, but when I looked around I saw nothing but blue and red lights flashing in my face. Even the old woman and her red toenails were gone, and, without a crowd, I wanted to get on that plane more than anything.

I couldn't believe the dart took him down, to be honest. At that point, I fully expected the kid to catch the dart in his teeth, chew it up, then swallow.

Later that night, we sat on a curb under the streetlights, answering the same questions with the same answers, never to anyone's satisfaction, watching the Keystone Cops and paramedics work on the kid in vain. When we were finally free to go, I was surprised they didn't load the comatose gator into the ambulance by mistake.

*   *   *

Me and Jesse sat on the red-eye (more like the "red-ass"), slumped as low in our seat as the stewardess would allow, painful sand working its way into the rivers of cuts on our jaw lines, chins, elbows, and backsides, as we both thought about our respective battles. At least I know I did. I hoped Jesse at least was worried about that gator ending up as boots, because he had it easy. Me, I was faced with one undeniable truth:

I had fucked with some kid's movie, and it had stopped his heart.

The movie on the plane was terrible, but we didn't say a word.

FORCED PERSPECTIVE

Like most American boys, my brother's injuries start in the garage. What begins innocently enough as a refuge from hot summer days with a promise of shade, cool, and concrete floors, usually ends up an obstacle course of cuts and contusions. And for one of his most dramatic injuries in our garage, we were barely inside it. Half in, half out, which might be all the proof you need that a garage is the most dangerous place on the planet if just the door can mess you up. If I get time, I'll tell you about when I tried to help someone cut down the swing door on an airplane hanger with a chainsaw, and how the spring unsprung and the spring block exploded, almost cutting me in half. I was in a doorway then, too.

But my brother's garage-door incident started with us getting chased home from the "mudpit," this milky, borderline-stagnant pond where we went fishing for Bluegill before, after, sometimes during school. It was filthy, but the only place to fish in Millbury, Ohio. And our grandma had made us a deal, a dollar for anything bigger than our hands. So we'd been pulling them out of the pond for her to fry up for our lunches when all the sudden these older kids in a jacked-up 4x4 were tearing after us on our bikes. It was after one of us made some smartass comment (hint: it wasn't my brother). They'd slowed down the truck to ask if we'd caught anything, and we'd gotten so good at it, it felt like a trick question, and I said as much. That day, in fact, we'd caught seventeen Bluegill total, maybe ten of them too small to eat, but they were all crowded in a bucket of pond water until we could make sure. And we were fishing with our fingers, too. I know, *all* fishing is with some fingers, but we just had fishing line tied to our thumbs, near the knuckle and the bottom of the thumbnail, where it didn't start cutting into our skin as fast. On the ends of our lines were some barbed Eagle Claw hooks, before the backlash against barbs. They were the bait-holder-style hooks, with thorns up the sides like a rose stem. We were putting wet balls of Wonder Bread on the hooks, so we didn't have much use for bait-holders, and we mistook those thorns for extra traction on the fish lips. But like I said, it didn't matter what we were using. That pond was shallow and stinky but teeming with Bluegill, and snapping turtles, who must have eaten more

Bluegill than we did. These were the only two creatures we ever saw at the mudpit, but there wasn't any money in the turtles.

So seventeen fish were in the bucket when the chase started, splashing and jockeying for oxygen. I don't remember what I said, or even when we pulled the fishing line off our thumbs. The next thing I knew, we were just flying down the road with a truck weaving and honking behind us. Since I had the shittier bike with no seat, I learned to pedal much faster that my brother, and I got back to our house first. I skidded into the driveway and glanced back to see my brother taking the last turn onto our street so fast his knees were knocking against his handlebars, his pedals a whirling dervish so dangerous that his feet were hovering up and out of the way. I dismounted with the grace of a gymnast and let my bike hit the wall of the garage, leaving a black streak of rubber across the furnace. In a panic, I remembered we were home alone, and I started pulling down the garage door as fast as I could. Right then, my brother came flying down our driveway at Mach 3, feet unsuccessfully trying to get back onto the blur of pedals to stop himself and *bang!* The garage door caught him in the top of the head and scraped him off his bike as quick and efficient as a boot decapitating a dandelion.

His bicycle, now blind, got one good bite on me, a fender clipping me hard in the shin and slicing off a triangle of meat. My brother was down, I was down, and his bike was running up my chest like a slobbering dog greeting you at the door, its front wheel still spinning in my face. The 4x4 rumbled up to the edge of our driveway, and a greasy-faced teen leaned out to survey the scene of me wrestling a bike and my brother splayed out Christ-like in the gravel.

"Oh, shit, he's dead," he laughed. Then the truck was gone with a roar. My brother woke up before the wheels of his bike stopped spinning, and he ran past me into the house screaming his head off. I don't remember who got in trouble for the crack in the garage door or the dent in the furnace, and nobody noticed the gash in my shin. It should have received a handful of stitches, but everyone was too worried about my brother's possible concussion with a football game coming up on Friday. For days, I dreamed of fishing line around my thumbs, strangling the kids from the 4x4 like an assassin with piano wire.

He lost the football game, but there's still a scar on my leg. And for about a week, what I thought about most from that day was the smell of that bike tire an inch from my nose and the tiny nipples of rubber on the tread that I'd never noticed before. Then we went back to the mudpit and saw the bucket where we'd left the Bluegills to die, tilted on a broken slab of concrete, water on all sides, and now a year rarely passes where I don't regret not dumping out those fish. My brother still swears he was the one who pulled the door down on me, but unconsciousness can make you an unreliable narrator.

*　*　*

When I dropped her off at her apartment, we sat in my Volkswagen Rabbit while she made some calls on her TV-dinner-sized phone to make sure this show was definitely going down. We called it the Walleye Derp, our name for the Walleye Drop, or Walleye Midnight Madness, a New Year's festival in nearby Port Clinton where fishing tournament trophies were handed out, and where a gigantic, sparkling fiberglass fish was dropped from a crane, similar to the New Year's Eve ceremony in Times Square. Well, as close as they could get to it anyway. So instead of a disco ball dropping at midnight, this fiberglass monstrosity would bust open on the ground and dump out hundreds of pounds of Swedish Fish candy, or so we were told.

My rusted car door shrieked when Jenny opened it to leave, and I watched her take out a penny and drop it into a cracked seam in the metal near the passenger's side window crank. It rattled around inside my car door like a piggy bank, and I laughed.

"What was that for?"

"Remind me to tell you a story later."

"Oh, okay?" I said, a little worried she was gonna break up with me again, and I watched her walk off, unable to shake the idea that something was wrong. I reached across the passenger's seat and shook the door, trying to rattle the penny loose. Unsuccessful, I didn't get much sleep that night, but we got to the Walleye Derp early. Like so early I was convinced the whole thing was an elaborate prank, but then five hours later, people started setting up the porta-potties along the river, and about an hour after that, a tent was erected for the band, so with toilets and music in place, I knew we were in business. Watching the crowd grow, then queue up to urinate, it felt a bit like a live-action version of the Monty Hall Problem, trying to avoid the goat as I went door to door, finding most locked and occupied. Finally inside one toward the end, the antiseptic smells of cleaners assaulting my nose, I was mesmerized by the voices surrounding me. Maybe I'd never been in one of these porta-johns when there wasn't some noisy concert or festival-type situation, so it's possible I never knew the little mesh half-windows on either side of my head projected all the conversations right down the line, amplified right into my ears like I was a bug crawling around some soup-can telephones during a conference call. I urinated fast, then stood there to listen in. I heard someone on the phone mad about missing the fish drop the year before. Never again, he said.

I looked out the right mesh and saw a conversation happening between two porta-potties on that side, at least four people down the row. The sound was so distinct, I could even hear the echoes of their urine in the plastic pans. Once, Jenny and I had visited C.O.S.I., the now-defunct science center twenty minutes away in Toledo, along the Maumee river, and they had a couple giant plastic satellite dishes about 50 feet apart where you could stand with the curve of the dish behind you and have a quiet conversation. Only our conversation turned into an argument, something about the social responsibility of an artist. I can't remember exactly, except that it echoed in my skull like we were screaming in a bucket.

That night, after dozens of men tried to get the most deceptive forced-perspective shots of their tournament-winning Walleye, and after the giant fiberglass fish was dropped but no one heard it hit the ground, we drove home with Jenny's legs up on my dashboard. She lined her feet up with her previous footprints on my windshield.

"What were you going to tell me about again?" I asked after I leaned over to breathe her in, all the sweat and sun trapped in the baby hairs of her arms.

"What?"

"You said to remind you to tell me something. When you put money in my car door."

She looked at me, considering, then sighed.

"Okay, so, I knew this kid who had this cracked piece on the inside panel of his door, kind of like yours, and it made this slot that was perfect for change, like pennies or whatever. It was a great way to save money, basically. And any time he'd stop at a drive-through and get change back, rather than dropping it into the jar to save cats or orphans, he's drop it into the hole in his door. But eventually, his door starts making jangling sounds, and rattling real loud when he takes hard turns . . ."

"Then what happened?"

"Nothing. He had a car full of money?" she shrugged, then reached into her pocket for a handful of change. She started feeding the coins into the slot on my door, one after the other, all of them rattling to the bottom.

"Whoa, whoa, wait a minute," I said. "Didn't it throw his car off balance?"

"What? Shut up."

I leaned back in my seat and cracked my neck on the headrest, searching my mind for a story from my past that would impress her, but the accident with the garage-door spring hadn't happened yet, and she was already halfway out the door. And as my brother could tell you, halfway in or out was the most dangerous place to be.

She blew a drip of sweat off her nose and smiled, then dropped her last penny into my car door.

* * *

Back in high school, I picked a fight with this dim-witted asshole everyone called "Squeegee." He got that nickname back in third grade when the bus driver caught him writing a bunch of profanity on the bus windows with his bad breath and knobby fingers. He was a hero at the time, especially when the driver had the principal meet our bus at the curb and march Squeegee into the building with all the gravity of a *Dead Man Walking* situation. But by the time he got to 9th grade, he was a bully and a monster, and one day Squeegee was taking too long at the water fountain and I said, "You want to practice sucking on something else and give somebody else a turn?" It wasn't my best joke ever, but at least I remembered it, unlike the crack at the mudpit that knocked my brother out, and there was a line of kids behind us who appreciated it enough to start hooting. So ol' Squeegee leaned in and told me to meet him behind the dugout at 8:00 that night so he could kick my ass. None of my friends heard Squeegee name the arena, but word got out, and they wanted to come and help me out, since everyone hated Squeegee, too. But right before my mouth formed the words to tell them to meet at the dugout, I got the bright idea to send them to a church parking lot instead. I wanted to take out Squeegee myself, and figured I'd be a legend after that bit of misdirection. So at 8:00 that night, my friends went to the church parking lot while Squeegee beat me half to death behind the dugout, and for years afterwards, I never lived it down, constantly getting wrong directions from my friends every chance they got. But I felt like my friends were a little impressed, even though they'd never admit it. But that didn't matter as much as the fact that I was impressed I'd gone through with it. Until my brother told me he'd followed me to the dugout and watched the whole thing from the bleachers. When I asked why he didn't help me out, he said his seats were too good.

I hated him for awhile, but then I'd think about the fish, and how five more Bluegill might have been enough for the bucket to tip over on its own. Or five more dollars in change.

I was lucky enough to run into Jenny while I still had scabs from the fight, and I told her about the dugout and the misdirection, and I watched her tune out completely. I heard myself telling the whole story anyway, going through the motions, but all the while thinking about the bowerbirds we learned about together in the Australian exhibit at C.O.S.I. How the video showed us the male of the species building this crazy tunnel of sticks, lined by an even more complicated avenue of rocks, with smaller rocks toward the front, and larger rocks toward the back, which he utilized to entice a mate. It was the only creature in the animal kingdom that messed with perspective to trick the female. But what we found most interesting was that this bird seemed to do all this work in order to appear smaller. It perpetuated its species and won the day with a show of weakness. Which is how it should be.

As she walked away, I thought about forced-perspective photos in trophy fishing and how I tried to get Jenny to take a picture of me at the Walleye Drop, my hand in the foreground, pretending to hold the giant fiberglass fish behind me. She wouldn't do it. At the time, she was too disappointed that it wasn't full of candy. Or that it never exploded on the ground.

*   *   *

My brother got hurt a lot more than me, or at least it seemed like it with all the attention. A lot of them were my fault though, and for awhile it seemed like I was chipping his teeth every week. It was only twice, but it was the same front tooth. The first accident involved a Nerf football and an Etch-A-Sketch. Remember those? Two dials, silver sand, and an invisible needle that drew on the inside of the glass screen like a Flintstones dinosaur toiling inside a tiny television. In case you ever wondered, there are all sorts of things waiting to be discovered when you crack open this amazing toy with a hammer in your father's garage. Like it stops working.

So, my brother was lying on the bed playing with this thing over his head, and I casually threw the Nerf football at him as hard as I could. The Etch-A-Sketch flew from his hands and bashed him full in the mouth. And after a couple seconds of silent bleeding, he tore screaming down the stairs, lips and mouth gushing. I know I got in trouble for that one, but less because of the tooth and more because I used the toy to scrawl "Aaaaargh!" on the screen, then tried to convince everyone this was the last thing he wrote on impact.

Accident number two. Days after he got his tooth fixed, with all of us kids jealous of his fang-like shard, we were skating on the neighbor's frozen yard when my brother wiped out trying to skate backwards and busted that same tooth all over again. Remember how I said our pond sucked? Yeah, imagine how bad it had to be if we preferred to skate on frozen lawns.

So now that I think about it, I didn't have much to do with his broken tooth that second time around, because that day I was too busy at the other end of the neighbor's frozen field, on my hands and knees with one skate off my foot and in my hand, chopping at the ice. I was oblivious to my wet sock growing heavier and heavier, soaking up all the snow and mud around my numb foot like a magnet, because I could see this fish just under the ice and I needed to hack my way down to it. For some reason, I thought setting it free into the winter air would save it. Or maybe I was going to rush it home to the toilet for rejuvenation. Either way, I was baffled. How could a fish freeze into someone's backyard? I had to have it.

It was a Crappie—I could see the spots—and I did chop it free with my skate, at the cost of half the fish's tail and a series of deep gashes across the top of my own wrist. When I got home to show my mom this miracle, she shoved me out of the way, the long phone cord wrapped around her neck as she screamed into the receiver at my father, telling him what I'd done to my brother "this time." I turned to see him sitting at the kitchen table with his hockey stick over one shoulder like a soldier, mouth swimming in blood. I walked past him and ran my wrist and the tail under the faucet and wondered how many fish lived in our yards. How many fish hid in our high grass all summer? The yards in our neighborhood were in a constant state of flooding, and you'd have thought we lived in a South Korean rice paddy instead of a Northwest Ohio suburb, but this field had only been frozen for a week. And it had just snowed the week before that. I started to wonder if any puddle sat long enough, would something be swimming in there when you looked away. After the fish in the field, I didn't feel as guilty about the ones we left behind. And this might have nothing to do with anything, but whenever I put a bucket under a leak in a ceiling, I have no problem leaving it overnight, even in the garage. But I rarely look inside.

TURTLE CAKE

At the funeral reception, Bolita Ramirez rocked and kicked the child's swing around and around some lazy figure-eights, letting her feet drag every fifth spin or so to keep her orbit just slow enough to seem distraught if the backyard full of mourners noticed. Most of the children were gathered around the plastic playground with her, particularly ones the same age as the deceased and therefore much more likely to talk freely about his short life and lack of legacy. Boli felt something like a kinship to 9-year-olds, as she understood the difficulty of imitating rational adult behavior the minute she became one.

She was laying low because the boy they'd buried that morning had died in a car crash that was collateral damage from Boli's latest crusade against wanton roadkill. The boy had been thrown from a car that had swerved to hit one of Boli's "turtles," a counterfeit Carolina Terrapene she'd crafted from cereal bowls, spray paint, a gutted Pound Puppy, and a bit of garden hose which, when compressed by a car tire, revealed a porcupine of carpenter nails almost guaranteed to result in a blowout. Any accident afterward was a bonus.

Boli had originally started her project with a World War II helmet her boyfriend had scavenged from an Army Surplus. She had this thing about vets lately, and he swore he was headed for veterinarian school once he shook off all that National Guard bullshit. But she quickly discovered they just didn't make things like they used to (or make cereal bowls like they used to make steel infantry helmets anyway), because even an 18-wheeler couldn't crush the cannon fodder of her box-turtle infantry. Colanders and popcorn bowls were too big, too, even though the popcorn seemed especially appropriate for the suspense of waiting in the bushes for the trap to spring. But there was something about any turtle bigger than a breakfast bowl that made people start worrying about their tires, and they wouldn't take that bait. Indeed, during her research, she'd read news reports of turtle shells piercing the white walls of some Lincoln when the driver exercised his God-given right to flex his *Great Santini* Syndrome ("It takes a mighty brave man to run over turtles!"). But a normal cereal bowl was the porridge that was *finally* just right, spot-on dimensions of the familiar box turtle, the perfect target that sadists steered towards on the highway the vast majority of the time.

Her new boyfriend, fresh home from Afghanistan, was no stranger to funerals, of course, but he wouldn't come near this one, and for good reason. He was feeling way too guilty about what they'd done, even though it was technically his idea to begin with. Okay, it was more about the day she saw that creature lying burst open next to his mailbox, where her letters had piled up unread, bloody string of intestine and Ping Pong balls trailing off into the gutter. And maybe she suspected he squashed it, but everyone blamed the mailman for everything. None of these things mattered. Her projects would always get complicated, intentions forever blurred in favor of effect, but they were always completed, too.

It was the cat that really set her off though. Her new guy had this cat, an obese calico with markings very similar to a turtle, but dimensions more similar to a cake. Once, Bolita tried to balance some candles on Turtle Cake's back, and the cat wasn't burned too badly really, as the candles fell off before anyone had a chance to blow them out. But after this incident, there was just no getting that image out of her head—cat, turtle, pancake, porcupine, birthday parties, or whatever-the-hell combination—but always with all those burning candles sticking up out of its shell. This image sort of morphed into a daydream, then smack dab back into fantasy, where she imagined evolution finally gifting mankind a turtle that could safely flatten out under compression, rather than die squirting out a streamer of omelets. Instead, drivers would get a bevy of secret spikes that would punish any bastard who purposely swerved to run over some poor critter. And her imagination and fat-cat wrangling led to that fabled *ding!* of a light bulb over her head. Well, maybe more like a *boom!* really, but definitely the blowout she was looking for.

A girl half Boli's age, but still twice her height, joined her on the swings, and it didn't take Boli long to get her talking about the dead kid in the box. Nose twitching in excitement, she told Boli how he'd led a terrible, but unremarkable life. He'd lied, bent stuff, broke stuff, stole stuff, in general put his filthy fingers where he wasn't supposed to, and Bolita felt a lot better and didn't drag her feet on the swing quite so much. She may have been happier if the driver who'd swerved to crush her precious turtle bomb had been the one who flew through the windshield instead, his neck snapping somewhere along that journey and ending up dead with bare feet swinging those lazy figure-eights in the willow tree and inspiring at least one internet-famous photograph, but justice was an imperfect science. Eggs got broke making omelets and all that.

She swung faster and faster on the plastic swing, black shiny shoes tapping the clouds now instead of the stones. She didn't feel bad at all anymore, not that she ever did, but this would surely put her new guy's mind at ease. And now she was confident they could step things up very soon. A relationship had to move forward, right? This was the real reason behind any funeral reception—good attendance cleared consciences. She knew that soon she could ask her new guy to take the next step, and she smiled as she imagined him pacing his half-empty apartment right now, memorizing recipes for homemade explosives, mostly forgetting about that leg he'd left in the teeth of an I.E.D. in Panjshir Province.

There on a rusty swing set that was about two more summers from disintegration, munching on funeral shrimp and thinking of her new guy, she realized only a psychotic hopes for a car wreck when someone runs over reptiles. Certainly there was room for improvement here. Personal growth. Wouldn't the driver's survival be favorable? So they'd learn something? Maybe, but if the crash also left someone with a loss of limbs and a more turtle-like appearance? Even better. This was something to shoot for.

She'd start working on a more lethal birthday cake when she got home. Something more like the mechanical roadkill that ate her new guy's leg for dessert in a desert halfway across the planet, where nobody swerved at anything for fun. Now that would be a turtle to reckon with when it got pancaked. The rabbits could still win all the races, but they'd fucking pay for it.

SHARKS WITH THUMBS

*"The fly sat upon the axle-tree of the chariot-wheel and said,
'What a dust do I raise!'"* —Aesop

You ever get the feeling someone is talking about you?

Like you're right at the end of the movie when the speaker starts popping and you hear that voice. Like once a week, right when you're finally starting to relax around this spider web of power cords and surge protectors, you're reminded you can never trust the wiring around here. Never move somewhere just because you like seeing a river out your window.

Remember when a nearby lightning strike fried something inside your picture tube and put a freaky green line through the middle of your screen? That green line was there for about six months, mercifully getting smaller and smaller and almost fading away until it was just a glowing yellow smear in the corner of the TV, like you'd smashed a lightning bug on the glass and never cleaned it up. You don't know if this room is some sort of electric Bermuda Triangle, not the game but the real thing, but you can't risk any more equipment. That's why you move fast whenever you hear a speaker snap, crackle or pop.

You're ready to pull the plug when suddenly you're hearing two voices from the speaker that aren't part of the movie. You know this because the movie was at the end, right at the part where everyone gets what they deserve, and all you should be hearing is gunfire, one-liners and big, dumb music. However, this whispered conversation is something you'd hear in the middle of a flick, maybe the beginning, when you're not sure what the characters are really up to and you're supposed to be all suspicious of everyone.

The sad thing is he has no idea I hate his guts.

You sit down by the speaker, actually thinking about getting a glass to put between the television and your ear to hear the voices better.

Remember his last story? Even the goddamn dog was rolling his eyes.

You adjust your legs to get comfortable, hoping the reception lasts a while. You know the "hearing voices" thing is supposed to make you nervous, but it happens in this building sometimes. A couple times, a year back, when your surround-sound speakers were still working, you picked up some random banter between truckers. It's the bad wiring that does it. Sometimes, you'll suddenly get three more people in the middle of your phone call, and you'll find yourself answering a question about the first time you stuck a finger up someone's ass instead of answering your grandpa's question about car insurance.

But those fractured conversations lasted a minute at the most, and they were nowhere near as clear as this. This is like you're holding the tomato cans between two people, but their strings are coming out both of your ears.

If that bastard had any idea what people say about him . . .

Right then, the speaker crackles and the voices are buried under static. You lean in closer and bang your head on the glass. There's a final *POP!* and you yank the cord from the wall. You sit with your back to the TV, feeling the electricity tickle your neck as both you and the equipment power down. You reel in the cord, wrapping it around your knuckles, working to bend the prongs straight. You hold your breath when you plug it back in. Thank Christ it still works. You stare at the green stain in the corner of the picture. It's back, but it doesn't bother you. You'd watch TV if the whole screen was green. Nothing happens in the corners of a movie anyway. A green sunset in this Western? The gunfighters wouldn't even notice.

00:00:03:57—"Love Without a Life Jacket."

When you claim there's a long list of things about her that used to drive you nuts, you're not talking about a sheet of paper, or even a stack of paper with both sides filled plus illustrations in the margin and a flip-cartoon in the corner to reenact the top ten, you're talking about the kind of list where you could stand at the top of the stairs and you let the pages drop and they bounce down the steps and unroll out the door and down the hill and across the street and over the cars and stray dogs are crashing through it like a finish line. That's how long your list is. And at the top of that list? Surprisingly, it's not how shrill her voice gets when she gets drunk. It would have to be the way she used to walk into the bathroom to use the phone. It drove you crazy. Well, maybe not *crazy* crazy, but crazy enough to ruin your day. Crazy enough to think about the word "crazy" until it renders the word meaningless. Luckily, that's one thing you don't have to worry about any more.

This new girl though? Sometimes she stares right at you, even when she's not on the phone. And she lets you listen to even her most embarrassing conversations. And she's never turning the volume down on the receiver in case the caller says something you shouldn't hear. She's never pressing the phone hard against her head, so afraid a secret would sneak out while she was talking. So hard her ear looks like a ripe tomato slice when she finally snaps the phone shut. This new girl though? She's got nothing to hide. Probably doesn't even own a phone. She's in the bathroom right now, and you trust her so much you're not even turning down the volume on the TV to listen to her piss.

Then the toilet flushes once, twice, and chokes on a third attempt. She walks back into the room, then slides down to her hip in a quick motion that would make any gunfighter shake in his boots. Your smile slips when you see her phone drop into her pocket.

"I thought you drowned," you tell her.

00:00:28:09—"Bugs Cannot Use Tools."

It's too cold to have a fly on the window, on either side of the glass. There's no leaves on trees. The birds are long gone. The morning before, you had to dig your car out from under the wake of a snowplow with red fingers. There's nothing alive outside without fur, nothing alive out there smaller than a rat, because you brought your rat inside with you.

But there it is.

One of those big, blue-eyed garbage flies, crawling around the edges of the glass like it was summer out there, like there isn't a kid kicking the head off a snowman two houses down. In a daze, you pull the black tape off the window, taking some of the paint with it, knowing it's going to take another hour to seal that window back up. You yank it up with a grunt, cold air freezing the snot in your nose.

It's the first time you've ever seen one trying to get in instead of out.

What the hell do you feed it? Usually, you're trying to stop a fly from drinking off the edge of your pop can instead of keeping it alive. So you just stand back and let it ricochet off the walls like a drunk hoping it'll find a stray cornflake or damp toenail to munch on. You watch it circle the room about six more times, increasingly confused by its behavior, cruising frantic figure-eights about a foot from the ceiling. Finally, you grab a stuffed animal still upside down in a corner from three ex-girlfriends ago and chase it toward the bathroom. If you're going to have a pet fly it should be near the bowl, right? You're a pretty clean person, but you figure if there's anything around this place a fly can eat, it's going to be in there. Shit, cats and dogs get water bowls, don't they? You consider writing the name "Spike" on the side of your toilet.

00:00:42:31—"You're Gonna Eat *What* Exactly?"

The next day, your new girl comes over to watch a movie. Halfway through, the speakers start popping again, and while you're screwing with the wires in the back of the box, she sighs and runs to the bathroom, and suddenly you're listening to her piss even though she's a hundred feet and a closed door away. It's splashing so loud you flinch and think she squatted down over your head, and that's when you remember the fly.

Same old shit, you know? Why do I even come over here?

The voice is fading, so you crawl over to your bookbag and pull out your headphones. Several books tumble onto the ground, but you don't retrieve them. The ones that land face-up are: *If They Move . . . Kill 'Em!: The Life and Times of Sam Peckinpah* by David Weddle, *Motherless Brooklyn* by Jonathan Lethem, and *Choose Your Own Adventure #2: Journey Under the Sea* by R.A. Montgomery. You don't have time to imagine the significance of those selections and you quickly try plugging the headphones directly into the TV and get zapped with static instead. Like a fool, you sit there, with the headphones unplugged and dangling, still listening for the voices. The headphones are new. They're the kind that go in your ears instead of over them, sometimes too deep, the kind that you might lose in your head if you scratch too hard. Like you always do. And just like they always told you would happen when people are talking shit, your ears really do start burning.

I have to go watch the rest of this horrible movie, if he ever gets it to work . . .

You're so excited about hearing someone's voice through unplugged headphones that, at first, you don't care what she's saying. It's not like the truckers you heard through the speakers before. This time you can only hear one side of the conversation. Her voice is a non-stop sigh, like the endless hiss of a tire valve.

Maybe I'll pretend I'm sick.

Then the toilet flushes, and it's as loud as a cyclone. You grab the sides of the TV in case you start spinning around a drain and get sucked on down. You're so wired about this discovery that you're smiling like a maniac when she comes out, struggling to keep your new eavesdropping skills to yourself. By the time you finish the Western, you realize it's not just the headphones. The fly was in there with her. Always the fly.

. . . the first time I've ever seen one trying to get in instead of out . . .

00:01:34:07—"Spiders Are Not Our Friends."

After she's gone home, you're thinking you should call NASA or whatever government office deals with the physical manifestation of metaphors. Or, at the very least, spy on about ten more people you suspect are talking shit about you. You're already making a mental list and considering how you might propose marriage to her when you go back into the bathroom.

The fly is dying. At least, it's moving slower. Your eyes follow its sluggish path until it vanishes into a crack in the porcelain box behind the toilet. You panic and shove the clock radio and empty box of tissues onto the floor and take off the lid, shaking your head in disbelief as you look inside. Impossible.

The fly is caught in a spider web, flailing like a drunk trying to navigate beaded curtains at a party. Spiders in the toilets? Flies in the snow? You wonder what's next.

Suddenly, you know what to do. You stick it outside the bathroom window still glued to a tangle of web, and, just as you hoped, the cold air seems to revive it. It's moving fast again, but it never gets back to full speed. It's not going to last much longer. You check the clock radio on the bathroom floor to try and estimate how much time the fly has left. The display is flashing a green "12:00 a.m." since you never figured out how to set it. Now you've got two problems. A time limit, you're not good with math, *and* you can't get everyone into your bathroom to spy on them.

Staring at the word "Spike" on the bowl, you decide you should take your fly for a walk. Once, your grandpa told you he used to stick flies to his fingers with honey when he was a boy.

"We were bored as hell back then," he said, "Now, don't think I'm reminiscing so I can tell you how it built character or any noble shit like that 'cause the only thing playing with flies does is make you wish you had toys instead."

He told you his flies didn't fly too long because he always smacked them just a little bit too hard to slow them down, sort of like your grandma did to you.

Yours won't last long either, you realize, and you have to move faster than you're moving. You look around the bathroom, find some dental floss the last girl left behind. You have no trouble grabbing it out of the air, and it's still sluggish enough to tie a leash around its body without risking a swat to stun it, but the floss is too thick for a knot. You look around and around and around, and finally your eyes stop on the answer stuck to the side of your toilet, underlining your pet fly's new name. You crouch down to get closer.

All this time you thought it was a crack in the porcelain, but it's a long, black hair stuck to the moisture on the side of the bowl. You peel it loose and hold it up to the window. Black. Thick. Curly as phone cord. One of hers. You half-expect it to twitch like a severed spider's leg, and even though it's just a hair, even though you haven't cleaned the bathroom since she left, you're amazed to find a piece of her still here. You'd be less surprised to find a five-foot-five layer of skin she'd shed, rustling and drying in a corner.

You tie the leash quick. Too easily. You decide it's because you had one of your hands buried in her hair for so many years that when they're not connected to her head any more they still know your fingers, and sometimes you can still get them to do what you want.

The fly grabs her hair and starts stroking it with two front legs. Does that damn thing have thumbs, you wonder?

Impossible. If bugs had tiny thumbs, they would have already invented a tiny wheel.

You tie it to your finger where the skin is still white from the ring she gave you, then you put on headphones plugged into nothing, a power cord dangling down and tucked into a belt-loop. You start your day.

00:01:09:13—"Bringing a Fly to a Fist Fight."

You're out the door looking at your watch, and you see it's time for free doughnuts. The gas station makes new ones and throws out the old ones at exactly 8:00 every day. They're always real cool about giving you those old doughnuts, but you got to time it just right. The fly tugs on its leash, circling your ring finger, then resigning to wrap itself around the steering wheel. You worry about a sudden turn breaking the leash, so you pull over and carefully unwind the hair without breaking it, thinking about the old Westerns your grandpa used to make you watch, and the way the cowboys made their horse stay put by dropping a leather strap across a bush or twig without even tying it up or anything.

Inside the gas station, the girl behind the counter smiles, and you grab one of each kind of doughnut before the kid can slide them into the trash. He sighs and waits for you to drop them into your bag, then quickly clears the case. You take longer than usual because you're trying to keep one hand behind your back. You don't know what would be worse, someone thinking that flies follow you around, or someone seeing that you keep one on a tiny little leash.

When she's counting the cigarettes behind her, you tie the fly to a bag of peanuts near the cash register, not really tying a knot, just winding the hair around the peanuts once, knowing it will stay, then you run out to pump your gas.

Inside, you see the girl at the counter talking to the next guy in line and he throws a thumb your way. You quickly pull the headphones from inside your shirt and pop them in to see if this guy is talking shit. Amazingly, he isn't. But she is.

He just tries to act like he had no idea they were free even though he was in here last night . . .

Your head down, you run in and grab your fly. For the first time since you started going there, she talks to you.

"You paying for those peanuts, asshole?"

You stop at the post office and check the stamp machines in the lobby. Just as you hoped, there's a wagging tongue of five three-cent stamps sticking out. You tear them free and put them in your pocket. Ever since the price of stamps went up, people usually leave the difference behind. Every little bit helps. It helps you stay on the periphery of responsibility but also feel like you have a job. For some reason, this feels like integrity.

The girl behind the counter smiles and waves as you leave.

He doesn't have three cents?

What the hell? You scratch your ears hard to see if the voice goes away. You scratch harder. If you could scratch your ears with your foot, you would. You don't understand. The headphones are around your wrist. The fly isn't anywhere near her. And neither are you. How is this happening?

You stick to your routine. You go to the diner. Are there females behind every counter? Do they grow them back there, just out of sight, ten more rising up behind every register, and you can't see them just yet because they haven't grown high enough for their heads to clear the cash drawer.

The waitress has a pencil shaped like a tiny pool cue. You stare at it, hypnotized, every time she takes your order. You asked her about it once, but she ignored you. Tonight is no different.

"Excuse me," you say. "There is a fly in my soup . . ."

She looks down at the fly tugging against its leash on your finger.

". . . and I think the little bastard just lassoed me."

She wanders away, a miraculous combination of expressions on her face that you didn't think was possible. You stop in the restroom on the way out. In the urinal, just above the line-of-fire, there's a sticker that declares: "You hold in your hand the power to stop a rape!" For a second, you think the sign refers to the fly crawling across your knuckles, and you're suddenly ashamed. "Is it so wrong to be a fly whisperer?" you want to ask the urinal cake. When you're zipping up, one headphone falls from your left ear and plops into the yellow water. You sigh, pull the rest of the wires out of your shirt and toss them all in with it. Your obsessions have their limits.

You stop at the garage to get air for your tires. Your VW Rabbit's always had this problem, but new tires are expensive, and if you find the right gas stations, air is free. This garage is one of the only places in town where you don't have to pay fifty cents to fill them up, and the guy who owns the place gives you a knowing smile and the better part of a wave. You wave back whole-heartedly and accidentally bounce your fly off your forehead. He's cool. The last time you stopped by, this man smiled and agreed that paying for air was "freaking ridiculous."

You get out, tie the fly to the compressor, snake the hose, hit the button.

How fucking low do you have to be to steal air . . . c'mon.

Was that a woman's voice? You thought it was all men in that garage. Could it be a girl from one of your earlier stops? What kind of reception does this fly get, anyway?

I heard of someone stealing dirt once, only that was from a construction site and that shit ain't cheap. But air? Nope. Never heard of anyone stealing air.

The compressor stops rumbling. Your fly strains on its leash, then curls back to land on a coil of hose.

I've heard of people stealing water once, but that was during the war.

You throw the hose. 29 pounds of pressure will have to do. In your tires and your brain.

Honestly, who the hell steals air . . .

You can't contain your rage any longer. You yell at the shadows in the garage.

"Well, who the hell *sells* air?!"

Two mechanics slide out from under their cars and into the sunlight. They stand and walk toward you, wiping grease from fists, blowing sweat off noses, staring at you like you're nuts.

00:01:45:22—"Fly Factory Revealed."

Do you ever get the feeling someone is talking shit about you?

You stop at the video store to steal some movie inserts. You do this because those throwaway pieces of paper in DVDs really are great reading. Sure, sometimes you get a paragraph of summary or some decent production notes or an interview, but that's not what you're looking for. You steal the inserts because you like to read the chapter titles. It's like a whole movie in ten seconds. The chapter titles tell you all you need to know.

You grab a random one as if to prove your point. Okay maybe not so random. You've read this one before:

Sharks with Guns

- "Love on a Lifeboat"
- "Sharks Are Using Tools?"
- "Are You Gonna Eat That?"
- "Dolphins Are Not Our Friends!"
- "Bringing a Shark to a Gun Fight"
- "Shark Factory Revealed!"
- "Duel to the Deaf"
- "Quitting the Coast Guard for Good"

See? What are you missing from the story after you read that? It's all there. The crisis, the love interest, the surprise ending. Didn't someone once say there are really only three stories you can tell? A stranger comes to town, and a man goes on a journey? Man sort of talks to fly?

You study the box and snicker. It's one of those pre-fab cult movies that are so popular these days, and you scoff. There's no way that shark could hold that chainsaw, much less a gun. They don't have any thumbs.

Now that would be a scary movie, you think. If they had thumbs, they could make a phone call, like a cat or a car. It wouldn't have to bite anyone anymore. Just show one shark whip out a phone and every asshole in the audience would start screaming their head off.

Could happen. You've seen more far-fetched things than that in a movie. One time, in the bathtub, your ex-girlfriend checked her phone underwater so you couldn't see who called her. You figured she'd ruined it, but it turned out the phone worked fine when you blew the bubbles off of it later that night to find the number she was hiding.

You slip some DVD booklets into your sleeves. You avoid the Blu-rays since they rarely have them. Then you go up to the counter and grab one of those free internet CDs. She *is* up there, and you see a strange light flickering in her eyes and realize this girl is watching something under the register with the volume turned down. You wonder when she snuck a TV in there and now you have to know what movie she's watching. Is she watching something she's not supposed to? Why else would she have the volume down like that?

On the way out, you finally see what it is. A security monitor. She was watching you steal those movie inserts the entire time, and you can see yourself in the corner of her screen, standing by the door, hunched and alone, unbelievably small, looking over her shoulder, guilty as hell and green as the sunset.

Sitting in the car with your hands on the steering wheel, your heart jumps. The fly is dangling on the hair like a suicide, so you turn on the air-conditioning, open all the vents, and hold it in front of the cold air. It starts to climb back up its leash like a spider. It's moving slow, but it's still alive. You realize that every time you hide the fly, it starts to die.

Sounds like a children's rhyme, doesn't it?

You have to get home. Or get it to the bathroom. Or a restroom. You think about how cold toilet water is even on the hottest day, and you realize that, even if you know what's been floating around in there, it's got to be tempting to swim in it when you're burning up. For a bug, you mean.

You drive fast, checking the size of the gas stations, trying to gauge whether they're big enough for a public restroom. You glance down at the fly and see it slump on the string and swing from the hair like a pendulum. You slam on the brakes and make a hard right into the smallest gas station you've ever seen. You ask the third-grade boy behind the counter if they have a restroom. He says no and turns back to counting the candy bars. In desperation, you hold up your hand with the limp fly swinging from your finger.

"Dude, my fly needs to drink from a toilet fast or it's going to die." The kid smiles over a huge piece of gum and stares at you for 13 . . . 14 . . . 15 seconds. Then he points to the door behind the beer.

"Hurry up."

Unfuckingbelievable. You guess he's seen stranger things than this. Inside the bathroom, you're assaulted by a stench worse than any outhouse, and you walk over to the toilet and cautiously lift the lid. The water is clear as a mountain spring, and you carefully lower your hand until the fly's head just breaks the surface. You think about the part of the buddy-cop movie right around the second act where the drunk partner has to get revived by the more wise-cracking partner, so he shoves his face in the bowl. You're much more gentle than that.

And it works. The fly starts to activate, cranking its legs over its head to clean itself off. You smile. A cool pool party can fix anything. It looks like it's playing a tiny air guitar. No, it would need thumbs to do that.

"Ears burning?" the clerk asks you on your way out.

You smile. They've been burning for years. Once, you read a story about a mythical creature that ate nothing but ears, left behind the rest of the animal, just snacked on them like potato chips, leaving a trail of stone-deaf barnyard beasts all through the Dirty South.

Sometimes, you envied them.

Back in the car, you wonder how many people would believe you're actually worried about this fly. You've never taken care of cats very well. And plants? Forget about it. But this feels like everyone's fly now. You feel the weight of new responsibility. You try to imagine yourself in the waiting room at the veterinarian with your fly. You'd be the only person who a kid with a sick hermit crab could feel good laughing at. You watch it perched on the radio knob, cleaning its wings, and you stab the gas pedal over and over, keeping the car in neutral, smell of hot metal in your nostrils.

You realize you've spent more time worrying about this fly than you worried about all of your ex-girlfriends combined. Even when that one had to get her appendix out. You mess with your stereo.

Equalizer, you think. *That's a good word.*

Suddenly you understand something. It just seems like you care about the fly more than her, but if you were to line them all up against the wall and put a little pencil mark over their heads, you'd find that actually your feelings about the fly and her are precisely the same. And it's not that you think more of a fly really, it's just that, the more you find out about human beings, and the more you listen to their voices when they don't think anyone is around who can hear, the less you think of them.

00:01:58:19—"Your Gears Are Burning."

One time you told her you were going to invent a phone that, instead of ringing, released a swarm of bees. You said it would guarantee she would answer the thing every time you needed her to. She didn't understand what the hell you were talking about. You think she thought you were talking about some special ringtone, and you said, "Okay, listen, how about just three small bees, just enough of a scare to buzz around your ears and make you swat the air in a panic every single time I called you?" She had no answer to that. Later, your uncle invented something that played cupid with telephone numbers and license plates, but you don't tell too many people that story, unless they've had as much to drink as him.

You walk out of the bathroom, and you see she was reading that same magazine again, the one with the prescription label with your ex-girlfriend's name on it. You told her once how this old girlfriend used to snort painkillers off those very same pages, which seems like a worse addiction than drinking, but it didn't really feel like it at the time. You'd think that alone would make her not want to read the thing, but she folds a page over to remember her place. You used to try to get a letter published in one of her magazines so she'd stumble across your name and accidentally listen to you.

Wait, did you say "prescription" earlier instead of "subscription"? Because that is exactly what you meant.

The speaker suddenly starts popping again.

Shit fuck shit . . .

You pull the cords on everything. You hate the wiring in this house more than you've hated anyone. It eventually destroys everything. You hear water running in the sink, and you figure she's going to be in there awhile. She does that sometimes. Runs the sink so you can't hear. Like you're really listening to hear her pissing? Come on. Then you remember something, and you quickly crawl to your box of old cassette tapes rotting in the corner. It's your worst, last pair of headphones. Huge ratty pink ones from the '80s that cover your entire fucking head. You hesitate to put them on. Your headphones are getting bigger and bigger, and you seem to be sliding further back down the headphone-evolutionary ladder. Once you're holding them in your hands and blowing the dust and insect shells off the foam, you realize they're older than you thought.

These are from the '70s, not the '80s, no joke, and they're also the only thing left of your mother. One time, your mom came up to you and put these over your ears, and you were pouting about something like kids do, so you didn't say anything, didn't even look up, but you didn't take them off your ears either. And you still can't remember the song she wanted you to hear or why she wanted you to hear it. Maybe there was something funny in the song? Maybe the lyrics meant something important to her? Maybe she thought it was your favorite band? You can't remember. You were too busy ignoring her for reasons long forgotten. And now you'll never know what song it was because you just sat there, arms crossed, mad about something stupid, frowning until the song was over and she finally shrugged and walked away.

The wind blows the dead fly around on its string. Your ring finger is white from lack of circulation, so you unwrap the leash from your skin, waiting for the blood flow to return and paint the white knuckle back to red. You're amazed at how strong her hair was.

The strange thing is, when you think back to it, you could have sworn you were outside, sitting with crossed legs and crossed arms under a tree when your mother walked up and put those headphones over your ears. The cord couldn't have reached that far, could it?

You hide in the bathroom awhile. It's true that the bathroom is the last place where the remains of a relationship will linger. Is it all those half-empty bottles and soaps—or is it just hairs around the toilet?

You're no scientist. And even though you still have at least one toy stethoscope, you're not that kind of doctor.

00:02:00:07—"End Credits and Ironic Theme Music."

The next day, you finally take out the trash. Not a second too late, either. You can see a box of sweet-and-sour chicken moving down there on its own, and suddenly that mysterious fly isn't such a miracle anymore because you can see at least three more green-eyed buzz bombs bouncing around in the bag with their snouts dipping in and out of a month of your scraps. Your grandpa used to say that tiny fish would appear in a mud puddle if it sat undisturbed long enough. Not true. He was lying. Those were mosquitoes all along.

You recite your favorite line from *Titus Andronicus*, the movie adaptation of the Shakespeare play everybody hates:

"'What dost thou strike at, Marcus, with thy knife?' 'At that that I have killed, my lord, a fly.' 'Out on thee, murderer! Thou killst my heart.'"

You know how they say the bathroom is the last place your girlfriend exists? You were wrong. You meant the garbage. You take out the bag, then keep walking past the dumpster to throw your headphones into the river before you change your mind. It's one of those rivers that looks good from a distance. Then you're standing next to it and you catch a smell of what's been dumped in there for years. Wasn't this the river that caught on fire because of the pollution? You'd think your toilet would have ignited from all the cigarettes she flicked in it. Is this the river where that little boy swore he saw the shark?

The headphones bob along, riding the brown waves, then something under the water takes a couple bites and finally pulls them down forever. There's a girl standing next to you when you turn around.

"You know what you looked like to me just then?" she asks. "You looked like the last scene of a movie. The part where the sheriff throws away his badge."

"Hold out your hand," you tell her, not expecting her to do it. And when she uncurls her fingers for you, you expect something to fly away.

"What's your name?"

"Maggie. But I go by 'Shell,' short for 'Michelle,' my middle name."

"Of course you do. I'm not calling you that."

"Then don't."

"I've seen you before, haven't I?"

"I live in your building."

"Have you ever had problems with your wiring?"

"No." She laughs. "Have you?"

"All the time."

"You look like you do. You should get a surge protector. Seriously. I have three of them."

You stare for 7 . . . 8 . . . 9 seconds. Then you write your phone number in her hand. Just for laughs you scribble a fly underneath it.

"Sorry, I like drawing flies."

"I know. They're easy to make. Like a smiley face. You know why everyone draws smiley faces? Because there are less than five lines you need before you can recognize it."

"I believe it."

You hear the buzzing sound again, and you know what it is before she even pulls it out. She smiles an apology and presses the phone deep into her face, quickly walking away before she starts talking.

You walk off in the opposite direction to give her some privacy. You think of your phone number and the fly you drew on her skin, and you cup your hand around your ear like a seashell. Even years later, when you're both miles away and her head and her hand are the only things visible above the waves smacking your face and filling your nostrils, you still keep your hand over your ear, and you can still hear every word of her conversation like she's swimming right next to you. Until you pull her under.

TACO HELL

Okay, no one believes we had a real, live movie based on our whirlwind relationship, but it's true. We didn't believe it either at first, but when we finally stumbled onto this flick, things started to go bad. It was kind of scary actually. We're watching . . . what was it called? *Conformity* or *Obedience* or *Sucker!* or some such shit. I can never remember. *Compliance?* Yeah, that's it. Too many people to count told us we had to *had to* see this movie. So we did, and we decided it wasn't too bad, maybe a little far-fetched, although it was purported to be based on a "true story" in the opening crawl. That's where things get slippery.

If you haven't heard about it, there was this guy pretending to be a police officer, who prank-calls a McDonald's, or maybe MacDaddy's, the sad knockoff, and he accuses one of the employees of stealing money from someone's purse so that he can get a manager to strip-search and eventually sexually assault some poor underling due to the overwhelming threat of Big Bad Authority looming on the phone. Or something like that. Not quite the Milgram Experiment, but interesting enough to fictionalize, with some fun exploitation of fast-food employees by the filmmakers. But, ironically, it's a little less interesting when I find out on Wikipedia that the movie wasn't lying like *Fargo* about it being true, because I immediately start second-guessing every motivation of the filmmakers or the supposed victims of the crime, because people are horrible, right? But then it was interesting all over again when we realized at just about the same moment (while staring at each other and watching our pupils dilate, the universal signal of affection throughout the animal kingdom), that we were the ones who caused it.

But we don't really know for sure until the movie's over. Because during the movie, Amy's not paying that much attention, and I just keep thinking, "Ha ha, we called a fast-food joint to fuck with them once. Glad it didn't get this out of hand!" And I'm into the movie, so it doesn't really click. The film itself is low-budget, artsy stuff, so mostly it consists of lots of dramatic close-ups of bad hand-acting and lovingly filmed Freedom Fries. You know, whatever they can do to make fast-food seem noble. But when it's over, and everyone in the movie is wringing their hands all like, "What have we become!" I do that little bit of research and find more details of the real crime online, and I see the list of calls to various fast food places during this supposed prank-calling crime spree.

Then we notice the location of the first phone call, "Taco Bell" and I think, "Whoops!" and I want to give her a kiss right there on the spot.

See, a couple years back, I made a phone call that went a little screwy, but it was a righteous cause, goddamnit! And it was her idea really, if you want to point fingers.

All I wanted was a taco, like as bad as Mike Muir wanted his Pepsi. And the last three times I asked Amy, my spanking-new partner-in-crime at the time, to please *please* pick me up some drive-through tacos on her way home from work, something happened where I ended up not getting any (tacos, that is). It got to be a running joke in our apartment, me standing there looking down at empty, no-taco hands because of various fights, fires, firefights, or simple confusion over store hours. And the Taco Bell was right next to where she was working nights for extra money once her first-year PhD funding at the University of Pittsburgh fell through.

So the night of the Presidential debates, back at the tail end of two-thousand-whatever, when there was no *way* that one motherfucker was getting elected, my unofficial farewell party to Pittsburgh, Pennsylvania, was no exception to my taco-free streak of bad luck.

The evening starts out innocent enough. Amy and I are having Jesse and Dee over. Maybe he was insisting on being called "Jay" again by then, who cares, but they represented both the last remnant of my childhood and the last splinter faction of our old University of Pittsburgh crew, and they'd come over to watch these debates, maybe some grab-ass and thumb wrestling later, definitely some laughs. I figure if we drink a Busch beer every time our no-way-he'll-be Commander-in-Chief fumbles and fucks up English like it's his second language (was this before or after that dim "W" cast a Bat-signal-like shadow over our nation?), also possibly cursing an entire generation to speak with tortured drunk-uncle metaphors and stuttering sentence fragments, we'll be on our way to being drunk fast enough not to care who actually wins. Or how badly his infectious grammar-cide affects us. With fragments, I mean. The worst.

An hour passes with me and Jesse bored and our brains defragmenting and confused at all the pre-debate interviews and Sunday evening quarterbacking. We wait and wait for Amy and Dee to get back with the tacos, eyes narrowing, desperate for that grease in our bellies to soak up some alcohol and extend our evening. The girls were put on Taco Duty since Dee lived by a Taco Bell, and we hoped they took this mission very seriously. We have high hopes is what I'm saying, in spite of how nervous our Never-Future President was looking. It's been years since my first half-dozen undergraduate Taco Bell incidents, so I'm almost ready to think of the joint as just another place to get food, and maybe no one gets hurt this time. But this Taco Bell was already different. It had burned down once before, or so I thought. We'd driven up one night thinking my luck would change securing the "illusive" taco, that mythical burrito, and instead we saw flames reaching up all the way to lick the top of the not-offensive-at-all, Mexican-church-looking steeple. So I was thinking, "Welp, at least there's no more suspense," but then in the morning, it was fine. Opened back up like nothing had happened. No smoking rubble, no grizzled firefighters coughing and shuffling through the smoke, though all their trucks had likely been converted into "party buses" by then anyway. But not a mark on the stucco, just business as usual. Everyone already called it Taco Hell, but now there was a good reason. Damn thing was fireproof.

And this place was, for some reason, considered in Pittsburgh to be a vaguely healthy alternative to the other fast food, maybe because you're able to get four different food groups into your hands in the least amount of time? Or at least four different colors. And didn't some sting operation prove it wasn't really meat? Just a fluffed-up protein powder in all their tacos, kinda like dog food? Shit, that was supposed to be some big indictment, but to Yinzers, that sounded even healthier! And, okay, maybe they weren't as fast as MacDaddy's or Burger Queen, but, hey, Taco Hell was pretty fast. Or so I'm told.

But getting fast-food at a drive-through is always the Great Reminder. Sure Amy was slumming by working at Starfucks or wherever until she finished her dissertation, but it was certainly nice to keep in mind that this existence wouldn't be permanent. And watching those dead eyes at that window makes you regret quitting whatever job you just bailed on, or being grateful for the shitty one you had, because, damn, it wasn't *that* bad, was it? Look at that sorry motherfucker hesitating to pull back the glass, torn between getting some outside air and having to decipher another stranger and his squawking carload of baby birds. And isn't there something about that window that always makes it real easy for small arguments to escalate out of control?

So when the ladies start running late with the food, I'm already uneasy, both worried that I won't get to eat and that, somehow, Amy picked up a job application there instead of a taco. So I call Amy again and ask her to *pleeeeeese* remember to hook me up with some tacos on their way over, just in case they started tittering in the car and talking smack about us and completely forgot. But there's no answer. I should have known, because now that I have a second to really think about it and stop the hyperbole, in spite of the dozen or so times I've walked through their door or rolled up to the drive-through window smiling, sweaty balls of money rolling around my hand like Captain Queeg, I don't think I've ever actually *received* a taco from this place. Or anything at all. At least three times in a row, something has fucked this up. Have I ever eaten Taco Bell in my life? I have no answer, and it feels like panic.

But throughout history, drive-throughs have always been a bad idea. Road rage mixed with hunger? Think about that. Honking, impatient drivers, garbled instructions, pictures of the food just out of reach? Why not release clouds of bees into the cars to raise the stakes even further? Or raise actual steaks above people's heads so they can't reach them. Or, I know, put the window up a steep hill surrounded by sprinklers? They already do that, you say? Right. It's the very definition of a recipe for disaster. Now add a strategically placed camera. Do they want people to burn it down? Amy thought they were a "fascinating rhetorical situation," especially with the addition of surveillance, and she had at least one unfinished essay about them.

But sure enough, right on cue a half hour later, in walks the two of them, empty-handed and visibly shaken from some kinda drive-through trauma. Their story comes out like this, but Amy delivers it a lot louder:

"So get this, we pulled up to the speaker to order your stupid food, and the chick inside was having trouble hearing us. So Dee says, 'No, not bean burrito, *beeeFFF* burrito.' And apparently by exaggerating the letter 'F' like this, and by stalling out your truck again—sorry—and then having trouble getting it started again, she sent this bitch into a downward spiral of madness. We pulled up to pay, and she takes the money—Mexican girl, cute purple braids by the way—I think it was one of my students—then she fired off all mad, 'By the way, don't *ever* get smart with me again . . .' so I'm like, 'What did you just say?' And she's like, 'You heard me.' And I'm like, 'I'm afraid I didn't.' And I'm wondering if I'm talking like this because of the expectation of the invisible camera, or do I always talk like this, and she just slams the window and walks over to another employee to rant 'n' rave about us, all waving her arms around like she's being attacked by bees . . ."

"Bees?!" I say "I fucking told you!"

"Told me what?"

"Nothing. Just my stomach growling." I'm smiling, but mostly because I'm familiar with this role we fall back on sometimes, sort of a comforting regression to white-trash stereotypes complaining about fast-food altercations. It's an alternate form of entertainment when you're limping through college. Amy explained that it's a defense mechanism caused by the Imposter Syndrome, something that will always sound terrifying as fuck.

"Can I finish?" she says. "Okay, so, at this point, it was taking way too long with the food. And Dee decided to ask for the money back because now she's thinking someone's going to do something . . ."

Then Dee jumps in.

"Yeah, I figured someone was gonna spit in the '*beeeFFFF*' burrito. Or worse."

Burrito? What is that? Sigh. It sounds delicious, doesn't it? I'll never see one in my lifetime. I'm sure glad I didn't try for that new, certainly unattainable "Choco Taco" dessert item (more like *desert* item, right?) that I saw advertised the other day. Oh, my Christ, I'd eat a hundred of those bad boys. Some day. Anyway, Dee's still talking, and she's legit white trash:

". . . so now we can see that her name tag says 'Kim'—she throws the money at me and snarls, actually fucking snarls, like she's not even a human female, 'You're lucky I'm in here or I'd come out there and kick your motherfuckin' ass.' So now we're were getting loud, too, and some other employee came over to calm down Crazy Kim, but she just shoved this guy up into the air, bonking his head off the heat lamp because now she's got that crisis-situation super strength, and yells out, 'Don't tell me to relax, I'm the shift supervisor!' By this time, everyone was swearing, and Kim was making these moves like she was really going to come outside and attack our car."

"My car," I say.

Jesse looks up at this.

"Actually it's your brother's truck."

"How is that important?" I ask him. "Just let her finish. Maybe at the end of the story, there's food."

". . . so Amy starts pulling away, loudly declaring that she's gonna call the 1-800 number on the window. You know, the one that asks how smooth the transaction went? Right under the one that says 'Always hiring'? Anyway, this nutty twat yells out, 'Go ahead, I don't give a shit! They're not going to fucking fire me!' And Amy shouts a final, 'What the hell is your problem?' And Crazy Kim answers back, 'Your mother!' who is kind of a problem, to be fair . . ."

Amy laughs, then jumps back in.

"Which is, of course, *ridiculous,* since my mother is at home watching Court TV at this same time every day."

"While your dad hunts coyotes," I add, then lean over and give her a little kiss on the cheek and she shrugs. Unlike most dads, he hunts a different kind of coyote down there in Texas, those monsters you have to pay to sneak over the border.

"But, yeah, that was pretty much it," she says. "The debate ended with hard stares right out of those crappy Westerns you're always making us watch. And after two or three stalls in your truck to ruin any dramatic exit, we were off! So, yeah, sorry. No food."

"Why me," I sniff.

"Hey, we tried!"

"No, that's funny. It's a good story," I admit.

"You know what I hate?" Amy says. "When you say 'That's funny' instead of just laughing. You sound like an asshole. What do you think causes this?"

But before I can answer, they start excitedly telling the story all over again, mostly just to Jesse this time because he's a little slow. It gets a little better the second time around as they start adding extra flavor, Extra Hot Sauce, extra steak sauce, and raising those stakes and sprinkling in some more important details about their nemesis's appearance. And by three and a half recitals, Kim's purple braids are not being described as "cute" anymore. But now I'm getting all worked up. Partly because, in my head, I'm picturing Amy or Dee stalling my truck over and over and looking stupid on their way out, and partly from being on the verge of fainting from malnutrition and lack of taco love. And there's something about how Amy acts when Dee is around that's a little horrifying. Her voice gets a little shrill. Not that Dee isn't great in a lot of ways. But she's like an earlier version of Amy, pre-college, who, though perfectly charming and acceptable in normal circumstances, is, to be fair, someone I could never fall in love with.

Looking around the room, everyone and everything looks like a giant taco to me now. Even the Nope-Nope President. Remember that old Looney Tunes cartoon with the guy imagining his buddy on the desert island as a huge steaming chicken? It's just like that but everybody's a taco. And there's no island. And there's three of them instead of one. And there's no steam, as most fast food requires reactivation via microwave or it reverts to its natural inert state, industrial plastic pellets or SeaMonkey dust. So, forget everything I said. They look nothing like that cartoon, but I'm dying. And now I also got a dilemma. If it was a *guy* that was threatening people at some drive-through, instead of Crazy Kim, I could just go over there and be all chivalrous, or *say* I'd go over there anyway, and maybe he'd say the wrong thing and I could pull the little bastard out of the window by his head, his crooked but carefully arranged oversized baseball cap falling slow-motion to the pavement. But here we have this girl-on-girl madness. And we're already 15 minutes into the Presidential throat-clearing that signals the true beginning of the debates.

But Amy has an idea. She's leaning on the tower of her overdue psychology books from the library, one hand thoughtfully flipping the corner of a shelf-worn dust cover—I remember this like it was yesterday—and now she doesn't really look like the troubling early version of my future wife. She looks kind of scary. But her plan is intoxicating the way she explains it.

So reservations aside, me and Jesse start rubbing our hands in diabolical circles and get working on Plan A. Or, should I say, Plan "Egg." This involves taking two raw eggs (I know, kinda weak, but that's all that was in the fridge, and we got big ones, like duck eggs for nostalgia purposes) and then us pelting Amy's archrival when she opens the window to take our money. But we need to think of a way to do this so that we can still get a goddamn taco. But I force myself to stop worrying about my stomach and think about the greater good.

So putting the new plan in gear, I plop two eggs in a plastic bag, and we're getting ready to roll, but then I start to think about collateral damage again because Amy's in my ear about some stuff. And it should be noted that the phrases "greater good" and "collateral damage" are at that moment being volleyed back and forth between the Not-My-President President and the Green Party candidate on our television screen at that very same moment. That and "compliance" to certain treaties. And something wacky called "a very real threat of World War III." But eggs are a serious issue. Amy is saying we have to consider innocent bystanders. Amy asks what if Kim is no longer manning the drive-through after all the excitement she just had? Good point.

So Amy has me call them up real quick to do some recon. Later I'll understand that this phone call was Amy's entire master plan. Because it was more than enough to do the job. The *huevos* were just props to get me into character.

When a teenager answers the phone, I do what Amy tells me to, and I inquire who is working the drive-through, claiming "Someone forgot my food!" And when an irritable female voice gets on the phone, sighing before she speaks, I know it's gotta be our pal Kim.

"I've never been so sure of anything in all my life," the "Send Halp!" Garbage President panders, and I clear my throat and ask Kim all stern:

"Am I speaking to the manager? Yes? Okay, did you or one of your employees just have an altercation with two girls about ten minutes ago?"

"Listen, sir, that's n-n-n-not what happened, sir . . ."

Almost instantly, maybe because of the raspy authoritarian tenor of my voice (due to starvation), she starts stammering and going into this alternate reality version of events where she's just a victim who wants nothing more than to happily take money and hand out tacos, love, and smiles forever. I'm confused about something in her tone though, how it doesn't fit with Amy and Dee's play-by-play. And then something starts to dawn on me. All her "sirs," stuttering, rapid-fire explanations, and defensive over-enunciation? Is she running for office?

Wait, no, I get it. But Amy's already got it, and she's nodding at me to keep going.

This dunce thinks I'm calling from that 1-800 number they were talking about, and Kim believes I'm some sort of authority figure. Holy balls. I clear my throat louder, and now I'm suddenly working for Taco Hell, and shit gets kinda strange:

"Well, I heard that you were physically threatening customers and swearing and . . ."

"That's n-n-n-not what happened, sir. They were causing trouble, and I was just reacting and . . ."

"Well, I'm afraid I must be privy to different facts than you are."

Privy?! Who am I, right?

But at this point, I'm just trying to imitate every similar dressing down I've received from a boss, but I'm also quoting our Alternate-Timeline President almost word for word as he denies ever saying Arctic wildlife "was an eminent threat to global warming."

This isn't where Amy first teaches me about "mushfaking." Angie taught me that actually. But she shouldn't have.

But Kim is on the ropes, and when she almost whispers the million-dollar question in my ear, I don't hesitate:

"Who is this?" Kim asks.

"Your District Manager."

Okay, it feels like a bit of a demotion after the Presidency, but after I pull this out of my ass, I figure the jig is up anyway. I wait for her to say "fuck off" and hang up because she's gotta know who her DM is, right? Wrong.

"Listen, sir, they were making fun of me at the drive-through, and I can't believe that I would get in trouble over this when it's just my word against hers and . . ."

"Well, it's not just your word against hers because (pay attention, I'm really proud of how fast I conjure up this next ass rabbit) there was a vehicle behind them and someone from that car also called the 1-800 number to complain about your behavior."

I should mention at this point that me, her District Manager, is wearing a homemade "I Fucked Your Martyr" T-shirt with the sleeves cut off, twirling two eggs in a baggy, and trying to stifle the three giggling heads leaning in to listen.

"Hey, they started it!"

Clearly she's scared now, and folding faster than Superman on laundry day.

"So you were threatening and cursing at customers because you thought they were being rude to you? That is simply unacceptable. Why do you think you can just . . ."

"They started harassing me first, sir! It's not fair that I should get in trouble for this and . . ."

"Okay." Big, authoritative sigh. "When is your next day off?"

"Tomorrow."

"Ask her to come in," Amy whispers.

"Yes, I'm going to need you to come in so that we can sit down and talk about this and figure out what should be done."

"Oh, no. It is not fair that I should have to come in on my only day off when I already rearranged my schedule once this week because it's my only day off and it's just not fair that I should be the one to . . ." And blah blah blah. Dee whispers in my other ear:

"Goddamn, this bitch is big on 'not fair'."

At this point, I hold out the phone in disbelief. I don't know what's funnier, the fact that this idiot really thinks I'm her District Manager, or the fact that me, her boss, can't get her to come in on her day off, even to save her job. On the television, the (can't say it) "President" holds a hand tight to his gristle-y, tomato-red earlobe, and a camera zoom reveals an earpiece buried in that swirl of piss-stained cotton candy that no one knew he had. Amy would have been all about any new debate-rigging technology, but she misses it. But Jesse catches it.

"Are they giving him the questions or the answers?!" Jesse really wants to know. Then, suddenly offended, Jesse declares this as "fuckin' cheatin'!" and I motion for him to shush and turn off the TV and pay attention to the eggs. Then I can't help but squeeze the phone painfully close to my own head, too.

After another minute of "not fairs" from Crazy Kim, and still being coached by my past-and-future wife, I finally give up and switch tactics:

"When do you work next?"

"Sunday. I open."

"Okay, don't worry about opening the store because . . ."

Time out. This is where some people who work in middle management may start getting a disapproving "You've gone too far" kinda look on their mug. But, hey, I've only been a District Manager for seven minutes, so I'm gonna make some mistakes!

". . . we'll take care of that," I go on, reading Amy's sign language. "You just come in later. I'll meet you at noon so we can sit down and figure out what we're going to have to do."

"Fine."

Wow. That was a cakewalk. Amy signs "I love you." Or possibly, "We need a worm farm." Apparently, it will always be infinitely easier to convince someone to stay home instead of coming in. It's a lesson we all remember from grade school where kids would rather get suspended for ten days instead of standing in the corner for just one.

I hang up, and we're all laughing our asses off, hoping she actually comes in late on Sunday and gets canned. We talk about it a lot, drinking and ignoring the end of the debates even after Jesse turns the TV back on. I do, however, catch one of the candidates saying something self-righteous about "never judging people by . . ."

By what? No idea. We couldn't hear the rest over all the fake applause.

And that's all I really remember from that day, because I spent most of my night fantasizing about being behind one of those podiums next to the actual District Manager of Taco Hell, carefully explaining our party's platform with purposeful hand gestures and reassuring nods. I would declare, "My fellow Americans, you can never judge people by the color of their purple hair. However, you *can* judge people by their favorite books, songs, or movies. You *can* judge people by how fast they yank clothes out from under a sleeping cat. And you can *only* judge people by how rude they are on the phone, or in traffic." Dramatic pause. "Or, of course, at a drive-through, the unholy bastard combination of both."

When Amy and I discuss the whole thing way later though, we're convinced that Crazy Kim flipped out because of the rhetorical dilemma of "the drive-through Panopticon." To translate Amy's high-minded theories for you, imagine a phone call where the person you just hung up on suddenly pops their head in the window of your house to get the last word. That would fuck you up, wouldn't it? And if you're more likely to be rude to strangers on a phone (like most people), you sure wouldn't know what the hell to do if their head suddenly popped out of your freezer. Instant confrontation at a drive-through window is an unexpected, awkward ending to what's basically a garbled, angry phone call between the hungry and the disgruntled. It's something that's not meant to happen, ever. Like time travel. Or a rational debate. Or cameras on cops. Or me ever getting to eat a taco. To be fair, Kim probably didn't know how to handle this. It's kind of like when you're in traffic and you're yelling at the car next to you for whatever infraction, then, three miles later, you're both idling at a red light together. Do you look over? You *have* to look over. A friend of mine used to be prepared for exactly this kind of situation. If someone was glaring at a red light, he'd slowly pull out the winter mittens, sunglasses, and motorcycle helmet that he kept in his glove box (yeah, it was a big-ass glove box), then he would stare them down, leaning on the steering wheel of his rusted-out '92 Fajita. Wait, Fiata? Miata, whatever. You know what though? No one ever raced him.

In retrospect, it sucks our debate party was full of such distractions because, since we moved to Pittsburgh, it was the most people we managed to gather around us in months. Although I suspect this had gotten more difficult because of the upcoming elections and my tendency to drop my pants and press my groin up against the TV whenever the Are You Kidding Me? Leader of the Free World was talking, which was a lot. I kept trying in vain to make Amy understand that the bigger the crowd means the less likely I was to exclaim, "Hey, look! The President's suckin' my dick. Again!" A few years ago, I'd tried to piss on the biggest, shiniest building I could find when I was in Chicago. Not easy. And now, of course, impossible.

Seriously. Where's the camera? We could make T-shirts and cut the sleeves off! Hold up, where are you going?

Okay, jumping ahead to the middle of the story, it's finally Sunday, and I've told everyone who will listen about our taco hijinks, actually kinda getting tired of the story and starting to doubt Kim really wouldn't figure that she'd been bamboozled in 48 hours or less. I was thinking that as soon as she mentioned anything at all to her store manager or fellow employees about our phone call, they would quickly call the District Manager (the real one, not me) and the cat's out of the bag.

So I'm as shocked as you are by the happy ending to this story.

See, I already told you Amy works at Starfucks near the Taco Hell in question, and Sunday afternoon she calls me to say she just told her coworkers all about the incident. Her words:

"So, at about 11:00, a couple of the second shifters went across the street to get lunch and came back to tell me the good news. Dude. There was a big sign taped to the door that read, 'Will not open until 1:00. Sorry for any inconvenience.' No bullshit, I swear. I got five witnesses who saw the sign!"

She even took a picture. The sign had scare quotes on all the wrong words, and on the TV a news anchor was explaining that, in spite of the candidate's mysterious earpiece and the clown wig to hide it, polls were predicting that shitbag actually won the debate over immigration. Or taco trucks, I can't remember. But the price of earpieces and red noses went up. Taco Hell's prices would forever remain the same, as invulnerable as roaches after the bomb.

"*Cyrano de Bergerack-ack-ack . . .*" Amy would sing, an Edmond Rostand/Billy Joel mash-up that seemed to make her very happy.

Postscript. A week later, Dee actually calls the 1-800 number to complain about those bona fide customer service issues, really just trying to get some free food out of it, and she's given the phone number of the store manager. This all-business woman named Angie Something then proceeds to tell Dee that she knows all about 'the situation' and that 'her District Manager is handling it.'"

Whoa, what is she talking about "her District Manager handing it"? Because I ain't handling shit. "It's not fair!" I would tell the reporters. I've got entirely too many new responsibilities that come with my new District Manager job title. Like the truck stop that puts too much salt on their omelets, the kid at the gas station who shorted me on change, that convenience store with the clerk who stares too much, the future murder of my wife . . .

I mean, I'm sorry, but there are just too many other stores in my district that need my attention.

Anyhow, "70 incidents in 30 states" is what they say on Wikipedia. Incidents? The incidents the movie was based on, or weird phone calls? You know why it's probably fast food joints that this crazy fucker targeted?

Because maybe they were asking to ask for it.

Seriously, a window where you reach out and grab food while you're driving by? How does that not end in blood and tears every damn day.

One last thing. Remember those two eggs? As I was packing up the last of my silverware for the Kentucky move, I noticed them on the windowsill, next to the phone charger, behind my dead plants and leaky squirt gun, still sealed in the bag though, fermenting in the sun to (kissing the tips of my finger and thumb) perfection. I'd like to say I used them to make a Mexican-style omelet. I'd like to say that I forced myself to eat it on the day of the election. I'd like to say that me and my betrothed went outside and placed those eggs at either end of a parking space and laughingly mastered how to drive a stick-shift and parallel park on a bright summer day without anyone losing their temper and wrecking my truck for the fifth time. I'd like to say that whenever she thought no one was looking, she would replace whatever article of clothing the cat was sleeping on with something equally comfortable so it didn't tumble onto its head like Sunday dinner off a tablecloth magic trick gone awry. I'd like to say that something meaningful happened to those two eggs, since this story introduced them but forgot about them as quickly, not like guns hanging over the fireplace. I'd like to say that they did, indeed, crack someone on the head and turn someone who deserved it into a salty omelet, instead of just getting dropped into the trash without any ceremony, or debate. But they didn't.

So if you check the dates of that first incident in the police report, you'll see it was me, which means it was her. And I run around telling the world we did this. I tell them this is when we fell in love, or at a minimum, knew our love was real until it wasn't, when she saw me for the first time as a white-collar professional. But no one believes us.

"Unrelated," they say. "Coincidence!" they add. All good points. But much like our President To Be (or Not To Be), New Yorkers and Texans who by definition must have complicated feelings about migrant workers, you'd assume incorrectly, I have no energy to debate any of this. It was just like dropping a rock in a puddle and watching the ripples, maybe more like dropping a Choco Taco off the Texas Commerce Tower. Or a Mexi-Melt off a Twin Tower.

The Taco Bell burned down again a year later, but it stayed that way this time, and there was nothing about it in the newspapers.

A VAST COMIC INDIFFERENCE

"A little water clears us of this deed."
—William Shakespeare— *Macbeth*

As I walked along the bridge, knuckles bouncing off the padlocks to get them swinging, I heard a car door slam and turned to watch the headlights of the Jeep flicker as a tall shadow rounded the vehicle to intersect me. All I really needed to see was the outline of the rifle bobbing on his back like a huge antenna to understand this was the father of my dead wife who had found me, and within minutes I was slammed onto my back with his beer breath in my nose and his knee in my chest. His gun was slung and loose and sliding down his shoulder, so I figured I had about a minute to talk him out of murder.

"Hi, Greg," I said from the ground, fingers gripping the slats of the bridge to keep from sliding. "How'd you know I'd be here?"

"I showed Angie this spot, Dave. Before she showed it to you. Just like I showed it to her mother, and just like my father showed it to me."

"She never showed me this place."

"Then why the hell are you here?"

"Are you gonna kill me or what?" Bold question, I know, but I'd learned this head-on delay tactic during my one semester as a psych major at the University of Pittsburgh, where I'd met my wife.

"Did you do it?" he asked, blinking slow.

"Do what? No, I didn't do it."

"Well, if you didn't do it, why'd you skip town?" The pressure of his knees on my sternum relaxed a bit. "You've gone a long way to convince everyone you've done something wrong, the way you've been acting."

"I'm not *acting* like anything," I said, as forceful as I could with most of his weight constricting my lungs. "Just because I don't grieve like other . . ."

"Grieve! You're on a road trip like this is some joke! The cops got a lotta questions for you, and so do our families, and you're out here on some

218 DAVID JAMES KEATON

Midwest tour playing *This Is My Life.*" The rifle strap was down past his elbow now.

Your Life, I thought, but I didn't correct him, and I didn't answer his question either.

"This was her favorite spot."

Now the gun was all the way down, the rifle stock in his hand, bloodshot eyes glowing with rage.

"You just said you'd never been to this bridge before, Dave."

"I know, this is where she was cheating on me."

Wrong answer. His fist gripped my coat collar as he yanked it up my throat.

"Sounds like motive," he hissed. "I should blow your head off right now and save the taxpayers the effort." He looked me over a bit. "But you've been on a bridge like this before, haven't you?"

I strained behind my arms to try and grab the fence, and I was able to pull myself up enough to catch one good, deep breath. Our struggle had rattled more padlocks, and his eyes shifted to the sound. I took the opportunity to crawl out from under his knee completely and managed a sitting position. He allowed this, hypnotized by the motion of locks, and I tried to keep him fixated on all that shiny silver and gold rocking back and forth along the guardrail so that maybe he'd forget about killing me.

"Is one of those padlocks yours?" I asked. "You and your wife's, I mean."

"Yes."

"Did you throw a key in the water, too, like you're supposed to?"

His eyes were back on me, and now he was smiling.

"You don't even know what you're talking about, do you? Do you know why you're supposed to throw a key in the water?"

"For good luck?"

"Right, good luck. And did you throw yours in?"

I said nothing.

"That's what I thought. And how's that luck working out for you?"

* * *

Even though we did the requisite "love lock" thing on our honeymoon in Paris, we'd learned from "Fabio," our full-time concierge and part-time snake-oil salesman of any and all tourist traps, that the original idea had actually begun in Italy. But all these romantic bridges with tiny, cheapjack padlocks had gone worldwide since then, of course, but no one promoted the impromptu riverside ceremony as hard as the French along their noto-riously love-struck Seine. By the time that Fabio was done shilling to us in the lobby of our hotel, I was unable to resist buying a handful of padlocks from him before the sweaty Americans behind us clamored for the rest of his bullshit stash of tiny mangled Eiffel towers key chains, getting so desperate one guy shoved me to the side and dropped his hotel key through the heating vent on the floor in the process. We knew it was a scam, but we didn't care. We were pretty sure Fabio got kickbacks from somewhere to push that junk and I could sympathize, and besides that, we'd brought our own padlocks anyway, and plenty of keys.

My wife had purchased a ton of them actually, which meant, what, a half ton of these keys? We even numbered them so they didn't get mixed up. Which was doubly ridiculous really, especially after we realized that most used the same key to open them, with only three possible variations. But despite both of us being pacifists and staunch opponents of firearms, there was just something intoxicating about that commercial that seduced her easily enough, mostly when the slow-motion bullet fails to penetrate the lock, and the spokesmodel give the blasted lock a tug, then a shrug, then chirps, "Nope, still holds tight!" I wrote off her excitement as the residual influence of her father. Remember, we still had Greg's NRA ("Not Really Aiming") stickers on the toolbox he'd given us as a wedding gift, which I couldn't get off no matter how much I picked at their corners. Angie wanted me to leave those stickers alone and "respect my elders" and all that, but she needn't have worried, as I was pretty sure the sticker factory used some sort of industrial adhesive so they'd haunt multiple generations with that logo, an embarrassing hitchhiker on so many father-in-law hand-me-down vehicles throughout this era in increased school shootings, movie-theater shootings, and open-carry everywhere. Which is probably how Greg was able to cross three state lines conspicuously strapped, half in the bag, and out for blood.

But even if we filled our new toolbox to the brim, I knew that after the honeymoon we'd have more love locks than we'd know what to do with. But, of course, at the time I didn't know there was a bridge in Ohio just like our bridge in Paris. And I sure as hell didn't know this was where she'd be screwing around with some research assistant, or musician, or medical oddity, or whatever the hell he was.

But I didn't argue with her about any of this at the time, or anything else really. So what, she got a deal on padlocks. And smuggling American-made, bulletproof padlocks for a bridge in Paris with our initials and our hearts scribbled on the sides of those bad boys? That nonsense had to be true love, man. That nonsense was forever. Only I guess I must have jinxed us by never throwing our key in the river like the ritual demanded. Fabio made it very clear you threw the key in after you clicked it shut, but even after Angie and I had dutifully performed our love-struck ritual of snapping our memento onto the bridge at the Passerelle des Arts, when it came to tossing the key, we got distracted by some unusual movement in the brown water below, some bright, strobe-like flashes that we first took for more keys, of course, but later became convinced were the reflections of eyes. Wide and glassy, but not just any eyes. Huge eyes where there shouldn't be eyes, and not moving like eyes should move, at least not the eyes they'd tried to teach me about in school.

But these flashes of light in the water shouldn't have been so much of a shock, as we'd heard the Seine was plenty polluted, and I, for one, had no reason to doubt this explanation. Come on. Tens of thousands of cheap, rusted keys hurled into the depths by the smitten masses? That couldn't be good for any ecosystem. But I figured any life it could sustain would be malformed and squinting at best. But these were massive, hypnotic eyes, and throwing a key at them in that moment didn't just seem wrong, but a weird kind of wrong. Not just the shame of littering in a foreign land, but some deeper violation. It was hard to explain, and we never talked about it later, but it was almost as if I had this incredible urge to swim the key down there myself, to hand the damn thing over respectfully, like a key to a city that wasn't my own. Throwing it into the water was a poor substitute after that impulse, but it was easy to imagine it as the only alternative for the sane couples who frequented the Parisian walkways and didn't want to drown after their lovelock selfie.

So we shook off these impulses moments later, at least I did, and when some street hustlers tried to scam us with the age-old "lost gold ring at our feet" trick, plucking it from near my shoe with the worst slight-of-hand ever and grinning with a "Is theeeeese yoursssss?"

I ended up just taking the key home in my pocket. Eventually, it found a home on my tiny Eiffel tower keychain.

*   *   *

"Gimme 'em."

The father of my dead wife was holding me at gunpoint, so I handed over my keys. Well, he sort of had me at gunpoint. The rifle laid across his forearm, and the stock rested near his shoulder. I wasn't exactly looking down the barrel or anything, but the night was still early, and that's the kind of stuff that happens at the climax, not the middle of the story when the bad guy is still talking.

I expected him to throw my keys into the Ohio River, and it would be a relief to get rid of the busted Eiffel tower which had started cutting my hands, but he needed to tell me a story first, the story of the padlocks and the keys, the story of the two rivers, the story of how we're all connected in ridiculous ways, the story of why so much was still at stake, even though we were both suffering this terrible loss. And he started with the story of his father, when he was stationed in Paris during World War II, and when he visited the bridge at the Passerelle des Arts, the very same bridge Angie and I were drawn to on our honeymoon. But somehow this bridge over the Ohio was that bridge over the Seine. And he was there, too, even though he was in Vietnam, playing "bug hockey" or something. It didn't make a whole lot of sense, but he'd just lost a daughter, so I tried to follow him best I could.

"He stood on this bridge in Paris, when it only had a few dozen of these padlocks clamped along its rails," Greg said. "Rather than the tens of thousands that adorn it tonight. We stood there and listened to the water splashing below as I kissed a French nurse, a woman who was not Angie's grandmother, and I only pretended to throw in the key, as it was just a rehearsal for the real thing."

"Wait, who stood on the bridge?"

"Don't interrupt me, Dave," he said, finger not on the trigger yet, but definitely dancing around it. I'd met Angie's grandfather, Harry, before his death, a great old guy with a flair for turning old satellite dishes into giant lawn-art butterflies. I had a feeling he'd deny all of this and calm Greg down with a squeeze of the shoulder. Her grandpa had a few of those gnarly World War II tattoos on his forearms, too, long turned green, one of the American flag, one of his wife's name. The poor quality of a veteran's tattoo only insured its authenticity, so I'd never mock one on purpose. But still, he got mad at me once for joking about it.

"I like my women how I like my coffee, too, Harry. With my name misspelled on their side!"

He'd never been to a Starbucks in his life, and even worse, Angie's grandma's name was misspelled on his arm, with "Peggy" looking a lot more like "Leggy," but that might have been on purpose, too.

Greg increased the volume on his story when he saw my thoughts were wandering and gave me a rifle barrel crack in the cheekbone.

"Hey! Pay attention. So, in Paris while he worked the booby traps under these bridges, my father learned that at the bottom of every river is a locked box," Greg explained. "Well, to us it's a box, but it's more the idea of a box, so it needs the idea of a key, and something in these rivers has been searching for those keys for longer than my father's father's father stood on this bridge in Paris, 4,000 miles away. He was lucky to have that bridge really, or any bridge under his feet, because being stationed in Paris after World War II meant that they'd saved those bridges in the nick of time. Hitler had prepared Paris's 50 bridges for demolition, even wiring up more than the Allies did, and this wasn't due to any discernible battle strategy, but because they wanted to bury something, forever. Some kinda secret."

"But what about *this* river?"

"You aren't listening to me," he said, hand squeaking on the rifle stock. "Any street crossing any river on this planet is one and the same. And you might think throwing all these little tin keys down there for years and years may have bought us some more time, as a race, whipped up a little confusion to keep those boxes shut. But they're worming their way through them keys right now. Trying every one in those locks. Sliding all over the river bed and curling and turning anything shiny."

"Tentacles?" I asked, despite my warning. He was drunker than I thought.

"No, no, no," he laughed. "People always get that confused. Just fingers. These are regular fingers. And regular arms. But with like fifty elbows each."

Oh, no, here he goes with that conspiracy shit again. We don't have time for this.

I thought about how I knew a kid in grade school who swore he had knuckles on his penis, but everyone was pretty sure there was something else going on down there. I kept this memory to myself and tried not to laugh. Laughing at the wrong time is what got me here.

"Have you ever heard of the Inverted World Theory?" he asked me.

Only about every time we saw you over the holidays.

Greg turned his back on me, unsure if he should continue, but I knew he was just getting started. Greg was all into that conspiracy stuff. His all-time favorite phrases were "Government's known about it for years" and "Let Buzz Aldrin try that crap with *me*." Astronaut Aldrin had famously punched a moon-landing denier in the face, you see, and Greg was always frustrated that conspiracy nut hadn't properly armed himself. With more facts, of course.

The real problem was her dad had discovered the World Wide Web way too late in life, and this was an especially dangerous time to teach an old dog new tricks, which is actually very easy to do. He was quickly neck-deep in dubious explanatory hypotheses, and that familiar, beloved "devil's advocate" style of most father figures turned out to be quite the unexpected liability when it came to unvetted internet insanity. I'd heard parts of this particular theory last Christmas when all of us were vacationing in Florida. And actually, in that part of the country, he sounded relatively sane, but on the plane ride back I realized how crazy it all was, all that babble about some guy named Sneed and machines with names that sounded like they were straight out of bad movies.

Greg wheeled back around, rubbing his own Marine Corps tattoo thoughtfully. His face was like a man possessed. No, that's the wrong word. This was more insidious, like an infiltration, or maybe an *occupation*. The world has been used to possession for hundreds of years, which is why we aren't prepared to deal with anything like this. And we should deal with it like it's our job.

*   *   *

In 1964, Russian astronomer Nikolai Kardashev first came up with the idea of Type 1, Type 2, and Type 3 civilizations, and he claimed "Type 3" was some fantasy about controlling an entire galaxy, which I'm pretty sure was the plot of *Men in Black*. But Type 1 wasn't just speculation. This was reachable. A true global civilization? Yes. Some scientists now claim the internet is our first tangible example of Type 1 civilization technology. But at what cost?

Not to keep sounding like science-fiction movies here, but on a timeline relative to the development of the human race, that machine destroyed us the second it was switched on.

"Did you enjoy serving, Greg?" I asked him. I'd known my father-in-law long enough to understand these kinds of questions rattled him, but he also found them irresistible and would buy me more time.

"What do you know about serving?" he said. "You haven't served any-where. Or anyone. You don't know anything about what's important, Dave. It's all a joke to you. I've known that since Day One."

One big step forward, and he was grabbing me by the throat. I yanked his grip free, his old-man fingernails slicing my collarbone, and he jumped back to raise the rifle and tap my head with the barrel. Almost gently, which was scarier. I held up my hands.

"Okay, okay," I said. "Please don't misinterpret the levity, Greg. Gallows humor, man! It's the only way I can deal with any of this."

"Gallows humor is reserved for those facing the gallows," he said, sliding the barrel of the gun up my cheek.

"That's exactly what I'm saying."

"No, it's crystal clear to me that you take shit too lightly, even before she died." The gun slipped a bit, and he looked uncertain again. "So for now, listen . . ."

And then he started throwing around his Inverted World Theory again, and I mentally mapped out escape routes.

They all involved the water.

I watched his eyes and his mouth as he talked. This goofy theory had always been his favorite, and it rolled off the tongue a lot easier than the "Illumi-naughty" stories his friends shared in chain-letter emails. This was some craziness about how the Earth was hollow, and we all lived inside it, and the sun was a ball only like 600 miles across. And when you moved toward the center of the void in this grumbling planetary stomach ache, the distance became exponential, and that's "where the infinite slept." Or maybe he said "stepped." Okay, sure, the theory was pretty dumb out loud. But the part about the critters was interesting.

". . . and if *distance* is exponential," Greg went on, "then the size of things can be distorted. So what we perceive as freshwater fish and frogs and crawdads are quite simply space monsters. They just look tiny to us up here where we're standing . . ."

I was sort of relieved that the pet lizards I'd neglected in my childhood had been potential world destroyers. It eased the guilt.

". . . so there is some level of infinity, but it doesn't involve holes at the North Pole, it doesn't involve the vast, deepest ocean. The infinite involves the cracks in the surface, the ones filled with water. And anywhere there is a river, you have a pathway to forever. That's what this bridge in right here."

"This part of the Ohio river is only 20 feet deep, tops. The Seine, too, if you still think you're in France right now."

"Doesn't matter. This is a different kind of deep. All these rivers are simply cracks in the façade, and all these cracks are connected. I mean that just like the leg bone is connected to your brain bone, the Mississippi is connected to the Amazon. The Mekong is connected to the Nile. The Danube is connected to the Thames. And, yeah, laugh all you want, the Seine is connected to the Ohio, or wherever this is."

"I'm not laughing."

"Boy, you don't have to do it out loud for me to know that there's something unsettling about your attitude in the face of this knowledge, and, more importantly, in the face of the loss you have suffered. Or will suffer."

His finger was flicking the trigger, and not ready to jump yet, I tried to keep him talking.

"Okay, but if this river is a crack that goes through the Earth and pops out the other side, wouldn't it be a river in China, not Paris?"

"Does this river look straight to you, boy!"

Good point, ya crazy fuck. I hadn't thought about that, but I'd thought about his other theories a lot more than I'd like to admit, like the one he presented over Easter dinner with the solemn production of a seminar paper, if academic conferences let you conduct panels with piles of carefully organized candy animals. He used chocolate rabbits and marshmallow peeps to explain that any and all creatures that you'd find in a river were actually from . . . somewhere else.

He said this was the great secret of the cosmos. At the time, he wasn't talking about keys letting anything out, here or in Paris, but he was asking us very sincerely, as a chocolate rabbit melted around his fingers, if we'd ever wondered why monsters were always drawn to resemble our more innocuous friends, particularly the fish and the frogs.

"Fish and frogs are behemoths," he said. "And vice versa."

"You mean the frogs are the fish?" I asked that night, grabbing for the bunny ears.

"What? No, no, no. Sometimes a big frog gets out and runs amok, yes. But all the hoaxes and Bigfoots out there help disguise them real good."

And by the time he let me eat some of that rabbit, he'd almost convinced me. Well, not really, but Angie and I thought it was all so funny back then. It wasn't funny now.

"And you know what, Dave?" he said, finger tickling the trigger. "Maybe you didn't kill my daughter. So maybe I just came here to make sure you throw that key in the water, or make you give a shit about her death, whichever comes first."

He looked around, as nervous as I'd ever seen him, almost stone sober now.

"Pay attention. By throwing it in, you're making a new promise, to something besides me."

"We're in this together? Is that what you're saying?" I asked cheerfully, still reaching into my single-psychology-semester bag of tricks. Too bad I got a C+ in that class.

He took a step back and stood up tall, looking me over like he'd just noticed me again. Then he looked around, checking the shadows for witnesses, or something worse.

*   *   *

According to *Wack-opedia*, the Conspiracy Theory hub of the only slightly more respectable *Wikipedia*, Cyrus Sneed, a chiropractor from upstate New Jersey, first proposed his controversial Concave Inverted Earth Theory in 1969, also referring to this head-scratching conjecture as "Cellular Comixology." Sneed and his devoted "Oneness Cult" conducted many experiments on the beaches of Florida, mostly a lot of equations drawn in the sand, eventually moving their studies to the many rivers and inlets, where they had to start writing on paper. Sneed's followers claimed to have mathematically verified the concavity of our planet with the use of his specialized "Rezonator," a tool which resembled, in many ways, the *Ghostbusters'* P.K.E. meter, (a conspicuous movie prop that had been recycled in several science-fiction films, such as *They Live* and *Suburban Commando*). This Hollywood toy "proved" conclusively, at least on a muffled YouTube video, that not only were we crawling around the inside of the Earth like insects in proverbial discarded soda can, but also that there was a rapidly escalating increase in distance as you headed toward the center void of any sphere. Or, according to the most recent interpretations, simply managed to touch the bottom in any marginally deep river. Or any river where you couldn't see the bottom. And sometimes your toilet. That part was less scientific.

But Greg was in love with all those numbers that confused people enough to prove nothing and everything. And he would point to the horizon and ask why it wasn't curved, once telling me over a campfire where he must have known the dancing shadows were doing that crazy stuff to his face:

"If we were living on the inside of the Earth right now, everything would be perceived exactly the same looking inside the planet, the same as we would have looking out."

We'd all laughed at this stuff at first, but I'd always suspected Greg took it all much more seriously. Especially after him and I waded into a creek in Minnesota one time to fish and he remarked on how quickly we were sinking into the muck and silt.

"This riverbed is rock," he said. "This shouldn't be happening."

"What?"

"Just keep moving or we'll end up in Australia."

He wasn't joking.

* * *

Every time I've ever been tasked to read an epistolary book, like *Dracula* or *Frankenstein* or *The Whisperer in the Darkness*, I would think to myself, "No way someone just stands there and writes or reads those letters. And no way someone just stands there and reads someone *reading* those letters."

And there's definitely no way someone sits still while a story such as this was being told.

Unless it was at gunpoint.

"The eyes aren't really eyes . . ." Greg said, wiping beer sweat or tears from his face with his forearm. "Bulbous frog bodies with a bit of dogfish thrown in for good measure. You want to picture what's down there? Imagine falling asleep underwater staring at that *Dogs Playing Poker* painting . . ."

"I don't have to imagine that!"

". . . sometimes those deep electric dreams and impossible arms can be seen when the water levels are low. They're often mistaken for various cryptozoological creatures, like I said, but it's altogether worse than that. Or better. Real, I mean . . ."

"What the hell are you talking about, Greg?"

I was now convinced that, just as it had done to so many miserable fathers lately, the internet had actually driven him insane. Then driven him straight to me.

"What the hell did you do to my daughter?" he asked, pressing the barrel hard into my cheek. "No, that's next," he said, easing back up. "What's important now is that we throw your key into the water. Like you should have done for her years ago."

"You're losing me, man."

"What the hell are you, boy? Your wife is killed on her way to work, left like garbage on the side of the road, somehow drowned in her car with no body of water in sight? No one knows what happened, and you skip town. Skip the funeral. So tell me, what are you?"

"That's a terrible question," I said.

That's a great question, I thought. But I dealt with her loss the only way I knew how. And I hated me worse than any of them could.

"I skipped town for the same reason you skipped town, Greg. Because we can't deal with not knowing, or maybe not caring."

"Why do you think the Eiffel Tower was never finished?" he asked, openly weeping now, squeezing my souvenir keychain until his hand bled. "You ever look at that stupid goddamn thing? Covering it with a million golden locks would be an improvement!"

Golden locks?

"Now I'm picturing it with hair."

"You look at these locks here. Sometimes you'd see a bike lock, and then a bunch more locks on that lock, like an addition on a house. You could have had a house."

"I could have, yes."

"Listen!" his voice echoed like a thunderclap. "Every one of these locks represents a new family, specifically the promise of a child, forever marked by that exchange between inverted rivers to be a part of something larger to come. You have denied our family a chance to be part of this. A lock weighs 300g and there are 1000 locks on one section of railing—that's the weight of about 4 adults. How weak are these bridges?"

"What's your point?"

"The point is they're unsafe, they're unsound, and everyone governing the infrastructure knows this. Yet one glorious day they will cover every bridge on this planet."

"You never should have gone near a computer, Greg."

Boom! The gun went off, and I sat down hard. A trickle of blood filled the corner of my eye, and I quickly checked childhood databanks of multiplication tables and my first kiss to make sure he hadn't blown off a chunk of my memories. I touched the gash on the top of my head, relieved I couldn't feel brain, but not knowing what it would feel like if I did. But my ears were ringing, one eardrum possibly ruptured, so I'm not sure I heard him right when he told me he killed her.

"I had to. She broke the chain. Three generations did it right, but you two were doomed the minute you walked away with that key."

I stood back up, hand on my head, as he explained the Myth of a Golden Age in America, how growing up in Duluth, they were always broke, and everyone he knew was broke, but now a different age was coming, one built on infinite river beds lined with novelty keys and bone. My ears were positively screaming, so I may have missed some of his confession, but there was something about endless coupling on those honeymoon bridges, and how the locks cursed any future child, insured there would be no reproduction as that union is forever committed to a search for the key to release it from the burden of the human race unless he threw my keys in the water to save their bloodline.

Or something.

You know, internet shit.

I took a swing for his jaw, and he brought the butt of the rifle down to my forehead and almost knocked me out. Cloudy, I watched him ratchet it again.

I knew our time was up even before he spoke. His words were ice cold, and terrifyingly sincere.

"We all have to make sacrifices."

*　*　*

It was hard to see, but I knew from the sound he was unlocking the padlocks one by one. He used any key on my chain and, of course, and they all worked, in every last lock. When he was on his tenth lock or so, I could suddenly feel the bridge creaking beneath my feet, wood screaming as if something terrible was going to happen, and something rose up in me, and I don't know why but I knew that he couldn't be allowed to do this, whatever it was he was doing. I threw a better punch this time, not trying to be the guy in the movie, but like the guy in the movie who was training the guy playing the actor in the movie.

"Aim for an imaginary space behind his head," the stunt guy might say. "Like if his head was a globe, and his eyes were the United States . . . you're punching Russia."

So I punched the shit out of Russia, but it was more like a slap really, as my fingers were also trying to grab the gun at the last second, but this desperate clusterfuck of limbs was enough to send him off balance.

"I'm going to make you show some emotion," my father-in-law said as he rolled against the railing. "Even if that means I take the blame."

The gun went off again, and the bullet plowed through a line of lovelocks, cheap metal raining down onto the slats of the bridge like chrome confetti.

So much for that commercial, I thought.

He cocked and fired again, missing me but detonating dozens more locks in the process, and now a bridge that was in no way architecturally beholden to the considerable dead heft of a thousand padlocks was suddenly tilting beneath us, dumping us onto asses and backs as we tumbled together into a collapsing lamp post. This post snapped against our tangle of bodies, and seizing my chance, I grabbed the shiny end and brought it down hard on his head, transforming his skull into its own concave planet, turning one eye completely backwards in its socket.

I hoped he perceived everything exactly the same looking inside his skull as he did when he looked out. I mean, I hoped that when he looked backwards inside his head, he . . . never mind.

I stood up and dropped the shattered lamp, then I walked to the edge of the bridge, broken Eiffel tower key ring jangling in my hand. I counted almost a hundred eyes watching the scene, then counted again just to be sure. I kept ending up on an odd number, which was almost more horrifying than their stare since you never saw odd-numbered eyeballs in nature. Then I heard the sounds of him walking toward me, and I didn't have to turn around to know he would be headless, and not really aiming, and seconds away from finding me with his final bullet.

He fired. And this unknowable subterranean audience, the first true global civilization, watched the muzzle flash chase me over the railing and into oblivion as I dove into those eyes, but the only one who blinked at the explosion was me.

DOUBLE PISS TEST

"The more you drive, the less intelligent you are."
—Repo Man

Maybe we should call the radio station and request a song.

Why don't you request a story instead?

Okay, here's one. I'm out of jail three days, and my girl starts telling me about how some asshole she works with proposed to her. This is her version. She says, "We went on this hike, which was his idea. We were actually lost for awhile, sweating and coughing when he finally got down on his knee to ask . . ."

Well, at least he didn't try to make it all perfect. More interesting with her all sweaty and all.

Just listen. That's when she tells me, "Yeah, it was fate. He actually found an arrowhead and gave it to me and said that it was symbolic, and that's why he'd decided to do it right there on the spot."

Red flag.

I know, right? My bullshit detector is in overdrive now. I go, "Wait, hold on, so he wouldn't have proposed if he hadn't found that arrowhead?" She thinks a second and says, "I guess not. So what?" So I ask, "What did it look like?" and she's all confused. I repeat, "What did it look like? Was it big? Small?" "That big," she says, holding her fingers about three inches apart like I'm doing right now. "What color?" "I don't know. Rock color." "Did you see him find it?" "Yeah." "Did you see him pick it up?" "I think so. Why?" she asks. "Nothing. Keep going," I say, and she goes on with her story, "So, it was great because the last time we went hiking out there, I found an arrowhead. And he said he almost proposed to me back then." "Whoa, back up!" I cough, "You found one years before?" "Yeah, so what?" "Okay, remember when you said you were lost? Who was lost?" She thinks hard, "He was. He's the one who goes there to fish, not me." "Yeah, no shit he goes fishing." I mutter. Then I almost grab her head so she'll pay attention to what I'm saying, "Just think about this for a second though. Don't you think that he may have just been pretending to be lost so he could find this arrowhead he'd stashed, or better yet actually got lost looking for the arrowhead he'd stashed just so he could find it in front of you and then act like it inspired him to propose?"

What did she say?

She got mad. But that was nothing compared to how mad he was when I asked him about it.

No shit. Arrowhead, my ass! I'd take that thing to the fucking lab. Try to find the bar code on the back of it. Maybe the ring, too. Hey, you should mail her a big-ass bag of arrowheads in the mail with a note saying "Thanks for your bulk order! Here's some more for anniversaries!"

He was right though.

About what?

That it was symbolic.

Why's that?

Because I stuck it in his fucking eye. Well, tried to. More like stuck it in his ear. No, I'm just kidding, man. Keep that door shut.

*   *   *

How far did you say you were going?

I can take you about 20 more miles.

Appreciate it.

Hey, you keep me awake, and I'll keep you moving. And if you're trying to scare me with that talk about jail, keep it up. I need to drive about ten more hours anyway, and that shit's better than coffee.

I wasn't trying to scare anyone. Just talkin'. I figured you didn't scare easy. Anyone that picks up someone under that sign.

What sign?

"Penitentiary: Don't Stop For Hitchhikers?"

Didn't notice.

Impossible. They're everywhere. Okay, you know what I overheard outside the gate? This mom and dad were talking to their daughter—she was real little—about some wedding, and they said, "You don't want to be the flower girl?" And this little girl, about half the size of a cricket, says, "No. I want to be the dragon!"

Ha! I want to see that wedding.

Loved it. What does that even mean?

What's up with this theme, man? I don't pick up an ex-con to hear about weddings. What else you got?

Hey, you're the one dressed like you just got back from a wedding.

What are you trying to say?

Whoa, man. Sorry. Just trying to entertain your ass, pay for my ride.

Do you smoke?

Huh? No.

Here, take one of mine. You should, you know. Hitchhikers are supposed to smoke. Makes you look more normal. Kind of like walking and eating a sandwich. Makes your odds go up. Getting a ride I mean.

Am I reading these signs right?

What?

Did I really just leave "Moon" and am now entering "Mars?"

Yep. Just outside Pittsburgh.

What time's that job interview again?

We're in the middle of it.

* * *

When you worked as a captioner, how many captions did you type a day?

I don't know. Thousands?

That's not that much.

Nothing ever sounds like that much. When an astronomer says, "There's hundreds of thousands of stars up there right now," it never sounds like enough, does it?

Not even close.

Who are you talking to?

Did you know that in closed captioning, you desperately wait for a man to be by himself so he won't fucking speak.

I can believe that. Wait, was that a hint?

Hey, you see that sign?

The one that says "Stay Off Shoulders?"

Exactly. I'm gonna have to ask you to cease that back rub immediately.

Oh, sorry.

I want to work on a train. That would be like being paid to be in a car without having to worry about the driving.

All the momentum. None of the responsibility.

* * *

Job interview, huh?

Yeah, it's the third one. I nailed the first two. Closest I've ever got.

Third interview? If you don't have the job after two, you should hang it up. What is there left to ask you about?

Well, the first one was the asking. The second one was typing. The third is apparently urine. Can't drive a limo forever, you know? Got to get back to my training.

Damn. Drug tests, eh? Well, you shouldn't have to worry about that. Now, if they showed you ink blots, then you might have a problem.

You should talk. All you'd see are a bunch of weddings.

No. I'm used to those tests. I already have a harmless list memorized no matter what they show me. "Dog, cat, duck, spider, lizard, crab, praying mantis." And if I'm up against the wall, "Half a duck." Hey, why do you keep talking about weddings when you're the one wearing a tux?

Good question.

So, how did you take a typing test with your hand like . . .

It doesn't change anything. Actually, it makes me faster.

I took a urine test for a new job once and found it to be a very nerve-wracking experience. Not because there were any drugs in my system but because I normally drink a shitload of water every day and it turns out that too much water in the sample can be considered "diluted." Add my pot-tokin' friend who said I should drink all the water I could because of the contact high from shaking his hands or taking his phone calls. So I chug about nine glasses, then grab a phone book to find the lab closest to me that did this testing. They were closed. And the next closest one was also the furthest. I call them anyway and I'm told they're closing soon but I might make it if I hurry. The girl on the phone says, "Fine. Hurry up. But please make sure you can urinate when you get here because we hate when people come in at the last minute and can't perform!" So I run back to the faucet and slam three more glasses of water and crash out of my house, bladder visibly swelling like a conjoined twin as I painfully stub my stomach on my car door. I drive slightly slower than the speed of sound and jump a curb as I come flying in hot with about ten seconds to spare. The angry girl from the phone meets me in the lobby with a cup and yells as I'm running to the bathroom. "Don't flush! Please do not flush the toilet or your test is disqualified!" "Why not?" I ask over my shoulder, zipper halfway down. "Because people use fake bladders and flush them all the time." I want to ask her more about this bizarre image or the bladder black market, but I have no time. In the bathroom, ready to burst, I hose the cup with the weight and velocity of ballistic missile exhaust. But I can't stop. And the waves are quickly approaching the brim. "Do you have any more cups?!" I shout through the door as the surface tension bubbles and strains around the edges. I hold my breath to try to lower the pressure. "What?" she asks indifferently. So I turn the broken hydrant toward the toilet in desperation and, I'm totally serious here, begin to fill that to the top, too. The water is just getting ready to pour over the rim and onto my feet when I reflexively reach out and flush. "What are you doing?!" she screams from outside, suddenly interested. "Saving your life!" I scream back. When I'm finally out and the tsunami has calmed down, she holds my cup up to the light, squinting. Proudly, I tug on my belt and say, "Got fifty more cups you need filled? Is there an orphanage on fire nearby?" But she just squints harder then mutters, "Hmm, they might send this back because it's too clear." I'm like, "What?! You just told me to drink a bunch of water, Doc!" And she shrugs and says "Maybe they won't. But we'll see." So I go home all paranoid and hit the internet. Big mistake. I read about people failing drug tests just for watching stoner movies three hours before their tests or even singing along to popular '60s songs on the way to the lab. It also says that people usually shave their heads so they can't do a follicle test on them, too. I start thinking, "Oh, no. I just shaved my head yesterday and I drink water. I am the most suspicious drug addict on the planet. I will never be hired again with such a smooth cranium and twelve gallons of crystal-clear piss that pours forth from my body like a pure Arctic stream!"

Did you pass?

I don't know. I started cutting the neighbor's grass instead. Less stress, lots of water to drink from a hose, and I could listen to music all day.

So, are you going to fuck up someone's wedding or what?

What?

Wait, am I reading none of these signs right?

* * *

I thought you didn't need gas?

Now I do.

But your gas cap's on the driver's side. Plus your car's about 20 feet away.

Yeah, but you're over here.

Don't point that nozzle at me.

Don't move . . .

* * *

So, how far are you going?

Next town's fine. Thanks for the ride, man. Never got picked up in a limo. Anybody back there?

Don't open that. You'll let out the air. Hey, I see you looking at my bad hand. Don't worry about it. It's the first thing a hitchhiker notices, since their thumb's been erect all day.

I wasn't really looking at . . .

Hey, you ever actually piss on someone's wedding cake?

Nope.

You ever burn one down? A wedding, I mean.

Why do you keep asking me about weddings? You're the one in the tuxedo, man.

You didn't see that cake in the road back there? That's the only reason I can think of for somebody throwing the whole thing away like that.

No. Just drop me at the next gas station.

Well, see that smoke? That's was the closest one. But you're not gonna want to go near it.

Why's that?

Some dumb bastard was smoking next to the pump. You don't smoke do you?

Nope.

Here, take one of mine. You should. Makes your odds go up.

A GUN NAMED SIOUX

"Heads hung heavy and they swore the Ranger would be mourned
But a boy had found Red's holster and filled it full of thorns
Filled it full of thorns . . ."
—Arty Stealins "Pig Iron"

Agua Fría, New Mexico. Midday sometime.

The shadow on the horse with the hole in its head sits frozen, a hand over his holster, towering over the four men standing in a loose circle around him. He's still blocking a sunset reluctant to disappear into the airish evening red. Then someone belches, and the sun is finally down, and he's out of the shadows, face brighter now than during any hour of the day, hat tipped back to show blazing eyes and rust-colored hair.

"I've been thinking, boys," the Red Rider says. "How many horses have I stolen?"

Al Mutters, a.k.a. "Mud," stands on one side of Red's horse, and Little Joe hides behind the other. Ned Parker, a particularly skeletal man they all call "Egg" stands near the sagging worm fence, his filthy legs blending in with the weary, wizened structure. Jack Hicks, a.k.a. "Jackass," kicks at the dirt near a post hole like it's the most important thing in the world. All the while, a fifth cowboy still has his hands high up in front of him, fear making his cracked fingertips shiver.

No one talks awhile, and soon all the scrawny, dust-covered men are straight and still, waiting to see what Red is going to do. Dread hangs in the air between them, the expectation that comes from seeing Red do many horrible things. Heads creak lower than normal, every face dark and hidden under the shade of their hats.

"At least 50," Fifth Cowboy sighs. He's the newest member of the gang, still missing a nickname, even missing a real name. Little Joe leans around the ass of the horse, mouth open to ask who he was, and Mud points at him to shut up.

"And how old am I?" Red asks everyone.

"23," Fifth Cowboy answers.

"And how many women has this here biggity bub fucked in this town?"

"All of them."

"How many's that!"

"At least 30? Back when there was 30."

"And how old am I, again?"

"Still 23, boss."

"And how many men I killed?"

Red holds a hand up before the man can answer. Instead he cocks a thumb back at Little Joe.

"I don't know, boss," Little Joe says. "I ain't been around you long enough. I've seen you kill at least 10."

"He's killed 20," Mud says, blinking slow, mumbling. "No blusteration."

Mud sports a long, droopy mustache, and sometimes his voice is buried behind it.

"And how old am I again?"

"Still 23, boss," Mud says.

"And what's wrong with those numbers?" Red laughs.

Nobody says anything. One of them starts muttering Bible verse to fill the silence.

"It's hard for thee to kick against the pricks . . ."

"I was doing some thinking, boys," Red says. "And I'm thinking that a man should have stole as many horses, fucked as many women, and killed as many men as the number of years he's been on this Earth. That means this can be the last horse I'll steal for a while, your sisters can be the last I've nailed to the counter for a while . . . but I'll be needing to catch up on that other number. Dang, I figure if I'm at least within three, I'll be satisfied."

"Why within three?" Fifth Cowboy asks, hands still up, palms out, legs together, but knees bent and ready to step back. Red studies him, smiling, noting the man's head isn't tilted ever so gently to the side, like his own.

"I don't know! Seems like good number, with the Father, the Son, and the Holy Spirit and all that shit. Within three, and I won't have an unhealthy obsession with numbers and bed men down for no good reason . . ."

He rolls his neck to crack it a bit. Bones pop like kindling.

"And then there's the fact we've all got three days to live," he shrugs. "That bad medicine hangs over my head a bit."

The men all kick dust and shuffle their feet, nervous. Egg is chewing on his lip like it's tobacco. Someone is still quoting Acts 9: 5-6.

"What wilt thou have me do . . ."

"Well, boss," Fifth Cowboy says, coughing. "If you're 23 years old, you're within that 'three' right now . . ."

But now that man has switched from staring down the nostril of a dead horse to staring down the barrel of a gun. Red drew so fast that no one saw or heard it happen. And everyone is suddenly scratching their dusty heads, like Little Joe, desperate to remember this man's name, just in case they get a chance to ever tell the story later in life. They won't.

"You're right, boy," Red says. "Only today is my birthday."

The handle of Red's revolver squeaks under his squeeze, and his finger curls around the trigger like the tail of a whipped dog. The trigger tilts the seesaw of the strut, and the hammer is loosed to fly for the bulls-eye on the base of the cartridge.

When men are dying of thirst, simple actions like this seem to take forever and become conducive to memorializing, but in spite of the apparent complications of the gunshot, no one remembers the man's name, nor the nature of his demise, before or after the journey.

*   *   *

Doña Ana, New Mexico. Noonish.

Arizona Ranger Bob Ford's rusted revolver explodes in his fist, showering his face and shoulders with shrapnel from the burst barrel and a warm drizzle of his own blood.

"Jesus Christ!"

The Ranger stumbles back and sits in the dirt, watching the raccoon blink at him in confusion then turn and run off with a red fistful of chicken. A man steps from the trees behind the Ranger and stands staring at the Ranger's back for a moment. Then he walks from the Ranger's shade and speaks. It's Tom McMaster, a young man in his 20s, one of the cowhands Bob flagged as eager for a law-enforcement father figure. The Ranger has always hated the genus.

"Got a letter for you, Ranger,' Tom says, then scoffs as he watches the Ranger pull his sleeve up over his wounded hand. "You know something? While I walked up, I pulled my gun and put it back in the holster six times. You never flinched."

The Ranger doesn't turn around. He just reaches back behind his back with his good hand and holds it open.

Tom waits.

He finally slaps the letter into the stigmata of his palm.

"No way you're that beef-headed to pull on me," the Ranger says. "So why lie about it?"

"You swearing us in tomorrow?"

"Everybody but you, Tom. Unless you quit asking."

Tom steps back to let the Ranger read the letter, shaking his head as he watches him get blood all over it.

* * *

Agua Fría. Same day. Dusk.

A young Mexican woman breast-feeds her baby in an adobe house full of starving, howling cats. Outside her open door, in the dying, lingering light of the day, a man on a horse with the hole in its head rides up to the porch and dismounts. He walks through the door, throwing his crushed hat against the wall in an explosion of dust, stripping a few rust-colored hairs from his scalp along with it. Red is a younger man in the shadows, strawberry blonde the last time he bathed, with a surprisingly innocent-looking face around the wild eyes, hatred, and dehydration. He has flecks of blood on one cheek outlining half a laugh he's saving as he walks toward the woman and her baby. He dangles a tangle of chicken wire, then throws it at them as she shields the child.

"Your chickens are dead, dummy. Use this on the windows to keep out the cats." He points at the baby. "Pretty soon those noisy animals are gonna stop beggin' for food and start takin' . . ."

He wades through the desperate felines, kicking the wire out of his way, stomping up in front of the cowering woman. His boot comes down heavy on the tail of a huge, ratty tom. It screeches and howls, and the rest of the cats scatter out the door, but Red doesn't even blink, not even when the cat twists around his boot, biting and clawing at the leather, its back legs rabbit-kicking Red's leg in vain. Red takes no notice of this at all, and the other half of his smile grows.

"Put that udder-sucker away. It's my turn on that thing."

The woman stares in horror at Red's boot heel still grinding the cat's tail, then quickly moves to lay the baby in its box. She tries in vain to release the child, but it hangs onto her breast by its teeth. The cat's howls are deafening, and combined with the baby now spitting milk down the woman's stomach and shrieking along with it, the woman fights the urge to crack her own skull against the dirt floor in despair. The cat bites hard into his boot, eyes crazed, and the woman relaxes a bit, imagining her own teeth sinking into Red's leathery face. Red crosses his arms, still oblivious to the discord and palpable desperation hanging in the dust. He nods at the white bubbles burbling between the baby and her tortured nipple.

"Come on, no kid needs that much to drink. I know you like it spicy, but you bean-eaters have to conserve like the rest of the town."

"With baby it's not '*drink*,'" she says in broken English. "It's '*eat*.'"

"You heard me. Hurry up before you yean another. Now where's my teat?"

With one hand, the woman hands him a bottle of whiskey, and he laughs and swigs half the alcohol almost instantly. With her other hand, she finally frees the baby from her body with an audible *pop!* and shakes the dirt off a blanket to tuck around its shoulders. The cat, still trapped but not giving up, strains to climb Red high enough and lock on the bit of bare leg where Red's jeans are shredded just above his boot. It stretches up and snaps into his calf, snarling so low the woman feels the triumph in her chest. Rivers of blood stain his leg like red lightning at dusk, but he just blinks a little slower. Seeming to notice the cat for the first time, he puts his full weight on its tail, and it howls so high it's actually inaudible for a good few seconds. Then Red coughs down the last of the whiskey, absentmindedly throwing the half-empty bottle against the wall. It ricochets and lands inside the wooden box makeshift crib, shattering over the infant's face. The baby wails so loud that the cat stops working Red's leg and tried to climb into his boot to hide. Horrified, the woman runs to their baby, hands shaking as she pulls whiskey-soaked shards from its hair. Red turns to leave, disgusted.

"Too goddamn noisy in here. Your *mamasita* been blacksmithing you again?"

"What you do?" the Mexican woman cries.

"Relax. That kid ain't had nothing but rocks for toys since it's been born. It's gonna *need* that drink."

"Go!"

Red kicks the cat through the open window, then tosses a pewter hip flask onto the floor near the woman as an afterthought as he walks out. She comforts the injured child as best she can, trying to lick her fingers to clean the cuts. After a moment of staring down at the flask on the dirt floor, mouth too dry to produce saliva and her body too dry to produce any more milk, she eventually retrieves it from the floor and takes a deep drink of whiskey. Then, sobbing in silence, she leans down to wrap the chicken wire around the baby's wooden box, the hexagons casting shadows like honeycomb over the pinched, pink face. The lullaby of creaking metal calms them both a bit, and no longer weeping, she finally presses the metal lip of the flask to the baby's eager mouth.

* * *

Bisbée, Arizona. Flashback to the summer of 1853.

Little Bobby Ford, long before he rode to Texas to become a big Texas Ranger, is aiming a finger at a hill in the distance while his father, Samuel, looks on. Bobby's dad is a big man with a sunburned face that masks his age. He is struggling to put a large revolver in his son's hands. Although Bobby will be a feared lawman one day, for now his hands are so small that he can only reach the trigger with the tip of his middle finger. And his father knows that's no way to hold a gun. A rabbit grazes nearby, and Sam is growing angry as Bobby drops the gun before he can get off a single shot. Furious,

Sam finally untangles his boy's hand and takes the gun away. Bobby is used to his father's anger, and he resumes pointing at the rabbit with his finger instead. In one smooth motion, his father stands tall with the pistol and fires. The rabbit explodes in a flash of blood, dust, and fur, and the Future Ranger blinks in shock at his father's lethal speed and casual cruelty.

Later that day, Sam and his son hover over a dozen weapons laid out on top of the display case in Sam's gun store. Sam is giving his son a fast history of each gun while moving him down the line to see if his small hands can wield just one pistol successfully.

"See these guns?" Sam asks. "These are my prize dozen. And they make my calendar, boy. I take one gun out each month and get to know it all over again. It helps me remember what month it is, too. Pay attention and one day you won't just be carrying no apple peeler."

He picks up what appears to Bobby to be the shell of an unfinished revolver.

"This is always my first gun of the year," he continues. "I take it out every January. It's called the 'Skeleton,' forged in 1880. All the springs and gears are visible, revealing that there ain't really much to guns after all. It was a prototype, created as an instructional tool to sell to the Mexican army. D.B. Wesson hisself made this creature so you could finally see all the organs for the first time. Legend has it that this skeleton of a gun was fired into the skeleton of a dog so that they could study the inside of the gun *and* the target simultaneously.

"They shoulda got a skeleton to shoot it, too!" Bobby laughs, reaching for the handle. But the Future Ranger's hand is too small for it, and Sam snatches it away, more annoyed at his son's joke than the genetic failings of his grip.

"Pay attention to what I tell you about these weapons, boy. A lot of folks will tell you stories about how this gun did this and this bullet did that. All bullshit. I'm gonna give you the straight history right now . . ."

They move down. Sam holds up a long, strange pistol with a large row of teeth surrounding the cylinder in its center.

"February," he says. "This was the first .44. First made in 1870 and called the 'Model 3 American.' Has more kick than a Big Fifty Sharps, and almost as long. This weapon here was a prototype where the firing pin rotated instead of the cylinder. No more guessing what chamber had a bullet in it, if you were one of those boys that liked to spin it after loading. Or one of those fools who like to guess. This particular gun killed 27 people the day it debuted . . . all during games of Russian Roulette."

Bobby smiles at his dad's attempt to join in with the jokes, but Sam doesn't let him hold this particular gun either. They slide down the counter to pause in front of a large, silver revolver.

"March. This is the .45 Auto Loader, originally built for government testing. You can take it apart into pieces that can then be taken apart into smaller pieces and so on and so on and so forth. Do you like magic tricks, son? No? Good, because I hate them."

In a flurry of grunts and hand movements, he quickly dismantles and reassembles the weapon. Bobby starts to point out the several pieces remaining sprinkled across the counter after the reassemble, and Sam brushes them off onto the floor.

"When I was your age, I liked playing with this gun every March because that's when your grandpa would usually finish putting together the jigsaw puzzle he'd started during the winter. That always made sense to me. Especially because you don't have to put the pieces of a jigsaw puzzle back the way they want you. Your granddad taught me that.

"Daddy, did you say 1870?" Bobby asks, glancing at the gun parts on the floor, then scratching at the wood on the corner of the gun case. There's a heart with a year carved inside it. A heart Bobby gouged into the counter years ago, but he suddenly realizes he got the year wrong back then. He's not sure, but he's now worried this may have screwed up his sense of time for good. He's not too worried though. He'd messed up the heart pretty bad, too. Although he'd heard once that a real heart *did* have three points on it, at least, and fingers. Kinda.

"Oh yeah, one more thing. They say you can reduce this weapon down to small enough puzzle pieces that you could swallow . . . if you had to. Of course, that particular feat don't mean too much. I saw a man eat a piano once. And I don't mean he 'bit the ground,' I mean he really, truly devoured a Baby Grand from teeth to toes. Hell, a man could eat an entire gun factory if he just kept shittin'."

Bobby backs up a step.

"You hungry, boy?" he laughs.

"But it's not March, is it, Pa?" Bobby shivers, trying to change the subject. "It's too cold outside for March."

Sam squeezes his son's shoulder.

"Settle down now. What kind of father would force his son to eat a gun? Because a bastard like that should get some kind of reward!"

* * *

Dona Aña, New Mexico. 1895. Present day. Morning.

The air's still cool, and Tom kicks around the rusted remnants of an exploded weapon scattered in the dirt, as the Ranger sits on the ground nearby. The letter Tom delivered flaps with the wind, smacking the Ranger's knee for attention. The name on the envelope reads "Wendler" in large, child-like script.

"Ain't it a little early to be resting?" Tom asks. "On the road, no less?"

"Not really," the Ranger says. "March is the first official month for sitting your ass on the ground. 'Nobody marches in March,' my dad used to say. And the last icicle fell three weeks ago."

Tom circles him impatiently.

"Well, aren't you gonna read it?" Tom asks as he reaches down to pick up the rusted cylinder from a gun that exploded that morning, as well as decades before. "After I deliver mail to you on a *Sunday?*"

He flicks some dirt to reveal a piece of the revolver's hammer.

"You could probably salvage this thing," Tom says. "Not that anyone should want to. Hold on a second. What was this made out of?"

He picks up the shard and sniffs it.

"This ain't pig iron, is it?" he asks as he sniffs again. "The smelt went wrong when they made this, that's for sure."

The Ranger says nothing.

"You don't make guns outta this shit," Tom laughs, flicking it away like it's a dung shard and wiping his hands on his thighs. "So you gonna read the letter or what, boss?"

"Why don't you just tell me what it says?" the Ranger asks, still not looking up.

"I don't read your mail. I just bring it. On a *Sunday.* Of course, if it was open already . . ."

Now the Ranger raises his head.

"Well, it *was* open," Tom says, looking guilty. "It's from some sheriff's wife. She says that they won't have any more water in Agua Fría in about two weeks. Not one drop to drink."

"Well," the Ranger sighs. "That's two years longer than I thought that town would last."

"She says that the wells are drying up, and any parties, too," Tom says, talking fast now. "She says in two weeks anyone who ain't left town will be dead because she says that it takes a week in every direction to get anywhere else. She says they have a bell tower in the town that's going to chime when they're past the point of no return. She says when the bell tolls, it's too late to even try to leave. She says a lot of people are gone or going, but some people are staying, too. Including her."

"Whoa whoa. What? How long ago was the letter sent?"

"A week ago?" Tom shrugs. "That bell she's talking about probably started ringing today."

"Why the hell would anyone stay where there isn't any water?" the Ranger asks himself more than Tom, chopping a heel in anger.

"Oh, yeah, one more thing. She says there ain't any sheriff there anymore either. Ever hear of a man named 'Red'?"

Hearing this, the Ranger stands up, face furrowing into knuckles.

"But you ain't going there for him either. You're going there for that sweet angelica. Tell your sister I said hello."

The Ranger stares at Tom until Tom has to turn, then he starts collecting the pieces of his exploded revolver. Tom holds it in a while, but eventually can't help but laugh, in spite of the beating he received last time he mocked the man.

"Yeah, don't forget your gun!"

*   *   *

Desert. Dusk.

The Ranger and Tom ride in silence. Tom's face is haunted by the dead dog on the wagon tracks in their path.

"I'm seeing that way too much," Tom says. "And it's something that will be hard to stop. An animal always wants to take the same path a man does."

"Who told you that?"

"Something I heard in church. He liked to say that a lot, before he started drinking Apache tiswin."

"One day, we'll walk on these dogs instead of the road," the Ranger says, still working on the rusted puzzle in his hands.

"A road without water leads straight to Hell," Tom agrees. "And we're already going in circles, which is the same thing," he adds, staring at another skeleton, wondering how anyone could restrain a dog that size with only the thin collar of a priest.

As they ride, they take turns sleeping with their chins against their chests. They don't realize that they share the same dream, even with the enemy.

It's a dream of Agua Fría twenty years ago. A 9-year-old Red is sitting on the bar drinking from a mug while a burly, red-haired man drinks from a bottle. The sound of a fight erupts from a card game in the back of the room, and gunshots ring out. The bartender ducks down as stray bullets fly. As Red watches, the red-haired man's skull and whiskey bottle both explode without warning and shower Red with glass, blood, bone, and gore. Little Red blinks as chunks of his father's brain drip from his nose, then he starts to laugh hysterically, dragging red streaks through his hair with his tiny fingers as if he's playing in the mud. The shaking bartender comes up from behind the bar to grab the child. Then he drops the blood-soaked boy in horror when he sees that he's laughing. Red falls for what seems an eternity, finally splashing down at the bottom of a well. Only when Red hits bottom does he finally start to cry.

"What the hell is so funny?"

They all wake up when the coyote skeleton speaks. It's also the bartender.

* * *

Bisbée. Flashback. Forty years ago. Midday. Weather Unpredictable.

Back in the gun store again. Little Bobby Ford, a Future Arizona Ranger, and his father, Sam, are still working their way through a special kind of calendar, consisting of a dozen weapons laid out on the counter. The Future Ranger's hand is too small for every pistol he tries, but Sam has high hopes for a particularly ornate shooter.

"This is April's gun," Sam says. "Very appropriate for 'April,' since it's a woman's name. Woman's shooter, too, probably. It's the .38 Single Action, decorated in silver and gold by Tiffany & Company. Polished to perfection. It was actually presented to General George Custer in 1869. It looks like it's made from cake icing because it's the most expensive gun in the case. But no one has *ever* thought about stealing it because they don't want the firearm that proved once and for all that Custer *was* a homosexual. You know what that is? On second thought, don't even touch it, boy."

They start to move down, but Sam stops and goes back.

"You know what this gun looks like to me?" he asks his son. "It does look like the kind of gun a girl would carry . . . if it was the kind of girl who *wouldn't* normally carry a gun. Get me?"

They move down to a long rifle, which Sam quickly picks up. To the Future Ranger's surprise, Sam breaks it in half over his knee.

"May," he says. "The Smith & Wesson Revolving Rifle. It looks like a rifle, but it's really just a revolver with a long, detachable barrel and shoulder stock. Developed in 1875, this particular gun saved its owner's life when he fell and pretended to smash his very own weapon. Then, when his attackers' backs were turned, in five seconds tops, he put it back together and shot them all down. Shot them in the back, you ask? No, of course not. You should never shoot someone in the back. He shot them in the back of their goddamn heads. And May is a good time to use this rifle, too. Lots of turkeys to shoot. And it's good sport to hone your talents because the back of a turkey's skull is real tiny."

Sam snaps the rifle back together and pushes his son past it to the next one.

"June's gun. This is the weapon built after both Horace Smith and Daniel B. Wesson survived their first gunfight. It's the S&W Model 1. Fired a tiny .22 Rimfire short cartridge . . ."

"They had a gun fight?" the Future Ranger interrupts. "Against each other? Did that really happen?"

His father ignores the question and moves down again.

"July. This is the .38 Super, built to compete with the Colt .45 and the .38 Colt Super Automatic. I'm not a Colt fan, but they say that Smith & Wesson are still, to this day, obsessed with topping this gun. They say that they're working on something called a 'Magnum' as we speak, whatever the hell that is. Sounds like a goddamn Indian name to me. Goddamn thing must shoot arrows and sadness. We'll see."

They move down again, then both stop to stare at a small, thin gun that resembles a child's toy.

"I fuck with this weapon every August," Sam says. "Built in 1887 and used in the 1908 Olympics, Smith & Wesson built this Target Revolver with the first adjustable site. They stopped building them because the 1908 Olympics were such a joke with rich, weak bastards having slap-fights and staring contests and other equally stupid shit. Did you know that the rules in the first Olympics were designed to keep real athletes from competing? Smith pulled the gun from the exhibition and publicly said they were embarrassed to be a part of it. Rumor has it that he did this after he saw an Apache laughing his ass off at the thumb-wrestling contest. Yes, son, the Apaches *did* invent thumb-wrestling, but their version is to the death. Or maybe that was 'Sue' Indians. Anyhow, I set up a little target practice of my own every August, when it's the hottest part of the year. Ever try to shoot the thumb off an eagle? They're the only animal besides us that's got thumbs, you know?"

"True story?"

"True story."

Sam picks up the next gun in the line, holding it over his head to show his son a long, metal chain dangling off of the grip.

"September. Built in 1861, this here's the Model 4 American. Actually it's a variation on the Model 2. But it turned out to be just too goddamn big. The extractor rod is attached with a chain only slightly longer than a bulldog's leash. In fact, that's what people used this goddamn chain for. Instead of throwing a stick, they'd throw the extractor rod, and the dog would bring it back. It was a good way to teach the dog to bring back the ducks you shot with it. Also makes a good splint."

Then they finally come to the small lump of a revolver so dull and dirt-covered that it's almost invisible. It seems to be made of rock, or maybe carved from a chuck of dead wood as a joke. The Future Ranger reaches for it excitedly, his small hand covering the grip perfectly.

Sam's hand smothers the boy's, and when they both squeeze the gun together, it's so cold that the boy's teeth start clicking, and little Bobby, the future Arizona Ranger, thinks his father has turned it to September just by speaking the word.

* * *

Agua Fría. Present Day. Mourning.

The Ranger and Tom are entering the city limits. Their first glimpse of the town is such an obscene vision of hell that it's almost comical, particularly to Tom. A broken signpost marks the border, as does a blazing bonfire of dead horses. A line of silent storefronts loom in the distance like tombstones, vultures perched on their rooftops. As the Ranger and Tom approach the fire of horseflesh and bone, Tom chuckles and points at the animals' legs protruding from the flames. The Ranger stops his horse, and Tom does the same, then clears his throat and points some more.

"You know what," Tom says. "I once rode into a town, and the first thing I saw was this giant butterfly made out of a dozen kinda flowers. All the children there had built it just to welcome us. Turned out that my stay in that town was perfect; no fights, no sheriff, didn't lose no money. Then, this other time, years later, I rode into a different town, and some little bastard hit me with a ball of fecal from the roof of the bank. And my stay *there* only got worse after that."

"Are you saying 'road' or 'rode'?"

"What's the difference?"

"I mean, what's your point?"

"Point is, I'm thinking there's good omens, and there's bad omens. And I look at a fuckin' bonfire of horses and, uh, I ain't a superstitious man or anything but . . ."

As they circle the fire, the Ranger struggles to stop his nervous horse when he sees a man lying on the ground nearby, his arms behind his head and his hat covering his face. The man seems to be relaxing, and as they get closer, they see the hat move as if the man's snoring or breathing hard underneath it. The Ranger dismounts and walks closer. When he gets in front of it, his black Mustang blows a stream of mucus onto the Ranger's brim.

"Do you think there's a solitary horse left alive around here?" Tom asks him. Then, "Does that Mustang of yours got some kind of infection or what? We gotta be careful . . ."

Tom trails off as the Ranger pulls back the hat to reveal the face of the cowboy on the ground. There's a boiling mass of maggots in the holes where the man's eyes, nose, and mouth should be. Tom stops laughing for good and coughs to stifle a gag. The Ranger starts unloading the gear off his horse.

"I ain't seen any flies in days. Or rain. Good thing I didn't pack my fish," Tom jokes, still horrified and hacking up some smoke. "Tell me now, how the hell can there be maggots without flies?"

The Ranger ignores this observation, and the follow-up.

"We'll camp here," he says, and Tom looks at him in shock for a moment, then dismounts and begins unloading his horse, too.

"Why not."

Tom plays a bit from his harmonica, unpacks some, staring at the legs in the flames a little more cavalier, like it's any other bonfire.

"If this isn't a good time to blow some spooky notes on a harp, I just don't know what is," he says between lazy puffs of music. "Got anything I can quirley with this tobacco?"

"Nope," the Ranger grunts. Then he ponders, "You know, if someone dragged these horses over to burn them, then that means there's people still here to worry about the stink."

Tom reaches into the fire and breaks off a horse's leg. Then he pulls strips of hide from the smoking limb as the Ranger gives him a curious stare. Tom stops skinning the leg and throws it back into the flames.

"Just a thought," he shrugs. "A charred horse hoof or a lathy bit of leg might look like a sweet, ripe peach to us in about 24 hours."

"How much water you got left?"

"Most of it," Tom says, patting his canteen and the bags near him. "Some jerky, too. But we have to finish our business tomorrow and ride straight the fuck out if we want to make it back."

The Ranger stands up and slaps some dirt off his legs.

"We will," he says. "If we don't waste time here telling stories."

"Ain't that what a campfire's for!" Tom says, punctuating this with some tuneless metal bleats.

"Not at all," the Ranger says. "A fire's something you stare at when you want to forget a story, not remember one."

"Whatever you say."

"Grab your squaw wood. We're on the move."

"Not till you tell me a bedtime story," Tom says as he reluctantly packs up.

The Ranger stares at him for a solid minute.

"Okay, here's a five-second fable for you," he says. "When I was young, my father rigged every gun he owned, every gun in his shop, to explode when it fired. For some reason, he thought this was a good thing to do. Thought it would make me a man."

Tom considers this a moment.

"That ain't no fable," he decides. "A fable has a point."

"So does your fuckin' head."

There's a rustling and crackling of something moving in the brush behind them, and they both spin around quick, hands on their guns. They see the shadow of a boy disappear into the dark. The men exchange a surprised look, quickly finish loading up their horses, and swing legs up into their saddles to follow. The Ranger kicks his steed hard to get it moving.

"You should lighten up on the beast," Tom says. "Might do wonders."

The Ranger waves this off.

"Have you ever noticed that everything bad that's happened to a man on a horse, happened to a man on a horse?"

* * *

Bisbée. Flashback. Thirty years ago now, give or take a decade.

The gun store is ragged but still standing, just like Samuel, and a teenage Bobby Ford, future Arizona Ranger, is arguing with his father like it's his first time.

"Goddamnit, boy. He is too fast."

"So am I," the Future Ranger says.

"He's faster than most. Faster than you for certain."

"How do you know this?"

Sam throws a bottle against the wall closest to his son.

"Because I caught him playing with himself when he was eight!" he says.

"Blarney."

"I swear, son," Sam says. "Listen to me. He was eight years old, and his hand was moving so fast it looked like a hornet trapped under a shot glass. His mother actually talked a doctor into tying his right hand to his side for weeks. And, of course, what a mistake that was, 'cause when that hand finally broke free from those belts and ropes and knots, his jerkin'-off hand was three times faster than it was before. Guess which one he fires with."

"You're so full of shit," the Future Ranger says, trying not to smile.

"I ain't lying. That's the real reason Red left town. He hasn't seen his mother or been back to Bisbée since the day he untied his shootin' hand."

"Bull. Shit," the Future Ranger says, turning toward the door.

Sam grabs for his son's arm to keep him still, but he yanks it away and keeps walking.

"Hey, this ain't no joke, boy! If it's a gunfight . . . you're gonna die today."

The young Ranger stomps out the door in disgust. Sam watches him go, brow furrowed.

"Thanks for believing in me, daddy."

* * *

Doña Ana, New Mexico. Flashback but not that far back. 12:03 p.m.

The Ranger, Bob Ford, is sitting in the dirt behind his farmhouse, looking down at the twisted wire of a chicken cage. The sides of the mangled cage are speckled with an explosion of blood and feathers. He squints in anger and disbelief at his skid marks in the ground, indulging in a bit of nostalgia, while a rusted gun rests on his knee. He's motionless, the sun sinking in the distance. A rolled-up stack of posters are on the ground by his boots. The visage of one particular poster has been stomped and kicked around, and through the mud stains, only the word "Wanted!" is visible. A large raccoon peeks out from the warped, wooden porch steps, and the Ranger levels his filthy revolver to kill it. The raccoon runs for the chicken innards, a streak of black and gray barely adjusts its beeline for the bloody cage, even when he cocks the hammer, and the Ranger laughs, wondering how the animal knows it has nothing to fear from his weapon.

* * *

Bisbée. Some day. Some time, a long time ago.

A Future Ranger and his father are standing over a small, dust-and-rust covered revolver, still trying to find anything to fit the boy's little hand. Ready to give up, Sam blows some insect shells off the worst gun in his store.

"October. With the droughts, Smith & Wesson had just went bankrupt like everyone else. That was the year this gun was coming out. So they had to build this with spare parts and substandard metal. It's a .30 caliber piece of shit, and you shouldn't even be looking at it. You've got a one-in-ten chance of it exploding in your hand every time you fire it. That's why it's my Halloween special for you! Trick or treat."

The Future Ranger never loses sight of the gray, featureless gun, continuing to glance back at it as they move down the line. His father's quick dismissal of the weapon makes it the most fascinating one by far. Sighing, Sam picks up a thin-barreled weapon to distract his son, a gun that closely resembles a water toy he picked up from a snake oil salesmen after the first of the brutal Arizona droughts. It looked real enough, minus the squeeze bulb.

"November. There's a good story with this one. Looks like that toy, don't it? You remember that Parker Stearns & Sutton USA Liquid Pistol you wanted so bad? I got suckered into buying that one 'cause they swore it could put out a fire. And there is something to be said about pointing a gun at some flames to make them go away, like the opposite of what you'd expect! Bullshit. It was the first thing to go once that fire started. But this gun only looks like a water pistol. Now, some say that Joe Wesson joined Smith & Wesson on November 11, 1880 at the age of 21. But I hear that's actually when him and Smith's youngest son had their first duel. And he was fast, too. He was so fast that, for awhile, that company was called Wesson & Smith. And this is the gun that boy used, because it looked like that toy, this crazy Luger-looking thing with a stripper clip you pulled to chamber the bullet. He called it the 'Blow Forward.' And I ask you, what kind of name is that for anything shaped like this?"

"But . . ."

"Wipe your chin and listen, son."

Sam takes his son's elbow and drags him down to the last gun on his counter.

"Finally! Your last hope! December. It was December, 1882, when Joe Wesson, D.B. Wesson's youngest son, developed this. It's the .44 Hammerless, also called the .44 'Humorless' by the boys in his office, mostly called 'The New Departure' by the boys in the factory, a name that stuck with the public, too. And it's good gun for December weather. No hammer to freeze and one extra trigger in case the first one locks up. See that? It has no hammer but two triggers. The lower trigger rotates the cylinder and cocks the invisible hammer inside. Look. Look here, I said!"

Sam holds the gun out to the Future Ranger. He holds it carefully but struggles to get his hand around it. He can only squeeze the bottom trigger with his middle finger, as it just barely reaches the top one. Embarrassed, the boy hands it back.

"Did you take the hammer off this?"

"Why would I do that?"

"I don't know, daddy. You did just lie about Smith shooting Wesson."

"So?" Sam says, smiling. "It's a good story ain't it? Leaves an impact."

He remembers when his father tried repairing guns for a living, before he resorted to sales, then finally to collecting. He ruined all the weapons he serviced, however, a reverse Midas touch, as his only training was based on a discarded Sears & Roebuck Co. catalog where all the "exploded" gun schematics had been printed in reverse.

"I don't know. Maybe I'll just take October."

He walks back down the line and reaches for the gray, lumpen revolver, and his father spins him around.

"Why the hell would you go for that? After looking at all these, you really want that? You don't want that."

"Tell me about it again. You said 'substandard metal.' What kind of metal did they use then?"

"Pig iron. Mixed alloy. Worst of all worlds. It looks like a rock for a reason, boy."

"How big?"

"How big what?" Sam asks.

"How big was the iron?"

"What the hell are you . . . no, I said 'pig' iron. Not 'big' iron, dummy."

Sam affectionately rubs his son's head in spite of his disgust, then cackles when he picks the gun back up.

"If that's what you want, fine. It's all yours, boy. Happy Halloween!"

"Daddy, how can these twelve guns be your calendar? There's years missing in between each of those guns. I don't get it."

"A man doesn't need to know what year it is. He just needs to know the month."

"But you thought it was March before. And now you're saying 'Happy Halloween.'"

Sam says nothing.

"So, I can have it?"

"I said you could, if you really want it. You realize they don't make them out of pig iron for a real good reason, right?"

"If I take it, how will you know when it's October?"

"Because I won't have a gun for a whole goddamn month!"

"Right."

Or a son."

"Right!" Not really getting the joke, the little Future Ranger claps his hands, trying to act like it doesn't hurt. "So . . . are we going to California like everyone else? I heard people talking about the wells running dry around here."

"Who was talking about that? No, no, no, that's five towns and nine years away if it ever happens. The Arizona droughts are over for awhile. Nothing for you to worry about. Right now I want you to worry about *right now*."

"Does it work?" the tiny Future Ranger asks, staring at his new gun, cocky but doubtful.

"No. I already told you. You picked the worst one."

"But it's the only one I can carry," the Future Ranger says, skinny arms crossed, belligerent.

"Maybe it'll do," Sam says thoughtfully. "Who knows? The man who traded it in said to me, 'Metal has rock and rock has metal, so it doesn't matter what you're pointing at another man to threaten him. As long as it ain't no apple peeler.'"

"What's that mean?"

"Hell if I know. Sounds like Indian bullshit."

"Does it have a name?" the one-day Ranger asks, fingering the trigger and aiming it at insects in the corners.

"I called it 'Sioux.'"

"I don't know if I want a gun named 'Sue,'" he says, arm and weapon sagging.

"No, not 'Sue,'" Sam says. "I said 'Sioux.' Like that Indian bullshit you were talking about. That's the name of the squaw who swapped it. Them Sioux were always sayin' shit that didn't make much sense."

"Okay. I'll take it."

"As if you ever had a choice."

The young and Future Ranger puts the gun in his belt, and his pants are tight for the first time in his life. Then pulls it out fast and points it at the window, the door, then his dad, in succession. Sam shakes his head and sighs.

"Life ain't gonna be easy for a boy with a gun named 'Sioux.'"

Behind the gun store. Later that day.

"You ever heard the word 'smelt,' son?"

"Yeah. It's a method of extracting metal from iron ore by fire. It's how men make guns."

The Once and Future Ranger stares at his father a moment, dangerously close to connecting over the symbolism of that term. Then his father shakes it off.

"Nope. It's a fish."

"Okay, it's a fish. So?"

"It's a little fish. Like you."

"How is it just like me?"

"Because that's a fish that everyone eats whole."

Sam is towering over the scene, blocking the sun, arms on his boy's arms, showing him how to hold the gun steady.

"Listen up. If you insist on playing this game, there's some rules," Sam says. "You listening?"

The Ranger squints down the barrel, the shake of the gun slowly steadying from the soothing voice of his father an inch from his ear.

"Rule number one . . . keep the sun at your back. Number two . . . maintain eye contact. Number three . . . keep your holster waxed. Number four . . . don't talk. Number five . . . shoot when *he* talks. Number six . . . always shoot for his buckle . . ."

The Rangers arms drop again.

"Now, why do I shoot for his buckle?"

"No idea. Quit wabblin' and don't ask questions."

"What day is it?"

"Man doesn't need to know the day. Or the year. Only the hour."

"What if he ain't wearing a buckle?"

"Then he's unarmed, and this shit ain't even happening."

"But . . ."

"Okay," Sam sighs. "You shoot for the belt buckle because with the adrenaline spike, aiming any higher will put the bullet over his head."

"And why do I shoot when he speaks?"

"Because when someone is talking, they won't know what hap—"

The boy pulls the trigger, and the gun explodes in his hands.

Past, present, or future, a gun will always explode in his hands.

CHANGE MACHINE

Gum Struck

"Goddamn it, whose gum is that?"

"Ours."

"No, I threw those away."

"I know you did. I rescued them."

"You did not."

"Yes, I did."

"Why? Nobody does that. Who does that?"

"We do."

"Wrong. So, whose gum was the pink one?"

"Yours, dumbass."

"Seriously."

"I said it's yours."

"You're lying."

She reached down to scrape them off again, and I guess I pushed her harder than I meant to. She stood back up and blinked in shock as I stepped in front of her to protect them. Then she shook her head, grabbed her shoe that had slipped off, and crashed out the door. Then the next door. I didn't follow her to the car. I was disappointed we hadn't been arguing in the bathroom. Whenever our fights started there, I'd get to hear her slam three doors on the way out. That's the record. You can't slam any more doors on your way out than three no matter where you are. Any house or apartment gets three slams maximum, a room in a room in a room. It doesn't seem like nearly enough.

After she'd been gone a few hours, I checked the gum, and I could have sworn they were closer together, even stretching out to touch. I scratched a line into the wood with my fingernail to mark where they were so I'd know for sure if they really were moving. There was still about three inches of wood between them. Two pieces of gum, one blue, one pink, teeth marks and shine like tiny brains, as if a child had cracked open the heads of two favorite toys, one boy, one girl, and found the insides to be frighteningly real.

My throat still hurt from yelling and my stomach bubbling dangerously low, I checked the 'fridge to find nothing but a jar of brine with a couple pickle stems bobbing in the back like something forgotten in a lab. Once, when I stopped her from throwing out that jar, I begged her to leave it alone for a year to see if the stems could grow more pickles. She shook her head and asked when I was gonna grow up and start buying groceries. It was a good question.

Dumb Struck

I'm driving around thinking that stealing a car for such a ridiculous reason is exactly the kind of thing that makes you assign crazy nonsense all sorts of significance. Of course, people I've known would sigh and say that I've been doing that all my life.

But after opening up a strange vehicle so easily, I'm thinking maybe keys are just an illusion of security, that maybe any of them will open any car at all.

It couldn't be chance. Dumb luck? No one is that lucky.

The gas tank isn't low, but I stop to fill up anyway. It started with a full tank, a nice surprise, like finding a plane ticket in a glove box. But it feels good giving it gas, like I'm making an investment, like I'm planting a flag and proving my right to drive, feeding the horse I stole instead of just riding it to death like they do in those stupid Westerns. They don't hang cowboys for that, right?

As I reholster the nozzle, I notice a sign on the gas pump that reads: "Stealing fuel could cost you your license!"

I stare a minute, then get so disgusted by this threat that I try to get the attention of the teenager on the other side of the pump.

"Hey, you see that?"

"What?"

For some reason she steps back and looks at the bottom of her shoe, making me wonder what happened the last time someone said those words to her. I rap the pump with a knuckle, keeping my bad hand hidden, the one missing a thumb.

"No, that. Right there."

She reads the sign.

"So?"

"So? Doesn't that make you mad?"

"Why?"

"Because it doesn't make any sense. That's like saying, "Stealing a car could cost you your fingers.""

She puts away her nozzle and opens her car door, lost in thought. She turns to me before she climbs in.

"No, it's not like that actually."
"Why not?"
"It's more like saying, '"Stealing a television could cost you your glasses."'"
Then she closes her door and is gone before I can tell her she's right. That is exactly what it means.

Love Tied

Then there was that pregnant girl. Well, maybe it was stealing the car. No, if I had to narrow it down, I would say neither was more important than the other. Except maybe putting my key in the wrong ignition and finding they fit.

I never for a second thought it would work. I mean, what are the chances? Seriously? I'd love to look someone in the eye and proudly declare that I did something as dangerous as stealing a car that day. But the truth is, I only drove off in a strange car because I didn't want to look stupid.

I was in the grocery store looking for some pickles, and I saw this girl I used to know. She was turning around right when my mouth was forming a "hello," and that's when I noticed that she was approximately eight months, three weeks, and two days pregnant. A carnival barker couldn't have guessed more accurately.

Pointing to her stomach then my jar, she's like, "Pickles, huh? How funny is that?" Then we walked around together for awhile, and I helped her grab stuff off the high shelves. After a few more lanes, I got comfortable walking around with her giant stomach, so I dropped my juice in her shopping cart and started pushing it around for both of us. We talked. She was married and happy, and I saw she had all four food groups in her cart. I told her I hadn't seen a cartload like that since I rode under one with my grandma pushing it. I told her I'd chew on the ends of the onion stalks that hung down through the cart, and my grandma used to yell out, "How'd a rabbit get in here?" Then, after a third lap around aisles we'd already been through, I started to notice that when other shoppers looked at us, they clearly assumed we were together. They seemed pleased we still had so much to talk about at this stage in our relationship. Maybe that's why I walked around the store with her for so long, to pretend I had a pregnant, happy wife, just for the afternoon. But I have no idea why she did it.

We rolled around about an hour, putting checkmarks down a long grocery list, even penciling in some extra stuff at the bottom. And even though there was a spot in the margin on her list where her husband had scrawled a note ("Don't forget the light bulb!") our illusion was never broken, and she seemed to be letting me enjoy it.

Then we were in the spotlight of the sun, and I was so distracted watching her walk to her van that I marched up to the wrong car and put my key into the door. The key unlocked it easily, and I sat in the driver's seat for at least five minutes before I even realized where I was.

On the outside, this car looked exactly like mine. Green, squat, orange brake dust on the rims, antenna crooked from being bent, then bent worse in an attempt to straighten it. Inside, however, it was like waking up in a strange bed. It reminded me of my old roommate Gary, who once contracted a hilarious combination of drunkenness and sleepwalking our first night in our new dorm freshmen year. He wandered off and woke up down the hall next to a fish tank half full of water, dead fish, and dirty silverware. Then he just sat in the middle of the floor waiting for me to wake up and tell him where the fish came from. We'd just met the day before and had only one day to memorize faces and room numbers. With nine floors of identical bunks and pastel-colored waiting-room furniture, that wasn't enough time.

He stayed down in that other room for half the day before a guy who actually lived there finally came back from exploring the campus and explained he wasn't me. Gary came stumbling back to our room, exclaiming, "I puked in a fish tank today, dude! Has the world gone crazy?!"

Later during orientation, he told me he'd never been more confused in his life and kept waiting, weeks later, for me to tell him I wasn't really his roommate either.

Point is, that's exactly how I felt when I looked around the inside of that car. But it didn't last. It was the windshield that finally convinced me I was lost. So clean that it was almost invisible, and not a spider web of cracks to be found anywhere. And then I saw the 8-ball air freshener hanging off an undamaged rearview mirror and knew I should probably run.

I was getting ready to bail when the pregnant girl pulled up next to me to wave goodbye one last time. And that's when I smiled like an asshole, waved back, and put the key in the ignition, fully expecting it to jam about halfway.

I couldn't believe it when it slipped in and the car started up. I sat there idling, ready to shut down and jump out any second. But the long line of traffic leaving the lot kept her van creeping along within sight for so long there was no way I was going to let her see me getting back out to unlock a second car. No way I was gonna stand there shrugging and waving to her like some mental patient.

So I thought I'd drive around the block once or twice. Then, once she was gone, I'd bring the car back and hope nobody saw me. Instead, I followed her out onto the highway and ended up so far away from the store that I just kept going.

And when she finally disappeared down an exit ramp, I shook my head and started checking to see what radio stations were programmed, amazed that I'd just stolen a car simply so I wouldn't have to embarrass myself in front of some girl I would never see again.

Tongue Struck

I find a car wash, thinking this will further establish the vehicle as my own, and try to feed the machine a five dollar bill. It's telling me to "insert coins only" so I go over near the vacuum pump and see a big green box marked simply "Change."

I sigh, having had bad luck with vending machines lately, worse than a slot machine, always trying for potato chips and getting the ancient 1975 chewing gum off the dusty bottom row instead. Someone else must have had the same problem, too, because an angry note finally appeared on it that read, "If this machine was used by air traffic control instead of just giving out tasty snacks, there'd be hundreds dead." I don't doubt it.

I put the five bucks in the horizontal slot, and it spits it back out. Without thinking, I drop a quarter in the vertical slot and stand there staring. I put my ear close to the box. Nothing. It apparently doesn't make change, just takes it from you. Not exactly false advertising.

I start laughing and give it another quarter so I can yell to a passing car: "Hey, notice anything different?"

On my way home in the stolen car, I'm suddenly worried what happened to my own vehicle. I decide to flip a coin to decide whether to go back. My brother used to tell me it was impossible to flip a coin without a thumb. He was wrong. But the quarter flies off my middle finger sometimes, and tonight it ricochets off my chin and disappears out the window into the dark.

At the end of the road, there's a parking garage in the middle of an over-grown field of weeds, the last thing to be torn down in a dead stretch of city too far from the heart of it to stay alive. When I was little, my brother and I would ride my bike out there, watching the trees and building along the streets get darker and older and slump to the side. It reminded me of when I'd put rubber bands tight on the tips of all my fingers to watch them turn red and the kindergarten teacher who ripped them loose so hard her fingernail cut a Nike swoosh along my pinkie. She screamed something about my fingers falling off if I cut off my circulation too long, then laughed and said maybe I should put one on my tongue instead.

But when I'd finally ride my bike to that parking garage, I'd try to get enough momentum to make it up that snaking ramp. I never had the strength or the guts to go all the way to the top, but it seemed like a victory anyway. My legs usually ran out of gas about a third of the way up.

So now I'm driving to the top, checking my gas gauge nervously, wondering how far I've gone. Wondering if I have the "guts," roads and innards forever entwined in my memory. My brother once told me through the bathroom door that the human intestine is curled up so tight that it was three miles long when you unwrap it. But he warned me you can only unravel anything once. He also swore our tongues actually stopped halfway down our throats. The ramp in this garage is just like that. Stretched out, I decide it would extend to either ocean.

Then the light is suddenly blinding me, and I'm on the sun-soaked roof. The headlights blink off, and I step out of the car, tracing a scratch along the hood, feeling an engine running hot enough to melt through metal. Looking down over the edge, I see the trees have shrugged off their leaves, and I see more roads than I ever have before. And on these roads are hundreds of splashes of color dotting the pavement in every direction. Is there really that much roadkill in the world? If so, why aren't they all red? I'd like to say I rubbed my eyes and the colors went away.

FASTEN YOUR MEAT BELTS

This year, I got to the festival so early nothing was going on, so it gave me time to scan for suspicious initials scratched into the love locks dangling from every fence. Three hours later, people were setting up the porta-potties along the river, and about an hour after that, a tent was erected for the band, so I went back to my car to stake out the scene in peace. With toilets in place, I knew that meant for real. I turned my Rabbit to keep my headlights on the tent, flipping through Angie's secret love letters, knowing that bravery often accompanied feeling as bad as possible, and me and my rat, Nero, chewed on either end of my last stick of Cajun-spice jerky, sort of like bush-league *Lady and the Tramp*.

Another hour passed, and I was half-asleep and digging around the back seat for more gas station rations, so I chugged a Gatorade that tasted more like a color than a flavor and headed back out to piss. Rather than adding to the litter box in the back seat of the Rabbit, I made a beeline for the tight formation of chunky blue phone booths, spring-loaded doors already banging as the roadies broke them in. Watching the swelling crowd queue up, I thought about the Monty Hall Problem the year before, but now I was trying to avoid a goatee instead of a goat. But when the doors opened, goddamn if the smells didn't remind me of summer concerts and hooked thumbs in the backs of her blue jeans, and I started to unzip my own but quickly became mesmerized by the voices surrounding me.

I remembered the little mesh half-windows on either side of my head from the last time I was there. And, as always, I heard someone in another toilet booth complaining on his phone about missing the actual "fish drop" the year before. "Never fucking again," he swore. It might have been me talking. Then came the scary stuff:

"I'm telling you, the guy has two dicks."

"Shit, I wish I had two dicks."

"Naw, two dicks only *seems* like a good idea. The second one is usually messed up somehow, so you have to suck or squeeze the extra one way harder. To like draw that shit out, like a toothpaste tube."

"I don't have to do anything, bro."

"True story though."

"Does he provide the emergency slide out the bedroom window so you can save time when you're screaming all the way to the parking lot?"

"There's a message buried in there somewhere, man."

"Yeah, the message is, 'Send help.'"

"No, I mean a *message* message, like a fable."

I remembered the argument last year about the social responsibility of an artist, the echoes growing so loud that the whole exchange almost makes me pass out, ricocheting around my skull like it had been hollowed out with a trowel. But somewhere at the bottom of the memory of this commotion, I swore I heard her confession:

"Would you rather your girl fucked a guy with two dicks, or had two dicks?"

"That's like asking someone if they'd rather fight Mike Tyson or talk like him."

"Hey, if you had two of those things, you'd never need suspenders."

"Fasten your meat belts!" I shouted before I could stop myself, and the voices ceased. Then there was one last ghostly comment as I held my breath.

"I heard he can play his keyboard with either one . . ."

Then came the laughter, and all the doors were banging open now, and I ducked down, heart pounding, mind on the most important question regarding my missing wife, something I hadn't considered.

Was she having an affair with a man with two penises? The shame game of former partners and genital size is bad enough for weak-minded dudes without me having to compete at that level. How many men are like this?

I was at least three relationships past looking through other people's phones, but I was suddenly consumed with the urge to scan Angie's for any evidence of these things. We'd both talked about how "dick pics" were an oddly sanctioned form of flashing these days, even without the added attraction of a diphalic freak show. Those phones ended up in evidence bags, most likely, buried in the back of evidence-room shelves, the only photographic evidence of the Loch Ness Monster forever forgotten, along with its two heads.

I was still zipping up in slow-motion when the door to my left banged, and the top of a man's head slid into view through the screen. He looked out through his mesh, not really seeing me, but I could have recognized those Wayfarers anywhere, even without the album covers.

It was Prince's keyboard player. No joke. The one who dressed like a doctor. I knew every goofy member of that band. Most of our wedding mix was Prince.

"One of those days, huh?" Matt Fink sighed, and I assumed he was talking to me. I listened close for any indication of a louder urine stream than normal.

"You know it!" I said, forcing levity, staring straight ahead.

"Can I ask you a question?" he asked, and I swear, this was happening.

"Sure," I said, cautious.

"What do you think is the social responsibility of an artist?"

It seemed impossible he could be asking me this, unless I'd been thinking out loud in my confessional. Angie always hated my standby answer, which he supplied.

"Because I think the artist has no social responsibility at all."

"I agree!" I liked the guy, even though the fumes in those phone booths could scramble your brains. And even if he was way too young to really be in Prince's band—cover band tops—something about the confessional aspect of our faces in the shadow of those vents really made me want to open up more than my shorts. I wondered if he was feeling this, too. Wait, did he say "The Artist" with a capital "A". . . ?

"Can I ask you a question?"

"Sure," he said.

"Did you fuck my wife?"

Then the door slammed, and he was gone from the vent. I stepped out, too, and looked him over in the sun. Though there was no way to put a finger on what was wrong, he didn't seem to stand like a normal human. His head was sort of bent to the side, just a bit, like he was perpetually balancing an invisible phone on his shoulder. But one of the big phones, from the '80s. Definitely not old enough to be a fake doctor in Prince's band, and too young to be a real doctor in real life.

"Sorry, sorry," I said, palms out in peace. "I was talking to another toilet."

"Right," he said, eyeing me suspicious.

"Are you a real doctor?" I asked, trying to appear as casual as I could leaning against the "Party Time Portables" stencil on the door.

"Yes. Why?"

This answer amazed me even further, because now I was either dealing with the fake "doctor" keyboard player from Prince's former band pretending to be a doctor out in the world for some bizarre reason . . . or a different "Matt Fink" entirely, who was an actual doctor, pretending to be Prince's old keyboard player? Who was also fucking my wife. Who would you rather have perform an operation?

I noticed his throwback '80s style and spiked hair, the style that was hot when I first met her. He was also wearing those goofy foot rubbers, those hideous toes with the shoes on them. His feet seemed remarkably small for a man with two penises, so I remained skeptical.

But I was still in a confessional state of mind, considering telling him all sorts of things. Like how we'd once arranged a threesome but couldn't swing an extra female and settled for my buddy Jay because I'd seen his dumb ass naked dozens of times. How that disconcerting moment when we both disappeared inside her had precisely the opposite effect I expected. Rather than a perverse feeling of power, I felt more like I'd been absorbed, devoured, teetering on being thrust inside-out and rendered negligible, and I realized this secret, hidden interiority of women's bodies made them infinitely more terrifying than the exposed meat of our own.

Afterwards, I couldn't look at Jay, and sometimes Angie couldn't look at me, but we tried to put it all behind us. Until I found the letters. And a level of detail betraying acts once thought impossible. Or improbable. And the question returned—if I had a choice, two men or one man with two . . .

And she'd confessed that day along the Maumee River, whispering that she'd tried it again, just to make sure. One man, or two men, or not that kind of doctor, it didn't matter. "For my own good," she screamed into the din of those buckets, and I could hear this clearly, even 50 feet apart. Because science was fucking scary.

"Excuse me," he said and started to walk away. I stopped him with a hand on his chest.

"Want to hear something funny? Me and my wife used to laugh about how she couldn't wait to bust people for saying 'Not that kind of doctor' when she finally got her PhD."

"What are you trying to solve here?"

"Nothing," I lied.

"Can I go?" he said, looking down at my hand still on his chest. "We need to finish setting up."

I stepped back for him to pass, then was shoved as another roadie crashed into the toilet I was blocking. I went back to sit on the hood of my car and watched the doctor mill around the stage. Finally, that stupid fucking fiberglass fish rolled out, too, but I was long over it. Like before, they claimed they were going to drop it from the top of a crane, right at midnight, that it was full of candy. If it really happened, one of the locals swore he was going to strap himself to it and ride it to the ground like a nuke. It just felt like more lies.

I sat through the entire band rehearsal. Maybe it was an ugly time for music, but I always enjoyed '80s tunes, and Dr. Fink did play two keyboards at the same time.

They dropped the fish on time, but the world is always too gutless to ever let it hit the ground. Or maybe it's still falling.

THE UNFORESEEN HAZARDS OF HITCHHIKING

"I used to have a large, nude pin-up on my cell wall.
It was there, across from the bed, doing time just as I was,
until I woke up from a wet dream and, in the half light,
thought a naked woman was in the cell with me.
When fantasies become that real, it's time to give them up.
The next time I pin up a photograph, it will be of something I can use.
Like a helicopter."
— Jerome Washington— *Iron House*

A white man is chained to a black man. They're both in their 50s, and look it. Though this wouldn't matter soon enough. They're on their way to become one of us, the eight thousand inmates of Eloy Prison, and once assimilated, their combined age would average out to zero.

The white man turns to the window beside him, and a sign on the road catches his eye:

"Do Not Pick Up Hitchhikers. Prison Area."

Under it, someone has spray-painted:

"How Many Ways Do We Have To Say It?"

He smiles, allows himself a small laugh. The black man looks over as if to say, "What's so funny?" then notices the modified handcuff on his seatmate's trembling, soap-white left fist.

"Name's Bill Bishop," he says, loosening his pause to steady his fingers. "Long story."

The black man doesn't respond, trying to decide if he's chained to a dangerous man or merely a damaged one. They both stare at the jangle of metal binding them. Bishop's restraints are gleaming and new, wrapped twice over with an extra loop of tempered steel crossing the lifeline of his palm and circling up between his two middle fingers.

"They made this special," Bishop says with a tug. "With a hand like mine, you can shake off cuffs like a broken watch."

The black man realizes Bishop is missing the thumb on his left hand. He doesn't ask for an explanation. Like all of us, he's been on long prison rides before, and he knows to wait for explanations. When one doesn't come, he offers a handshake best he can.

"Thomas Jefferson Jones. Forgive my metal."

"That's quite a name. You a founding father?"

"Yes, I am," he smiles. "And that's a longer story than yours."

Bishop thumps the window with the side of his head.

"Any idea when we'll get there?"

"You in a hurry?"

They bounce along in silence for a while, until a young, excitable voice from the back of the bus calls out.

"Hey! Asshole! I know you!"

Jones closes his eyes. Recognition in these situations is rarely good. Bishop stares out the window to tune everything out.

Another sign rolls by that reads: "Heavy Machinery On The Road When Flashing," and an orange light blinks its warning.

*   *   *

Inside the prison walls, the new arrivals walk past rows of cells, strangely quiet as we gaze from our cages. Our eyes look through them easily, like X-rays, and Bishop whispers to the nearest inmate shuffling next to him.

"Aren't they supposed to spit on us or something?" Bishop asks.

"*Shit* on us?" he laughs. "No, that comes later."

We clear our throats, thankful for the reminder, and a wad of saliva hits Bishop in the back of the neck, and he smacks at it like a mosquito. The guard behind him shoves him to walk faster, and a shrill, familiar voice pipes up in his ear.

"Welcome to Eeeeee-loy Prison, fuckface!"

Bishop looks back into the sea of orange and the wide face of a young man in an unusual lime-green jumpsuit, grinning from the middle of the stone-dead glares. He has a crazy, lopsided blonde sweep of hair, like a wave crashing on top of his head, and this, combined with the jumpsuit, earn him an instant nickname from a young black man behind him. It was the name we attached to every white kid we marked as doomed. Eventually even the nicknames fade away though.

"Shut the fuck up, Gumby," he says with a shove, and Bishop notes the huge number "7" tattooed on the side of the black man's neck.

"That's not a real place," Bishop says to no one.

As Bishop walks on, he sees black bodies corralled and steered up some stairs by the guards and white bodies steered up another. It's a quiet, almost casual segregation, and he looks around to see if any of us is protesting this as he's marched up to the second tier. A steel baton taps his chest and stops him in front of a cell. He steps inside and turns. Minutes later, as the shadow of the bars slide across his face, he makes eye contact with the man with the number "7" on his neck, and notices it actually reads "187," circling his throat completely. Numbers are popular in prison, both assigned and self-inflicted. Bishop gives him a nod out of habit, and the inmate stares back a moment, then backs up into his cell until he vanishes in the dark.

"Listen up!" a voice echoes. "You are Level One! 24-hour lockdown for 30 days! Level Two allows some freedoms, depending on how you handle Level One! Each month, you will be given one jumpsuit, one bar of soap, and two rolls of toilet paper! Run out of toilet paper and you'll be wiping your ass with your soap! Which makes more sense if you think about it! But that's neither here nor there! Use this time to screw your heads on straight."

There's a flurry of footsteps above and below Bishop's cell, as he stares at the tight bundle of mattress and pillow curled in the center of a sagging metal bed frame. He sits on the floor.

"Lock it down!"

There's a heavy iron *BOOM!* as a distant door is slammed shut, and a low rumble of unseen machinery sliding deadbolts into place. We're asleep in seconds, but Bishop stares at a stain on the bars, waiting to see if it crawls away. His eyes grow heavy before he finds out.

Hours later, Bishop's eyes snap open to the distinct click of slow, polished shoes, the clank of riot sticks, and the muffled grunts of a struggle. He's still sitting on the floor of his cell, mattress roll and pillow untouched on the bed frame. Over the rail and across the drop, he catches a glimpse of a cell door rolling shut, and he sits up straight to squint into the dark. Nothing else happens, and he joins us again in dreams, where we all swim in the sky just above the razor wire.

*   *   *

A silver Saab 95 with a police boot locking the front wheel gleams as the sun races over its hood. The sky grows bright, then dark, bright then dark. Days fly by, and bird shit appears across the windshield like a Jackson Pollock.

In a nearby house, shadows stretch as fingers flutter around a small mechanical creation. The hands are a blur of motion as the shape of an airplane becomes clear, twirling knobs and buttons on a large remote control until the tiny propeller starts to spin. Time slows a moment to reveal the hands of a young girl.

Miles away, the sun chases ants through infinite spirals in the sand, circling a jar propped next to their hill like a monolith. Almost imperceptibly fast, the flicker of ants scramble, climb, and tickle the glass, as sunlight pulses around them. Once inside the jar, they are unable to climb out, and their motions slow, then cease, dried and dead with their legs above their heads. Slowly, despite the sun and moon racing overhead, a large, sun-burned hand reaches into the jar, and new ants are dumped inside. These new ants pile over the dead and dying, in turn scratching and spiraling around the base. Eventually they slow, then die, too, and the huge, red hand drops more. Then more. Over and over, the cycle repeats for days, then weeks, until the jar is filled to the brim with husks.

Inside the prison, days pass, and we race around their cells, the cafeteria, the yard. Everyone, men in gray, men in blue, men in black, with shields and plastic faces, all buzz the halls like insects, sometimes stopping to fight, racing back to dark corners of their cells just ahead of the whistles, then out again, until we slow, slow, as time returns to normal.

The confined new arrivals trace a smaller circle than us in their floors. It's now a month since Bishop arrived, and he still sits on the cement, his mattress roll untouched. And although time has leveled out, his heart remains fast, and he still sucks in his breath at the metal *BOOM!* and the rumble of our cell doors.

* * *

A huge prison guard looms at the corner of the yard like a human watchtower. His thumbs and forefingers frame a director's square in front of his body. If anyone was standing close enough, they would hear the ticking of his tongue as he imitates a movie camera, but we never dare approach.

Each gang takes a turn inside the guard's square, until he settles on a shot of our white bodies. There are only nine of us leaning against the wall. We're silent, looking over shoulders, listening to rap music sung by men with country accents, our stereo balanced on an old pair of shoes like a car up on blocks. The guard squints to get a close-up on Bishop, who is approaching our black bodies, and there he finds Thomas Jefferson Jones leaning up against the fence, as we all watch the interaction between these new arrivals. A short man steps in front of Bishop, who the guard recognizes as Wilkins, the best-dressed of us, and one of the only black prisoners with glasses. He's small, with a neat, crisp appearance, and he notices the guard watching. The guard puts away his director's square and resumes a perimeter march. Bishop speaks to Jones, but looks at Wilkins and points to the radio.

"I didn't think they allowed those in prison."

Jones says nothing, just turns his head toward the sun. They're overheated but happy to be outside. Wilkins snorts a laugh.

"This ain't *Footloose*, man. They encourage as much music as we can stand. They figure the shit keeps us calm."

"Does it?"

"Sure. It's all the same beat though, like a TV knob stuck between stations. I don't even hear it anymore."

Bishop tries again to catch Jones' eye, but Wilkins steps closer. Yes, he's the best-dressed of us but also the second-most aware of us, as well.

"Now that you know everything, why don't you take off. You're over there. We're over here. This ain't the playground, motherfucker. Your team has already been chosen."

Bishop turns away and sees the latest Gumby running toward them, pointing to a shadow high in the sky. Some of us squint off into the distance, too, and Bishop hoods his eyes until he gets a better look.

It's an airplane on the horizon, headed straight for the prison, old news to us. But Bishop hasn't experienced our curious air-traffic situation, and he clearly thinks this is a real problem approaching, maybe flying lower than it should, maybe a potentially action-packed sort of scene. He doesn't notice how unimpressed we all are by this seemingly remarkable incident. We're turning back to conversations, or changing tapes in our radios. Some of us even trying to scratch hard-to-reach spots on our backs. The New Gumby is the only one who's excited.

"Is someone trying to bust someone out?!"

We part to reveal the huge prison guard, the one with the ridiculous director's fingers, heading for the strange lack of commotion. He's walking slowly, sort of stalking his line of sight with this plane in the distance. He punts one of our boomboxes out of the way, and it sails a good 30 feet before crashing down, and now the music seems faster.

This guard is easily twice the size of the rest of the screws, even bigger than most of us. His thick face is pale white, a hard-living late 30s, red curly hair, piercing blue eyes, with ragged scar tissue tracing his throat. We've always though he resembled a burly lifer someone dressed as a cop for Halloween, but we'd never say that to his face.

"Who's that monster?" Bishop asks.

"Jim Wayne," Wilkins whispers. "He'll tell you to call him The Duke, but I wouldn't talk to him at all."

The Duke pumps his shotgun, and an unbuttoned sleeve falls to reveal a black-and-blue splotch on his forearm. A closer look and Bishop sees it's not a bruise, but tattoos over tattoos, now rendered unreadable. The Duke watches the sky, smiling, apparently unconcerned with this grievous breach of air space. He cracks his knuckles, then pinches one eye shut to aim.

"Does he really think he can shoot down an airplane?" Gumby asks anyone.

"Wait, the engine, it's all wrong . . ." Bishop trails off, backing up to prepare for a crash.

The airplane flies over the wall with a shrill whine, skimming the loops of razor wire and dipping down towards our heads. The Duke raises his shotgun and fires a single, well-placed shot, and the airplane explodes, a cloud of plastic and metal shards fluttering to the sand-dusted concrete. Bishop shakes his head and finally realizes he'd been watching a small, remote-controlled model airplane after all. The show over, we all turn away again, as if we've seen this happen a million times before. Maybe not a million. More like fifty. Some of the new guys, however, remains confused.

"Damn! What kind of gun was that?!"

"It was a friggin' toy," Bishop says.

"Toy guns don't do that."

"A toy airplane, dumbass."

The biggest Mexican of us walks over, and the new white men are noticeably agitated. He's in his 40s, with faded green homemade tats on his neck and hands.

"That was nothing," he says regarding all the excitement. "That motherfucker used to swat those planes down with his bare hand, like Kong's orangutan brother. We're all getting soft."

Bishop looks the man over, and he smiles.

"Salvador Francisco," the biggest Mexican says with an introductory nod. "You notice anything weird about this place yet?"

He holds out a hand to Bishop, shaking it slow enough to study Bishop's missing thumb.

"No, just everything."

* * *

In the cafeteria, Bishop walks past The Duke eating alongside his ant farm for company, and Bishop's curiosity gets the better of him. On his way by, he glances down to see The Duke hugging his plate with one huge, ink-stained arm, and hugging the ant farm with the other. Buried in his tattoos are a green eyeballs, bursting from the swollen knobs of bone on The Duke's wrists. He catches Bishop staring.

"Hey! You want me to read your fortune?"

Bishop keeps walking past, but The Duke stands up, smiling.

"You wanna look in my crystal ball that bad?"

Bishop picks up his pace as we all look up, a wave of nervousness riding the tips of our invisible antenna.

"Hey!" The Duke shouts. "I'm talking to you."

All activity stops. Frantic radio chatter between the guards is discernable as Bishop turns to face The Duke.

"You," he says to Bishop. "Keep walking. Back to your seat, boy, and wait for the whistle."

But Bishop can't help studying those arms, and suddenly The Duke is standing over him. He leans over to rest his chin on the top of Bishop's head. "Are you going to be a problem? Is that it? Tell me now, 'cause we got alotta problems around here, so maybe we can just get yours out of the way right now."

Bishop looks past The Duke to avoid his eyes.

"No, sir. Just here to eat."

"Tell you what," The Duke says. "You don't worry about my scars, and I won't worry about yours."

As he says this, The Duke reaches down and pulls Bishop's left hand up high, twisting Bishop's fingers until his hand is the shape of a gun. The Duke rubs the angry pink pinch of skin where Bishop's thumb used to be, then pulls the hand up to point at his own head.

"Damn, son, I'd blow my brains out before I gave up a thumb! You left handed? I guess you *could* hold a gun, but you couldn't cock it, could you? That's the point though, ain't it?"

The Duke lets Bishop's hand drop back down to his side.

"I *know* what you did," he whispers to Bishop, barely audible.

Bishop looks into those dead eyes a moment, then blinks.

"Sorry, boss. I got distracted by the jar. Won't happen again."

"Fair enough," The Duke says. "A man's eyes are drawn to movement. To momentum. Hey!" he shouts to a smaller guard walking up. "You notice how lizards won't look you in the eyes? A wolf won't either. Dogs do though. The wilder the animal, the less likely the eye contact."

He turns back to Bishop. An almost endless ten seconds passes.

"Too bad about that hand. You have my sympathies."

The Duke suddenly bangs the table and digs through his pockets.

"Almost forgot!" he shouts, positively giddy. "Your fortune for the day! It was foreseeeeen!"

The Duke pulls a black scorpion from his pants and unscrews the top of his jar to drop it in. It's long dead, and the ants ignore it. Unfazed, the Duke scoops a gummy bite of mashed potatoes, talking through his mouthful to his ant farm as we all go back to our routines.

"Remind me again why I keep any of you creatures around."

* * *

When our dreams swim again, we all flashback together. We all join Bishop back on his front lawn, to see the day of his arrest. Bishop is face down in the grass, a knee in his back as a police officer cuffs him. The blood on his hands and arms is making this difficult.

"I tried to stop it. . ." he mutters. "It's my blood. . . not hers. . ."

"Shut the fuck up."

Bishop struggles to raise his head. His daughter Jenny glares at him from their driveway. She's 16 years old, face pinched into a red fist of anger.

"It's my blood," he explains, and turns away toward the front door of the house. Bishop strains harder to rise, veins pulsing across his forehead, desperate to stop her from going inside. Another officer jumps on, and more hands slam the top of his head to keep him still.

"Stop, please," he says to the pile on his back. "Don't let her go inside. Are you going to let a child see her own dead mother!" he howls.

"Stand him up. One. . . two. . . up!"

Bishop is lifted to his feet, and he watches helplessly as his daughter opens the front door of their house. He clenches his teeth so hard that he bites through his tongue, and he slumps. The cops loosen their grip, and because of all the blood, they're unaware of Bishop's left hand and the thumb he removed earlier that day in his garage. His left hand slips out of the handcuffs, and his arm comes around fast and shoves the cops off. He's loose and moving toward the house, bloody cuffs dangling from his right wrist. His daughter stops at the door and stares at her father reaching for her, but she barely recognizes him through the carnage, and she's crying as she reaches for her father's good hand. Their fingertips are inches apart when the police tackle him again.

"Did he break the cuffs?" one cops says, amazed.

"Naw, his hand is fucked up. Thumb's gone," the other cop says. "Get the zip ties."

"How'd you miss that shit?"

"Ain't got time to be counting fingers, son. A scene like this don't come with instructions. . ."

"Well, they're gonna need the instructions with those two bodies in there. They'll be sorting out puzzle pieces for hours."

One cop laughs as he removes his knee from Bishop's head to whisper in his ear.

"If they find an extra thumb in there, we'll save it for you."

"Yeah, we'll make a lucky keychain for you, killer. . ."

Bishop strains his head under all the fists, forearms, and knees and actually manages to force his chin up again, just in time to watch in horror as his daughter disappears inside the house.

* * *

Back in the prison cafeteria. Bishop is at a table with Sal, Gumby, and Jones, questions flying.

"Why does The Duke eat with the inmates?"

"I hear he *is* an inmate. Some kinda cost-saving thing. 'Let *us* police *us*' sorta shit."

"We never saw him come in. Never heard him come in, go out, nothing. He's just there sometimes."

"We got other things around here to worry about."

"Like what?"

"Like the fact that we might not get to do that 'time' they promised us," Jones says. "First Number Seven is gone, who's next?"

"That wasn't a number seven," Bishop says, but they keep talking.

"Maybe this prison is built over an old Mexican temple. . ."

"Spooky!"

"Did you know they played basketball with heads?"

"You guys keep saying 'Mexican' when you should be saying Hispanic, or Chicano, or Latino," Sal says. "Why we all gotta be from Mexico?"

"Just trying to simplify."

"Well, it's got to be 'Mexican,'" Jones says.

"Why?"

"Because of the joke."

"What joke?"

"We're the joke. A white man, a black man, and a Mexican walked into a prison. . ."

"It's supposed to be, 'walked into a bar.'"

"Why?"

"That's how jokes start."

"Well, I walked into the bars!" Gumby cackles.

* * *

A week later, Jones brings it all up again.

"You know what I think?" he says. "I think we're the 'three blind mice.' Only we're three blind mice of three different colors. Like that three-flavored ice cream you can get."

"You don't even know how that story goes," Sal says, cracking his neck, and everyone gets comfortable.

"Three blind mice are sitting around the bar. The first mouse downs a beer, slams his mug on the table and says, 'I'm such a hard-ass, when I run into a mouse trap, I spring it and catch the bar. Then I bench-press it until I get hungry enough to eat that fucking cheese.'"

Jones leans back and crosses his arms like he knows where the story is going. Bishop rubs his hand absently as Sal goes on.

"And the second blind mouse, he slams a shot of Tequila, throws the glass over his shoulder and says, 'That ain't shit, holmes! I'm so bad, when I trip over the rat poison in front of my hole, I pull out a razor blade, cut it up into lines and boom, baby! I snort that shit until I'm *flying*.'"

Jones smiles in spite of himself as Sal wraps it up.

"And that third blind mouse, he slooowly drains a thimbleful of water, stands up even slower, looks around . . ."

"He can't look around, the fucker's blind."

". . . he *sniffs* around, sighs and goes, 'Boys, I ain't got time for this bullshit. I gotta get home and fuck the cat.'"

We share a big laugh together, and Jones stands up.

"I'll see you guys in the rec. room. Gather under the TV, there's that good show on."

He walks away, and Bishop notices The Duke watching him go, thoughtfully tapping the curved glass walls of his ant farm. He's studying his forearm, too, like he's mapping something out. Bishop looks around the cafeteria, seeing arms around trays, all covered in tattoos, quotes, cartoons, philosophies, shapes, meaning. . .

He turns back to his food, swirling everything together until it's gray.

*　*　*

"What's he hiding?" one of us asks one day soon after.

"Who?"

"The Duke. At least three layers of ink on his arms. He get kicked out of the Marines? A fraternity? Is that his serial number? Expiration date? Bar code? What?"

"Remember what they say about the imagination being the last thing to go during incarceration."

We turn their attention back to the sky when the buzzing starts again. And we watch as another plane is coming in hot, a little desperate, out of control. We all watch it come in low like the other ones, wobbling in the desert wind. It dips its wing and turns, heading for a spot by The Duke on the basketball court, who waits eagerly. It follows a clear line The Duke has scuffed into the concrete with his boot heel. We watch as the plane touches down safely, skipping on tiny wheels across the sand and finally stopping obediently at The Duke's feet. The propeller still spinning, a huge, red paw covers its snout as The Duke claims his prize.

*　*　*

The next day, The Duke sits alone, the toy plane parked next to the ant farm. And when the airplane's motor begins to buzz, his red fist crashes down to smash it like a horsefly. The propeller chops tiny gashes into The Duke's wrist as he pounds the plane into silence, and Gumby takes advantage of the distraction to run up to him, where he amazes us all by snatching The Duke's prized ants. He holds it high over his head, then smiles like he's on stage, which he is.

"What the hell is he doing?" Bishop has time to mutter, then Gumby spikes the jar to the ground.

"Touchdown, asshole."

Ants, sand, cricket and spider husks fly everywhere, riding glass shards and rotten food across the cafeteria floor. Almost in slow motion, a solitary ant arcs all the way to Bishop's tray, where it uncurls and antennas taste the air. Then a guard clocks Gumby in the face with a baton, and another guard gets his arm under Gumby's jaw, and Gumby is floating off his feet when a third guard buries a boot deep into his stomach. Gumby vomits up his beans, and they let him pitch forward onto the tile. The Duke strides over and delivers a brutal kick to Gumby's skull, parting that green wave of hair forever. He stands over him while blood drips from the propeller gashes in his arm. We almost look away. The latest Gumby never lasts too long.

"I hate it when they stop moving like that," he says, kicking again, harder with each blow. "Why bother?"

Eventually, the Duke holds up a hand to stop the boot-and-baton party, and the last Gumby is quickly dragged from the room, all our eyes following the blood-and-bean streak across the cafeteria floor.

"You know what I think?" Jones says, pointing toward the remains of the plane.

"What?" Bishop says, finally breathing again.

I think we just missed our flight out of here."

* * *

Ink, the wisest of us all, sits high on his throne of stacked plastic chairs, cleaning his needle and blowing dust from the motor. Around him, pins, needles and hollowed out ball-points soak in urine. Two more black inmates, Hobbs and Waters, the most unremarkable of us, drop their porno rags when Bishop walks through the open cell door.

"You lost?" Hobbs asks, blocking Bishop's forward progress.

"Quick question," Bishop says to Ink.

"You don't hear him?" Waters asks. "You don't see him standing over you, blocking out the sun?"

"One question, then I'm gone."

"I don't doubt that!" Waters laughs.

"You want branded?" Ink asks, squinting. "Whatchoo want on your arm? A heart? A cross? 'Mom' . . ."

We all laugh, and Bishop waits.

"No joke," Ink says. "You ain't getting shit from me without giving up some skin."

Bishop nods expectantly, and minutes later Ink is hunched over Bishop's arm, the shell of an empty ball-point with a needle taped to the front, poking and wiping blood from Bishop's skin as we talk.

"How long you been here?" Bishop asks him.

"Only thing I don't keep track of. Was that your quick question?"

"Were you here before The Duke?"

Ink stops a second, then resumes poking and wiping.

"Go take a walk," he says to the bodyguards, and they walk out as Ink resumes his work. Bishop flinches with each prick.

"You were, weren't you? When he first came in."

"Why did you cut off your thumb? Did you think that would stop you from doing something bad?"

"I just want to know about The Duke," Bishop deflects. "Or the planes. How long have those toy planes been coming over the wall?"

"You seen them, too! I've never seen these airplanes everyone talks about. Just a UFO once, and they shot that fucker down. But the guards? I'm trying to tell you, it's all true. The guards here are serving time, too. Just like us."

"The Duke?"

"Well, he's something different altogether."

"Different how?"

"I heard those planes tried to smuggle in a bullet once. . ."

"Different how?" Bishop repeats.

"Why are you asking me this shit?"

"The tattoos on his arms. Did you cover them up when he was still a prisoner?"

"Who says he's not still a prisoner?"

Bishop tries to respond to this, and Ink suddenly jumps back, throws his pen and needle against the wall and wipes his hands on his thighs.

"We're done."

Bishop looks down at his arm and frowns. His bad hand is shaking again.

"You can't leave it like that. What is that? A frog?"

"Finish it yourself. Or don't. They're all misspelled these days anyway."

Ink hands him an ink-stained ball-point shell with a black needle taped to the end of it. Bishop pockets it and leaves the cell. As he walks, he rubs the blood away from the new letters on his arm. Just under his wrist, the shape of a heart. Inside the heart reads:

"Jenny Frog"

Bishop runs, blood seeping through his sleeve as his bad hand, now rock solid, digs at the stain.

* * *

Back in his cell, Bishop pulls his new pen and needle from his mattress-roll stash, and shakes a black puddle between his knees. He dips the tip, and his bad hand pricks his arm, then stops. He cranes his head to check for guards, then crawls back to his needle, dabbing it like a quill in an inkwell. Eventually, he switches to a black-and-blood-stained fingernail on his bad hand and tries to finish what Ink started. Wincing, he scratches and smears until his arm finally reads something close enough:

"Jenny Frogive Me?"

* * *

That night, all our conversations through the pipes are almost deafening, and Bishop is on his knees in front of his own metal bowl, ready to mimic some fake puking if a guard wanders by. Our shrill toilet voices echo around the blue stained water, shimmering with bad ideas.

"Tomorrow," one of us says. "We go for it."

A toilet flushes deep in the works, and Bishop pulls his head up from his bowl, then sticks his head back in. He clears his throat.

"Hey, who is. . ."

Our loudest voice echoes through the block, so deep it vibrates the walls as well as the plumbing:

"We're trying to sleep! Hang up the phone!"

* * *

Another uprising squashed, riot guards stand over us again. Bishop is handcuffed on his stomach, and Jones buries his own face in the asphalt before he's manhandled like always. The guards step over us, but we always sneak looks at each other when we're able.

"They'll never try this again," Jones says.

"Not true," Sal says, as a foot clips his ear.

"He's right," Bishop says.

"What's not true?"

"That's what they used to say in court," Sal goes on. "You see, it's not that they don't believe you. Or that they think you're 'guilty' or 'not guilty.' They just think that your story exists somewhere between 'true' and 'not true,' just like our heads forever exist between the foot and the floor."

Jones rolls over to spit some dirt, and a guard steps over him while he quickly buries his face again.

"You sound like one of your bullshit nursery rhymes," Jones scoffs.

"Now those are true!" Sal says.

"Okay, time's up," Jones says, eyes darting around after another boot grazes his head. "If one of y'all was planning on some dramatic ending here, you're burning daylight . . ."

"Fine," Bishop says, climbing to his knees. "Here's a rhyme for ya. Three little kittens lost their mittens. . ."

"Don't do it."

Bishop slips his blood-soaked four-fingered hand easily from the riot guards' handcuffs, then stands up tall. To our amazement, he continues to recite the nursery rhyme as he steps forward, ignoring commands from guards and inmates alike.

"Get the fuck *DOWN!*"

"Face-plant, motherfucker! Hands over your head or you're dead!"

"Do it, bro!"

Bishop calmly wades through the minefield of our faces at his feet, still reciting.

". . .but they smelled a rat close by. . ."

"On the ground! Three seconds!"

Bishop walks over one of us that The Duke has kicked into oblivion, then he turns and makes the shape of a gun with his trembling, thumbless hand. Our shouting increases as his eyes find the sun and actually stares it down until a cloud finally makes it blink.

Then there's a scramble in the guard tower and a weird whistle in the air. High-school athletics instincts kicking in, Bishop reaches out to pluck something arcing toward him. It hisses against his chest, gripped tight in his hands, and for a second he thinks he's cradling some sort of animal. Then the military surplus tear-gas grenade explodes, and a bloody football-sized hole flowers from Bishop's ribs. Bishop goes down hard.

On the ground, he stares at a tiny drop of blood on the tip of his finger, and we follow it with him until it forgets his skin and drops to the sand. Tiny fireworks spark around the bubble a moment, sunbeams tickling its rim as if it's still alive, or maybe still swimming with our collective dreams in the starlight above the wire. Then the blood bubble bursts, and the desert soaks him up like he had never been there at all.

* * *

Bill Bishop lies stiff in the prison infirmary, eyes wide open. A sliver of moon sneaks through the bars on the window, illuminating one of us in the shadows, gently sliding Bishop's blood-freckled arm from under his body. A small flashlight clicks on, revealing the face of Ink, the wisest of us all. He licks the corner of his gray shirt to swab the dry, black blood from Bishop's cold skin, then takes his pen-and-needle rig to fix the mutilated tattoo.

The work complete, the flashlight beam takes one last lap around the body, tracing the number "188" and the beautiful Old English script in a twitching circle of light that reads:

"Jenny Forget Me."

The flashlight lingers on a corpse in the corner, shining on the remote control bagged and balanced on the dead prisoner's chest. Then the beam is gone, and we're all gone, and Bishop is alone again, and the only light left is the faint reflection of moonlight flickering in his black, dilated eyes. Finally, the moon looks away, too.

BAD REACTION SHOTS

One of the things that was probably gonna be held against me once I stopped driving was how I didn't call anyone to tell them that she died. How I just got into my car with a stray cat-like something or other and hit the road without spreading the bad news as required, like a cellular infection. I can understand that.

And her funeral would be coming up, too. That was something I couldn't face. I'd been dodging funerals all my life, and people understandably started thinking, "Awww, poor Dave can't face death," and no doubt they'd write this off as an even more legitimate reason to duck the ceremony. But that wasn't it at all. The truth was I was too caught up in studying others and what I perceived as their inappropriate, sometimes self-serving displays of public grief that I couldn't get out of one without a scene, or at least a dangerous blood-pressure hike. Watching people react to tragedy just made me angrier than I can reasonably describe. After I got old enough to have some friends and relatives start dying, I realized with some horror that it was my reaction to the reaction of others in the face of death that was so insufferable.

So, yeah, I didn't tell anyone about her death. But I didn't have to. I'd played every possible version of those hypothetical conversations in my head as I drove, so there really was no need at all. I heard me trying to sum up the insanity of the past 24 hours filtered through tiny speakers pressed tight against everyone's ears, and it made me want to bash my head open on the steering wheel. But steering wheels are for pussies these days, all rubber and soft like those Fisher Price dashboards. So even that suicidal daydream was a cop out, not that I'd ever consider copping out and killing myself, of course. I remembered one particular steering wheel from the old Buick Regal my dad used to drive. It was hard and slick, polished like a high-school basketball court, like the court where I slipped and broke my nose the first time, and sweaty hands would slip right off on any sharp turn.

I wanted to do the right thing, but if I called anyone right now, instead of refueling my flask and my Rabbit with fuel, I'd just have to relive it all, but also translate through my urge to make anyone on the receiving end feel better about how my life was destroyed. As I drove, I imagined a swap, and some sorry bastard like yourself hearing me play-acting like those cops on my doorstep. How bad could it sound?

"This isn't easy for me. Wait . . . hold up," you would say while I waited for you to gut me with the news. "Someone's on the other line." And then you'd take forever to click back over, and I'd have already crashed the car in anticipation. Or I wouldn't get there in time, so you'd have to leave me a message, too long, as usual, with your usual brand of suspense accumulated from decades of hating fucking phones, something like, "I know we haven't talked for a year, but if you call me back, I'll tell you who's dead." Then you'd hum along with a song I couldn't hear and try to get in a dozen belches and some beatboxing before the beep. A seductive voice would tell you my message will be saved in the archives for only three days, and even that computer would sound oddly threatening, so I'd call you back within the hour.

"What's up?"

"Are you sitting down?"

"Of course I am. I'm driving, asshole, not running."

"You could be running."

"Come on. Who the hell is dead?

"Guess."

And then you'd tell me. I'd think I was ready for this moment, but I won't be.

"Seriously? How?"

"No one knows. They found her in a guitar case. Shot through the head. Then dumped in a river. I'm no detective, but either she killed herself or someone else did."

"You deduce that all by yourself?"

"What's the difference?"

"What do you mean?"

"I mean, what's the difference? Murder, accident, suicide. She's still dead."

You will think about this until you understand the difference. You won't say it out loud, but you'll realize that if it wasn't suicide, you wouldn't be dwelling on it nearly as much. Out of character, he will fill this silence with some actual sympathy. It will give you the creeps.

"I'm really sorry, dude."

Then you'll drive a little more and think about those days when you and her used to watch movies together, and how you'd know immediately that it's a bad one and she's gonna fall asleep with her face in the microwave popcorn if the camera kept lingering on the reaction shots. You know these bad movie moments well, the ones designed to tell the dumbest viewers when to gasp, laugh, or cry (coincidentally, the typical reactions to murder, accident, and suicide, in that order). Picture the scene. An actor does something shocking like, say, pulling his eyes out of his goddamn head. That should say enough to the viewer, right? Well, a bad movie won't be content with this. A bad movie will cut to someone screaming, maybe even shouting out, "Oh, my god! I can't believe something so crazy has occurred! Imagine the pain!" This is infinitely worse if the bad movie in question is trying to make you cry.

"Are you sitting down?"

You'll decide that I only asked you to do this because I saw it in too many movies. Unless it's the scene where three authority figures come knocking on the door, that's how the phone call always starts. The movies always tell you that it's the hardest job ever, delivering the news to the wartime widow, but you're too smart for that nonsense. You've noticed that they never have to actually say anything at all because just like everyone else they've visited, you will always collapse on the stairs before they even speak, before I even speak, sometimes before I even open the door. You've always been convinced those motherfuckers have the easiest job of all time.

But after you soak in the news, you'll start calling other people, all the way down the line of people who care a little less and less, and eventually you will discuss her death with people who need to prove a connection, and a bizarre competition will surface that neither of you will be consciously aware of. It will sound familiar to anyone leaning in to listen because you've said it all before, even outside of the worst movie you and her watched together.

First is your bizarre rush to react the most inappropriately ("I guess she won't be needing that five bucks back!") quickly followed by a scramble to be the most respectful ("I'd drive nine hours to her funeral if I had to.") then you'll start the world's most subtle duel about who really knew her better ("I remember every word of her alligator poem." "You mean 'crocodile poem'?") then you will say something about there being nothing you could have done to change things, but you'll actually be hinting that even an extra word in the last sentence between you would have changed everything that followed ("I almost forced her to miss a plane by not calling her back.") then you will subtly attach meaning to the most insignificant interactions ("I'm the one who named her dog, even if she never realized it.") negated by a hasty downplay of the most significant ones ("She brought me that article on love being a disease, but she probably showed it to everyone." "Oh, yeah, did she write your names on a padlock and seal your love onto a bridge halfway across the globe?" "Yes, well, halfway across the country.") then you will offer up something embarrassing, knowing that although no one can prove her feelings for you, you can change your own depending on who's around

("I hesitate to even say this, but I always wanted to sing Karaoke with her watching from the crowd, and, God help me, sing it well.") then you will make it clear your special connection allows you any joke no matter how many crickets are chirping ("Tragedy minus time equals comedy, but this clock ain't workin!") but then you'll make it clear you wouldn't allow anyone to do the same thing ("Imagine her mother in the car with us before you say that stupid shit again.") then you will desperately try to attach yourself a little closer to the tragedy hoping that there's at least one person left that hasn't heard so you can ask if they're sitting down, too ("If you haven't called her crazy dad yet, let me do it.") then you will remove yourself from the drama ("The funeral reception is too far away, and her body won't even be there") in direct opposite proportion to your relationship with the deceased ("I'd hitchhike if I had to, even though she probably wouldn't remember me.") then you will take advantage of an opportunity to settle old scores ("I'll tell him I don't want to talk about it if that asshole has the bad judgment to want to reminisce.") then you will minimize her best accomplishments ("I think people should be honest and admit that her poems needed work.") or maximize them depending on the accomplishments in your own life ("I told her that one day we'd all rent hot-air balloons when we're millionaires, then put some heart-shaped padlocks on a thunderstorm") then you will, of course, fall back on the ridiculous contest of who-knew-her-best since it was never decided ("Once, I saw her hold up a line of traffic while she walked down the middle of the road with her headphones on, everyone honking and yelling over her shoulders.") however, you'll never ("I know, I know, that's so her, isn't it?) no matter how hard you try ("Actually, it wasn't like her at all.") really declare a winner.

Unless you get caught with a mouthful of something and spray it everywhere in shock when you hear the news, you can always count on your reaction to be unsatisfying. And you can't just fake it and hold milk in your cheeks and wait for the punch line like they do in the movies. You're talking about that split-second after your drink washes over your teeth, that instant before your throat flexes to swallow, that moment that's harder to nail than anyone actually realizes. And if you do spit uncontrollably all over everything when they tell you, then maybe, maybe, you'll believe that you reacted honestly. But you won't.

Just understand that an honest reaction to the news of a tragedy has never happened in the history of the human race. That's what we are.

For example, notice up there how many more times you will say "I" instead of "her." This is because the only people who handle tragedy worse than high school kids are college kids. And the only people who handle tragedy worse than those little bastards are everyone else.

* * *

If you drive long enough, even with a stray creature climbing on your shoulders, the only relationship you can cultivate is hatred for authority figures who claim more than a reasonable share of your road. You will also begin to think of every cop, fireman, even paramedic as the same person, blissfully ignorant of the destructive influence this blind generalization has had with other relationships in your life. This is mostly because, much like the initial giggling skirmish you had over that theater armrest on your first date:

You simply cannot tolerate anyone asking you to move over.

So when you almost get pulled over, your instinct is to call someone and tell them all about it. In the movies, the hero never bothers to tell anyone what just happened, no matter how strange or remarkable, even though it is the only time a reaction shot would be justified. This is not the case in real life.

But someone will call you first, and you'll be getting the news about her suicide all over again. You will imagine everyone out there fighting over phones to tell you again and again.

You will want to take the high road when you answer, but suddenly, even though this caller will be more sincere than the first and won't play the game nearly as well, your old reflexes will be back before you know it:

First, you'll ask each other all the sexual details that you've always suspected ("I swear I never fucked her.") minimizing or maximizing in relation to what the other one reveals ("My shit was up against her shit, and that's all.") then you'll Monday-morning quarterback the crime scene with a decade of police shows under your belt as qualifications ("I think they need to track down if she got the gun from the same hardware store she got the padlocks.") then you'll decide that since you're not directly involved, no one should be involved ("I think that it's not our tragedy to claim because with every death someone else has earned the right to be more upset than you.") then you'll decide no one can grieve unless they've got identification to prove they're her mother, father, brother, or sister by blood ("I honestly don't think a stepbrother should get the first call.") then you'll complain about how families are the only ones who get to know conclusively if it was really the most unlikely suicide of all time ("I know for a fact her parents knew her least of all.") then you will try to make someone feel better, but only because jealousy motivates you to try to dismiss their influence on her last days ("I'm telling you, it's not your fault. She was upset about someone she just met, not you.") then you will try to make sure no one writes about it without changing everything ("If you're gonna put it on your website, I think you should say her cat died recently, not her dog, you know, to protect the dog's family.") or else you'll decide that no one can write about it at all until you have the time to try ("I honestly think posting an online tribute for her relatives to stumble across when they're searching obituaries is the equivalent of crashing a stranger's funeral.") then you will mourn the loss of the most important password you can think of outside of a high-tech heist film ("I tried to befriend her on Spacebook, but she told me it was just to log in and access other people's sites, making hers out of reach forever.") then you'll swallow your disgust as you compete with people suddenly claiming things that can never be verified ("Good thing I'm the only one that can access her profile, until I forgot her password and ruined it for everyone. Oops.") then you'll either say it's a god's fault ("I saw thirty people today that deserved to die before her.") or a dog's will ("I know there's a plan because his tail curls when it rains.") then you will try to hint, as tastefully as you can, that by talking to her last or by not talking to her last, you were responsible for her death ("I want you to admit that you're actually proud you made her cry, not just because I am, too.") because no one is allowed to ever admit such a thing out loud even though it's in our fucking DNA.

This second conversation will be what they called during the Cold War a "race to the bottom," but you will fail to recognize it. And you'll struggle to recognize actual guilt under all that bullshit. And the real problem is you never will. You can only feel guilty about having inappropriate reactions to tragedy, never about the tragedy itself. You may finally understand that for humans this is simply impossible, always has been.

But the quickest way to gauge how close you were to the deceased?

How eagerly would you use her death to get out of a speeding ticket?

This is the real reason that talking on the phone while driving is now a crime in seven states.

* * *

One last thing. I just want you to know that the worst movie you ever saw would have been fine if it wasn't for all the reaction shots. I know this for a fact. The opening, ending, and everything in between was just this long chase where the monster was on a rampage and working its way through a campground. But all momentum was destroyed when the camera constantly kept cutting to the faces of the teenagers to show them looking horrified, even though you were the one who was the most traumatized by the way the movie failed on every level.

Your phone will ring, and you'll finally get to tell someone the news. But you'll do it all wrong right out of the gate. You'll even forget to ask if he's sitting down, and oh, shit, here we go again! Then you'll confide to me . . .

"You know, just between you and me, I might have fucked her."

But first comes something that no one can prove ("Just kidding, I probably never fucked her.") quickly followed by something else no one can prove ("He never fucked her either.") then some shady denials ("I swear.") then you'll try to come up with the best theory no one's thought of yet ("I'd kill myself if my dog died.") then you will discount everyone else's ("I know for a fact that a dog can't affect someone like that, even if they gave birth to it.") then you'll try to suggest she was thinking of you ("I sent her a text message the day before it happened.") at the same time you suggest your absence drove her to extremes ("I should have answered the cryptic message she sent me back.") then you'll feel the need to demystify her ("You and I both know she wasn't perfect.") in direct proportion with anyone who dares romanticize her ("Remember when she told us about her sister slashing her wrists on Thanksgiving?") by proudly letting your imagination fill in any blanks that her family won't ("I'm thinking there is no sister, never was.") then you'll convince others, as you convince yourself, how well you really knew her and how important your friendship was compared to everyone else's ("Today I realized she never knew your middle name, just the initial she wrote on a heart-shaped padlock.") then you'll try to set the record straight on something that will only make you feel better ("I hated how she tried to be one of the guys, telling us 'bros before hoes' whenever we didn't include her.") and ignore the awkward silence when you're finally honest enough to get to your point ("One of the guys, my ass. It was clear that she just wanted to get with you, not me.") then you'll try to make light of it since this said more about you than it did about her ("I told her 'prose before hoes' and went home to do my homework that night since she just wanted to stay out longer with you.") then you'll throw out a bit of trivia ("Once she was up before the sun and called to brag, but it only lasted two more mornings.") then shame mixed with relief that you'll only admit to yourself ("I'm sort of relieved she can't ever tell anyone I couldn't get it up.") then you'll try to shock the conversation to a close and be disappointed when you can't ("Remember the day all three of us walked through campus for the first time and she couldn't take her ears off you?") so you'll try harder ("I actually thought about killing you so that she'd listen to my stories instead.") then you'll project a bad memory of the last time a cop came to your house and searched your face for the right reaction, as if this explains your behavior since ("They always act like it's hard to knock on the door with some bad news, but they love that shit. Don't let them tell you different.") then you'll gratefully acknowledge your forever-second-place position in this competition and try to end the debate quickly ("I think no one knew her at all, not just me, I mean, not just not me.") then you'll make a surprise connection ("She was the sister I never had.") but you will mock anyone else's similar revelation ("You mean the sister you never fucked?") then you'll want to get off the phone fast when you remember there's one person out there no one's told yet, someone who might still be standing up for bad news.

And you'll never ask yourself why you've never cared if it was suicide, accident, or murder or which order those three words belong in because you're too excited about giving someone the news. As you stab the gas, all you will know with certainty is that, despite what a murderer in the worst-made movies may believe, the embarrassment over things you said to someone when they were alive never dies with them.

This will be your best chance yet to tell someone first. You will be the closest to her. And she doesn't have a phone. You threw it out of the car when she wouldn't show you who called. It was knocked out of her hand when you called her and distracted her long enough to be abducted. They were right. There ought to be a law.

Soon, you will pass more and more cars that look exactly like one you used to own.

You will consider the collisions.

RUMBLE

"I'm a hard hallucinator with an axe to grind,
Shooting from the hip like a porcupine . . ."
—Machine Gun Fellatio— "Mutha Fukka on a Motorcycle"

Jake pulled his gloves slow and tight like a doctor in a horror flick and kick-started his bike. He revved the engine loud, louder, louder, the rumble growing deep in his chest, then moving up to thrum the tuning fork of his spine to finally nest in his brain. He looked both ways down the intersection, then leaned back and gave Cherry a last kiss on the red apple of her cheek. He cranked the throttle and raced through the next two lights before they changed, angling his wheel for the rotten tomato stand and the yawning mouth of the abandoned corn maze behind it.

But they never got there. Jake saw the blur of something he took for a wooden baseball bat jamming into his spokes and exploding into toothpicks as he lost the bull rope of his handlebars between his legs and rode the fender onto the street. The gong of his brain bucket painted his world black a second or two, eardrums rattling like an old man's newspaper. Then he sat up on the road, counted his heads, and started flicking stones from his face embedded deep as ticks. When he finally focused, he looked around for Cherry's splashdown, and that's when the hairy fist found the hole under his nose and sent him flying back into his shredded saddle. Rolling to his feet, Jake flailed for a weapon, hoping to find a shard of the bat, maybe with the "Louisville Slugger" stamp still visible, but there was nothing but confetti and paper in his spokes, ticking like playing cards as the wheel spun. Later, he realized he'd been taken down by grass-stained stakes and a rolled poster urging people to vote for the local noise ordinance. Exactly the kind of shit that turned farmers murderous. But it wasn't a farmer that clipped him this time, he was sure of it. Kicking away the poster strips, he stood up to find the owner of the fist long gone and tried to pinpoint the buzz of a dozen dirt bikes in the distance. Suddenly remembering the love of his life may have ended her run as a bloody rooster tail along the ragged hieroglyphics of fading white lines, his pulse spiked.

It took a good ten minutes more before he was sure his bike was drivable and his heart finally slowed back down.

* * *

Fingers bloody from shucking strings off guitars, they're sitting on the hood of Jake's '57 Eldorado, holding hands and enjoying the show. Cherry always liked watching red police lights flash in the distance. He calls these lights "cherries," too, but everything's cherry to him these days. They're on a hill, overlooking a lopsided crop circle. The cops have found the first body, still clutching 100cc's of Baja motocross nonsense. But she's playing her own game, too. Not just refusing to answer the question anymore, she's stopped speaking altogether. But it's hard for Jake not to ask the question, and it squirts out of him again before he realizes.

"What are you thinking?"

He can't help it, watching her watching cops from the hill with her cold, button eyes. He wishes they could hear them crunching the dead, brown stalks, figuring it all out, maybe see flashlight beams crisscross their faces as they kiss. He wonders if she's thinking of the 4th of July, the red-and-blue fireworks and their second kiss, their first real kiss. He thinks about how she watched the shirtless men lighting the rockets instead of watching the explosions and how he hoped she was waiting for someone to get hurt.

Jake squeezes her hand the wrong way, watching those dolls eyes for a reaction. Nothing. He knows it's his fault. Sure, he promised never to ask that question again, but Jake can't believe she's chosen now to punish him, when everything came together so perfect, after the accidental serenade of those broken guitars. He pulls back her thumb like he's cocking a gun, hoping she'll recoil, asks again like a fool.

"What are you thinking?"

Still nothing.

* * *

Jake's uncle was on his sagging porch, fighting with a sticky switchblade, peeling apples so perfect they looked like cue balls.

"Are those even apples?" Cherry asked Jake as he kicked his car door shut and walked up the cinderblock steps, carrying her like his bride. He crushed a mosquito into a smear of war paint on her cheekbone without answering, then clucked his tongue and pretended to knock an invisible door until his uncle looked up. Jake's uncle was blonde and big, just like Jake, but wind-beaten and scaly, not quite like he'd been through a fire, but more like he'd stood too close to them all his life.

"Hey, Jake!"

"Hey, Jake!"

Jake's Uncle Jake even wore the same red-white-and-blue Highland High jacket as his nephew, the dog-eared "HHS" hanging by a thread, holes worn in red leather elbows faded almost pink. Jake dropped out a full year earlier than his uncle though.

"They look good, don't they!" Uncle Jake beamed, pushing the button on his blade, which was jammed up and sluggish with sugar.

"Almost too juicy," Cherry said. "Are they rotten?"

"You're rotten, Cherry," Jake whispered to her, as he gently set her on the swing and sat between them. His uncle studied her, confused, eager to say a whole lot more, but he got stuck on the name like Jake knew he would.

"What the fuck did you call her?" Uncle Jake asked him.

"Baby, this is my Uncle Jake," Jake wrapped one loving hand around her back to give her neck a squeeze.

"Not another one!" she laughed a little too loud. "This is your namesake?"

"I guess."

"You ever seen *The Two Jakes*?" she asked them.

"Yeah, right here on my porch, numbnuts!" Uncle Jake answered, and Cherry snickered, having never been called that before.

"Oh, you think that's funny?" Then to Jake, "What did you call her? Don't even . . ."

"This is Cherry."

"Another Cherry Bomb, huh. Or is it C.B. for short?"

"Hey, it's a popular name," Jake shrugged.

"Mm-hmm. So you *want* to be confusing, eh?" Uncle Jake laughed, and Jake frowned.

"Where's *your* Cherry anyway?"

"In the garage."

"Garage? Well, I was hoping we could all talk about . . ."

"What are you guys whispering for?" Cherry asked, and Jake's hand stroked her neck to sooth away some questions. He suddenly had less control of her than he'd had that morning.

"So, what the fuck happened to you, kid!" Uncle Jake barked, some of his confusion giving way to understanding. He finally noticed the road rash across his nephew's face, "Where's your ride? Back to the El Diablo I see."

"Someone 'Jake Braked' him," Cherry said cheerfully. "Both of us, really."

"What the hell does that mean?"

"It means someone jammed a baseball bat in the spokes of his Harley," she went on. "Sent us flying."

"Well, it wasn't a baseball bat," Jake corrected.

"Never mind that," Uncle Jake said. "Is she telling me that's what they'll call it when someone jams something in your spokes, kid? *Jake Breaking?* It happens so often to you that they named that shit?"

"Guess so," Jake laughed nervously. "Here's the thing. I was hoping I could raid your garage for—"

"No, not Jake Breaking. Like 'Jake *Braking*,'" Cherry interrupted, impatient to explain. "It's actually called 'Jacob Braking.' You know, engine braking? You get it installed on your diesel, and when it lets the air out of the cylinders, it slows down your truck. Saves your brakes, but it sounds like a little boy making a machine-gun noise with his lips. People in the 'burbs hate it, and—"

"I know what fucking Jake Braking is," Uncle Jake said, still looking at Jake. "The question is, why is that the name for getting dropped like a bitch?"

"Because when he hit the ground, it let the air out of him with a big ol' hiss," Cherry said, voice low. "But mostly because his fucking name was Jake."

Now he was finally looking at her, so Jake took an apple from under his uncle's knife and took a big bite, eyebrow up. Turned out they weren't apples at all, but those damn kiwis again, back in season. He loved kiwis. Jake looked down between his feet and saw the fuzzy green skins piled under the swing. His uncle kicked them out of sight in disgust.

* * *

She still won't talk to him, but there's something Jake is saving. A last resort. A kind of "Break Glass In Case Of Emergency" expedient he can no longer resist.

There's always been a strange muscle somewhere in Jake's head. He doesn't know what it does, or how he flexes it, but it's somewhere behind his eyes, or between his ears, perched above the hinge in his jaw. And when Jake squeezes something deep in there—like biting down, but more like biting with his brain—he hears this . . . rumble. Like holding a seashell up to his head when a train goes by. He's never told anyone about it, as his greatest fear is that it does nothing at all. His earliest disappointment as a boy, discovering that the rumble between his ears didn't start fires or stop anyone's heart, was almost too much to bear. But as he got older, he thought maybe he could use the rumble to move things. He worked on real cars first, then toy cars. Then he tried it on the older boys, the ones with the best bikes who would smack him upside the head whenever he rode by on his Schwinn Stingray, faking motorcycle noises with his mouth as required. But he never crashed them with his brain either. Sometimes out of habit, he'd still make a wish, flex that muscle, and see if that could bring down an airplane.

So tonight he doesn't need to ask the question. Tonight he's going to use the rumble to know exactly what Cherry's thinking. He's suddenly convinced this is what the rumble in his head was always meant for.

He forces her into the back seat. There's resistance when her legs go the wrong way. No words, but a squeak he translates as laughter. To him, this tiny, normally almost undetectable scoff sounds something like a thousand rotten apples falling into helicopter blades, spraying endless pulp over his face as the entire planet laughs along with her. He almost gags.

Then he flexes the strange muscle in his head harder than he ever has, and it must be working this time, because the rumble transforms into the sound of her voice, and she can't help but tell him everything that's been on her mind.

*   *   *

"Hey, Uncle Jake! Where's your other jacket? I wanted to show off your gang colors."

"Oh, shit," Uncle Jake said, stabbing his blade into the wooden swing arm to hold it. "You talking about Deuces Wild?" He leaned over to rub Cherry's knee. She didn't blink. "Our gang was supposed to be called 'Deuces Wild,' right? Only the loopy crone that sewed up our satin jackets for us can't spell, right, so we get 'Deuches Wild' instead. On all five of 'em. You know, *Dooshes Wild?*"

"Oh, no!" Cherry squealed.

"But here's the thing," Jake said. "His gang was so tough, they left it. How badass is that?"

"Yeah, right," Uncle Jake laughed. "Running around, calling ourselves douches before anyone else can, I guess that's a preemptive strike? And big letters, too! Right under a couple of dice. Of course, the dice looked like boxes with air holes cut in 'em for catching fucking frogs. Cherry, it sounds like a joke, but we were tough, I swear. The girls back then went ape over a tough guy with a nice mix of stupid."

Jake laughed.

"We'd kill you though," Uncle Jake said, all serious. "Well, not you, baby," he added as he rubbed Cherry's knee a little longer, trying and failing to tickle it. His nephew pulled her away.

"Go get the jacket, Uncle Jake. Please?"

"Nah, it's in the garage soaking up oil." He wrestled his blade loose again. "I'll bet some of those other mooks still wear theirs around though. Mine had 'Uck' sewn right here over the heart, right where this HHS is hanging. My gang name was 'Uncle Duck,' you see, which everyone twisted into 'Duncle Uck' when they got buzzed."

"Where'd that come from?" Cherry asked.

"My hair was more yellow back then, like your boy's there. And I had that duck's ass in the back, bigger and higher and badder than anyone. But nobody really called me 'Duck' too much, especially this motherfucker, huh, Jake? He wants to be me so bad, he can't stand it."

He punched his nephew harder than necessary, and the swing rattled and shook.

"Did everybody have a nickname, Uncle Jake?" she asked.

"I ain't your uncle, girl! Fuck, I'm not his either. I'm his *Uncle* Uncle Jake, if you want to get technical. Great Uncle or some shit. But they never proved it."

In the distance, someone rolled down their window to sing along with the Stones.

"I see the girls walk by dressed in their summer clothes . . . I have to turn my head until my darkness goes . . ."

Cherry turned red, and Uncle Jake put his foot down to stop the swing.

"She looks just like her, you know?"

*   *   *

The rumble of her voice fills his ears to the brim. Finally, everything she's thinking, rolling like thunderheads . . .

I don't know why he's looking at me like I'm scared. My first time wasn't scary. And it sure wasn't him. And it got real easy once I knew I didn't have to get naked. All you need is one leg out of your jeans. God damn, why do they try so hard to scare us . . .

Jake kicks off one of her shoes and works her pink leg out into the night, her joints are loose, her skin smooth as bone. She's limp, but her voice is getting louder.

It doesn't mean anything if I've done it before. Does he get this?

Her voice echoing, Jake tries digging his fingernails into her leg, scratching for a grip through his own sweat. He sees the red smiles he'll leave behind when a nail flips back.

Why's he trying to steer me by my pelvis? Did he get that from Elvis? His fingers are so fucked from smashing too many guitars.

Jake buries a thumb between her legs, searching for heat and finding none, using it to pull her higher. His movements are abrupt, petulant. The resistance mocks him, and now the crickets are drowning out her voice. Even downing out his rumble.

How many crickets are there in the world? Don't know. I read somewhere if they rub their legs together hard enough, they can catch fire. They have to jump to flame-out or they'd all burn up. And that's how you get lightning bugs . . .

Jake can't believe she's heard the same ridiculous story about fireflies, something he made up as a boy but told few people, and he tries harder to get a better grip. But it's hard, she's hard, and his wet fingers keep slipping off the handles of her bone, pitching him forward and off balance. He locks an arm under her throat before she can laugh again, and in desperation tries to work all his fingers inside her. Up to his wrist, he watches her black eyes for a reaction. He almost screams when he feels the snakebite of a splinter enter his finger.

*   *   *

"Let me tell you the best advice I ever heard, boy. Hold your nose and eat a spider first thing in the morning and nothing worse will happen to you all day."

"You said that before, Uncle Jake. But I thought it was a frog."

"What's the difference?"

"The amount of chewing, for one." He started rocking again, staring at the girl, her unblinking eyes and her glassy, almost translucent skin, slick as a Coke bottle in the sun. He followed her blood-red hair down the middle of her back, the blood you'd find in movies, too bright to be real. All of her consisted of colors you could not find in nature.

"Uncle Jake . . ."

"Do me a favor. Just call me 'Jake.' That two-uncle thing just ruined it forever."

"Okay, but it's gonna get weird," Jake shrugged.

"You know what, boy? Your Cherry reminds me of my Cherry. That's no accident, is it?"

"Well, there *was* an accident actually—"

"You had a Cherry, too?" she asked, as Jake twirled ruby hair behind her ears.

"Sure did! But my Cherry was a little different. She had this game she liked to play."

"What game is that?" Cherry sounded worried about where the story was going, but Jake just smiled and mimed like he was buckling a seat belt for a good yarn.

"It was called Dead Girl On The Side Of The Road."

"Whoa."

"I know, right!" Both Jakes stomped their feet. "Wanna try it?"

"Uh, no?"

"Aw, come on! You kids don't know fun if it bit ya. It was a gas. My Cherry swore she made it up, too. Here's how it went down. First, she'd make me take her out for Chinese food ,to go. Sweet 'n' sour pork. Them Orientals were only a decade out of the camps back then, so they were working their asses off, even outside of Chinatowns, so we'd get plenty of rice. But we'd get an extra order just in case. White rice. Not that healthy rabbit-pellet shit. Then we'd drive out to a dead-end road off a dead-end road and drop her off with the grub. Then I'd come back a little later, playing like I'm just driving along, right? And she'd be lying there, waiting—"

"I thought it was Japan in those camps," Jake muttered.

"Was she playing possum?" Cherry asked.

"Ha, more like playing pussy!" Uncle Jake laughed. "So, she's lying there, and she's got rice and noodles sprinkled all over her body, corners of her mouth, her ears, eyes, between her legs . . ." He felt the two scooting away and stopped. "What? You know, like maggots and worms! More rice on us than newlyweds running from a church. Come on, keep up. So I come across her lying there, and I pretend I find a dead girl on the side of the road, you dig?"

"So, then what?" Cherry asked, not really wanting to know.

"Then I brush off the rice and fuck her! What do you think? I'm telling you, that shit's better than a honeymoon."

The two of them shook their heads as he picked up speed.

"No, no, I ain't done. I ain't done. So, the last time we do this, I'm working to get her jeans off, but her knees were locked tight, right? You punks today and your tight asses had nothing on a Teddy Girl in the '50s. You'd need your blade to get her out of that denim, to tell you the truth. And normally I probably woulda used one. But here the struggle worked with the game, because it was like rigor mortis, you get it? But at that moment, since she's so stiff, I'm also thinking she's changed her mind, like maybe I'd waited too long to come back and she had time to think how ridiculous it all was?"

"Can you blame her?"

"Listen, when she wanted to, her legs would lock so tight you could hear them humming like an oncoming train. So I started whispering to her. Pillow talk. Like, first I just told her to snap out of it, 'please baby, baby,' but then I started telling her other stuff, too. Pleading for real, even some weird sincere shit. Then I don't know what happened because her finger is suddenly jabbing me in the ribs, and she's looking at me all strange, but with love, you know, too much love for a crazy girl who just smeared Jap food all over herself."

"Wait, so what are you—"

"We'd fallen asleep, I guess. She was asleep before I got back. But then I crashed there, too. And when we checked our watches, it was actually earlier than when we'd started."

"I don't get it."

"We slept there on the side of the road until the next day! Dead? Alive? I don't know. Shit gets weird on the road. I just know we spent 24 hours together in a ditch with rice on our faces like a couple of open assholes."

"You know what we did?" Cherry said, sitting up straight. "We made snow angels in a ditch once! Well, dirt angels. There's a reason they do it in snow, you know. Got our elbows all bloody, like this . . ."

"Shut up," Uncle Jake said, looking around for his knife. "I'll tell ya though, the side of a road is more comfortable than you think. Don't jump to conclusions if you see a dead body. Might just be a catnap."

Jake glared for a second, mad how his uncle talked to Cherry. But the sun was going down, and his Uncle Jake was one of those guys who smoothed out once the sun went down.

"Where did you meet her?" Cherry asked him.

"A bar! Where else?"

"What were you doing?"

"Playing fool? Playing pool? What else was there back then?" he laughed. "It was at The Bone Yard, so the pool table was jacked, of course. About as level as my balls in a hundred-degree weather. Hey, I stole their sign once. Everybody stole their signs to hang 'em over their bed. Drove Ray nuts. But Ray stole my sign right back for his own bed. Remember my music store? The Cherry Tree? Any guitar your heart desired. Electric or neutered. Les Paul, Neubauer, Albanus, Gibson, Radio Tone, Fender, Alamo. Remember the Alamos?! Still got a pile of broken Radio Tones in the back . . ."

"The Cherry Tree!" Cherry laughed. "No way."

"Would George Washington lie about a name like that?"

"The Bone Yard, huh. I've heard of that place, too. Isn't that where Gay Busted Elvis hangs out?"

"Yep! One and the same. Except back then, we called him High-Strung Elvis. He was just this big plaster Elvis bust someone glued rainbows of string all over for hair. Only later, like the '70s and '80s, did people start calling him 'Pride Elvis' or 'Rainbow Elvis' or whatever, which is what led directly to the 'busted.' Have you seen his face lately? Cracked right down the middle, so he's only half-a-fag now. Two thirds at best. Well, they'd have to weigh him to be sure. You've been there, right, Jake? But back then in '56 and '57, The Bone Yard was like most dives, every goof in there trying to imitate some Limey café hangout in the movies with their flitty Café Racers. All day long, every one of 'em bullshittin' about bench-racing imaginary cars, every one of 'em a photo finish. Except instead of Frankie Limey and The Fuckin' Teenagers 'Why Do Fools Fall in Love?' on the jukebox, it was all Elvis, all the time. And all his goddamn songs were questions, too. Those were the worst! 'How's the World Treating You?' 'How Do You Think I Feel?' 'What The Fuck Are You Thinking?' My favorite from '56 was always 'Paralyzed' . . ."

"What was wrong with the pool table?"

"It had an extra hole, for starters. Right in the middle where balls would go airborne on the break. Someone tried to fix it by filling it with tree sap, but that just made it worse. The night I met Cherry, I'd been slinging hash with these guys, buncha candy asses claiming to be Stone Grease outta Chicago, and they were swearing up and down that the hole in the table was really a bullet hole. And it was working, impressing these twits at the bar. So I jumped into the story, too, trying to help a brother out. Now, I wasn't as good with stories back then as I am now, so I just said, 'Yeah, they're right! There was this fight, and the punk who lost came marching back in at closing time like Stagger Lee, right past the guys that beat his ass—not regulars either, Big Four, or at least associates—but instead of lighting them up, or popping the bottles behind the bar or the fins off the ceiling fan or any of that shit you're supposed to do in a story like this, he just walked up to the pool table, put his snubnose flush against the green and *BAM!*' Well, the debs were impressed as all hell with my story, and they kept feeding the table quarters all night to play these dudes, so they finally got drunk, and their game started to slip enough for me to start betting. Then Cherry comes walking in. She's wearing a red T-shirt and jeans, Kool-Aid or cherry stains all over her or something, crisp blues way too long—the only time I ever seen 'em that way—and rolled up to her knees. And she points at the hole in the pool table and proceeds to blow my whole story out of the water with a story of her own. It would have been okay if she'd just told her fable and that was that, but hers was much better than mine. Plus she acted it out in a way I never coulda topped."

"I've heard this!" Jake shouted.

"You might have. It's like this loony barfly variation on 'The Princess and the Pea' she starts doing. First, she jumps up on the pool table and lays back, eyes closed, then she tries to guess what balls everybody's knocking into the holes—get this—by just the *feel* of them under her body. She does this awhile, us banging away, her maybe getting her guesses right, maybe none, but it doesn't fuckin' matter with those white knees high up in the sky like that, and all us assholes are drooling on her, and *then* she starts fingering that hole like it's a *real* asshole and telling us how she's only in there looking buy fireworks from Ray the bartender and how he shorted her last time. See, fireworks were like bullets back then. Meaning they were everywhere . . ."

"I thought she told a story."

"I was getting to that. Fuck. Let me think. Okay, so, laying there on her back, she tells us all that she played this 'Princess and the Pea' action in The Bone Yard once before, but someone tried to trick her by taking one of Ray's M-80s or whatever out of the back, and then dropping it down the corner pocket after the 8-ball when she wasn't looking. Rattle rattle rattle rattle . . . *BA-BOOM*. Something like that. Wait, it wasn't an M-80. It was a cherry bomb. Of course it was a cherry bomb! But really, my story was better, only I don't have the knees for it. Oh, shit, and when she pulled up the back of her shirt to show us a scar on the sweet spot of her spine from the cherry bomb. Well, fuck it, game over. No one even remembered I was talking. Except for Rusty."

"Oh, no. Not Rusty." Jake knew all about Rusty. The enemy of every biker with clean chrome between his legs was a "Rusty."

"Yeah. See, there was this other guy, Rusty Games, who was always eating big red apples all sticky and sloppy all over the pool sticks. His dad had an orchard, see? He got that nickname for being terrible at 8-ball, but sometimes we just called him 'Games.' Or even 'Rusty Names.' Hey, at least we didn't call him 'Rusty Dames,' I guess. Anyway, Rusty Games puts 'Walk Fuck Like a Man' on the jukebox—"

"Wait, what song?" Cherry asked.

"You never heard that?"

"I think you're mixing up two songs there, Uncle Jake."

"You're nuts. But Games, he was a goddamn storyteller. Told wicked stories all the time. The one I remember best he told us that night. How he stole his daddy's Buddy Holly album and hid it in his own stack. And his stack was up to your neck, right? Most people only had 45s, so that was a red flag right there. But Games says his daddy's threatening to tip 'em over, and he says he daddy says he better dig it out careful if he knows what's good for him. Now, going through a stack like that to find one record is no easy task. That's heavy. By 'heavy,' I mean *heavy*, like real work. So his daddy pulls a fucking gun and says, 'Boy, you gimmie my *Chirping Crickets* el peeeee!' and Games says he says, 'Fuck you!' and snatches his daddy's .45 . . ."

"The record or the gun?"

". . . which is the gun, not the record. Swipes it right out of his hand, goes over to this leaning tower of pizza and says, 'Pick a card! Any card!' Which I guess was his way of saying, 'Guess how many records the bullet goes through,' right? And Games says his daddy's worried now because *The 'Chirping' Crickets* by Buddy Holly and The Motherfucking Crickets is probably near the top of the stack. But it's too late. Games puts that gun in the middle of the stack and fires straight down. *BLAM!* Turns out he shoots right through the doughnut holes! Swore he didn't scratch a single record. Or kill a single cricket. Didn't send anything flying except maybe the songs themselves. So, after this story, Cherry's all in love, totally smitten. So I clear my throat and say, 'Bullshit!' And that's when Games punches me in the mouth."

"Oh, man. We know a fucker like that, too, don't we, baby?" Jake said, petting her head. "Except he punched my bike in the mouth. Did he ride a little dirt bike like a bear on a unicycle?" But Jake knew he didn't. He knew Games had heavy metal just like him and his uncle. Jake knew all about Games. Uncle Jake practically raised Jake after his dad died, and he talked about Games a lot. So he knew how this story ended, but sometimes the stories in the middle changed.

"So I sat pouting, rubbing my face and listening to him more stories. After that punch, everyone was listening really."

"Did you guys rumble?" Cherry asked, and Jake's hand squeezed the back of her neck tighter than normal to quiet her down.

"Don't say 'rumble,' baby. In this family, it doesn't mean what you think it does."

"Both of you, zip it," Uncle Jake said. "So my heartbeat's in my lips, but I'm still in earshot when Games starts laying it on thick, sniffing her neck, nuzzling and telling her stories like this one about two cats that used to fuck under the hood of his Mustang when he was a kid. The way he tells it, you'd think this was a sonnet. He whispers to her how he heard these alien sounds in his car, followed them to their source, and his daddy said, "Don't look under there!' said it was probably just a brain-damaged cat licking antifreeze. But Games says he says he was so sure it was the ghosts of all the roadkill his Mustang had rolled over that he *has* to look, baby . . ." He nuzzled up to Cherry's cold neck, and she didn't twitch. ". . . but all he saw were the tails, he tells her. But that's enough. Three Elvis songs later, and they're holding hands. Another song later, and they're holding even more. But I watch him close all night. I knew he had a blade by the outline in his back pocket. Knew he'd cut someone recently by the wet stain around it. Which, come to think of it, is exactly what's going on in his front pocket! But he played the part, you know? Had the Jesus boots like me, like you, like all of us back then. But just like us, this motherfucker had to piss eventually, and that's where I decided I'd get back on his radar."

* * *

Still ain't working, is it, Jake? You remind me of that joke. Boy sticks in a finger. Girl says, "One more." Boy sticks in another finger. Girl says, "One more." Boy sticks in all his fingers. Girl says, "More!" Boy sticks in his whole hand. Girl says, "Stick in your other hand, too." Boy sticks in both hands. Girl says, "Clap your hands." Boy says, "I can't." Girl says, all smug, "Tight, ain't it?"

Jake loses sight of the numbers on his watch while Cherry's feet violently drum the window over his shoulder from his effort. When it shatters, Jake sighs.

Those windows aren't so easy to come by on a Cadillac, *he thinks.* It was hard enough finding a new door after I opened it on that kid's face.

Jake's car is streaked with gray primer from the door handles on up, so he calls it his Great White Shark. Tonight, with the windshield busted, he imagines it swimming around upside down, mouth wide open.

No room in here, Jake. You know, I saw a girl in a Russ Meyer movie once, one of the early ones, the nasty ones, says she fucks hundreds every year, but saves her ass for whoever she loves. Maybe that was a dream. There's a moral there somewhere.

Jake puts more weight on the arm across her throat and pulls his hand out far enough to see the numbers on his Eterna Automatic. He was sure having it inside her would make it stop from more heat and pressure than any timepiece was built to endure. He thinks about the clocks that stopped when they tested the atom bomb. He thinks sun-dials the size of football fields and the thunderclouds that render them useless. Then he goes in deeper.

I don't know why you think you can do any damage. You'd have to fuck me with something bigger than a fist, bigger than a baby, bigger than a baby riding a motorcycle . . .

Jake tries to think of things babies can do and decides fingernails are the answer. Babies never scratch anything but themselves or they'd scratch their way out. He wonders what keeps kittens from escaping their mothers' bellies with their claws. Her voice in his head is loud but bored, a lethal combination.

You'll never be half the man my daddy was. When I had my first exam, the doctor waited and wasted time until daddy was back in the room and next to me, then he asked if I was a virgin. Bastard's fingers just discovered I wasn't, you know? He thought daddy would be angry. And he was. But not at me. Daddy climbed over a plaster model of diseased ovaries on the desk and punched that motherfucker so hard his hand disappeared. Then he took me home. That punch was so loud, sometimes I feel I could ride it like a saddle.

Jake starts scratching and digging like a kitten, trying to find something inside her no one has before. And he does. Something small and hard. He traces its outline, squeezes rubber that feels like a wheel. He hopes it's not a toy, and his fingers curl tight to wrestle it out. He imagines chains rattling and oil bubbling and the groan of an engine as a car is slowly dragged from a swamp.

Too bad I never saw that doctor again because my daddy wanted to stick something in there to surprise him next time. Give him the surprise of his life. There never was a next time, but it was a good idea. Almost as good as this one . . .

That's when Cherry twists her hips so hard and fast that his middle finger cracks at the second knuckle. He pulls out, a silent scream circling his mouth, a knee in her neck to keep her down as he feels around in the dark to trace the new trajectory of his digit. He counts two extra knuckles he didn't have before and feels shattered bone rolling under the skin. It reminds him of the stone in his elbow from the last time he got dumped off his bike riding a corn maze.

Serves you right, Jake. My teeth are clenched, yes, but it's just the way I'm made. It's not the silent treatment, I swear. Hang it up.

Jake uses the heel of his injured hand for leverage and tries again, rotating his shoulder for power. He remembers playing doctor when he was a boy, and a girl on the playground asked him to unwrap his apple then wrap that aluminum foil around his finger to stick it down her throat. They thought it would make his finger a mirror, so they could see deep inside her body. This memory had always haunted him. Especially when she threw up all over him, and he kept fighting to keep that silver finger inside her to find her heart. That's how you play doctor for real.

Then his finger finds the trigger, and he pulls it, and her mouth finally blows open to let out the smoke.

*   *   *

"If you've been to The Bone Yard for longer than three beers, then you know the toilets are always broken. And Ray the bartender—sorry son-of-a-bitch never rode a bike that wasn't crop-dusting with a blown rod—he'd play this crazy game where he'd put Siamese fighting fish in 'em to see how long they'd last, just as a joke at first."

"Never heard that joke."

"You never heard that joke? Doctor says, 'I need a blood, urine, semen, and fecal sample.' So the patient hands him his underwear? Well, that's the toilets in The Bone Yard in a nutshell! But those fighting fish? Sometimes they wouldn't die. Ray's funny like that. He also likes to roll his quarters on the bar when he cleans out the machines, something dumbasses like me used to think were dangerous as brass knuckles. So while I'm standing there twirling my church key and killing time, not ready to pop the top on another Coca-Cola because someone will swipe it when our fight starts, I palm a roll of Ray's quarters and keep them close. Then finally Games struts in there to piss. I move fast. I'd already put the loudest song on the jukebox in case he screamed—I had a long time to think about it with his endless stories, you dig. So I walk right in behind him, and I punch him over the ear, and the paper breaks and quarters explode everywhere. But it's enough of a shock for me to get both his arms locked behind his back before he knows what the hell is going on. He doesn't yell out. Instead he uses all his strength to get one arm free. Then, at the last possible second—you gotta picture this shit—I'm pushing his head towards that black water in slow-motion, where a Siamese fighting fish is fighting a turd or worse, and right before the tip of his nose is gonna go *Sploosh!* he reaches up and catches the chain to flush that bitch."

"Chain?"

"It was a different time. Everything had chains back then, not just us."

"But you said these toilets don't flush."

"That's what I thought! Turned out they worked fine. Just no one ever flushed 'em!"

"He didn't get dunked? Aw, man! He beat you again."

"You don't know the half of it. Story ain't over. So his face slaps the bowl, and it's nasty, but not as nasty as that black mud aquarium. But I'm so surprised it flushed that he gets the best of me, and after some slap-happy bunny punches and slipping around on quarters, suddenly I'm over another bowl that's even worse, one where the Rumble Fish is floating and never had a fucking chance at all, and now I'm heading for the dunk of the damned. But he's only got one of my arms, just like I had on him, and I go for the chain, too, because I'm a quick study. And . . . I catch it at the last second like I'm going off a fuckin' cliff."

"Whew! Close one, Uncle Jake."

"Close one, my ass. Imagine this. Freeze the scene with my face in the same spot his was. Then move your camera up the toilet a bit. See that box? Inside that box, the chain goes down, and this little metal bar goes up, and there's another little chain, see? A little chain that Games cut earlier that evening with his switchblade. And when I pull my chain, it only makes this little chain swirl around a bit, barely even tickling the rubber plug that would have been my savior. All that clear, cold water in the box could have saved me from a mouthful of shit, piss, blood, and dead fish. And quarters."

"Man, he must be psychic. How do you know that he cut it?" Jake asked.

"The stains on his back pocket. That's why his blade was wet."

"Come on now, how would he know to do that? How did he know what you were going to do? How would he know which toilet to pick?" Cherry wanted to know.

"The one with the fish, of course. He knew I'd aim for the fish that was still fighting, and that left the toilet with the dead one."

"I guess. But why would he—"

"Hey! You think I'm pulling your chain?" Big smirk. Then, "Listen! You ever seen those little flies they paint inside urinals nowadays, down near the drain? It reduces piss stains by a thousand percent. It's our lizard brain—we can't help but aim for living things."

"Girls don't use urinals."

"Not your best idea following him in there, huh, Uncle Jake?"

"Not my worst idea either. I'll tell you about *that one* some time, when me and your dad tried to make a haunted house out of your grandpa Jake's garage? Let's just say, if you like scary haunted-house fog, or you like *life* a little better, don't back in your motorcycle and pump it full of exhaust."

"So how'd you end up with her?" Cherry needed to know.

"Huh? My bike?"

"No. Your Cherry. If Games got the best of you, how'd you end up with her?"

"'End up with her.' It's funny you say it like that."

* * *

Jake drives around in his shark, wind drying his eyes, taking a twisted route so the sun is always coming up behind him. He tries not to look at his bent, throbbing finger, a bloody maraschino topping the sundae of his wheel. After a couple miles, he finds a boy on a bicycle, a Stingray just like his, and he cruises behind with the muscle rumbling loud in his ear. It's not a dirt bike, but it'll have to do because it's the boy's voice he hears now.

What the hell is he doing up so early?

The boy glances back at the shark and kicks his heel down on a generator connected to his back tire. Jake sees a tiny wheel snap down on the white wall, and the red tail-light on the bike's fender grows steadily brighter. Jake realizes the boy is pretending he's fired up some sort of engine, imagining his tiny tail-light is some kind of rocket. Jake gets closer and sees cards in the spokes, not playing cards but some goddamn role-playing game with dragons instead of hearts, and now Jake is furious. This is even worse than a dirt bike and has no business on his road. But it's still just a kid. So he reaches back behind his seat and plucks ammo from his 8-ball collection, racked in a triangle, all the pool balls he'd stolen mid-game to impress Cherry during their courtship. He'd steal a ball and get chased out the door, then steal a kiss from her behind the dumpster. He had 8-balls rolling free around his shark until one rolled under his brake pedal and he couldn't stop without almost doing a headstand. He took out five mailboxes that day, but it could have been worse. And they worked a lot better than his piles of vinyl 45s he winged like exploding frisbees when challengers wanted to race him at a red light. Perfect for situations like this.

He used to collect those "magic" 8-balls with the water in them, the toys that lied and pretended to tell you what you were thinking. He even had one on his dashboard for awhile, but half its liquid guts evaporated in the sunlight, leaving the exposed die stuck with just one answer on the window, "Concentrate and Ask Again.” He tried taking this advice, but it ruined him and his girl forever. Even with a bullet finally blowing her mouth blown open for good, he knew she'd never talk again. Not just because of what he stole from her.

* * *

“How did I end up with her? Well, me and Games decided we'd have to earn her. So we agreed on a story. We agreed on a time. We agreed on a road . . .”

“For a rumble!”

“I told you not to say that word,” Jake said, rubbing his head.

“For a race?” Cherry asked, sheepish.

“No, no, no. I told him this, ‘I'll be with Cherry in my car, romancing her best I can. I'll try to tell her a ghost story, you know? Get her to believe it. He had this key ring for his bike made out of a green apple—no, a kiwi—with a little plastic sword sticking out. He said it came off some weird drink Ray made for him once, and he called this thing his “Martian Pussy.” And it really looked like something he'd been fucking, right, even though he swore he wasn't going to fuck it once it turned brown—”

“What kind of bike did he ride?”

“Oh, he rode one of those dustbin fairies, a Moto Guzzi. Into that new streamliner shit. So, he gives me the Martian Pussy for bad luck, and we choose our roles. He decides he'll be the ghost, and I'll be the ghost story. And may the best man win!”

“I don't get it.”

“I'd rather be the ghost.”

“It goes like this—I'd take Cherry down Mantis Trail in my car, right around the bridge where we'd watch submarine races . . .”

“What car?”

“You know what car, Jake! The same two-tone shitbox I gave to you!”

“Ha! Submarine races!” Cherry squealed. “I know what those were.”

“That ain't slang, girl. Naw, up by Mantis Trail was this big delta with an Army base about six miles up, so we could see real submarines on test runs. Wait, what did you think it meant? Fuck it. Anyhow, yeah, the bridge, that's where I'd start the story. Games would be doing about 90 per, since he's the ghost and all, then I'd reach a point in the yarn where I'd stop cold, take the Martian Pussy from the ignition and throw the keys off into the creek. Not my keys, but she doesn't know that. I'd have an extra key for later, tucked under the saddle of my bike. Then, when I've locked us out, or she thinks I've locked us out . . .”

“How are you locked out?” Cherry asked. “Now you're on a bike? You just said your ‘saddle’—”

"Without keys, you're locked out in the dark. Get it? So she'll be scared, thinking we're stuck. And right about then, I'd get to the part of the ghost story with a phantom bike or some spit, I don't remember exactly . . ."

Uncle Jake stopped to lean over and squint into a spider web on the rail. A grasshopper was struggling mightily, and its panic caught his eye the same time as the wolf spider living in his tunnel. But Uncle Jake moved quicker than the spider, quicker than Jake thought possible, and plucked it out first. The grasshopper puked on his finger, and he crushed it in disgust.

"Where was I?"

"A phantom bike or some spit," Cherry said.

"Right."

"What kind of bike did you have?" she needed to know.

"I have a hog! Same as yours. I mean, his. You know that. Orange and black. Called it my Halloween 'Sickle.'"

"Sickle, like 'motor-sickle'?"

"No, you know, a *sickle*. Like the Reaper carries."

"Ah."

"Harley '56 HK, a bobber by accident right now, but the same bike Elvis posed on that very same year for the cover of May's *Enthusiast*. Yeah, it's a 'Hardly Ableson,' the only thing they allowed up in Sturgis or the Black Hills. Thirteen-forty see-sees, two-valve vee-twin, swing-arm pipes so you don't go gunnin' it without watching those corners. Otherwise you'll drop your pumpkins, Ichabod-style . . ."

"What?"

"You can't throw a pumpkin if you don't have a good center of gravity!" He patted his bear belly hard, laughing. "So. Ghost story. We're standing on the bridge, just talking. It wasn't dark enough yet, and it was a hot night, one of those steamy ones. And that's when the fog broke, and we saw this boy on the water, frozen in a dive, hovering above the surface."

"What do you mean 'frozen'?"

"Frozen. Like a snapshot. It was this kid, caught coming off a diving board, stopped just above the water a split second before his hands would have pierced the waves. First, I thought it was just some boy surfing a submarine. But as he floated closer, I couldn't get my brains around it. He was too far out in the river to have jumped from anywhere but the motherfucking sky. So we're staring as he moves with the current, still locked in this crazy dive. Then the boy's legs start twitching, then scissoring, then pedaling the air. I thought I was losing my mind for sure. Still up and down arrow-straight, he's moving towards us while his legs pin-wheel, his fingers spread like he was stretching the surface tension, looking for a way in. I'm wanting to punch myself in the mouth to wake up from this dream, when the fog finally breaks and give us a clear view. I can see the boy's hands, see hands fanned out, and I finally understand, and my heartbeat returns to normal. He's on a raft, you see. It was just a boy doing a headstand on a raft. I didn't realize it then, but now I know that he's the reason it all went wrong that night. After seeing something like that, with no words needed to paint the picture, there was just no way any story that came out of my mouth could compete."

*   *   *

The last time Jake was on this road, he was under it. He had crawled into a drainage tunnel near the railroad tracks because he was in love with a girl but didn't have the nerve to tell her. So he spray-painted, "Ask me what I'm thinking" on the wall of the tunnel and took her to find it. When they were creeping towards it, flashlight bobbing around like an erection, so proud of his surprise, a train thundered over them, and she started backing out. He got angry and told her there was something she had to see. But she didn't care. She was scared of the noise, then scared of him. So he started to lie, claimed there was a strange opening in the wall, some nonsense about miles and miles of mysterious tunnels leading into the dark. He thought she'd need to see that, but it only scared her more. She was running down the tracks back to his Stingray before he could even back out. He stood under the rumble of the train, and he knew what she was thinking. They rode home in silence, and nothing could get her back down there. Not even when he hooked her antenna with a 45 while she was idling at a stop sign. And when he finally did say those three words, they meant nothing at all.

Jake taps the gas pedal, flashes his brights, then flips the switch on the heater, imagining he's triggered a ragged, chum-dripping mouth under the grill to scoop up his upcoming roadkill. His shark drifts over the double-yellow, sniffing for blood. Then Jake leans out his window, thinks something like, "Outlook Not So Good," and side-arms an 8-ball into the boy's spokes.

The fantasy cards flutter in the rooster tail of rocks as the boy squeezes his front brakes and flies headfirst over his handle bars. The bike chases his cartoon tumble into the ditch, greased chain still clicking smooth when they land. Jake backs up to see where the boy vanished, hissing through his teeth when he pulls the gearshift too tight and a greenstick fracture splits through his skin. The shark dances backwards on the rumble strip, then skids in the gravel as Jake pops the passenger door and shadows his crime. Jake looks down into the ditch for about ten seconds, then grabs the .45—the gun not the record this time—that still rests between Cherry's legs where it was born. He puts one bullet in the boy's head, then another in his mouth just in case, then stabs the gas and goes hand-over-hand on the steering wheel to spin around and leave the ditch behind. When the shark straightens out, he wrings out his wheel like laundry and sucks his broken finger some more. It's changing colors again, and he remembers the first time he ever buried it in a real, live girl back in sixth grade and how scared he was when he saw it turn green under the glow of the dashboard lights.

Then the sun is coming around to face him again, and it hurts to turn and stay ahead it. The roads will be filling up soon, and suddenly he knows what everyone will be thinking, without even squeezing the muscle in his head. He adjusts his radio, but the rumble grows louder.

* * *

". . . because I'm so caught up in the game, she starts telling me her own ghost story first! And now I know I'm fucked. She goes, 'Picture it, you're driving down the road . . .' She's saying this while she's flicking thorns at my face, right, long, crabapple thorns from Games' orchard that stung like a mother, so I turning away, and she grabs—"

"What kind of orchard grows crabapples?"

"That's what I'm saying. Him and his brothers had a cornfield that grew nothing but dirt-bike rallies, too. Anyhow, she grabs my jaw to straighten my head and goes, 'Okay, you're driving down the road . . .' Then, nose to nose, she puts one finger on a nostril and blows snot in my face. I jump up with, 'What the fuck?!' and she laughs and says, 'Bugs on your windshield. Pay attention, you're driving down the road . . .' And at that point, I just let her do what she wants to do, thinking it's all downhill after the bugs, but now she starts holding up her palms and taking long karate chops past my ears. 'Oncoming cars,' she tells me. Whoosh, whoosh, whoosh, her hands flying by my head. 'You're driving down the road . . .' she keeps saying, then, 'Now close your eyes.' And that's when she punches me in the mouth just like fucking Games. 'Never close your eyes when you're driving down the road,' she shrugs, smiling while blood drips off my bottom lip again like a fuckin' schoolboy."

"Sounds like a handful, Uncle Jake."

"Every time I took her riding on my hog, she wanted switch places."

"You were just afraid to be seen in the bitch seat."

"Humbugs! Nothing wrong with that. Lines you up perfect, like doing it 'donkey style.'"

"Don't you mean 'doggy style'?"

"I mean what I mean. Donkey style. Now, let me ask you kids a question, mostly you, Jake. And your answer means everything. What's worst? Fucking a dead dog on the side of the road . . . or lying about it?"

"Uh . . ."

"Don't answer yet."

"Can I not answer ever?" Cherry said.

"Okay, back to that night. She tries another story on me, going, 'Picture this, you're running through the river . . .' and she's got this beer bottle she snagged from the side of the bridge that's full of foam and mosquito eggs and spunkwater—stanky shit, rank, we're talking upper ranks, rank of First Lieutenant at least—and she's shaking it up with her thumb over the spout, getting ready to splash me, and I go, 'Whoa, whoa, whoa. I'm not running through the river. My turn.' She says, 'Fine,' so all spooky, I say, 'It was a year ago tonight. And you're running through the woods . . .' And now *I* start punching the air near her ears. She smiles, thinking no way I'm gonna hit her, right? 'You're running through the woods,' I say, swinging fists past her head, zip, zip zip."

The swing tilted as Uncle Jake reached around to get closer to his nephew and chop the air past his ears.

"You're running through the woods, Jake. Zip, zip, zip. That's what I tell her. Then I'm all like, 'Close your eyes.' You heard me, close 'em!" he yelled.

Jake closed his eyes, and his uncle heeled him in the forehead with a sound like a steak dropped on a countertop.

"No way you hit a girl," Jake sighed, hand cupped over his eyes like he was saluting a lower rank.

"Says you," Uncle Jake scoffed. "Had to get her attention. 'It was a year ago tonight,' I was saying. That's how every ghost story starts. Then I switched to 'It was a week ago tonight,' thinking it would be scarier, but it just sounded dumb. So I take a jar out of my saddlebag, and I set it down on my front fender in front of the headlight, 'cause beforehand me and Games had filled it up with apple and kiwis, get me? Apples on the top, kiwis on the bottom. Red light, green light, got it? So if I click my highbeams, it gives him a red light, meaning the scare is off. Too dangerous."

"Wait a second," Cherry said. "What's dangerous? And why the colors?"

"In case he blinks. I don't know. Didn't wanna take any chances. We can see red and green from miles away."

"How do you know green to him is green to you?" Cherry asked, and got a heel to her forehead in return. Her head went back so far, the two Jakes were surprised it came back. But that was always a good question.

"So I try my ghost story, some B.S. about a kid killing his best friend over a girl. Nothing new. Some horse hockey about a headless motorcycle rider like *Sleepy Hollow* or something. But she interrupts me with her own story again. This one is about a horse, and it's fucking better than mine. Again."

"You're just not a storyteller, Uncle Jake."

"Guess not. Unless I'm telling stories about other people's stories, I reckon.

Anyhow, she tells me she was 6 or 7, on her uncle's ranch, obsessed with their horse named 'Serendipity'—'Sir,' for short— and, oops, now 'Sir' is giving birth. She says she remembers the sucking sounds because it's the day the crickets stopped, and she can hear everything, from both ends of the barn and both ends of the *horse*. Sir kicks up some dust, and Cherry tries her hardest not to look at the tunnel under her tail. Eventually, she closes her eyes and makes a wish, she tells me. She says she wishes the little horse that comes out of that hole will look like the horses she used to draw, like all little girls used to draw when we we're too busy drawing motorcycles. She wishes for a centaur or a Pegasus, one with a man's head or one with wings. Either will do. Then the worst thing happens. Her wish comes true."

Jake never heard this story before, and he had one eye shut as if expecting another blow.

"The thing that came out of that hole haunted every farmhand in three counties to his grave. One rancher tried to pull her away. One cocked a shotgun while her father was pulling the thing out from under the whiplashing tail, one hand in front of his face like he's warding off the worst news in the world. She said there was this sudden blast of fluid, and that's when she sees the whole thing for the first time. It was deformed, of course, but to Cherry she just saw this shriveled snout, almost like a pig under glass, and a bunch of afterbirth stuck to its back that Sir is now hellbent on eating. It's not just afterbirth she's munching though. Most of its insides were suddenly on the outside, and with every bite, the foal was screaming. The sac was coiled, and wet, wrapped around its ribs, and Cherry tells me that, in her young mind, she was sure this was the wings. Like a bug slipping from a cocoon, wings straining to unfold. She was sure she got her horrible wish, and now Sir is chewing those wings right off its back. She's convinced she caused this, suddenly sure this is what it would look like if a goddamned flying horse really happened in real life. It wouldn't be something beautiful. It would be a horror. She tells me how she watched Sir tugging on the back of the howling foal, ripping away those wings, and how all the men were shrieking like children. Two shotgun blasts finally stopped everything, but not before she said she saw that foal standing up strong, soaking up buckshot like it was nothing, and spreading the rest of those tattered wings wide as an eagle. She swore she saw huge wings beat dust and spider webs off the walls—and not the kind of noble wings you'd see on a drawing of some mythical creature, more like something you'd see on an insect, blue-veined like our balls, or the wings of a fly drowning in your drink. Then her story's over, and she asks me, 'So, what were you saying then?'"

"Wow," Cherry said.

"Speak for your own balls," Jake said.

"Ha, we all got the same balls, boy. On a hot day like this, they all hang the same, like a plastic bag of guppies you buy to feed your fucking turtles. Swinging low and sloshing, trying not to touch your body to keep them fighting fish from boiling."

"Ew."

"So, this is what happened. I get so caught up in her story about the horse, her whispering that shit in my ear, head against my back, that I take my thumb off the brights. Her hand comes around to work me and my zipper, but I shake it away. No way I'm in the mood now. See, I was gonna give Games the red light no matter what, I really was. He'd stop the bike right before he went under the bridge, right before his neck got to the spot where I'd strung up the wire. A line of guitar string from my brother, your dad's Stratocaster, or maybe it was grandpa's piano—whatever's stronger—and Games would look at that wire and know he almost ended up with half a face, worse than Gay Busted Elvis. They'd both know what I almost did. But you know the rest. Her story was better than mine, so I had to step it up. I left my headlights shining green through those kiwis. All because Games was coming . . . but I wasn't."

Cherry laughed. Jake did, too. He knew the ending.

"The piano wire sank into the dark meat of that kid's throat like fishing line cracking through sunburned fingers at the end of the day. Maybe not quite like fishing line. More like a *finish* line. And I'd strung his finish line on an angle like a guillotine so the wire would work with the speed of his Guinea racer and cut fast and deep. But the motherfucker's head stayed on! From up on the bridge, we saw his headlight flutter with the impact, and I imagined those same hands that had stuffed my head in a toilet earlier that day wrestling with his own machine, maybe one hand coming up to keep his head on, too. Then he probably rode his bike to the ground, one hand still squeezing the gas, one hand squeezing the lawn sprinkler gushing from his throat. He might have made it another hundred feet, but the front wheel tangled around some weeds like spaghetti on a spoon—that's how real dagoes eat that shit, you now—and there it stuck, him bleeding out, engine screaming like it knew what I did."

"Damn."

"When we ran up there, he must have still been alive because we saw his fingers just starting to loosen up—like when you spread them over a flashlight—and all that red came rushing out. The back wheel was still up and spinning, yearning for the road to get at me, you dig? And that screaming wheel was probably the last thing he heard, I guess. I tried to get in the headlight so he'd see me and know who won, but he was already gone. But at least the bike knew."

*   *   *

What are you thinking?

Jake stands over the dead boys and their bikes. He strung guitar string through the corn maze where they raced and rode wheelies around the dead, muddy field, butting horns like rutting steers. But Jakes' snares caught more than he'd hoped for. He figures if he ties enough guitar string on the strongest stalks, or the tallest campaign crossbars, one day he'll snag the same dirt bike who lanced his spokes and brought down his horse so easy. He just has to keep laying down more mouse traps.

More like bug strips, *he thought.*

But he doesn't know what to do with the rest of the day stretching out in front of him. Jake thinks about famous maniacs, the ones who left the body hanging or made half a snow angel or propped a victim up against some cryptic song lyric or left a head on the plastic Big Boy burger, and how everyone always thinks it's a message. Not at all. They just didn't want to clean up afterwards. Maybe they were too bored to burn it or bury it or chop it up or even roll it in the water. Maybe the real nasty murders that get left all fucked up are just some nut going apeshit with the body because he's too damn lazy to start working.

The dirt bikes are as bent as the boys, necks still hanging on by some gristle, and Jake wonders if piano wire really is stronger than guitar string. And there's not enough blood either. He flicks the exposed tendons and muscle on one boy with his steel-toe, catching a bundle of tissue like puppy scruff. Jake is startled when his boot makes the boy kicks out a foot like a dog having nightmares. He heard once if you can pinched the right wires, you could make a body talk, just like a dummy. And he's already proven, for the record, that if you carry around a dead body and do the talking for it, your ventriloquism skills don't have to be top-notch with a corpse on the porch swing as a distraction.

"What are you thinking?"

Jake shudders to knock the question loose then wonders if a bullet in the head would be as unimpressive as Cherry's own death at the doorway to a labyrinth of corn. One bullet, just a tiny black dot, the period at the end of the third-grade love letter she threw away, embarrassing to read even an hour after Jake wrote it, but not nearly as excruciating as decades-old barroom tales.

Jake piggybacks Cherry to the car, pulling her arms tighter around his neck. This Cherry talks even less than the Cherry that died here, but she's certainly seen enough. She'd sleep on his shoulder everywhere now, even off the bike.

*   *   *

"When we got up to the wreck, we couldn't make sense of what we were seeing. Maybe it was the shock of it all, but we couldn't tell where Games ended and the bike began . . ."

"Where the games ended!" Jake laughed.

". . . and the color of the oil mixed with blood, what little we could see, didn't seem like blood at all. Once when I was a kid, I flipped backwards off the edge of my brother's—your dad's—new, above-ground pool. And when I picked myself up off the grass, I found three white holes in my leg where the exposed bolts had punctured my shin. I ran to the house, expecting a gush down my leg any second, but even after a full five minutes, nothing. Just white holes. I panicked, might have passed out, because that blood never came. I blacked out not because I'd popped three holes in my freakin' leg down to the freakin' bone, but because I thought I had nothing inside me. And I felt that same panic when we saw Games. Like we were made of some kinda shit that I knew nothin' about. But Cherry, she was panicking for other reasons, saying something about how tangled up he was with that motorcycle, his feet locked under the tailpipes, hands twisted behind his back and invisible. He was 'half boy, half bike,' she said. We were scared, sure. But something our dad—your grandpa—always said about killing a bug in your hand helped. If you squeeze it, it can bite, so remember to roll it in your fingers. That'll break it up easier than you ever knew. See, that's what we should have done with him, you know? So he wouldn't bite back. Get it?"

"Not really. You mean the grasshopper? So, did you get in trouble?"

"Hell, no. Cherry took off running first, and she started my panhead before I could climb onto the saddle behind her. Yeah, behind her. Donkey style! She'd stolen my keys when I thought she was playing with my zipper. And we rode home, me with my head on *her* back this time, and I thought about her ghost story and the creature she'd made for me. Half bike, half boy. A green-eyed monster. A perfect centaur. With wings. And wheels . . ."

"Endgame," Jake said.

"Two childhood drawings combined," Cherry said.

"Your dad always hated that nickname," his uncle. "But not as much as he hated you and me."

They sat in silence for about nine more swings.

"So, can I get that stuff from you, Jake?"

"Sure, Jake. Take whatever you need. All our parts are interchangeable."

* * *

Jake looks deep into the smoking hole where her mouth used to be. She doesn't know they're back at the scene of the crash, where his wrecked bike slept in the shade of a sign screaming "Hell Is Real!" unnoticed by traffic, patiently waiting for his return. He half-expects the bike to be teeming with wedding rice, and he guns his shark on past. He'd started the morning with a ghost story, even ate a spider so that nothing worse could happen to them all day, but he worries he should have eaten the frog instead when the rumble starts again and won't stop. He thinks of a warning from the dried-up Magic 8-Ball, before the words got stuck to the window.

"You May Rely On It."

He takes a sharp turn and hears the echo of gutted guitars clanking around the Eldorado's trunk. He stomps some pedals. Then his brain is Jake Breaking again. Right in two.

* * *

The two Jakes stood in the garage, somewhere on the border of morning and night. One said the other could take whatever he needed, and the other said pretty much the same thing.

Jake laid Cherry in the corner, near a pile of uprooted political posters, next to his uncle's Cherry, her dusty plastic head slumped to the side, puppet strings cut. He watched his uncle give him a look like, "That'll work," then bent down to give his girl a last kiss on the red and cracked Raggedy Anne dimples of her face. His uncle's Cherry was a crash-test dummy in a previous life, who'd also served as a ballistics mannequin when she never showed damage after the brutal crashes at her old Kawasaki plant. This was before they brought in the new dummies, jam-packed with metal and electronics. Rotten fruit was smeared across her face, and paint chips framed the four-quadrant circle on her cheek, a yellow pie with two pieces gone. His uncle's Cherry had holes drilled in exactly three places, originally to gauge her impacts in the factory, later slathered with motor oil to become something else entirely. Her long, ruby-red hair slid off her head with a whisper when Jake picked her up, revealing the chipped jawbreaker of her skull. Uncle Jake thought about how most kids needed new models because of the upkeep. But his nephew was raised better than that.

Jake ducked under the door with the mannequin in his arms, smiling at the weight, smiling at how easily things were replaced, nuzzling the wear and tear, the history on her face, already wondering what she's thinking. Her head lolled off his shoulder, and he shook her like a baby, hearing the heavy rattle deep in her belly. He wasn't sure if he could pull his uncle's gun from her mouth or between her legs. Both seemed impossible. He put her on his back.

Then he went for the pile of smashed Alamo guitars and started loading them in the Eldorado's trunk. He drove away with her head on his shoulder, listening to new stories.

Back in the garage, Jake's engine rumbled, and the sweet fog of exhaust smoke billowed around his knees. Everything rumbled. Rumbling was a tradition in their family. Just like 8-balls. And he collected all three; acrylic, testicular, and "magic." Both Jakes knew the magic ones were full of alcohol, having bashed open dozens to get drunk on special occasions. Like tonight.

Uncle Jake turned his new Cherry's head around so she couldn't watch, careful not to slip a finger into the yawning void at the base of her fractured skull. Then he stood up straight in the mirrored chrome of the hardtail fender and put on his uniform.

He pulled leather chaps over his ratty jeans, snapped and buckled and zipped and zipped again. Chains rattled, and gloves squeaked, and his boots scuffed black skids around his motorcycle in anticipation. He swapped out his Highland High jacket for Douches Wild, stinking to high heaven of gasoline and mothballs. He reached into the front pocket, flicking away an empty pack of Beeman's and gathering up a slick, heavy nugget of Socony 990 that had pooled there. Checking his face in the fender, he streaked his grey hair black with the wad, finished buttoning up the jacket with the reverence of a wedding tux, then with one last hand through his widow's peak, got down on his knees and mounted the bike from behind for the ceremony.

Even though they would have been great to grip, he was relieved they weren't old enough to need saddle bags. And as he unzipped his fly and squeezed his shit until the end got red and angry and mushroomed in his fist, he coughed a swirl of sweet carbon monoxide and laughed. He remembered all her nicknames, once "Hardly Driveable," but now a genuine "Hogly Ferguson" if he ever saw one.

He greased the edge of the tailpipe with the rest of the goop on his oily palms, and jammed himself in. The pipes were made skinny back then, so the hot metal pinched the head, sizzling all around the purple helmet, crackling on the chrome plating like a steaming helping of bibimbap, burning fast to seemingly protest his thrusts. He bit his tongue and pushed harder, fucking her hoggy style, her favorite, smelling the old scars on his meat crackling like bacon, scraping rust flakes into his white bush like tinsel on a sagging tree with every stroke.

The bike idled high, and the rockers on her V-twin boogied until they blurred. But Jake could still see his reflection in them and mumbled something about bikes and bopping being a way of *life*. Then he wondered if a cooling ring on the exhaust could keep him hard a bit longer, as his vision got hazy in the fumes, and he imagined something about hogs trying to buck him off. The engine revved, and Jake looked up at the throttle where he swore he saw his brother hang his helmet on the handlebars, a helmet with his head still inside and smiling. His lips now cherry-red from the vapors, Jake fucked the bike harder as he worried his brother Rusty, head be damned, had been banging her when he wasn't around.

He pushed harder and felt his scorched foreskin stuck tight, then peel back even further, layer after layer, until he half-prolapsed like a tube sock stuck on a toenail and rolled inside out. The hot pipe had finally opened his urethra so wide he'd become one with the motorcycle, sharing with it the same heart, lungs, regulator, and now, exhaust system. She pumped her hot smoke deeper into his bladder, deepest into his balls, filling his body with the lifeblood of her machine.

EPILOGUE:
VIETNAM BUG HOCKEY

When we stopped for gas, Mag swapped seats with Matt and curled up next to Zero and they both slept for hundreds of miles. Next to me in the passenger's seat, Matt took his turn rifling through my wife's yearbook, and I made a mental note of the pages he was stopping to study as if he'd seen them before. Over the better part of an hour, I slowly turned down the radio knob with my knee until it was off. He didn't notice until the click. The sun was coming up, and he looked to the horizon, eyes clearing.

"How far are we?"

"Pretty far. What did you find?"

I could feel him staring at the side of my face for longer than necessary, then he went back to the pages.

"Nothing," he said. "Just the stuff I copied for her once. Did you see this though?"

He held up the sealed envelope I'd marked "Invisible Prison."

"Yeah, don't open that. I'm not ready for that yet."

I would likely never be ready to prove I'd been wasting my time.

"What about this?" Smiling, he held up the map I'd found early on, the stained hand-drawn diagram of what I took for an unknown military skirmish.

"Yeah, what is that? Napoleon's last stand?"

Matt flipped it around in his hands and laughed.

"Yeah, it kind of looks like Waterloo, doesn't it? But that's mostly because Waterloo essentially looked like hockey."

"What looked like hockey?" I was lost.

"Our game."

Now I looked him over good, remembering the feel of his body retreating as I beat on it. He was different now, bolder. Bold enough to use "our" when referring to himself and my late wife. Maybe he was ready to give up some new information without another beating. So many beatings on this road trip.

"Tell me, Matt. What did you guys talk about when she came to your library?"

"Not a lot. She worked hard."

He caught me glaring.

"Yes, she was my friend," he said. "You can't make that many photocopies without becoming close."

"Uh huh. What game?"

"This game," Matt said, holding up the military map again.

"Am I supposed to guess? You were both in Desert Storm."

"No, Vietnam," he said, deadly serious. "We were in that library for ten hours a day some days, so we had to find games to play. And this was one of them. We called it 'Vietnam Bug Hockey.' It was a game we created together."

"Bullshit," Mag muttered from the back. "That's an old game. We played it as kids."

"Oh, boy," I muttered, reaching forward and scratching the crack I'd punched in the windshield. It was getting wider, spreading out to all corners of the glass now, reminding me of the crack the kitchen staff bashed into Sutherland's windshield in *Invasion of the Body Snatchers,* the second adaptation, not the first one, or the third one, or the inevitable reboot. I looked at Matt and thought all about "adaptation."

"You ever see *Invasion of the Body Snatchers*, Matt? Donald Sutherland played a Mental Health Department representative, and he finds rat turds in the restaurant's soup and was looking to shut them down, so they vandalized his car."

"And?"

"Maybe it was just 'Health Department' and not 'Mental Health Department.' Either department probably ends up on feces patrol though. My point is, nobody likes getting bad news."

He put the map down and closed his eyes to get some sleep.

I fiddled with the vents to blow the steam off my glasses and to distract myself from punching the windshield anymore and changing our course yet again.

* * *

Above the tree line to the left of the highway, the orange glow of a fire blazed somewhere nearby. When it was close enough to make our nostrils flare and wake everybody up and resume their upright positions, I rolled up my window to keep from coughing.

I remembered a fire my wife and I had walked through in France. It was a "gorse fire," the locals explained, something they called a "fire-climax" plant, an organism that encouraged fire and its own destruction. It had given

Angie something to research on our trip, even though she promised not to crack any books or computers until we got back. She told me that the fire recurrence periods in these kinds of plants were every ten years. This was known as a "catastrophic climax," and the seeds that shrugged off the gorse during this cycle grew right there in the middle of its own scorched earth.

When I first started driving, I expected the road to have some sort of profound effect on my brain wrinkles, those deep memories buried in the folds of the gray matter, any effect at all really. But all this drive time had really taught me was that on the tenth listen, Billy Ocean's terrifying "Get Outta My Dreams and Into My Car" sounded like it should be sung at gunpoint, and Sheryl Crow spent an inordinate amount of time describing what Billy was doing at the bar. Those two songs were apparently every DJ's favorite, and if there was one thing that every town had in common, it was shit DJs.

One time, Angie and I rented a van to check out the California coast, and the vehicle came with satellite radio and all those new-fangled specialty stations, which was at least an eclectic selection of songs for once. And during that vacation, the satellite station was running some kind of special "road-trip station" special (or maybe it was just a scheme to suck in tourists like ourselves), and we debated this supposed bargain.

"Aren't all car radio stations 'road trip stations' by definition?" she asked me. "I mean, you're definitely *driving*. Unless you're in a parked car in your garage listening to them. And in that case it should be a limited time 'suicide station.'"

The other thing we discovered during our satellite radio/marriage trial period was stand-up comedy, and after we logged about 30 hours of stand-up snippets on those channels, one thing that became clear was that stand-up had recently entered its post-modern phase, as around 2/3rds of those comedians would stop and comment on how weird their joke just was, how they delivered it, how it's received, etc. It reminded me of novels about writers, and the lack of sincerity in most fiction, and had something of the same effect as we cruised along, the landscape alternating between lush and Martian, real and imaginary, strange mountains marbled like muscles.

* * *

To break up the miles, after we stopped for gas and snacks, I put aside my pride and asked Matt to explain the game he played with my wife, and he was excited to tell me and Mag all about it. He smiled and said it was actually mostly *his* game, just to be clear, a game he used to play with the other kids on his street when he was a boy, and one of them first named it "Bug Hockey," not Angie. Originally it was a game to play with ants, which fascinated Angie the most, although Matt preferred spiders. And he said his dad told him spiders weren't "bugs" at all, then killed one in front of him, but he was never sure what that was supposed to prove. He said that Angie inspired their new variation on the game when a research dead-end led her down a rabbit hole of the history of the "Zamboni," and hockey rinks in general, but the kids' version was real brutal . . .

He said this all pretty fast, and I decided that would be his last 5-hour Energy Shot.

"First you take a soldier. . ." Matt began.

"A soldier ant?" I said. "I thought you said they were spiders?"

"They're all soldiers. They're in 'Nam, remember."

"Oh."

"We'd play this in this one kid's overgrown garage, crouched down over a split in the concrete where Triffid-sized weeds were pushing through. One almost touched the ceiling. His dad parked his corvette on the lawn. Angie was fascinated by the genesis of the game, see, and how it evolved. But this map I drew? That goes on the bottom of the shoebox. That's the 'theater.' I told her how this one kid, Shawn, had a shoebox with the diagram for a little hockey rink drawn on the bottom, face-off circle, the crease, red lines, blue lines, everything. It was a skate box, come to think of it, not a shoe box. And the 'Vaughan Gear' logo was in the center of the bottom—I remember that well—and that completed the illusion of the theater."

"Don't you mean 'arena'?"

"No, a *theater* like a war theater. This is how we weeded out the toughest ants."

I wanted to correct him again and say "spiders," but he was in some nostalgia zone, and it was too easy to imagine my wife listening to him tell this story the exact same way. He was rambling much like I did after too many Cokes, or Angie after too much wine, and I felt close to them in that moment, I guess. So I let him go on.

"To play we needed the 'theater,' a pencil, and a book of matches. For now, like I said, the game was still evolving. But Rule Number One was, if the ant touches one of the four face-off dots, then you used the machine gun. The machine gun was a pencil. You just stabbed, rapid-fire, until it moved off the dot, or it got stabbed, or both. The pencil was used for a lot of the weapons."

Matt made motions like he was stabbing the shit out of something, thankfully not making machine-gun noises with his mouth. I wondered how Angie reacted to this.

"Rule Number Two, if the ant crawled across the red line, then you used a flamethrower. The pencil was the flamethrower. You took the tip of the pencil and, starting at one end of the theater, drew a fast zig-zag across that line, fast and hard. A little like a heartbeat."

"Like a heartbeat on a heart monitor?" I said.

"No, no," Matt laughed, nervous. "More like a Richter scale actually. Anyhow, Rule Number Three was if the soldier marched across one of the blue lines and made the mistake of stopping, then it was time to radio in the tanks!"

"The pencil is the tank!" Mag and I said at the same time.

"Yes, exactly, and you dropped the pencil on its side so that it was resting about a finger's length from the soldier, then you rolled it. Just once. And real fast with your palm. Just one roll to grind up the soldier if you could."

"I'm guessing when the 'tank' showed up, the game was usually over."

"Kinda."

"And Angie played this game with you. While waiting for copies."

"There were a lot of ants in that library, at least down in the basement copy room."

I remembered a couple times when I'd tried to call her when she was out of town at his library, and it was impossible to reach her when she was making copies, due to the best copy machine being buried in a basement. So this part of his story checked out. But I didn't like the idea of them crouched down over a shoebox and killing ants together. It was like they were retroactively creating a childhood memory to share. And, of course, it was rumored this guy had two penises. I wasn't sure when I'd be able to bring that up, if ever.

"Rule Number Four," Matt went on. "If the bug touches any of the four corner face-off circles, then you threw a grenade."

"Let me guess. . ."

"Yep, the pencil was the grenade. You pound at the bug with the eraser end of the pencil, and you kept pounding until the bug exited the circle. The chances of this were always slim. But Angie usually let them go."

"I believe it," I lied. Yesterday was the kind of day where I'd believe anything. But that day was over.

"Rule Number Five. If the spider crossed into the 'icing' zone, this meant it hit some trip-wires. So you'd tear out the eraser and hit it with the raw metal ring on the end. We had to be careful so that the eraser could be stuffed back into the ring again though. Grenades were too popular to lose."

Rule Number Five made me flinch. Angie used to tongue pencil ends where the eraser had been worn away, absentmindedly leaving circles on her taste buds while she typed. I remembered one time when Angie had me unclog our tub, and I tried a shortcut with a toilet plunger. And on my first plunge, it popped loose and cracked the top of my hand against the metal mouth of the faucet, which left a deep, cookie-cutter wound right down to the bone. It took forever to heal, and the scar was way more interesting than that story, but the scar was exactly like one of her tongue circles on my hand, and it would be there forever now, so I was glad it happened.

"Rule Number Six, if the ant or spider or whatever touched the dot dead-center in those four face-off circles, you could use the napalm. This is where the matches came in. Just light one and drop it. You got one shot. One match wasn't quite the opening sequence of *Apocalypse Now*, but it was usually plenty."

Matt rolled down the window to let in some of the smoke from the nearby fire. His nostrils flared alarmingly wide.

"No way you were dropping matches into a shoebox in the basement of a library archive," I said.

"Correct. We never used the napalm. I just made a 'whoosh' noise with my mouth. Rule Number Seven, if the bug stopped crawling in the center circle, I mean if any leg or claw or fang or antenna or anything touched that logo, you had to call in the air strike. I mean the *President* called in the air strike. 'All mighty, All mighty,' that was the codename. And if this happened, after you said that shit, you lit all the matches in the matchbox and dropped it in the box. For this you got as close to the bug as you wanted. We never did that either, of course."

"Of course."

"I know it sounds like all the rules were the end of the game with a dead ant, but this one was *definitely* the end of the game. But there was a Rule Number Eight, believe it or not. If your soldier ant stopped and didn't move for more than ten seconds, the use of nuclear weapons would be authorized. This meant your foot. Oh, and Rule Number Nine, if the bug made it into either goal, those squares cut in the bottom where the hockey nets would normally be, it was considered 'home safe.' Then you had to let the critter go. Or put it in a jar. Or the library microwave. Wherever. But it couldn't really leave. Raise the combat theater up around it and into the air, whatever you want, but you left the soldier there on the floor. And Rule Number Ten, you already know that one."

"I do?"

"If at any time during the game you feel the spider or ant or person has cheated death one too many times, like you think there is no logical reason that it would not be dead, you can bring down the Knuckles of God."

I liked the sound of that one. I searched his face for evidence of my own fists.

"And that one happened a lot. Or you could bring in the Foot of God, or whatever. This was what Angie called the 'Zamboni.' Whatever the label, though, it wiped the arena clean. I loved the knuckles myself, when we were kids, I mean. Not when I played the game with Angie. We couldn't wait to punch the bottom of that box, punch like we were straddling someone in a fight with everybody watching. Later, we came up with a Rule Number Eleven, when we remembered the name of the game was 'hockey' and we hadn't incorporated any ice skates. So the skate became 'helicopter blades,' and Rule Number Eleven got kind of complicated. It was hard enough keeping Shawn from bringing out the God knuckles as soon as *anything* hit the bottom of the box, so imagine him when skates were introduced! But what we realized back then was that the bugs rarely left the box anyway. Even if they won. Even if we felt bad and turned it over and tried to shake them out. Then hung on throughout it all. At first I was disgusted by this, but now I realize I'd probably do the same thing. Just to keep the game going, you know?"

He looked at me, and sucked on a swollen lip.

"Bring on the fists. Right, Dave?"

"Right."

I remembered Mag and checked the rearview mirror, and I saw her huffing steam on her window and then writing 'Help' in her breath with her finger.

*   *   *

A few more miles, and my wife's letters were strewn everywhere in the car. We'd all had some 5-hour Energies, bringing the car total to about 25-hours of energy, and theories were getting thrown around. Matt was arguing with Mag, and now she wanted out of the car. Even after Mag had checked the folds Angie had made in her map and saw that it lined up perfectly with the Vietnam Bug Hockey diagram and told us this was the answer to everything. Maybe her heart wasn't in it anymore. But hitchhiking was always a crapshoot.

"That's amazing," Matt said. "But probably ultimately meaningless."

"How can that be meaningless?" Mag asked him. "If this is the safe path for an ant to take through a war zone?"

"So?"

"And Dave here mapped this same path onto our windshield."

"So?"

"With my fist!" I added. It still stung from punching those cracks.

"So?"

"So it just makes me feel a lot safer."

"Well, that's the important thing," Matt said, then his arm came around his seat and snatched the sealed envelope away so fast that Zero retreated to the back window.

"I'm opening this," he said.

Mag slapped him in the back of the head and grabbed it back.

"No, I'm opening it."

"Please, don't," I said. Those words she wrote would be the last thing she said to me before her disappearance, and I couldn't bear to imagine it was a suicide note. Or worse, if it was meaningless.

"Why not?" she said.

I stopped the car fast enough to bounce it up on two wheels again.

"What if it's nothing?"

"That's why you need to open it."

"No, what if it's nothing." I looked at her, then him. They seemed to get it.

"We'll make it something," she promised.

I felt so close to them in that moment that I almost cried, and she ripped it open.

"Open the envelope!" I said all dramatic, even though it was already happening.

It was a single piece of notebook paper. Angie's tight handwriting.

"What does it say?" I asked.

"Well, it lists in detail the 'Rules for Fake Prisoners and Guards in Phillip G. Zimbardo's 1971 Stanford Prison Experiment.'"

"Don't you mean 'Zamboni'?" someone said.

We sat silent for a moment.

"Yeah, she was into that stuff," I said finally. Then I blew a kiss to Zero in my rearview mirror.

"I think his litter box is full," Matt said.

"Meow, just once, goddamn it, so we know what you are," I said to the mirror as we all drove on. "We're in this shit together, you know, and not just because we're in a car."

ACKNOWLEDGMENTS

Big thanks to the party bus pit crew who got grease under their fingernails on this: J. David Osborne who brainstormed the concept with me when it was still riding training wheels, Matthew Revert for the primer and paint, Tony McMillen for letting me be a fireman when I grow up, as well as all my early test-drivers, Amy Lueck, Cody Goodfellow, and Jeremy Robert Johnson. And, of course, a tip of the trucker cap to my head mechanics at the Red Room Garage and Lube, Randy Chandler and Cheryl Mullenax. And a final shout-out to my first car ever, my cherry red '84 Pontiac Fiero. They used to call me a poor-man's Magnum P.I. in that goofy thing, even though Magnum was already poor. And squatting in someone else's house. And that Ferrari wasn't even his, so how sad was that shit? What high school kid had two thumbs and was deluded as hell about his ride? This guy! I ended up wrecking it, and it actually burst into Bristle Blocks, the poor-man's LEGOs. Shoulda used those two thumbs to hitchhike instead. And last but not least, thanks to the dude in the neck brace sitting next to me on the airplane who said I forgot that armrest-squeezing chase in *Body Parts* where the hero and the villain were in separate cars but still handcuffed together. Which is exactly like being stuck next to someone on a plane!

ABOUT THE AUTHOR

David James Keaton's fiction has appeared in over 100 publications, and his first collection, *Fish Bites Cop! Stories to Bash Authorities* (Comet Press), was named The Short Story Collection of the Year by *This Is Horror*. His second collection of short fiction, *Stealing Propeller Hats from the Dead* (PMMP) received a Starred Review from *Publishers Weekly*, who said, "Decay, both existential and physical, has never looked so good." His novels, *The Last Projector* (Broken River Books) and *Pig Iron* (Burnt Bridge) have also been optioned for film. Recently, he was the co-editor of the anthology *Hard Sentences: Crime Fiction Inspired by Alcatraz* (Broken River Books), and he teaches composition and creative writing at Santa Clara University in California. He can be found at davidjameskeaton.com.

CPSIA information can be obtained
at www.ICGtesting.com
Printed in the USA
LVHW012303260219
608881LV00007B/226